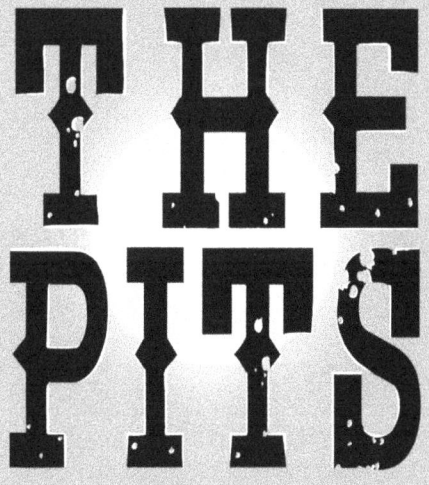

THE PITS

KATY L. WOOD

This is a work of fiction. Names, characters, places, and incidents are the product of the author's imagination or are used fictitiously.

Text © 2023 by Katy L. Wood
Cover Illustration © 2023 by Katy L. Wood
Cover Layout © 2023 by Katy L. Wood
Interior Illustrations © 2023 by Katy L. Wood
Book Design and Layout © 2023 by Katy L. Wood

All rights reserved. Published in the United States by Aspen & Copper Publishing. Special hardback edition published 2023.

www.Katy-L-Wood.com

contact@Katy-L-Wood.com

Educators, librarians, and others interested in arranging an appearance by Katy L. Wood at their event should contact her at the above provided e-mail.

Summary: In an alternate 1870s Colorado there are not Rocky Mountains but instead mysterious pits the size of mountains and full of magic. When Clarabella's girlfriend Emilia is forced into a strategic marriage by her father, Clarabella turns to her wayward outlaw sibling Royal for help only to end up dragged into the world of magic she never believed in. Together they head deep into the Pits in an attempt to find and rescue Emilia, suddenly finding that things might be much more complicated than they had anticipated.

Kickstarter Special Edition Hardback ISBN: N/A
Hardback ISBN: 979-8-9861137-6-0
Paperback ISBN: 979-8-9861137-4-6
EBook ISBN: 979-8-9861137-5-3

The Pits don't keep people. Not like this.
They steal from them. They make them go mad.
They kill them. But they don't keep them.

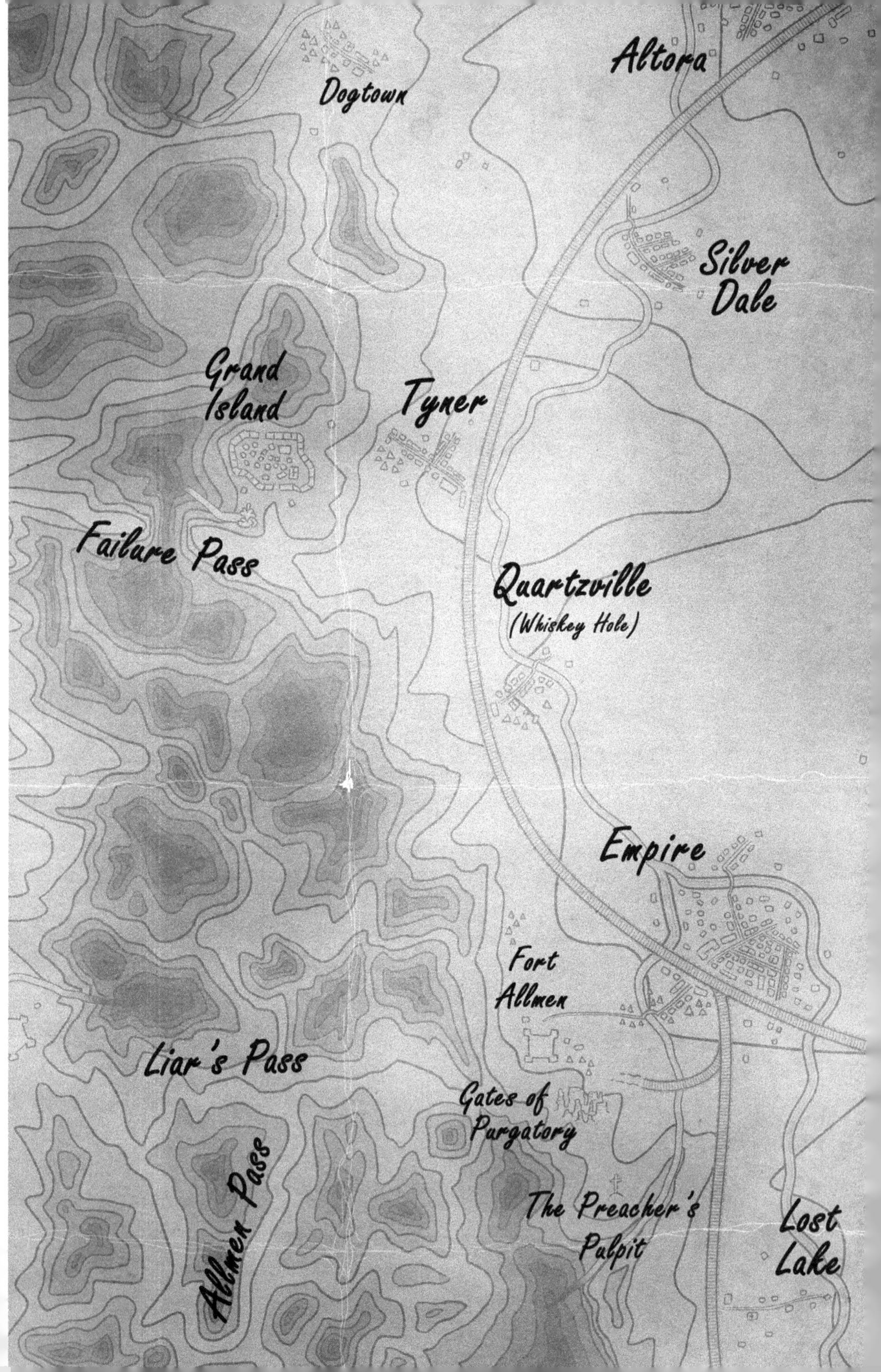
Altora
Dogtown
Silver Dale
Grand Island
Tyner
Failure Pass
Quartzville
(Whiskey Hole)
Empire
Fort Allmen
Liar's Pass
Gates of Purgatory
Allmen Pass
The Preacher's Pulpit
Lost Lake

Chapter 1
Finding Royal

July 1879

Royal was a person and a problem, and that's about where all useful description of my eldest sibling ended. I'd been attempting to track them down for over a week now and in that time I'd learned three things: one, according to the wanted posters, Royal had about a dozen colorful pseudonyms including "The Coyote of the Cliffs" and "The Black Pit Bandit." Two, no matter their other crimes, whatever town they'd last been in tended to also have a stray report of books going missing. Three, any sort of physical description got me nowhere when I questioned people. Royal was too good at shifting their appearance for that, just as likely to be described as a lanky man in dirty black clothes as they were a demure young woman in a lovely dress. There were, in fact, at least three wanted posters I suspected to be Royal, though it was hard to say what was a resemblance and what was a quirk of the artist responsible for the portrait.

What seemed to work better was tracking crimes that sounded like the sort of things Royal would get into, then seeing if any books were reported stolen in the same area around the same time. Outlaw or not, Royal was predictable, at least to me. I just had to hope this would be enough to allow me to catch up before it was too late.

I let my reins drop, trusting Shelly to wander in more or less the right direction for now, and to not fall into anything. Sun beat down on my shoulders through my light brown blouse, cooking my legs under the gingham skirt I wore and sending sweat rolling into my eyes.

"Should have taken the train," I muttered.

Problem was, the train only hit a handful of towns in the area, while I needed to hit all of them. Rumor had it Royal was still in the area. Somewhere.

Pulling out the penny map I'd purchased back home in Altora, I spread it out on my lap to examine. I knew the swirling lines indicated elevation, somehow, but what good was that when everything as far as the eye could see was flat? If I had been trying to navigate the Pits there would have been landmarks aplenty, even if they were just mountain sized holes in the ground. The closest thing I'd seen to a landmark out here in the last hour was a broken down old conestoga wagon that looked like it had been there for years, rotting away with every summer storm.

I was relatively sure I wasn't lost; I knew the train tracks were to the east, on my left side, and the Pits were to the west. Somewhere to the south of me was Quartzville, the town I was aiming for. I'd either hit the town or miss it and hit Empire Station, which marked the start of the only safe pass through the central span of the Pits. Either way, I'd end up somewhere with people. It would have helped a lot if I had the faintest idea how to mark distance out here, though.

Probably, I should've tried Grand Island first after exploring the growing mining camp of Tyner—if Royal was anywhere, Grand Island was a likely spot—but I had chickened out at the last minute, unsure I could find the way. Nor was I sure I wanted to go anywhere near there even if I could find the place. It was rumored the roads had been designed to trick and trap and confuse those who didn't already know the route. It was also rumored to be the most degenerate town on the whole front range of the Pits, which was saying quite a lot.

Huffing in frustration, I folded the map up and stuck it in my pocket.

Tyner and Quartzville were about eight hours' ride apart from one another, and I'd been riding for six, so it shouldn't be much longer. It wasn't like I *could* miss it, honestly. Anything taller than sage or a stray buffalo would be visible for miles.

"You better be in Quartzville, Royal."

When I finally spotted Quartzville I wasn't sure I had the right place. It seemed even smaller than Tyner, but it was supposed to be an actual town. The gate marking the entrance to the town—three skinny wooden poles in a lopsided arch over two wagon wheel ruts that passed for a road—looked one good gust of wind from blowing over. It creaked ominously as Shelly and I trotted up to it. On the top beam was burned the name of the town, proving I had in fact reached the right place, but beneath that hung a crude, hand-painted sign that said "Whiskey Hole."

"Charming." It certainly smelled like a whiskey hole.

Shelly seemed just as unsure of the arch and its strange noises, pinning her ears and shying away from it, so I led us around the side.

Based on my map, I'd known Quartzville was a tiny spit of a town but, looking around, it seemed like the map had oversold it. A rough mainstreet housed less than a dozen buildings, only two being more than a wooden facade with a large tent behind it. The closest real building was a ramshackle structure, gaps between the wall boards and a lopsided cross crudely nailed to the point of the roof. I found it somewhat sad to look at. Churches were meant to be beautiful centers of the community, not this.

At least the town would be easy to search, though I didn't like the idea of staying for the night. Shelly needed to rest, though, so I would find somewhere.

Passing the church—Royal would hardly be there—I headed for the saloon at the other end of town. It was the only other real building here and, unlike the church, it seemed well made. Wellish. Rising two stories, it had real glass in the windows (most of them, anyway) and recently painted glossy green trim shining against the whitewashed walls. A sign protruding from the front wall and swinging in the wind marked it for what it was, a whiskey bottle painted on it and nothing else.

To one side of the building was a small paddock with a water trough and a sign that horses drank free with the purchase of a whiskey by their owners. It also said violators would be shot and their horses sold to the local Ute. A series of crude pictographs along the bottom echoed the message for those who couldn't read. Another sign next to it said magic was banned on the premises.

I dismounted, patting Shelly's flank and rolling my eyes at the sign about magic. My legs ached from riding normally, rather than my usual sidesaddle. That saddle had a broken cinch, however, so I'd been forced to take my regular one instead.

"I'll buy whiskey this one time, just for you," I told Shelly. "Though, if they really believe in Pits Magic here I'm sure I could just lie about it and they wouldn't know the difference."

Shelly chuffed, heading straight for the trough. Securing the gate, I turned to eye the saloon. There was still plenty of daylight keeping away the raucous crowds, if any such thing existed here. A raised wooden porch ran the length of the front of the building, the steps up to it creaking under my calfskin boots. The outer set of full doors were propped open, leading to a little vestibule and then a set of batwing doors. Peaking between the gap in the batwing doors, I tried to gauge what the inside was like. A pungent mix of spilled liquors and what was likely vomit greeted my nose, accompanied by the noise of someone plinking lethargically at an out-of-tune piano. As suspected, the crowd inside wasn't a large one, made up of what appeared to be out of work bums and cattle herders draped over stools. All the sort of people with nothing better to do than eavesdrop and gossip, which was what I was after.

The man behind the bar was older, hair gone wispy and white, skin carved by years of living under the beating sun. He had a jovial smile, letting out a few notes of whistled tune here and there as he wiped down glasses. A grandfatherly sort of man. I could work with grandfatherly.

Patting my chestnut hair, I tried to assess how wild it had gotten from the intermittent wind during my ride. It felt frizzy at best, lots of strands loosened from the simple, twisted up style I'd put it in that morning. Without a better option, I attempted to pat down the flyaway bits and arrange them in a way that would come across as charming rather than disheveled. Sliding my hands down my sides, I pushed my periwinkle riding skirts lower to hide my ankles somewhat. That was as good as it was going to get.

Shoulders curled in slightly, I pushed one door open and peeked in around it before taking a few careful steps inside. Several people glanced up, including the bartender. I locked eyes with him and nibbled my lip, clasping my hands behind my back.

"Excuse me, Sir? I was hoping you could help me with a spot of trouble I have found myself in?" I asked.

All the patrons were eying me now, a few of them sliding their eyes up and down my body. It made my skin crawl, but I ignored them.

"This ain't the best place for a young lady such as yourself, dear," the bartender said.

"I know, I know," I replied, taking another step closer. "But, you see, I'm trying to find something that was stolen from me. Well, from my father. A thief accosted him and stole a very expensive broach. It is a family heirloom and very precious."

The bartender stared, face flat with skepticism, still wiping away at glasses. Fishing in my pocket, I pulled out a rough sketch of the broach and offered it to the man. It was an ornate, gaudy thing. My actual father would have called it "the poor taste of new money." But it had been stolen from a man in Silver Dale three days earlier, and the town librarian had come into work the morning after to find an entire shelf of her books missing.

"This is it, sir," I said. "My father and I are prepared to provide a *large* finder's fee to whomever helps us locate it."

He continued to stare, eyes going to my breasts instead of the paper. "Ain't right, a father sendin' his daughter out to dangerous places after thieves. Should be doin' such things himself."

Okay, sure. I could work with this too.

Putting my feet on the bar rail, I hoisted myself up and crossed my arms on the unsettlingly sticky bartop, leaning forward over them to make my chest more prominent. This close I could smell the tobacco on his breath, and his rotting teeth, could see the yellow in his scleras.

"You're right, Sir, of course, of course. But my father was injured by the thief." I took a deep, slow breath, holding the air at the top of my chest. "A cut across his cheek, and it has become badly infected. I just want to get the broach back to him before—"

A vice-like grip clamped around my left arm and a familiar voice hissed in my ear; "And the family calls me manipulative."

I glanced sideways to see Royal's familiar blue eyes—a mirror of my own and the only trait the two of us shared—glaring at me from under a silver rimmed cowboy hat with only the right side of the brim folded up.

"Well, maybe if you kept an address so I could write to you I wouldn't have to resort to tracking you down in this manner!" I snapped. Now that I'd found them, there was room to be mad for a moment that they'd made this so hard.

"You can't just come into a back-alley saloon and start waving yourself around without being prepared for consequences, Clarabella," Royal growled.

I arched an eyebrow and stepped off the rail. Reaching down to fish around under my skirts, I came back up with the six-inch long blade that had been in my boot. I held it up between us without comment.

Royal eyed it, looking deeply unimpressed. "That's too big for someone as tiny and inexperienced as you to use effectively. And it took you far too long to get to."

I huffed, not bothering to resist when Royal took the knife away.

A click interrupted us, drawing our attention back to the bartender who now had a tiny pistol in hand.

"Calm down," Royal said. Shoving a hand into a pocket of their duster, they pulled a couple little gold nuggets out and sent them clattering across the surface of the bar towards the old man. "No problems here, agreed?"

The bartender snatched the nuggets, eyes shifting to all his other patrons to see if any had noticed his prize. Satisfied that they'd all gone back to their business long before the appearance of the precious bits of metal, he gave a curt nod.

"You just carry gold in your pockets?" I asked incredulously.

Royal didn't respond, instead pulling me away from the bar. Without letting go they took me to a back corner I hadn't noticed; an alcove tucked behind the stairs leading to the rentable rooms above. It was lit with several gas lamps and there was a small group of people there—six in total—draped across several tattered couches and tables. There were even a couple women in the group, or at least a couple who appeared to be women, though they were dressed much like those who appeared to be men. Glasses and bottles were scattered everywhere, and a card game lay abandoned on a low central table. Everyone watched Royal and I's interaction as if the group expected me to be a danger to Royal. I wasn't sure what to make of this. I'd never known Royal to have friends.

"What are you doing here, Clarabella?" Royal asked, depositing me in the middle of the group and blocking the exit.

Putting my hands on my hips, I took a moment to give Royal a once over. This was the first time I'd seen them in the three years since our parents kicked them out for robbing the mayor. They'd always looked somewhat wild, never really paid any mind to impressing anyone, but now they looked every bit the Pits outlaw. Heavy canvas duster—black that was fading to patchy dark gray in spots and stained with mud, thick and flexible cowboy style boots with climbing spikes strapped to the toes, toughened canvas pants, ratty dark blue silk bandanna around their neck, a brace of long-barreled pistols, and a well filled belt of bullets. There was even a silver and turquoise ring on their left pinky, despite Royal's constant claims to hate jewelry. Their deep brown, near black, hair—several significant shades darker than my own—was longer than I remembered. Almost enough to be contained in a ponytail but not quite, stray strands falling around Royal's sharp, lightly freckled cheekbones.

"Is something wrong at home?" Royal prompted, looking annoyed. Royal's friends shifted, clearly coming to attention at the tone of Royal's voice. Not just casual acquaintances, but actual allies. Interesting.

"Home is fine," I replied. "Mother and Father still pretend you never existed, Eliza's in trouble with Mother for knitting lewd messages into the socks she makes for the church to give to veterans, Daniel broke his leg last month messing around in the creek but the doctor says he'll be just fine, and little Josephine now knows three new words and all of them are terrible ones she picked up from grumpy old Miss Wilton next door."

A flash of amusement went across Royal's face but was quickly tamped down. "Sounds exactly like normal, then. *So what are you doing here?*"

I pointedly glanced around at Royal's friends, then back at Royal. "You're running with a crew now, I see."

Royal rolled their eyes and threw their hands up. "Can you please just answer my question you petulant little brat? I don't appreciate reminders of the family that gave up on me showing up and shouting about my exploits. That is the sort of thing that draws far too much attention."

I didn't point out that tossing around gold nuggets like cheap sweets was also the sort of thing that would draw a lot of attention.

"Mother and Father disowned you because you stole the horse. I did not," I said simply. "I am here because I need a thief, and you are the best one I know."

This brought Royal up short, their hands hanging in the air in front of them, fingers and face shifting in confusion as they tried to come up with a response. "You...need a...thief? *You*? Little miss church-going, college attending, sidesaddle riding, princess *needs a thief?*"

"Don't call me a princess, *Royal*," I snapped. "And yes, I need a thief."

Royal opened and closed their mouth a few times, hands still fluttering with movement, clearly at a loss for words.

"What, exactly, would we be thieving for you?" Said a deep, brogue voice from one of the couches.

I turned, matching the voice to a man that would probably be even taller than Royal when standing, which was impressive given that Royal was a lanky six feet. Not only did he appear to have some height on Royal, he was easily twice as wide, if not three times as wide in the shoulders. If the devil needed a face, he would've picked this man's.

He had a wiry red beard that came to a point several inches below his chin, a mustache that he'd twirled up at the ends, and curly copper hair hanging to his collarbones, gone wild with the wind. Under thick eyebrows deep-set brown eyes sat above a thick splash of freckles that faded out into the less sun-touched portions of his face. Something in the dim lighting of the alcove made the brown tones of his eyes seem almost red. A mischievous twist graced his thin lips, matching the curve of his mustache. It was the sort of face that knew you had things and knew how to get them from you without you ever noticing. He didn't look much older than Royal, who would've just turned twenty.

"Don't you dare encourage her, Shiloh," Royal snapped, familiarity rather than anger behind the words.

"I'll encourage anyone who can shut you up so quickly," Shiloh said. "Don't happen often. Might have to ask her for a lesson."

"Agreed," said a black woman at a table in the corner. She was nursing a nearly empty glass and looked deeply amused. Her hair was in dozens of dreadlocks, each capped at the end with what appeared to be brass. Her dark gray coat looked like it would reach the middle of her thighs when she stood, and had thick, folded up cuffs that went halfway to her elbows. A man who looked too well put together for a place like this in his nice vest and spectacles was sitting next to her, eyes dancing around between everyone and looking just as amused.

"I don't talk that much!" Royal spluttered.

This was met with a chorus of disagreement from the rest of the group, which resulted in more spluttering from Royal.

"So, are you going to tell us what you need stolen?" Shiloh asked, leaning forward with his elbows on his knees. The suspenders over his shoulders looked like they were glad for the break from him sitting upright.

I surveyed the little group. They hadn't factored into my plans, and I wasn't certain what to do with that. It was one thing to ask my singular thief sibling to help pull this off, it was another to ask a whole group of people I didn't know to help out. But it didn't seem like Royal would be keen to leave them behind, nor that they would be keen to let Royal leave.

I was out of options and nearly, if not entirely, out of time.

"Have any of you heard of the American Princesses?" I asked the group at large.

Some of them shook their heads. A couple watched without acknowledging the question at all. The black woman in the corner went deadly still but said nothing.

Royal was the only one to speak. "Daughters of rich American men married off to poor European royalty. The rich men get to say they've got a royal in the family, a nice duchess or baroness, a princess if they're determined enough and have the money to throw around, and the royals get a much needed influx of cash from the dowry."

Something in the group shifted, all coming to attention at once. It was subtle, but everyone had straightened or leaned forward or narrowed their eyes. The black woman shared a knowing glance with Royal, something unspoken passing between them.

"That can't be a thing," Shiloh said, breaking the moment. "Well, I suppose it is well in line with how landed men in this country behave, but I had hoped we were moving beyond them selling their daughters."

"It only started happening recently," Royal said. "It was mentioned in a paper I got my hands on months ago. Just a few sentences. It wasn't even about the daughters, it was about all that 'precious, hard-won American money' being sent out of the country."

"Disgusting," Shiloh said. Everyone else echoed him with either nods or words.

"Glad you agree," I said. "I'm assuming that means you'll be willing to help me kidnap back my girlfriend before her father ships her off to a Duke who currently lives in California, then?"

Chapter 2
Lilac Letter

I followed Royal outside through a back door. After my request they hadn't given anyone else a chance to respond, just grabbed my arm again and herded me out.

"What?" I said, planting my feet in the dirt and pulling my arm free.

"You tell me," Royal said, arms crossing. "What girlfriend? Who is her father? How do you know what's going on?"

"Do you not trust your crew to hear those answers?" I asked.

"I trust them with my life and more," Royal returned, moving on before I could ask what "and more" meant. "And I respect them enough not to drag them into whatever this is without knowing a lot more."

"*Excuse me?*" I said, voice getting louder than I'd intended. "My girlfriend got abducted and is getting married off and you're calling it 'whatever this is'?"

"Who is she?" Royal asked.

I shifted from foot to foot. "...Emilia."

Royal freed one hand and rolled it in a circle, urging me on.

I hesitated, knowing Royal wouldn't like the answer.

"See, this is why I took us outside. You may have grown in the last three years, Clarabella, but you still look exactly the same when you're hiding something."

I let out a long puff of air through my lips, knowing there was no way around it. "Emilia Pierce."

Royal's eyebrows knitted together as they mouthed the name a few times. "Emilia Pierce...*the judge's daughter*?!"

I gave a curt nod, scuffing my boot against the hard-packed dirt.

"The judge who sentenced me to a year of hard labor for stealing a horse? That judge?"

Another nod.

"No. Nope. Not doing it," Royal said, shaking their head and holding their hands up, palms out and fingers spread wide. "Of all the people you could have dated, you picked Emilia Pierce? You know what her father did after I skipped town before he could lock me up, right?"

"Royal—"

"He's got a bounty on me, Clarabella. A big one."

"Dozens of people have bounties on you now!"

"Yeah, and that's why I avoid said people! Not go traipsing around after their daughters! Emilia Pierce. Honestly."

Royal turned and stomped back towards the door. This time, I was the one to reach out and grab their arm. "Royal, please, hear me out! Emilia's not like her dad. Not at all. She's sweet and wicked smart, she isn't afraid to bite back when people underestimate her, she loves strawberries and the color lilac, and I really, really love her. I didn't even realize she was the judge's daughter until months after we met."

Royal watched me, still looking frustrated. "How the hell did you not know she was the judge's daughter?"

"We met in college, way on the other side of Altora from where we both live," I said. "Both of us are—were—staying in rooms there. I never knew her at home aside from occasional glances as we passed in the street. I didn't realize who she was."

Royal's jaw worked side to side. "How long has she been gone?"

"A week," I said. "I came home from the market one afternoon and found her room cleaned out. She left me a letter telling me what was happening." I scrambled to pull it out of my pocket before I lost Royal's attention.

The paper was soft from how often I'd read the words. Royal took it and skimmed the short few paragraphs.

> My Dear,
> I am so sorry to leave you with only a letter, but my father has come to retrieve me. It would seem a marriage has been arranged between myself and a Duke who is living in California. To think we were just laughing about the American Princesses the other day! Such is the humor of fate, I suppose.
> I have truly cherished these last months with you, despite how distracting your visage could be in our shared lessons! You made the nights away from home far less lonely.
> Please remember me fondly, for I know I will remember you the same.
> -Your Lilac

"Well?" I said.

Royal ran a thumb along the edge of the letter, remaining silent as time stretched out. "This letter doesn't really say much."

"I know, that's why I need help," I said.

Royal finally lifted their gaze back to mine, handing the letter back. "Clarabella—"

"Please, Royal!" I said, feeling my emotions start to get the better of me. "She doesn't want this, I know she doesn't. Don't tell me you think it's right for a girl to be married off like this?"

"Of course I don't! That isn't the point."

"Then what is?!" I said, voice getting loud again. "Are you really so afraid of the consequences of stealing one horse three years ago? You've done so much worse since then!"

Royal glared, rolling the fingers of their right hand into such a tight fist their knuckles cracked. I swallowed, but didn't back down.

"Leaving was your choice, Royal! I know Mother and Father disowned you for stealing the horse, but you could have stayed and faced the consequences."

Royal barked out a laugh. "You keeping bringing up that they disowned me for stealing the horse."

"Well they did," I retorted, hands on my hips.

Royal's thin lips twisted into an almost pitying smile. "I left, Clarabella. Not saying it wasn't after a huge fight with them over stealing the horse, but I left. They never disowned me, at least not until after I was gone. I couldn't stand them anymore. Not after the way Mother treated me my whole life, not with the horrific opinions Father clings to. Knowing Father was going to pay off the judge to keep things quiet was just the final straw."

So much of what they'd just said sent me spinning, I didn't know where to start.

"The way mother 'treated you'?" I stuttered, finally. "She is a great mother! She's always been there for us!"

"Not for me," Royal said, no anger in their voice anymore, no emotion at all. "I was her business partner at best. Everything was a negotiation. Everything was a deal. Everything had to be earned. She was never my *mother*. Not once did she tell me she loved me without me having done something to benefit her first."

"Royal—"

"You're too young to remember, but her mother, Ephemera, I adored her. One day I realized she hadn't come to visit in a while, so I went and asked Mother when she would be coming by. You know what Mother said? 'Oh, she died six months ago.' I cried for three days, and she yelled at me for it, for being lazy and not doing my chores. I was seven, Clarabella. Seven."

I inhaled sharply, unable to parse what Royal was saying with the mother I knew. The one who took me blueberry picking, who had taught me how to read, who always bought me whatever books I wanted.

Royal carried on, gaining steam, voice still passive, though the passivity seemed more and more forced. "She was never cruel, but she was never kind either. And father—" Royal trailed off with a shake of their head, sending spots of sunlight glinting across the ground from the brim of their hat.

I swallowed, looking down at my boots. As much as I wanted to argue with what Royal said about our mother, I knew that whatever was said about Father, there would be no argument.

"He's a sweet enough man to us," I said weakly.

"It doesn't matter how he is to us," Royal said. "It matters that he pulls the buckboard closer to puddles to splash black people on the walkways. It matters that he calls them lazy and entitled and thieves and a thousand worse things. It matters that he still has the flag of the south tucked away in his and Mother's bedroom, even though he publicly proclaims to be against what was done in the war. No matter how he treats you and Mother and the rest of our siblings, he is not a good man. He does not care for a moment about the harm his words cause, or the terrible situations he perpetuates."

I sniffed, trying to hold in my tears. Royal wasn't wrong about any of it. But I loved my father. I loved when he taught me new things. I loved him when he'd fought for me to get a college education. I loved him when he told wild stories of his childhood in the North Woods around a summer fire in the backyard.

Royal came over and gently placed their hands on either side of my face, calloused thumbs sliding to wipe away the tears that had begun to fall. I tilted my head up to look at them, finding their face in a sad smile.

"They aren't good parents," Royal whispered. "I'm sorry, but they're not. I'm not saying that they didn't try, or that they weren't better for you than they were for me, but at the end of the day, they've failed me. I'm an orphan now. No grandparents, no parents, no aunts and uncles and cousins, not even really any siblings. I hardly even recognized you when you walked into the saloon, Clarabella, and that felt like a kick to the gut, because we used to be so damn close." Royal paused, swallowing heavily, but not breaking eye contact. "I'll never learn Mother's secret recipe for the biscuits I love so much, or have Father show me how he makes such amazing saddles, or help my siblings with their lessons, or attend the weddings of my cousins, or any of it. And that hurts. It hurts so damn much to lose all of it. But I couldn't live like that anymore, because every single thing, every word, was tainted. Dinner tasted sour because I could only think of Father calling the Mexican shopkeeper a slur under his breath as we left, all because she hadn't let him sneak two extra eggs like the old shopkeeper did. Mother was always after me to help her with the accounts for the saddle shop, but never once showed the slightest care that I had learned how to keep accounts in the first place because I wanted to start my own shop. I just couldn't do it anymore, Clarabella. Even if you say they've gotten better, I refuse to put myself back in that life, back into that constant pain. Even though it hurts to have cut myself away, that pain was one occurrence. It did not drag on and on, renewed every day by some fresh wound they caused."

The air had gone thin between us, and my tears hadn't stopped.

"I'll teach you how to make the biscuits," I said after a minute, not having the faintest idea what else to say.

Royal let out a laugh that turned into a sigh as they pulled me into a hug, arms draped over my shoulders and chin resting on my head. I tucked myself into it, burying my face into their chest and breathing in the dirt and leather and sweat, arms locking around their waist. It made me feel small, reminded me of childhood summer nights climbing into Royal's bed whenever it stormed.

"I just want to protect my girlfriend," I whispered into Royal's shirt.

Royal hummed, running their knuckles up and down between my shoulder blades.

"All you have is the letter?" They asked. "No other indications of where she may be? What her father's timeline is?"

I shook my head.

"Being a week behind...the chances of finding her are slim, Kitten," Royal said, using their childhood nickname for me. They'd given it to me after I'd broken up a schoolyard fight between two boys when I was six. Royal claimed my angry dressing down of the boys had reminded them of a little kitten trying to poof itself up so that it seemed bigger, despite the fact it was actually tiny and useless in a fight. I'd always found the name annoying, but now its familiarity was comforting.

I pulled away to look up at Royal again. "Please. I have to try."

Royal sighed, still looking unconvinced. "Alright."

Despite their agreement to help, Royal still seemed discontented with the whole affair. I wondered if perhaps I'd pushed too far, brought up too many old wounds that I hadn't even known existed.

"How'd you get here?" Royal asked. The harsh, falling sun had begun to cast their face in total shadow under the brim of their hat, preventing me from gauging their expression.

"What?"

"Did you ride? Take the train? Take a stagecoach?" Royal rattled off.

"I rode, though I don't see why it matters."

"What horse?"

"Shelly, if you must know."

Royal groaned, bringing one hand up to pinch the bridge of their nose.

"Shelly is a fine horse!" I insisted, stepping back and putting my hands on my hips. I'd helped birth the little paint, nursed her through two sicknesses. "And she was the one I had at school with me. I couldn't exactly go out and just buy a new horse, let alone stop at the house and pick a different one up!"

"Shelly is seven years old and has not had a single thought in those seven years," Royal shot back.

"Well that's rude!"

"Clarabella. She goes to an empty trough and acts like she's drinking because she doesn't realize there's no actual water in there."

I spluttered, trying to come up with a retort. The problem was, Royal wasn't wrong. Shelly did the same thing with food buckets. Probably, without a human around to tend to her, she'd starve out of sheer inability to realize she wasn't being fed.

"Look, she's a good town horse. I'll give her that. She's not a trail horse," Royal conceded. "If you're so determined to do this, then you need a different horse. We'll put Shelly up in the church stable—I know the priest well, he'll take good care of her. You can send a letter to Father to come fetch her, and I'll get you a better horse to ride. Deal?"

"A telegram would be faster," I pointed out.

"The town isn't connected. The train doesn't even stop here more than once every couple weeks."

With no other options, I gave in. "Deal."

Stepping back inside I nearly jumped out of my skin when I caught Shiloh out of the corner of my eye. He'd been standing just inside the door, clearly listening to us.

"Really?" Royal said. "Did you think my tiny little city-girl sister was a threat to me or something?"

"Nah." Shiloh grinned. "Just bein' nosy."

Royal rolled their eyes and shook their head, traipsing down the short hall to find the rest of the group exactly where we left them. Shiloh followed us and I was none too sure how I felt having him at my back. Royal seemed to trust him, at least, even if he was nosy.

The whole group greeted us with silence and expectant looks.

"So, seems I'll be splitting off for a bit to help my sister. I'll meet back up with y'all in a week or two," Royal announced.

The black woman with dreadlocks rolled her eyes. "Hiyá."

"Yes, Akhíta," Royal said witheringly.

She arched an eyebrow in response.

"I can handle it," Royal said.

"Never said you couldn't," the woman, Akhíta, replied. "But if you honestly think we aren't going to come back you up, you would be incorrect."

"What Akhíta said," Shiloh echoed. "You know me, always down to save a dashing damsel." He winked suggestively at Royal.

"I saved you, dumbass," Royal said dryly.

"And now we are all going with to save this girl," Akhíta said. "At the very least I am, and you know that."

"This isn't a bunch of people trapped on an old plantation, Akhíta, it's…family," Royal said.

Oh. That's why she'd seemed so interested. I eyed her, adjusting my assumptions to fit this new information. Stories of smugglers helping people escape the south were plentiful. Perhaps I'd even read about her without knowing about it.

"And we are family, are we not?" Akhíta replied.

"Well, yes, you are now, but this is old family," Royal tried.

Akhíta shrugged. "I don't know, I am quite liking this little sister of yours. She seems plucky."

Royal huffed. "Must you collect every wayward child you come across?"

Akhíta gestured at the rest of the group. "Seems to be going well for me so far."

Royal threw up their hands in defeat.

"So it's settled then, Akhíta and I will be going with Royal and Clarabella. Anyone else?" Shiloh said, looking around at the group.

Glances and shrugs traveled between everyone until all had raised a hand to indicate they were coming along.

Royal rolled their head onto their shoulder to look at me with a withering stare. "In three or so days, when you start to regret this, remember that it was your idea."

Chapter 3
Planning

It was agreed that while Royal and I took Shelly to the church, everyone else would go meet up with the rest of the gang who were apparently camped outside of town. Akhíta informed me that, not including Royal and herself, there were ten other people currently traveling with them.

Despite saying we could handle trading horses on our own, Shiloh insisted on coming with Royal and I.

"Must you be so obnoxious?" Royal asked him.

"I will continue to be obnoxious for as long as your grumpy face continues to be adorable," Shiloh said, snagging a thick arm around Royal's waist and pulling them in for a sloppy kiss on the cheek. Royal laughed and tried unsuccessfully to squirm away.

"Oh!" I said without thinking. "You two are...dating, then?"

Royal let out a long, over dramatic sigh. "You rescue someone from a sheriff *one* time and suddenly you can't get rid of them."

"Poor you," Shiloh said. "Also, I think it is the other way 'round. You saved me, but I brought you back to Akhíta and now you're the one who won't leave." He gave Royal a final squeeze before letting them go.

"You people have grown on me," Royal relented. "Now, are we going to trade horses or what?"

Shiloh swept out a hand in the direction of the front door, letting Royal lead the way. The bartender seemed to be glad to see the back of us, though his eyes did stray to Royal's pockets. Now that evening was falling more people were wandering in, but none spared us more than a glance.

"We should give her Marigold," Shiloh said as we descended the front steps.

"I was thinking Eagle would be better. He's more Clarabella's size, and a smoother ride," Royal responded.

"How long have you two been together?" I asked, desperately curious. Royal dating was as much of a surprise as them having friends. Their whole life, before they'd left, Royal had been far more likely to hole up in some secluded spot with a book than to bother with other people. Twice our parents even thought they were missing to the point of gathering a search party.

"Bit more than two years," Shiloh replied. "My turn. What was Royal like as a kid?"

Royal stopped in their tracks and spun to face us, boot spikes gouging the dirt as they did. "Oh don't you two dare make friends and start trading stories!"

I grinned, liking this game. "Well, all the adults around us would've said obnoxious, asking too many questions and all that."

Royal groaned.

Shiloh snickered. "Not much has changed then."

"You said you two met when Royal saved you from a sheriff?" I asked. Shiloh nodded. "What did you do to have the sheriff after you, and how exactly did Royal save you?"

Royal closed their eyes and pinched their nose, letting out a huff. "Can we get back to what we are supposed to be doing, please?"

"Oh, we'd broken into the same bank," Shiloh answered. "But as we were leaving only I was recognized, and considered a threat, as Royal was in a lovely blue gown and red wig at the time. Royal got themself away, then came and broke me out of the jail later that night."

"They never suspect the woman," Royal said. "Now, can we get back to the horse issue, *please*?"

"Sure," Shiloh said. "Clarabella and I will have plenty of time to trade stories when we're on the trail."

Royal shook their head and turned around, heading for the paddock. "This trip will be the death of me."

Shiloh and I grinned at one another before following. I still wasn't sure how I felt about Shiloh, but he was growing on me. As much as he and Royal seemed to pester one another, it was clearly with deep fondness. It was nice to know Royal had someone like that. Someone who loved them enough to watch their back as they got into everything they got into.

The paddock now had three horses in it. Shelly was tucked way at the back, looking distrustful of her companions. She'd never been the most social horse, only friendly towards my Father's roan. Royal patted the butt of a buckskin that stood in our way, moving him forward to clear a path to Shelly. Upon seeing me she trotted up, dipping her head to bump it into my chest. I scrittched under her chin and kissed between her ears.

It wasn't until I pulled away that I noticed Royal standing by Shelly's saddle, jaw tense. Their fingers were hovering in the air above the embroidered swirls and flowers, tracing the designs without touching them. After our conversation earlier about Father, I didn't have the heart to say I'd done the embroidery myself, under our father's tutelage. He'd been giving me lessons since just after Royal left. I struggled with tooled designs, unable to get the smooth, professional curves he could create, but I enjoyed the difficult work of embroidering the leather instead. It wasn't something I ever intended to pursue beyond a hobby, but I still enjoyed spending long afternoons in the workshop when no other work was pressing, threading away at the saddles Father had made but not yet adorned in some manner. I'd always assumed Royal felt the same; that the saddles were lovely but they were our father's creations, that both of us would go on to other things. Now I wasn't so sure.

Royal swallowed heavily and stepped back, dropping their hand. Shiloh reached out and squeezed it lightly, earning a flash of a tense smile.

"Let's go," Royal said.

I nodded and took Shelly's reins, following Royal out and down the road to the church. This time, no one spoke.

Hidden behind the ramshackle church were three stalls and another paddock. A preacher was there, mucking out one of the stalls. When he spotted us approaching he stopped and leaned on his pitchfork.

"Whatever trouble you're bringing, I don't want it," the preacher said.

"I thought you said you were friends with this guy," I muttered.

"No, I said I knew him and that he'd take good care of your horse," Royal said.

"We gave him money to help rebuild the church last year after it burned down," Shiloh said cheerfully. "He was annoyingly suspicious about the origin of that money, however."

"I can't imagine why," I said. "Why'd you help rebuild the church?"

Shiloh shrugged. "Towns die without their churches, and Whiskey Hole does have its charms."

I quietly wondered if it was Shiloh or someone else in their gang that was responsible for the name "Whiskey Hole" in the first place.

"Evening, Father," Royal said, leaning on the top rail of the fence.

The preacher did not come closer. From our position at the fence I could see that his clothes were as weathered and worn as his church. Age was beginning to turn his black hair to gray.

"Evening," he said, clear distrust in his voice.

"We were hoping you could watch this horse for us until we can get someone to come fetch her," Royal said, indicating Shelly with a wave of a hand. "We'll pay."

His eyes dragged over each of us one by one. "Your bounties would pay as well, Coyote."

"Aww, don't play like that, Father," Royal grinned, resting their chin on their folded arms. "You haven't turned us in yet, why start now?"

"To earn some peace and quiet?"

"A quiet life is a dull life," Shiloh said.

The preacher let out a long breath through his nose, shaking his head. "What are you paying and what *exactly* am I doing?"

Royal slapped the fence, causing it to release a puff of dust from the brittle wood, and stood upright. "There we go! Five dollars. We just need to leave this horse with you for a bit, and if you could send our letter on the next stagecoach north, someone should be here to retrieve her shortly after."

He eyed Shelly. "She's not stolen, is she?"

"Oh, no, Kitten here owns her free and clear. We're just taking an unexpected trip and need a horse better suited for the trails," Royal told him.

The preacher held up a hand. "Fine, fine. I do not want to know any more than that."

"You'll do it?" Shiloh asked.

He nodded.

Royal straightened up and clapped their hands. "Wonderful."

"Very. Except I don't have any paper to write a letter," I pointed out.

"There is some in my office, come with me," the preacher said. "Not you two," he added when Royal and Shiloh moved to follow.

"Ah. Making sure we haven't kidnapped her?" Royal asked.

"Of course." He indicated for me to head up the steps to the back door first.

I obliged and stepped inside, finding a dark, cramped office. A rickety desk, covered in papers and several bibles, sat in front of the only window. Beyond that the room was unadorned aside from a crucifix over the door I presumed led to the church proper, and a coat hanging on a rack next to that door. It smelled of incense, something I was surprised to find at a small, rural church. Such things were difficult and expensive to get out here.

"They haven't kidnapped me," I said.

He hummed and pulled out the desk chair, indicating for me to sit. I did, smoothing my skirts down once I was seated.

"My name is Father David," he offered.

I hesitated, remembering how Royal had called me Kitten outside. Perhaps I should use a false name? Though, I was sending for Father to get Shelly. It wasn't like he, at least, would not realize that I was here. He was equally likely to realize who I was with if he asked about it.

The thought made me somewhat uneasy, I realized. Father hadn't even said Royal's name since they'd left. I doubted he'd take it well if he found out what I was up to now.

"Kitten," I answered. "I promise, Father, that I am with them of my own volition. Royal is helping me to retrieve something I lost, that's all."

Father David sighed, glancing out the window. I looked as well, watching as Shiloh lifted my saddle off Shelly's back and set it against the fence where my bedroll and saddlebags were already resting. Royal laughed at something Shiloh said, but I couldn't hear either of them.

"Well, as long as you're sure," Father David said. "You get that letter written and leave it on my desk. I have some chores to attend to in the church."

"Thank you, Father," I told him.

He hesitated in the church doorway, looking at me. "You be smart, young lady."

"I will."

He left, the door smacking closed behind him.

Shuffling through the papers, I found a blank one. Hidden under a bible I found a pen as well and began to write. It was likely that, by now, Father had received word I'd left school. He'd be worried. Maybe mad. But I couldn't risk him finding and stopping me, so I kept the letter short. Just an assurance that I was alright, and would return home shortly.

Folding it up, I searched around for an envelope. Unable to find one I settled for writing my father's name and our address on the back. Setting the paper on top of a bible, I slipped outside.

Shelly was turned out in the paddock now, Royal brushing her down. The other two horses were nosing at Shiloh, who had produced a carrot from somewhere, and was breaking it into bits for them.

"You still owe him the money before we leave," I reminded Royal.

Royal dug into an interior pocket and pulled out a five dollar note, holding it up between two fingers.

"How many pockets does that coat even have?" I asked, going to get the money.

"A multitude."

Shaking my head I went back inside and placed the money under the letter.

"Leaving?" Father David said from behind me, making me jump a bit. He apologized for startling me, and I waved it off with a smile.

"Yes, we'll be going now. Thank you so much."

"May I give you a blessing before you go?"

"I would like that very much."

I took my rosary out of my pocket, thumbing across the beads as he came over and placed one hand on my shoulder. I bowed my head and he used his other hand to trace a cross in the air in front of my body, lightly tapping his fingers against me as he spoke. "To the Father, the Son, and the Holy Ghost, may you protect this child as she wanders these lonely trails."

I lifted my head. "Thank you, Father."

"Be careful, my child. These lands can be cruel. They may take things from you that you are not ready to give."

"To camp?" Shiloh asked, hefting my saddle up into his arms, my saddlebags already slung over one shoulder. He didn't have to heft it nearly as much as I did. He did, however, manage to make it almost look small.

"To camp," Royal agreed.

I picked up my bedroll and we headed out along the back of the buildings on the main, and only, street, walking in the direction of the river. Everything was painted red in the setting sun and the sounds of people eating supper floated out from the tent buildings.

"And then?" Shiloh asked. "What is the plan to retrieve Clarabella's damsel?"

I was curious to know as well, though I hardly would've called Emilia a damsel. Despite seeking Royal out, how they were actually going to help eluded me. Finding them had been an act of desperation more than anything, because who else would even help?

"Well, Emilia's father is taking her to California," Royal said, hooking their thumbs into their belt. "Quickest way there from Altora is the Allmen

Crossing, and I doubt he'd want to keep the Duke waiting by going farther south to the next crossing. That would add a couple weeks, at best. Wouldn't go north, with the last of the Northern Lakota continuing to raid overlanders."

"And the rails still haven't made the Allmen crossing," Shiloh picked up. "So they'll be going by wagon. They'll be slower."

Royal hummed in agreement. "Until they meet back up with the trainline at Lacey's Hideout on the other side of the pass, then it'll be a straight shot to California for them."

"As happy as I am that Emilia and her father will be slowed by taking a wagon, they really need to get the rail line finished," I said, trying to sound like I belonged out here. "It is absurd to still have to use a wagon in this day and age."

Royal shook their head. "That rail line is the worst thing to happen to this country. All of them are. Carving the whole damn world into pieces. Worst invention humans ever came up with."

I scoffed. "It's progress, Royal! Progress is good."

Royal and Shiloh shared a long glance, then both shook their heads and fell silent. I rolled my eyes but stayed silent as well. I'd debated Royal over the merits of modern technology enough times to know it was a lost cause. Anything newer than a gas lamp was interesting to them in a general knowledge way, but the actual application of it tended to annoy them for some reason I'd never understood.

At the edge of the river we found a smattering of tents around a campfire, a dozen or so horses corralled in a rope paddock a short distance away. Akhíta was there, along with the others from the saloon and several people who hadn't been there. The scent of cooking meat wafted out from a large cooking pot hung above the fire, a man stirring it as he conversed with Akhíta.

"'Ello!" The man stirring the pot called jovially. "I'm Theo. We did not have a chance to be introduced earlier. Lovely to meet you." Closer now, I realized he was the same man that had been sitting next to Akhíta in the saloon. Something in the inflection of his voice made me think of people I'd met from New York City, but there was something else to his accent that I couldn't place.

"I am indeed. Lovely to meet you as well."

Shiloh set my saddle and bags next to a tent and went over to smell whatever was in the pot. Theo swatted his hand away when he tried to dip a finger in for a taste. Suddenly a little girl, no more than a few years old, popped out of one of the tents and dashed for Shiloh, clinging to his legs. Her sleek black hair was fastened into a single plait and she had on a skirt covered in colorful Mexican embroidery.

"S'iloh, S'iloh!" She said, giggling as he scooped her up and tossed her into the air, catching her as she came down.

A child was the last thing I'd expected to find in this camp, and I was somewhat alarmed by it. How could anyone bring a child along with what Royal and their friends did? What parent would risk their toddler getting caught in the middle of a gunfight, or worse?

A young woman emerged from the same tent the girl came from. "Dios mío, Shiloh, must you toss my daughter so high?"

Shiloh grinned, tossing her once more. "She likes to fly, don't you, Dahlia?"

Dahlia giggled and flapped her arms. "Tweet tweet!"

"You know he'd never drop her, Hazel," Royal said.

"Well...no flying after dinner," Hazel said, going to kiss her daughter on the cheek before coming over and holding out a hand to me. "Hazel Gutierrez."

I shook her hand. She looked exactly like her daughter, aside from the fact that one of her irises was distorted and clouded over. "Clarabella Sutherland."

"Oh, so that's Royal's last name!" Hazel said with a grin.

Royal groaned, taking my bedroll and stomping away to another tent, vanishing inside.

"Royal is just Royal now," Akhíta said. She stood up and dusted off her pants. "Let me introduce you to everyone, Clarabella." She pointed around the assembled group one by one, introducing them.

Little Mountain was a tall, Native woman wearing a knee-length elk-skin dress under a wool blanket draped over her shoulders and secured at the waist with a belt. When Akhíta introduced her she also used her hands to sign the conversation and I noticed Little Mountain watching the signs in between glances at me. Daiyu was Chinese and didn't look any older than myself. Pedro wore a sombrero around his neck and a bright red sash around his waist; he seemed to be the oldest of the group, though he couldn't be more than 25. Oliver was white and looked like he'd be at home in a circus strongman act, his form even thicker than Shiloh's. Fox too looked my age, was also white, and something about him reminded me of Royal. Nadair was black and had an arm slung around Fox's shoulders.

I repeated the names in my head several times, trying to commit them all to memory.

"Well, it is good to meet all of you," I said. "Thank you for coming along."

Little Mountain's hands slid through several intricate motions, watched closely by Akhíta.

"Royal's family is our family," Akhíta translated. "Their siblings, anyways."

I nodded, touching my fingers to my chin and pulling my hand out slightly in the only sign I knew. "Thanks."

Little Mountain smiled.

Royal had emerged from the tent while introductions were being made, their hat and duster left behind inside. Underneath they had on a short sleeved, dark gray shirt that looked well worn.

"Have you learned sign since I saw you last?" Royal asked, mirroring the words with their hands.

I shook my head. "No, sorry. I just know 'thank you.' Not even sure where I learned that one."

"Eh, Little Mountain and the rest of us will teach you. She always starts with the insults, though," Royal said.

Little Mountain stuck her tongue and made what I assumed was some sort of rude sign that made Royal laugh.

"Soup's up," Theo said.

Everyone crowded in around the fire, taking bowls of chili as Theo ladled them out, then finding a place to sit within reach of the fire's warmth. Even in July, the nights on the plains got brisk. Blowing on a spoonful, I took a little bite to see what it was like and was pleasantly surprised. Too often I found that chili was made spicy at the expense of actual flavor, but Theo's did not seem to have that issue.

"This is wonderful," I told him.

He beamed. "Glad you like it."

Familiar chatter enveloped the group as we ate. Dahlia sat on Shiloh's lap, sharing his bowl of chili. I leaned over to Royal, keeping my voice low.

"Is Shiloh her father?" I asked.

Royal laughed. "Oh, no. She just adores him. You know how kids are. They deem one person their favorite and stick to them like glue. Dahlia's father is some cad who hid that he was married and put Hazel in the family way after making a bunch of false promises. Had Hazel chased out of town before anyone could realize she was pregnant."

"How horrible."

"Indeed."

"But…why not find somewhere else to live with her daughter?" I continued, voice still quiet. "Somewhere…more suited to a child?"

Royal set their half empty bowl on their lap and looked over at me, their head tilted slightly. "You know, if you're going to be out here with us, you're going to have to start putting away many of your preconceived notions of how life should be. Things are not as cut and dry as they may seem in cities and books."

"I didn't mean—"

Royal waved a hand and shook their head. "Whatever you meant, the statement stands."

Chastened, I went back to my chili.

"Royal?" I asked several minutes later.

"Hmm?"

"How'd you know I was in college?" It had been bothering me all evening, ever since Royal referred to me as "college educated" at the saloon. I hadn't started attending until late last year, long after Royal left home.

"Ah…." Royal let out a nervous chuckle.

"Have you been keeping track of me?" I asked, warmth spreading in my chest.

"Clearly not well enough if I didn't manage to catch you dating the judge's daughter," Royal said.

I reached out and patted Royal's knee. "I guess you'll have to settle for being a better thief than a spy."

Royal huffed and took my now empty bowl, pointing over their shoulder with their thumb. "Go get some sleep. We're leaving before dawn."

Leaning over, I kissed Royal's cheek. "Thank you for doing this."

With that I went and crawled into the tent, finding my bedroll spread out next to Royal's and, presumably, Shiloh's on Royal's other side. An extra woven blanket was thrown on top of mine. Only bothering to kick off my boots, I crawled under the blankets. For the first time since Emilia had been taken by her father, I let myself hope just a little that I'd find her.

Chapter 4
Making Camp

Royal's proclamation that we were leaving before dawn proved overly ambitious. Dawn came and went with everyone still scrambling to pack up. I tried to help but it seemed like I was more in the way of the group's rhythm than anything. When I reached for the cooking pots to pack them up, Theo got there first. My attempt to pack Royal's bedroll while they tacked up the horses was met with an already rolled bundle. Fox took pity on me and let me help him fold up several of the tents, though I was much slower at it.

"Why not stay in town?" I asked as I struggled with yet another fold. The heavy canvas was nothing like the thin fabrics I was used to folding.

Fox shrugged. "Eh. Too many of us. And hotels are expensive. Better things to spend money on. Less chance of being noticed out here too." There was something interesting about his voice, like he was forcing it to be deeper than it really was.

"I saw Royal tossing around gold nuggets like they were pebbles yesterday," I pointed out. "And don't you have money from robberies?"

"Those things? They *are* pebbles. Just a magic trick. One of Royal's favorite ways to get out of situations they don't want to deal with." Fox sounded fond about this, if not a little enamored. "And yeah, we have money from robberies sometimes, but why waste it on something like a hotel?"

I shook my head, unable to wrap my mind around it. Given the choice, I would always pick a hotel over sleeping on the hard ground, and I couldn't fathom why someone wouldn't.

"Are you and Royal close?" I asked.

"They tried to rob my parents' bookshop 'bout six months back," Fox said. "I'd been up late reading and fallen asleep in there. Caught 'em. But when I saw what sort of person they were, I asked if they'd take me with."

"What sort of person they are?" I tried to puzzle out what particular aspect of Royal's personality Fox was referring to.

Fox lifted their eyebrows, mouth twisted in amusement. "Of a different fashion? Unfond of the norms of society? Living under a summer name?"

"Oh! You mean because Royal isn't a man or woman?"

Fox nodded. "Never met someone like me before. Well. Sorta like me. I'm just a guy, but Ma and Pa always insisted I was a girl. Got tired of it. Royal showed up and I took my chance."

"Our parents mostly ignored it," I said. "They were far more worried about whatever bit of minor crime Royal was getting into than who they were that day."

We were interrupted by a shout to stop lollygagging from Akhíta, sending us back into motion to finish with the last tent. Once it was bound up, Fox threw it onto his shoulder and carried it off to the horses that Royal and Little Mountain were saddling up and packing. It was the first time I'd really looked at the horses and one in particular brought me up short. The mare had every aspect of a thoroughbred, except she had to be at least twenty-two hands tall. Far taller than any thoroughbred had any right to be, and taller than every other horse in the little herd. Her colors were strange, too. Mostly a chocolatey brown, but she was speckled with black in a way I'd never seen and her left front leg was completely white up to her shoulder.

Shiloh noticed me looking and grinned. "That's my girl Astro."

I looked between him and Astro, eyes wide. "Astro is...a significant amount of horse."

"She was born in the Pits. A shallow part, though. Be too mean to ride if she was born deep. Being born shallow just made her smart, and big."

I shook my head in disbelief, wandering over to look closer. There'd always been absurd myths of the Pits being full of strange animals, and changing any animals that went into them. Logically Shiloh had just happened upon a horse with a very unexpected set of traits. Something rare but totally explainable. Shiloh was likely messing with me, expecting the city-girl to be enraptured by the myth.

Astro, her eyes as blue as the sky, watched me as I got closer. A soft breeze blew from behind her and into my face, bringing an unexpected scent of what I thought might be gun smoke. Slowly her head tilted to the side in a manner that was almost unsettling. I stopped out of biting distance, to be safe. Keeping her head tilted to the side, she slowly dropped it down toward the ground, now looking up at me. Clicking her teeth once she picked her head up and turned around, trotting away to the other side of the herd.

"She doesn't like you much," Shiloh called. "But don't take it personally. She doesn't really like anyone."

"She's bit me three times," Akhíta offered from nearby.

"Twice!" Royal added.

Little Mountain held up four fingers.

Wonderful.

By the time we got going it was at least an hour into the day. There'd been an attempt to stay for breakfast, but Akhíta put a stop to that plan. It was roughly a ten hour ride to Empire, the town at the eastern mouth of the Allmen Pass, and at this rate we'd be lucky to reach the place by sundown. Instead we were eating crackers and hard cheese in our saddles as we followed the river south.

The group had provided me with a sturdy little gelding named Eagle that they normally used as a packhorse. He was indeed a smooth ride as Royal promised. Next to Astro, he looked like a toy. None of the other horses seemed bothered by Astro which backed up my belief that she really was a regular horse who happened to be large, rather than something magical.

It hadn't yet reached the temperatures of the previous day, aided by patches of shade from clouds that rolled in overnight. They only covered about half the sky, and no scent of rain came on the soft wind, so no one seemed worried about them.

Around me the whole group chatted in several languages, slipping from language to language depending on their current conversation partner. I caught bits of Spanish, German, French, Dutch, and several languages I couldn't identify. It was a bit overwhelming. The only languages I knew were English and a passable amount of French from my mother.

Unsure how to break into any of the conversations, and unwilling to let my thoughts stray to the direness of Emilia's predicament, I leaned back and dug blindly through my right saddlebag until I found the new dime novel I'd stuffed there. I was only a few pages in and wasn't sure how I felt about it yet, but anything was better than my own thoughts.

Before I could start reading someone to my right laughed. It was Daiyu.

"Royal's sister indeed," Daiyu chuckled. "They have a rule that they read all books from our jobs before we sell them on or give them back."

"You can't go wrong with a good book," I replied.

"Is that one good?" Daiyu asked, nodding towards it.

"I haven't decided yet," I told her. "It's a cowboy novel."

This resulted in another laugh from Daiyu, one so hard she clutched at her stomach and had to catch her breath, curling over the horn of her saddle. "Oh. Those things. Royal and Shiloh are competing for who can get written into one first. Akhíta is already in some. She claims three but Royal insists only two."

So perhaps I had read about her. I tried to think over everything I'd read, attempting to match her to a character. None came to mind, except in pieces.

"How does she know it's her?" I asked.

Daiyu shrugged. "Who knows. I don't like those books. Too wrong."

"Wrong?"

She threw a hand out to gesture at the group all around us. "How many white people in your books? How many men? How many here?"

I glanced down at the book. While the outside was a simple black cardstock with just the title, the very first page was illustrated with a dramatic black and white tableau of a gunfight. Even in black and white, it was clear the hero was a white man, as were the people cowering in the surrounding shops. The villain was too small to make out his race, but that wasn't any sort of reassuring. It was the second time since I'd joined this little band that I'd been told my expectations of things were wrong, and it hadn't even been a day. It felt like I should apologize, but I wasn't sure how. Daiyu had moved on, though, now chatting with Oliver. I returned the book to my saddlebag.

When I looked back up it was to find that Akhíta had trotted her pinto, who I thought was named Mouse, up next to me. I still wasn't quite sure what to make of Akhíta. As far as I could tell, she was the closest thing to a leader this little band had, but the position was a loose one. She and Royal were close, though, that much I was sure of. Their movements echoed one another like they'd been friends their whole lives, and I'd already seen them share a conversation through nothing but glances twice. There was nothing intimate there, just a deep bond. I wondered what had made it so strong in only two years.

"Morning," she said, giving me a little nod.

"Morning..." I replied hesitantly. There was a tone to her words that indicated more than a simple greeting, and I wasn't sure how to respond.

"I wanted to ask you something." Her gaze was locked on Royal's back a dozen horse lengths ahead.

I shifted in my saddle, trying to figure out where this was going. "Ask away."

"The girl we are going after, her father is the judge who tried Royal for stealing the horse when they were seventeen?"

I nodded.

Akhíta nodded as well in response, going silent for several minutes.

"Royal has told me a lot about that arrest," she said eventually.

"Oh?" I knew several versions of the story. A glossed over one from our parents. A sensationalized one from the paper. A truncated one from

Royal right before they left.

"You haven't seen them since," Akhíta said. "I have. Shiloh has."

"Okay...?"

She finally looked over at me. "You don't know what things were like for them after. We won't let the judge be a threat to Royal when it comes to physical harm, but that doesn't mean we can protect Royal from the bad memories."

"Oh." I frowned, looking down at the pommel of my saddle. Somehow, I'd never really thought of how the time immediately after the arrest had been for Royal. I'd been so mad at them for leaving there had never really been time to consider it.

"I want you to promise me, Clarabella, that you'll look out for Royal too. That you won't drag them any farther along in this than necessary. Not a promise like the ones your government is so fond of making, some useless scrap of paper that they turn around and ignore in a month, but a true promise."

I swallowed and nodded. "Of course."

"Good. And for what it's worth, if it does come down to pulling Royal out of this, I will continue to help you on my own, because I think what is happening here is wrong."

"Oh," I said, realizing I was saying it a lot. Akhíta kept saying things that required so much thought, the simple syllable was all I could muster out loud. "Thank you."

She nodded and knocked her heels lightly against the sides of her horse, speeding up to ride next to Royal and their bald-faced chestnut mare and leaving me alone once more.

We made a short stop for lunch to give the horses a rest and a chance to drink at the river's edge, but then it was back on the trail. Eventually even the sage petered out, giving way to swaying buffalo grass. Royal, several lengths ahead of me at the head of the group, turned around to grin at everyone, bouncing their eyebrows up and down in an implication I didn't understand. They were met with several happy whoops and tongue clicks as the group fanned out.

Shiloh took off first, Astro moving into a gallop so quickly it almost seemed like she flickered out of existence until my eyes caught up. The rest of the group followed in quick succession and, without prompting, Eagle took me with, clearly used to following his herd without input from a rider. I desperately gripped the reins, instinct telling me to pull them in and slow him down, but if I did that I'd be left behind in moments. Royal was somewhere behind me, their horse not yet in motion when Eagle decided to go.

I had never ridden so fast. This wild galloping was leagues beyond the steady trots I used to get to church when I was running late because I'd lingered too long over the morning paper after my father cast it aside. It felt wild and dangerous, my hands going slick with sweat and my knees aching from clinging to the hardened leather of the saddle.

A wild howl came from behind me and I risked turning my head a fraction of an inch to see what was going on back there. I didn't want to turn too much, though, for fear of sending Eagle off in the wrong direction. Out of the dust kicked up by the horses came Royal, standing in their stirrups, arms thrown wide and head thrown back, howling with joy. Their quarter horse beat a steady pace underneath them, nostrils wide and muscles churning, unconcerned by Royal's antics.

The rest of Royal's crew laughed, some standing on their own horses as the grassland slid by underneath all of us. Royal, arms still thrown wide, hat flapping in one hand, settled their gaze on me, a calculating look in their blue eyes. I wondered what they saw. A wayward sister come to ruin their fun with a silly quest, probably. Someone who didn't know what she was doing out here in the wilds, away from all the comforts and safeties of a town.

With the slightest, barely detectable twist of a leg, Royal urged their horse closer to mine, coming up right alongside me so close their feet were almost bumping mine. Royal lowered their empty hand, holding it out to me with a cocky, expectant smile.

"You're mad!" I shouted over the pounding of hooves and hollering of Royal's friends. My hands clung tighter to the reins.

Royal just waggled their fingers.

"No!"

"It's Sunday!" Royal shouted, sweeping their other arm out over the endless landscape around us. "This is our cathedral! Stand up!"

I glanced around, trying to see what Royal saw. It just looked like scrubland to me. Soft, undulating hills coated in overgrown grass with an occasional hardy sprig of Indian Paintbrush or Lupins. Reddish rocks sprouted up out of the ground in several places, none bigger than a wagon.

"Look up!" Royal said.

I did.

There was plenty of blue sky, but the clouds had grown, boiling upwards to unimaginable heights. They were bigger than the town I lived in, bigger than the New York City I so longed to visit. They towered so high it made my neck ache trying to see all the way to the tops.

"Why shut yourself up in a little box with a cross on the door when there's all this out here?" Royal said. Their hand was still out.

My rosary hung heavy in my pocket, but I could sort of see what they meant. Tentatively, finger by finger, I pried the hand closest to my wild sibling off the strip of leather that felt like my only lifeline. Shakily, and without looking, because looking would make it real, I lifted the hand up towards Royal. They took it, warm, calloused fingers much steadier than my own.

"Keep looking straight ahead, lean forward a bit, and put your other arm out for balance!" Royal instructed. "I won't let you fall. Count of three. One, two, three!"

I pushed up, my hand holding Royal's so tightly I wondered if they'd have bruises later. But Royal didn't object, and didn't let go. Really, standing only put my butt a few inches above the saddle seat, but the feeling was indescribably different. Wind grabbed at my skirt, wrapping it tight around my legs and snapping it over and over in the wind behind me. The motion of the horse undulated through me in a completely different way and for a split second I was sure I was about to fall, until something clicked and I found the rhythm, adjusting my movements to match.

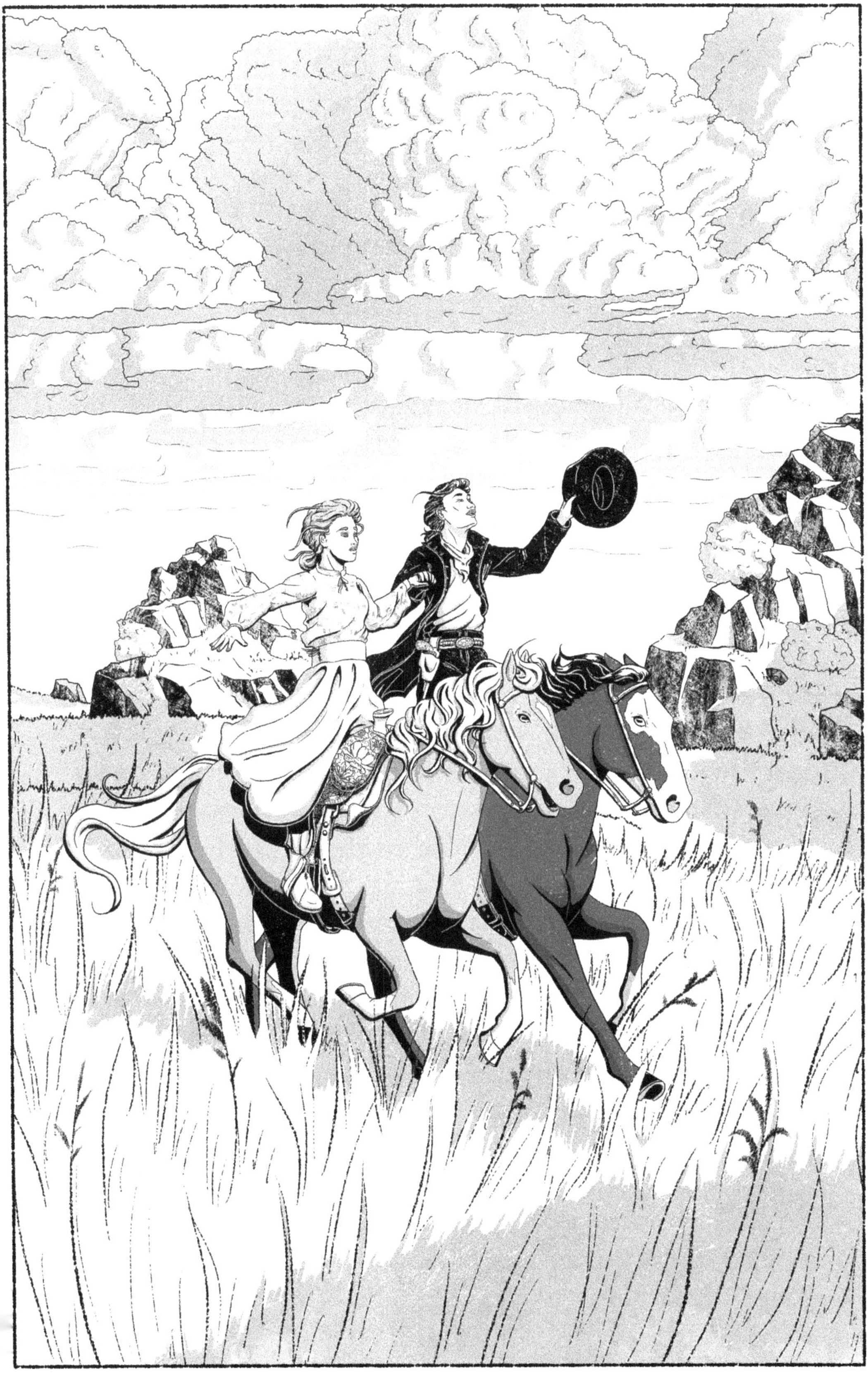

Royal let out a joyful holler, one echoed by the rest of the group. I didn't dare look around to see what the rest of them were doing. I wasn't that sure of my footing. But I was sure that this was the closest I'd ever felt to understanding Royal. To understanding the wild, restless need for adventure that pounded through their veins and pulled them in every direction except home. Royal, in turn, was looking at me like they'd never been so proud.

Our wild gallop didn't last long as we didn't want to push the horses too hard. The rest of the ride passed uneventfully and we reached the outskirts of Empire shortly before sunset. It was a good sized town, though only about a quarter the size of my hometown of Altora, and sparkled with newly installed electric lights in several of the buildings.

The town was nestled in a fork of the river, the train line bridging the gap between each side to create something of an island for the town to sit on. Empire had always done quite well due to its position at the mouth of the crossing, but with the rail line finally set to conquer that crossing within the next year or two, it was poised to become one of the biggest cities between Chicago and San Francisco. The exploding growth showed in the shanty camps around the city's edge. Without enough room at the Grand Empire Hotel, let alone the money to afford it, most people camped outside while they waited for their turn to cross. The papers had an article every other week with local politicians clamoring about the dangerous and degenerate people in the shanty camps and how said politicians were the right man to clean the place up, so everyone should be sure to vote for them in the next election. It always seemed to get ignored that many of the people in those camps were the same ones building the rail line over the pass and thus bringing so much money to the town in the first place.

Akhíta stopped us at a quiet, open spot well outside town. The closest tent was so far away it could hardly be seen. I knew most of this group were wanted, but it still seemed absurdly far. I didn't say anything, though, too ready to get off my horse.

Once more I found myself unsure of how to help as everyone set up camp, feeling guilty for just standing there. Fox tried to have me help with the tents, but my lack of knowledge about knots made me far too much of a hindrance. I could tie up a horse, maybe string together something of an impromptu bridle, but that was it.

Theo made dinner again, an onion soup this time.

"Do you think she's here?" I asked Royal, who was sitting next to me.

Royal lifted a spoonful of soup and swallowed it, looking off towards the glow of Empire. "We'll find out tomorrow."

"Not tonight?"

Royal shook their head. "We've had a long day. We need our wits about us. Empire's glamor hides a lot of rough characters, and I doubt our particular questions will be appreciated."

I agreed, reluctantly.

Royal knocked their shoulder into mine. "I was proud of you earlier."

I smiled down at my soup. As terrifying as it had been, it was also somewhat fun. Not something I'd ever be trying on my own, though.

"Since when do you care about church?" I asked.

Royal shrugged. "I wouldn't call myself Christian, or anything else, but when I look out at this world, I do tend to think there must be something behind it all."

"That's fair, I suppose." Perhaps that would be enough to save Royal's soul whenever their actions caught up to them. A loose belief was better than no belief. As long as they repented in the end, they'd have a good death with Heaven waiting for them on the other side.

With the soup finished, everyone lazed around the fire. Royal sprawled out next to Shiloh, one leg hooked over one of Shiloh's and head propped against a log, hat over their face. Shiloh, meanwhile, took out a chunk of wood that was shaped vaguely like a horse and started carving away at it, revealing more of the horse as he went.

"So, what did you think of your first day as an outlaw?" Shiloh asked with his usual grin.

Royal snorted under their hat.

I thought of what Daiyu said earlier about my novel, and what Royal said to me the night before. "Honestly, not quite what I expected."

"How so?" Akhíta asked. She was recapping several of her dreadlocks with what I had realized during our conversation earlier were bullet casings. It seemed like a very dramatic aesthetic, outlaw or not.

"It's the lack of robberies, isn't it?" Shiloh asked. "We can go hold up something in town if you like."

"No," Royal said, voice deadpan.

I laughed. "No, it isn't the lack of robberies. I think it's more...how comfortable you all are? That isn't quite right, though. You just...you all seem to fit out here so well, and with each other. I'm not sure I do."

"Aš, give it time," Akhíta said. "No one joins a family in a day."

"We've learned to live with and accept the magic of this stretch of country, that's all," Shiloh said, flinging the bits of carved off wood into the campfire.

I huffed, annoyed that he was treating me like an easily tricked city-girl again. "There is no such thing as magic, not anymore. We figured it out and now it is called science."

Royal gave a little shake of their head. "Stop being naïve, brat."

I aimed a kick at Royal's boot. "You're the one who brought up that I am college educated, excuse me for using it."

Royal let out a long, slow breath that echoed in their hat before sitting up, taking the hat off and settling it on their head. They looked dangerous with the firelight carving their features into an even sharper relief. I'd never actually thought of Royal as dangerous before, even knowing they were an outlaw, and I wasn't sure how I felt about it now.

"Okay, you want to play this game, let's play," Royal said. "Tell me, then, how the Pits were formed? Tell me what geological process could carve an inverted mountain range into the ground across the spine of a continent instead of shoving it up into the sky like everywhere else on earth? Tell me why this is the only place in the world with Pits? Tell me why the people who go into them never come back out?"

I stared at Royal, watching the firelight dancing in their eyes, turned navy by the night. As proud of me as they'd looked earlier, they looked the exact opposite now. The longer Royal looked without breaking eye contact, the more that gaze made my skin itch. Royal and I had had our fair share of disagreements and petty fights over the years, but this felt different. Deeper. Like it held more risk of tipping us over an edge we couldn't come back from.

The rest of the group had dropped their own conversations and were now watching us quietly, making me feel every more awkward and out of place.

"I don't see what that has to do with magic," I said eventually.

Royal sighed, shaking their head. "I wouldn't expect you to."

I wasn't sure what this meant, but Royal turned away, ending the conversation. They sprawled back out in the dirt, this time with their head in Shiloh's lap. Shiloh continued to carve, some of the little flecks of wood falling onto Royal's hat, which was back over their face.

Akhíta stretched out a leg and knocked her foot against Royal's, who knocked theirs back.

The silence that hung over us now made me feel chastened, despite the fact I knew I was right. I didn't know the others well, but could Royal of all people really believe in *magic*? That was absurd. Royal was too smart for that.

Unsure what else to do, I bid everyone goodnight and crawled into the tent. Once I was settled, I pulled out Emilia's letter. It was too dark for me to read, but the feeling of its feathery edges was comfort enough. I just had to find her. As soon as I found her everything would be alright.

Chapter 5
Emilia's Father

I was the first one to wake in the morning, slipping out the back of the tent so as not to wake Royal and Shiloh. Hazel was next to the campfire, a red and white mantilla draped over her shoulders. She was working on a long, thin, weaving, tied to a strap around her waist on one end and a stick held to the ground by her feet on the other. In the dirt next to her Dahlia was playing happily, trotting the wooden horse Shiloh had been making along a track she'd traced in the dirt.

Hazel looked up and smiled, her fingers continuing to roll expertly through the strings. "Eager to get going?"

I nodded, sitting down next to her. "What has you up?"

She gave a weary sigh. "Children never sleep when you want them to."

I couldn't help but smile, knowing exactly what she meant. My youngest sister, Josephine, had been much the same for several years. She was only five now, but she'd gotten much better about sleeping on a normal schedule in the last year. We sat in silence, save for Dahlia's horse noises, as the sun began to warm our backs. The strap Hazel was making grew longer at an astounding speed, an intricate pattern of squares and diamonds appearing inch by inch. Hazel finished just as sounds started to come from the other tents, deftly tying up the ends.

Rolling it up, she handed it to me. I took it, feeling confused.

"For your bedroll," she explained. "That cord you have is barely holding it together."

"Oh!" I ran my fingers over the surface, feeling the woven bumps against my skin. It was a mix of browns with threads of teal and a bit of white. The same colors as my outfit, nearly. Something this well made, this beautiful, would cost a pretty penny at a market. Yet this woman, who hadn't even known me two days, who lived with nothing to her name that she couldn't carry, handed it over without a second thought.

I held it to my chest and smiled. "Thank you, truly. It's beautiful."

She smiled back, gathering her remaining materials and tucking them away in a bag. Royal emerged from their tent, looking mussed, Shiloh right on their heals. Others began to appear, all in various states of wakefulness. Whatever outlaw mystique they'd had the night before as Royal talked about magic, they didn't have it now. None of them had on more than a loose shirt and long-underwear. Even Akhíta looked like a normal person with her dreadlocks tied back and thus mostly obscuring the bullet casings on the ends.

Royal plopped down next to me with a yawn. "Okay, so—" they yawned again. "Sorry. Anyway. Hotel first. If Emilia and her father are, or were, in town, they'd be at the Grand Hotel."

"I don't think I should go with you," Akhíta said, sounding nonchalant in a way that felt forced. "I'll stand out too much."

Royal grimaced. "You could coil your hair up, tuck the ends in and put on one of my dresses."

She snorted. "Royal, you're about as skinny as a cornstalk. My shoulders would shred your dresses the moment I lifted my arms, not to mention how much taller you are than me. No, I'll ask around the camps. See what gossip there is about the crossing."

"I'll go with Royal and Clarabella," Shiloh said, only for Royal to shake their head.

"Less people is better. We don't want to draw attention," Royal reasoned. "Clarabella and I can handle town. You help Akhíta check around the camps."

Shiloh and Akhíta glanced at one another, then said, at the same time, "Don't do anything stupid."

Royal scrunched up their face in a playful pout. "You two never let me have any fun."

An hour later, after a breakfast of biscuits and gravy, Royal disappeared back into their tent. When they reemerged, it was as a different person. Gone were the black duster and pants of the days before, replaced by a crisp, pinstriped red button up, clean dark denim pants, and a bolo tie with a piece of turquoise in the center of the silver medallion. They'd traded in their black and silver hat for a plain brown one with a flat brim, hair pulled back tight under it, and they'd used some sort of stage trick to create a layer of fresh stubble over their chin. The only thing that remained of their previous outfit was the little silver ring on their pinky. I wondered where they'd been hiding all of these clothes, especially the hat.

Scanning my eyes up and down over this new look, I got a suspicious feeling. "Royal...what are you known for in this town?"

Royal grinned, buttoning on their paper cuffs. "May have robbed a wagon train or two. Just the rich ones, though."

I sighed, deciding it was better not to ask for more details.

"You ready to go?" Royal asked.

I looked off towards Empire, biting the inside of my lower lip. "What if she's not there?"

Royal shrugged, buckling on their gun belt. "You said it has been a week, right? How many days exactly?"

"Eight-and-a-half, now."

"And you have no idea how they may have traveled?"

I shook my head.

"Well, doesn't matter. Let's assume they took the train, as it would have been the fastest way to Empire. The journey from your college on the far east side of Altora to Empire would have taken about half a day on the train, putting them in Empire sometime last Sunday. Crossings start every day, but comfortable ones that a man like the judge would take? Maybe a couple times a month. Alternatively, he commissioned his own guides and gear to make the crossing, something that would have taken days at best to put together, though he could have arranged it ahead of time. There's really no way to know for sure, but I'd say the odds are fifty-fifty that they're in town based on all of that."

That hardly made me feel any better, but clearly there was no time to waste. Hazel and Dahlia wished us luck as Royal and I set off for town, me trailing behind. If Emilia wasn't here, I had no idea what I'd do. Go to California and start asking around for a recently married or soon to be married duke whose name I didn't know?

"What *is* the crossing like?" I asked Royal as we walked.

"Hot. Dry. There's no water source the whole way through. You have to bring it all with you. And there's a bit in the middle called Liars Pass. It looks like you should be able to keep going directly west, but if you try you won't come out. The whole stretch is nothing but sands, and anything bigger than a coyote sinks in those sands as quick as if you were in water. You have to turn south forty miles in and make a big U. A good trip takes about two weeks. A bad one can take three. A single person on a good horse can do it in about ten days, though."

I tried to imagine Emilia out there, her lovely blond hair gritty with sand and clothes caked with dried sweat. She hated the heat. More than once she had gotten in trouble for improper dress because she'd stripped off her underlayers when the days got hot.

My heart ached with how much I wanted to hold her, to feel her body against mine and know she was safe. If I was lucky, that could happen within hours. If I wasn't....

Empire was loud. Loud and busy. People dashed everywhere, carriages and wagons and stagecoaches crowded the streets, and everyone seemed only capable of communication by shouting. It was nothing like the quiet, tree-lined avenues of Altora. Royal threaded through the crowds with ease while I had to practically glue myself to their back to avoid getting jostled and separated.

The people were of all sorts. Businessmen in pressed suits, beggars on the corners, cowboys that matched Royal, a few scattered Natives, grubby children, women rolling carts selling flowers and maps and perfumes. Around us were buildings of just as much variety. A large, modern looking hotel soared five stories high and appeared to be made of stone while across the street stood a lopsided wooden saloon. The whole place smelled like a neglected barn.

Without the faintest idea of where Royal was headed, I followed them along the street in front of the hotel. The main doors were set back from the street a ways, making room for a large, ornate garden behind a short fence. Women in extravagant dresses sat at shaded tables in the garden, pointing out at the people passing by on the street like they were some form of entertainment. Royal made no move to walk up the main path when we reached the wrought-iron gate, instead walking by like it wasn't even there.

"I thought you said we were going to the hotel?" I questioned, still struggling to keep up against the crowd.

"Did you not see the two Marshals at the door?"

I glanced back because, no, I hadn't noticed. But there they were. Guns on their hips, polished stars on their chests. They nodded to each person who came and went through the main doors.

"Do they always have Marshals at the hotel?" I asked.

"They've been having them more and more," Royal answered. "I doubt they're anything more than untrained local deputies, but we still want to avoid them."

Royal continued on until we reached the alley between the hotel and the next building, turning down it. The alley was empty, however coming out the other end we found the back was as busy as the front, but in a much different manner. Horses were being led too and from a basement stable, carts of luggage and linens and food went in every direction, and servants dashed to and fro trying to keep everything in order.

Royal went up to a young black man who couldn't be any older than me. He watched us warily. Royal held up their hands to show we weren't a threat.

"You don't have to answer, but is there—or has there been in the last week—a man named Judge Pierce staying here?" Royal asked.

The man's face darkened. "Oh him. Rude man."

My heart jumped into my chest. They'd been here.

"Is he still here?" I asked breathlessly.

The man nodded. "Tried crossing a few days ago, but his daughter wouldn't have it. I was away, takin' care of my Mam for a couple days, but I heard it from the other servants there was a big ruckus."

"Do you know their room number?" Royal asked.

The man shook his head.

Royal stuck their hand in their pocket and pulled out a few folded bills, passing them over. "Thank you."

The man quickly stashed the cash inside his uniform jacket, gave us a curt nod, and went back to work.

Without taking the time to say anything to Royal, I started towards the hotel only to be pulled backwards by my shirt.

"Hey!"

"Slow down," Royal said, still holding my shirt.

I flung my arm out at the hotel. "She's right there!"

"Then what?" Royal asked.

"Then…what?" I repeated. I just wanted to get to Emilia. Royal had accomplished what I asked by helping me find her and now they could go back to their gang without an annoying city-girl sister tagging along.

"What are you going to do once you find her?" Royal asked. "Do you think the judge is just going to say 'oh, I'm sorry, forget the Duke! You and my daughter are so adorable together, I could never come between that!'?"

My mouth dropped open.

"And let's say you do find her, and manage to get out of there with her, what then? Take her back to college and hide her under your bed?"

"I…well…I…." The truth was, I hadn't thought that far ahead. Getting to her seemed like the most important thing. "Once we're together we'll figure it out."

Royal shook their head. "No, you won't."

"Oh forget it. You helped me find her like I asked. Job done. Go back to your gang and your false magic and old myths," I snapped.

"My job wasn't to fucking find Emilia," Royal snapped back. "I honestly don't give a damn about her, at least not compared to you. And I'm not letting you march into this alone without even a semblance of a plan."

I hesitated. "That's why you came along?"

Royal sighed, one hand on their hip and the other pinching the bridge of their nose. "Yes. Sorry for shouting. Of course I came along for you. You're my little sister. I love you. Why the hell did you think I was doing this?"

I shrugged. "Because it was fun?"

Royal was silent for a long moment, staring at me assesingly. "You don't have to earn my affection by offering me some fun adventure, Clarabella. Love doesn't work that way. It isn't something to be earned like a wage, even if our parents acted like it." Before I could respond Royal turned and strode along the back of the hotel. I followed quickly behind.

None of the doors back here had Marshals and most stood propped open to allow staff quick access in and out.

"We still need to be careful, but one of these doors should work," Royal said, acting like our previous conversation hadn't happened.

"Okay. So, do *you* have a plan for what to do when we find her?"

Royal shrugged. "Not really. But at least I have some experience stealing things from the judge." This last bit was said with a cocky grin that made me roll my eyes.

"Emilia is not a horse."

"Not at all. She's much easier to steal than a horse. She'll actually be quiet during the escape and won't get me caught."

I huffed.

We walked the full length of the hotel before Royal turned back around and pointed at a set of open double doors just off center. "That one. Shoulders back, face forward, act like you belong," Royal instructed, taking off before they finished speaking.

Scrambling to catch up, I followed them into what turned out to be the hotel kitchens. Several people glanced at us as we continued through, but none said anything, all too busy with what appeared to be the beginnings of lunch preparations. Once in the hotel proper, Royal stepped to the side of the kitchen doors to look around.

The place was extravagant down to the last detail. Plush couches were scattered around the lobby, many occupied by rich men and women in the latest fashions. Golden filigreed trim lined the walls, and roman columns held up the soaring ceilings. In one corner stood a large piano without a single smudge on its shiny black surface. A young man sat at the keys, playing a classical melody.

Royal spied a coatrack in one corner, several elegant suit coats hanging from it. Without hesitation they grabbed one and slipped it on, buttoning it up. Taking off their hat, they hung it where the coat had been.

"Your pants don't match," I pointed out.

"I'm worried about first glances, not second," Royal replied. "Go ask the clerk if anyone has turned in a yellow scarf that you misplaced, then meet me by the piano."

Realizing I was a distraction of some sort, I went up to the check-in counter and smiled at the clerk. "I am so sorry to be a bother," I said. "But I seem to have misplaced my scarf. It's yellow, with little white flowers stitched around the hem. Has anyone turned it in?"

The young man said he wasn't aware of one, but offered to go check the room where they stored lost items. I thanked him and, as soon as his back was turned, I saw Royal approaching out of the corner of my eye. Forcing myself not to look at them, I waited for the clerk to come back. With a shake of his head he informed me there was no sign of the scarf. I sighed and thanked him, saying it was only a cheap scarf anyway, before heading off towards Royal.

The piano player had disappeared, leaving the corner where the instrument sat quiet and empty. Royal was there, leaned against a column that blocked them from the view of most of the room. They had the guestbook of the hotel in their hands and were paging through it.

"'Judge Pierce and Daughter'" Royal quoted, pointing at a line in the book. "'Room 308.' They checked in a week ago and haven't yet checked out."

My heart swelled and once again I tried to take off only for Royal to grab a fistful of my shirt to stop me.

"Would you stop doing that? Running headlong into a situation you know nothing about is a good way to end up in trouble, especially with your emotions in the way."

"You're one to talk," I said, crossing my arms.

"Yes, I am," Royal said. "I learned the hard way so listen to me, would you?"

My lips twitched in annoyance but I gave a curt nod. I just wanted to see Emilia.

"Good."

Royal dropped the book on the piano bench and led the way down the hall until we found a door marked "Servants Only." Pushing it open, a set of narrow, rickety stairs was revealed. They hooked back and forth, bringing us right to the third floor between rooms 312 and 314. Muffled shouting could be heard, the words becoming clearer when Royal cracked the door open. Royal put a finger to their lips and we listened.

"I paid you to escort her!" A man bellowed. "Not laze about in town at the saloon while she ran off!"

"The judge?" Royal mouthed.

I shrugged. I'd never actually talked to the man beyond a simple hello in town. Royal would have much more reason to recognize the voice, even if it had been years.

Whoever responded was not shouting, making their words much less apparent. Something about a preacher, maybe?

"Get out there and find my daughter you useless wretches! If she doesn't end up where I have sent her, I will have you hanged on charges of obstructing the railroad."

This time Royal threw an arm out to bar the door before I could even try to take off. A door down the hall slammed and two men appeared around the corner, both looking angry as they stomped down the main stairs and out of view.

"She's missing!" I gasped, my heart crawling its way into my throat.

"She's not missing, she left her father. That's probably a good thing, in the grand scheme of this whole affair. Just breathe. At least we won't be searching for her across everywhere between here and California."

I gulped down several deep breaths and nodded. Royal reached out and pulled me into a hug, kissing the top of my head. I hugged back, taking a minute to center myself before stepping away.

"We need to talk to him. Find out what exactly is going on," I said.

"Or we could go after the searchers," Royal said, gesturing in the direction they'd gone. "It sounds like they'd be easy to pay off, given how the judge is treating them."

I shook my head. "Who says he told them everything? Who says he told them the truth? The only way we can know what's really going on is if we talk to the judge himself."

Royal groaned and rolled their head on their shoulders. "Fair point. Let's go. And Clarabella?"

I paused halfway out the door to look back at them. "What?"

"If there is one thing I remember about the judge, it is that he loves the sound of his own voice. If things start to get dicey, find a way to keep him talking."

I nodded, though their words made me hesitate. What sort of dicey was Royal expecting? I remembered the promise I'd made to Akhíta, doubting she'd take it well if things got out of hand.

"Are you sure we shouldn't...go back and get Shiloh and Akhíta?" I asked.

Royal looked surprised at the suggestion. "What happened to sprinting off towards your girlfriend?"

I shrugged. "You're the one who said things might get dicey."

"We're fine," Royal replied. They stepped around me and led the way down the hall.

We made it to door 308, but Royal stopped me from knocking. They pressed an ear up against the door and listened for a moment. Seemingly deciding it was alright, they tried the brass handle. It only moved a fraction of an inch before the lock caught. Expression unbothered, Royal fished around in the breast pocket of their red shirt, pulling out a folded scrap of soft leather. Inside was a little key, no longer than my pinky and made of a pearly, translucent material that looked like some sort of stone. Opal, maybe?

"What is that?" I whispered.

"Magic you don't believe in," Royal replied. They inserted the key into the much larger lock and twisted it. I was astonished, and frankly confused, when the lock clicked open. Royal pulled the key out and stashed it back in their pocket.

Filing away my confusion for later, I followed Royal into the room. It was as decadent as the rest of the hotel and seemed to be a full suite made up of several rooms. The one we'd stepped into was a sitting room and on one of the couches, surrounded by piles of scattered papers and maps, was the judge. He was somewhat disheveled, huge bags under his eyes and short, graying beard unkempt.

I swept my eyes over the maps, hoping to glean some clue as to what was going on. They were just maps, though. Notes were scrawled across them, most indecipherable from this distance. A few jumped out, the handwriting a bit neater, but none of them made any sense, or seemed relevant. "Work Camp 1." "Fort relocation option 3." "The Preachers? Must remove."

It wasn't just the judge's things scattered around, though. Emilia's favorite straw sunhat was on a hook by the door and one of her journals sat open on an end table next to a recent edition of Godey's Lady's Book. An empty box, labeled as coming from "Montgomery & Sons Corsetry" was tossed carelessly on the floor, finger smudges of ink marking its cream surface. Through an open bedroom door I spotted several dresses laid out on the bed, and her Paisley shawl. That shawl was one of her favorite things in the whole world. Not a knockoff, but a true Paisley. It had cost her father $500.

"You!" The judge shouted, jumping up and shoving a finger in our direction. We both stopped and glanced at one another, clearly unsure which of us was the object of his ire.

"Judge—" Royal said.

He stomped over, getting right in my face. He was thin, but not as tall as Royal. Still tall enough to loom over me, though. "You're that harlot my daughter went to school with! I found your picture hidden in her things!"

"Excuse me?!" I shouted, trying to duck around Royal who took a quick step between us.

"She told me all about you! The ideas you put into her head! I bet you're the one who helped her escape!" The judge shouted, trying to get around Royal as well.

Royal, for their part, was doing an admirable job of staying between us.

"You seem to be a chapter ahead, Judge," Royal said. "We haven't the faintest idea where Emilia is, though we would also very much like to know."

The judge stopped trying to get around Royal and instead stared at them through squinted, contemplative eyes. "I know you too...."

"You certainly do, but that isn't particularly important at the moment," Royal replied.

"No...I know you," the judge said, tilting his head a bit.

Royal pushed on. "As a matter of fact, we would like to volunteer our efforts to help find your daughter, so if you could just tell us how she disappeared, and where, that would be a great help."

He sneered, jutting his chin out towards me. "Ask her. It's her fault."

"I'm asking you," Royal said.

"She ran off," the judge said warily, clearly still trying to figure out who Royal was. "Pitched such a fit when we tried to leave to make the crossing on Tuesday we had to come stay here for a few days. Told her she only had two options. Go to the Duke, or do a favor for me. Kept her under lock and key while she decided."

My eyes slipped back to the bedroom door, and I realized for the first time that it was splintered around the lock, as if someone had broken out from inside. A sick feeling settled in my stomach.

"What choice did you offer her?" I demanded.

He snorted. "Such aspects of business are far above the minds of young women such as yourself. But if you must know, she was to choose between marriage to the Duke or a more...direct manner of helping me recoup my lost investment in the railroad now that the market crash has ended. The Duke's connections in the timber and iron industries would have been useful, but there were other options available."

Royal was squinting suspiciously at the judge now.

"In the end she chose not to marry the Duke," the judge continued. "I paid a couple men quite handsomely to escort her, but someone interfered and the little minx slipped them. Now she's vanished. Rather than own their failure and repair the damage, the idiots felt they could get drunk on my money like there would be no consequences. They claim they searched after she vanished, but say they can't find hide nor hair of her." He shook his head. "Never should have let her go to college. It gave her ideas far beyond what any woman should have."

Royal's jaw clenched, as did their fists.

"How dare you talk about your daughter like that?" I shouted over Royal's shoulder.

"Quiet, harlot!" The judge thundered. "The opinion of a woman has no value here, especially the one who corrupted my daughter."

"Watch it," Royal said, voice low.

The judge squinted at them again, then their eyes widened. "You stole my horse!"

"Fuck," Royal muttered.

The judge's eyes jumped between me and Royal, getting even wider. "The Sutherlands! You're the oldest Sutherland kids!"

"Fuck," Royal muttered again.

"You low down, thieving little—"

Before he could come up with a proper insult, someone threw the door open behind us, sending it smacking into the wall. Royal and I both spun to find the two men from earlier, now with two more, all four with guns drawn.

Royal grabbed my arm and hauled me behind them, one of their own guns drawn so fast I missed it happening. Royal held their other arm back, keeping me corralled right up behind them.

"Was gonna come tell you to suck an egg, Judge," the man in a green shirt said. "But we heard shoutin'. What's this then?"

"Thieves!" The judge proclaimed. "The girl was my daughter's lover, if anyone knows where she has run off too, it is these two."

"Once again, we have no idea where she is," Royal said, voice surprisingly calm. "I doubt this fine establishment would be appreciative of bullets in the walls, so why don't we talk this out?"

"Shoot them," the judge said.

The four gunmen glanced at one another, then the judge. My heart pounded in my chest and I clung to Royal's gun-free arm, desperate for something to hold on to. All I'd wanted was to find my girlfriend. Now she was missing in a brand new way and I was trapped in the middle of whatever this was. A gunfight? Did it count as a gunfight if no one had fired a shot yet? Whatever it was, it certainly didn't meet the terms of my promise to Akhíta to look out for Royal.

"I ain't the smartest tack," green-shirt said. "But it don't seem wise, shootin' the people you think know where your daughter's at."

"A very sensible conclusion," Royal replied. "Guns away?"

No one put their guns away. Several of the gunmen did come farther into the room, though, surrounding Royal and I. This left green-shirt as the only one between us and the way out.

Royal shifted slightly, pushing me towards the door a fraction of an inch.

"So the judge would like us shot, but everyone else agrees that is a bad idea, correct?" Royal said, shifting another fraction of an inch. "But, seeing as no one is willing to put their guns away, what will break this standoff, then?"

No one seemed to know, all staring at one another.

The next several things happened so fast my mind could barely put them in order. With their free hand Royal grabbed my skirt and yanked me towards the door as they fired a shot at the green-shirted man who dropped like a stone. I stumbled over something, my own feet or the man's, and nearly ended up sprawled out on the carpet of the hallway. Before I could hit the ground more shots rang out and a hand grabbed the back of my shirt to haul me upright before pushing me forward. Throwing my hands over my head I dashed for the main stairs, clinging to the banister to keep myself balanced as I leaped down them two at a time.

People screamed, bolting out of the way as more shots rang out. Metallic gunpowder hung heavy in the air and on my tongue, wisps of gun smoke dancing with it in the light of the gas lamps.

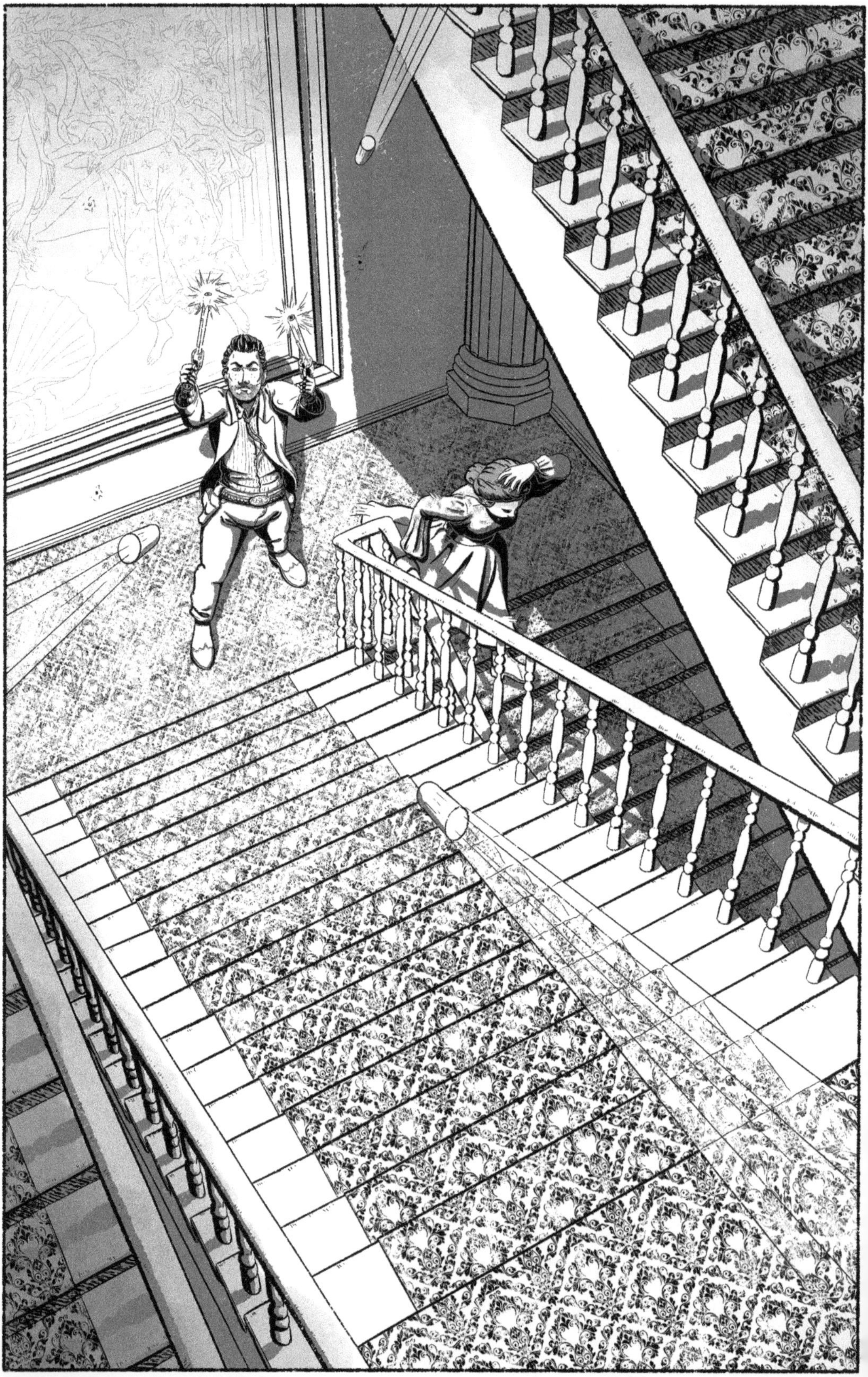

When I made the turn down the next flight of stairs I was relieved to catch a glimpse of Royal right on my heels. They made the turn as well, pausing for a second to fire up at our pursuers, then thundered after me.

We spilled out into the lobby to more screaming people all making for the front doors. The two Marshals we'd seen earlier were trying to fight their way in but couldn't make it through the crush of scared bodies.

Unsure where to go next, I froze until Royal pushed me in the direction of the kitchens. The servants took our chaotic, bullet heralded entrance better than the patrons. They hid rather than screaming and making for the exits, leaving them open for us.

How many of the men were still behind us? I didn't know and didn't dare look.

We made it outside and kept running. My feet smacked the ground so hard it hurt, shocks of pain rattling up through my ankles. It occurred to me that I hadn't run since I was a child, let alone run like this.

"Hide!" Royal gasped behind me.

Not letting myself over think it I took several random turns then ducked into a dilapidated barn. Royal followed, tugging the doors shut after them. We both stood in silence, panting and listening for sounds of pursuit. There were shouts, but they seemed far off. As we listened Royal thumbed more bullets into both of their guns and, in a thin strip of light filtering in between two of the boards, I caught sight of a smear of red across Royal's fingers.

"You're hurt!" I whispered. All thoughts of our pursuers were gone as I reached out, intent on finding Royal's injury.

They batted my hands away. "A graze. Leave it. We need to lie low until it's dark enough to slip out."

I hesitated, watching them for a moment. They didn't seem to be in any pain, and they were breathing alright. A serious injury would have been effecting them more, I thought, so I let it go.

So much of me wanted to leave now, desperate to find Emilia. It would be ages before there was any sort of useful amount of darkness to hide in. So much could happen in those hours. The judge could call in every lawman in town to look for us, even have them deputize any townsperson with a gun and nothing to do. Emilia could run into someone dangerous and get hurt, or worse. But the ache in my lungs and stitch in my side made it clear further running was out of the question for the moment. We needed to at least catch our breath, especially if Royal was any level of injured.

Royal and I retreated farther into the barn, taking cover in a moldering stall and sitting on several creaky crates to rest. I worried at my skirts while Royal sat silently, one gun resting on their lap and the other put away. Their only movement was fiddling with their ring, turning it around and around with the thumb of the same hand.

Time passed painfully slow, marked only by the shafts of light coming through the walls. The only thing occupying my mind was Emilia. Was she in town? She had to be. Emilia wouldn't have been able to survive out on the trail without any supplies. Probably not with supplies either. And she wouldn't have risked going home, nor back to school. I had to find her.

How long had she even been gone? I regretted not asking. And what could she possibly have done for her father to help him with his lost investment in the railroad? The terrible thought that he'd sold her off to a brothel crossed my mind, but I quickly cast it aside. That would not have gotten the judge any useful amount of money, no matter how pretty Emilia was.

I pulled out my rosary and fiddled with it as I turned the thoughts over and over in my head. After awhile they became so tangled I felt a headache coming on.

Bit by bit the light shifted, no words passing between Royal and I the entire time. No one came to the barn for any sort of search, but that didn't mean much beyond the fact that they hadn't gotten here yet. I wondered at what point Shiloh, Akhíta, and the others might get worried enough to come look for us. Even if they hadn't heard the gunfight, news of it would spread quickly. They didn't come either, though. The minutes dripped by, afternoon fading to evening. It wasn't fully dark yet, but it was getting there.

When Royal finally stood up to go, they swayed slightly and closed their eyes, taking a shaky breath through their nose.

"Royal?" I whispered, resting a hand on their arm.

"'m fine," Royal said.

I frowned, trying to place what seemed off about their face. It was hard to tell in the near darkness. Reaching a hand up, I placed it on Royal's cheek. Their skin that should have been several shades darker than mine was now several shades lighter. Gasping, I pulled apart the lapels of Royal's stolen suit jacket, despite Royal's feeble protests. I didn't need good light to see the blood staining the bottom half of Royal's shirt.

Chapter 6
Injury

Royal gasped out a sound that had my heart ripping its way up my throat. I'd never wanted to hear one of my siblings making noises of such pain. We'd made it out of the barn and out of town, Royal draped up against my side with one arm around my shoulders, but our progress was slowing and we still had a long way to go before we made it to camp. I'd wanted to fetch a doctor immediately, but Royal wouldn't let me, insisting we get back to the gang. Guilt over being the cause of this tapped at the back of my mind. I shoved it away. There wasn't time.

"Royal—" I said, about to lower them to the ground. It couldn't be smart to be moving them like this, not with their stomach pierced by a bullet. I wasn't sure exactly where the wound was, aside from somewhere near their navel. There'd been too much blood and Royal had been too insistent on leaving for me to examine them closely. The air was getting cold as well, now that the sun was down, which couldn't be good for Royal either.

"Shiloh," Royal gasped, one arm clasped across their abdomen, the other still over my shoulders, grip painfully tight. "Get me to Shiloh."

"I can run and get him," I tried, feeling tears pricking at my eyes. "It'll be faster." Royal was so much heavier than I'd realized, their wiry frame stacked with layers of muscle I hadn't expected. And Royal's damn legs and my damn skirts kept tangling in the dense grass we were fighting through, as well as with each other. There was no way I could get Royal all the way back to camp.

Royal shook their head and gasped out, "Not 'nough time."

I strangled down a sob and started helping Royal forward again, babbling at them the whole time. I didn't even know what I was saying, if I was managing full sentences. I just wanted to keep Royal awake.

I heard the campsite before I saw it, snatches of conversation carried to us on the breeze.

"We need to go look for them."

"They should be back by now, even if there was a gunfight and they had to lay low."

"We need to be careful. If they're hiding, we can't draw attention to them."

"Let's *go*."

I tried to shout, but no one answered, the wind that had carried their voices pushing mine away.

When I saw the campsite coming into view, everyone just starting to head towards us, towards town, I started screaming. Shiloh heard me first and instantly started running flat out towards us, the others in his wake. Without a word he scooped Royal up and turned back to the camp, running just as easily with Royal in his arms as he had without. I struggled to keep up, exhaustion pulling at every fiber of my being.

When I made it to the camp Royal was on the ground where they'd laid with Shiloh the night before, the entire gang crowded around. Royal's lips, chin, were smudged with blood now and they continued to hack up more. Nadir ripped off the bottom half of Royal's shirt, revealing the large hole there as it continued to bubble with blood and something that was certainly not blood. I tried to get closer but there was no room for me.

Akhíta was kneeling on Royal's other side, burning stick in hand as she leaned in to examine the wound. «What happened? Royal, what happened?"

Royal tried to answer her, but only managed to cough up more blood.

Shiloh was madly digging through packs, throwing things into the dirt without care, until he produced what looked a roll of ratty linen, only about three inches wide, and it looked like it had been cut down at some point.

"You can't use that as a bandage!" I protested as Shiloh began to layer it across Royal's abdomen. The thing looked filthy and would certainly cause an infection.

"Shut up, city-girl," Oliver spat.

"But—"

"He said shut up," Theo said. He, however, backed the statement up by pointing a small black pistol at my face. His face, meanwhile, was extremely passive.

Shocked at this shift in attitude from Theo, I snapped my mouth shut, eyes locked on the midnight black of the gun barrel. Akhíta, still knelt next to Royal, glanced at the gun as well, then at me, and did not tell Theo to put it away.

Forcing my eyes away from the gun, I looked down at Royal bleeding out in the dirt. Except something very strange had begun to happen. Royal's breaths were coming a little easier now, less blood foaming at the corners of their mouth. Looking closer I saw the terrible, dirty bandages seemed to have some faint writing on them in no language I recognized, barely discernible in the firelight. It looped and spun across the rough fabric, only a few shades darker brown than the linen itself, but as I watched the words—were they words?—got lighter and lighter until they were gone.

Shiloh grabbed the now blank bandages off Royal, using them to wipe away the blood and revealing nothing but a well-healed scar underneath where moments ago there had been a deadly wound. Royal struggled to their elbows, glancing down at their abdomen as I tried to wrap some logic around what just happened.

"Well," Royal said, voice weak. "Guess we won't be selling that bit of thievery. Shame. It would've fetched a good price."

Shiloh let out a slightly delirious laugh, wrapping his arms around Royal and pulling them onto his lap, planting a messy kiss to Royal's temple. Royal, still looking incredibly pale, melted into Shiloh's embrace, head tucked against the crook of Shiloh's neck, breathing immediately evening out into sleep.

"What—what was that?" I asked, managing to find my voice even though it shook.

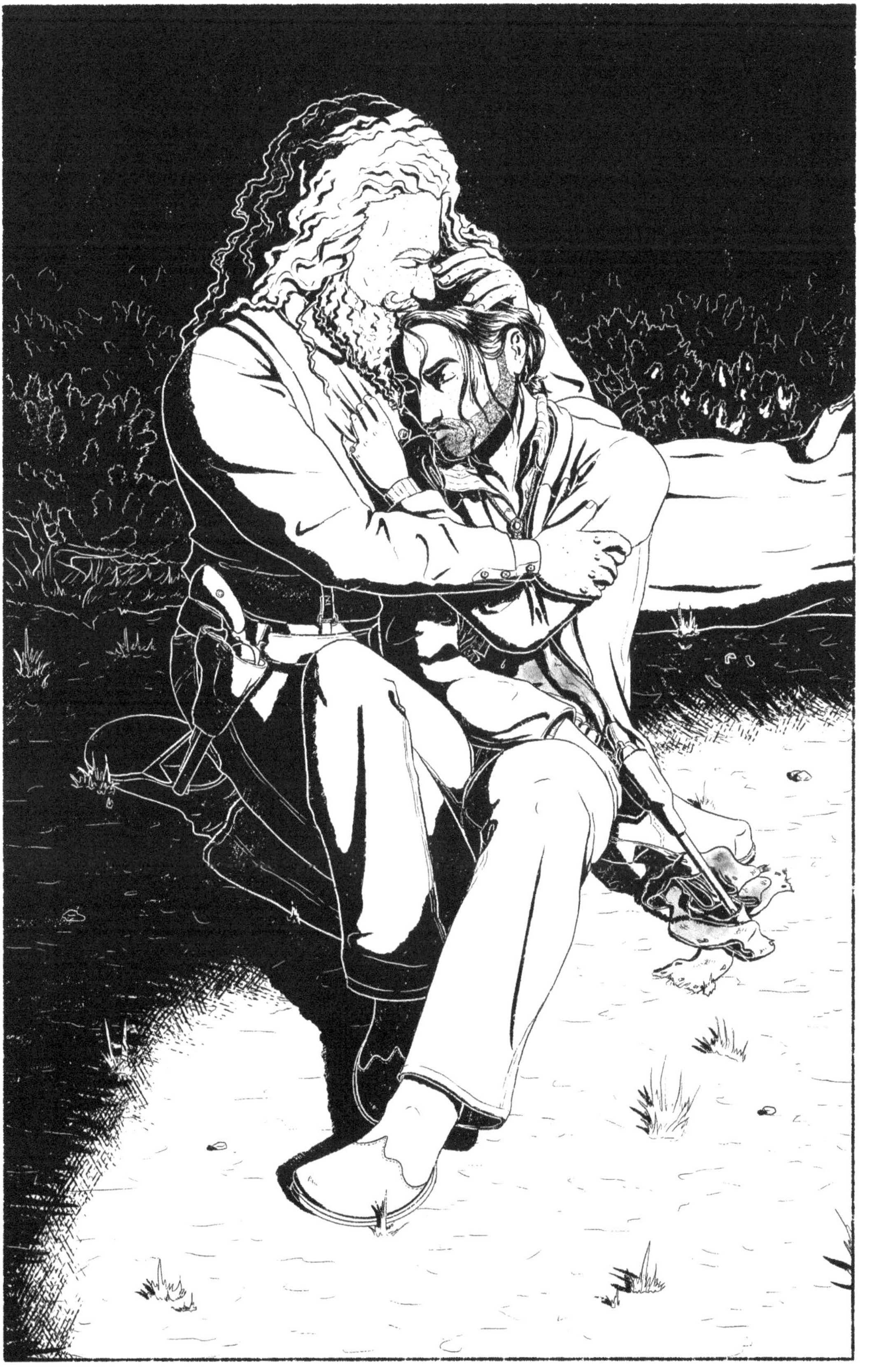

Shiloh leveled his eyes at me, assessing quietly. His arms were still protectively wrapped around Royal, one thumb running back and forth across Royal's bicep. The rest of the gang stared as well, seemingly awaiting Shiloh's response before they decided on their own.

"That, Clarabella, was magic," Shiloh said at last.

Several protests floated through my mind. All died on my lips. I couldn't deny what I'd just seen. Royal had been seconds from death, yet within those seconds they had instead been healed by a scrap of ratty cloth.

Theo finally dropped his gun, but did not put it away.

"What happened?" Akhíta said, voice low. Her tone wasn't threatening, yet it was clear it could easily turn that way.

"I—we—there were—" Tears prickled at my eyes and I couldn't get the words out, too overwhelmed. Akhíta stepped closer, posture tight. Gulping, I wrapped my arms around myself, hands on my shoulders, and took a step back. "We found the judge, and went—went to talk to him, but Emilia had run away. The judge had paid some men to escort her, and then again to find her once she ran off, I think. We were trying to get the judge to explain more when the men came to the hotel room, and everyone started shooting, and we ran, and we hid, and I didn't—I didn't know Royal was hurt."

"Who shot first?" Shiloh asked.

"I don't...I don't know? Royal, I think?" It had all gone blurry in my mind.

"We need to go," Hazel said. "If Royal was in a gunfight in the hotel of all places, no matter who fired first, every lawman in twenty miles will come out of the woodwork after us, especially if anyone else got hurt or killed."

There was a murmur of agreement and everyone spread out to start tearing down camp except for Akhíta and Shiloh. Akhíta continued to stare at me.

"No. You stay here," Akhíta said, voice still tensely calm.

My eyes widened, but Shiloh answered before I could.

"Akhíta, we can't leave her here."

She turned her gaze to him instead. "Look me in the eye and tell me that Royal wouldn't have gotten out of this unscathed if they didn't have a useless waiscu city-girl in tow?"

"Tell me they wouldn't have gotten out of this unscathed if you or I hadn't gone along with the pair of them?" Shiloh returned. "We knew the judge might be a threat to Royal, but we had no idea other people would be involved, so we didn't go. We thought this would be simple. It's on us too." Shiloh returned. Akhíta's jaw clenched. "What happened happened. Clarabella is Royal's sister and what happens to her is up to Royal, not us. We need to at least help her out of the area, then Royal can decide what to do next when they wake up."

Akhíta continued to stare at Shiloh for a moment, then shifted her eyes back and forth between us several times before stepping up to me. She brought her hand up, pressing a curled knuckle to my stomach in the same place Royal had been shot.

"That is the best friend I have ever had lying half dead in the dirt right there," Akhíta said, voice low and even. "They are in that dirt because of your actions, because you broke the promise you made to keep them safe. Because you dragged them into some half-cocked scheme to find your girlfriend. Because you seem to think this is some delightful book you'll be able to tuck away in your saddle bag when this is all over. It is not a book. It is the real world, and it is full of blood and pain and disease and death. It is not fair. It is not kind. It is not cut and dry. Royal nearly died because you don't understand any of that. The fact that Royal is alive at all right now is because of the magic you don't believe in."

A fresh wave of tears rolled down my face. Akhíta stared at me for several more seconds, knuckle still digging into my stomach, before she pulled away, walking off to help pack up camp.

I glanced over at Shiloh and Royal. "I'm sorry."

Shiloh shook his head and didn't respond.

No one even looked at me as everyone worked, let alone tried to offer me a way to help. I hovered at the edge of everything, just watching. The packing was much hastier this time, things thrown into any place they'd fit and tents mashed into lumpy bundles. Everything was ready to go within twenty minutes, all the packs full and horses saddled.

Shiloh, who had since wrapped Royal up in several thick blankets and dribbled some honey-water down their throat, whistled long and low, calling Astro over. The large horse came, leaning down to sniff at Royal's head. Shiloh scratched Astro's forehead, asking the horse to lie down. She did without hesitation. Shiloh stood, Royal in his arms, and threw one leg over Astro's back, settling into the saddle. Someone had put a thick, folded blanket over the horn of the saddle, giving Shiloh a place to rest Royal. Shiloh clicked his tongue once and Astro stood in a smooth motion that barely jostled her riders. Normally, the weight of a man as big as Shiloh coupled with the weight of someone Royal's size would've been too much for a horse, but it didn't seem like Astro even noticed.

Fox came over with Eagle's reins in hand and passed them to me without a word or eye contact.

"Thanks," I said.

Fox didn't answer, his back already turned.

Everyone mounted up, turning their horses north west away from town. Settled in my saddle, I looked down and realized my skirt and blouse were both stained dark with Royal's blood. It had fallen so thickly parts of the fabric were still wet, smudging onto the embroidered leather beneath me.

Once we crossed the traintracks the lights of Empire began to fade away behind us. After awhile, we started to swing south. Starlight spread out above us, the Milky Way a river of vibrant colors from one horizon to the other. No moon nor cloud cut through the sparkling display. A warm breeze with the scent of sage and dirt pressed against our faces. But none of this really managed to penetrate my awareness. My mind was caught in a cycle between a dozen other thoughts.

Royal. They were hurt, had nearly been killed, yet they'd also been healed. Somewhat healed. Sure the wound had closed, but Royal had still been pale and immediately passed out. What if there were still injuries inside?

Emilia. Where was she? Was she safe? How in the world was I meant to find her now? And, as Royal had pointed out earlier, even if I found her, what then? We couldn't go home. We couldn't go back to school. This had all seemed so simple a few days ago. Now I couldn't tell which way was up.

Magic. I'd seen magic today. Twice. A little crystal key that opened a door it didn't belong to, and a roll of old bandages imbued with healing powers. Things that belonged on the pages of novels, not in the hands of real people like Royal and Shiloh.

Over and over these things rolled around my mind, bouncing off one another and splitting into new thoughts and new confusions.

I loved Emilia.

I didn't know what I'd do when I found her.

I loved Royal.

It was my fault they'd nearly died after I dragged them into this.

I'd seen magic.

Magic wasn't supposed to be real.

Akhíta blamed me for what happened to Royal.

Everyone blamed me for what happened to Royal.

They'd all see me dead long before they let anything else happen to Royal.

Emilia was out there somewhere.

If I found her, we couldn't go home.

If I couldn't go home, I'd never see my family again.

I wanted to go home.

I wanted to curl up in my own bed.

I wanted to put my adventures back in a book, because Akhíta was right, this wasn't anything like the stories I loved.

No one bothered to look at me as we rode, letting me trail behind out of the way. Akhíta was in the lead, Shiloh to her right. Royal was still asleep in Shiloh's arms. Royal's horse walked to Shiloh's right, now loaded with both Royal and Shiloh's packs in lieu of a rider.

I wanted to check on Royal but knew I'd be rebuffed. All I had was the knowledge that if something was wrong, Shiloh would sound the alarm.

Repeated glances back showed that no one was pursuing us and I wondered if that would last. Hazel was right. A gunfight in a crowded hotel was going to draw a lot of attention. Had anyone else been hurt? Killed? Bullets had been going everywhere. It would be a miracle if there weren't other victims. What if there had been children there? A fresh wave of guilt rolled through me.

Never going after Emilia would have killed me, yet going after her seemed to have consequences even more dire. I couldn't figure out the right way to turn now, or if there had ever been a right way.

Slowly, though, I settled on a best way. It wasn't good, but it at least limited the damage to everyone else. As soon as I knew that Royal was alright, I would leave. This was my journey, my girlfriend. I never should have brought anyone else into the line of fire, so now I was going to take everyone else out of it.

Chapter 7
Morning

Setting up the next camp made it clear that the several hours of riding had not improved anyone's feelings towards me. I stayed out of the way, hovering on the outskirts. Royal was still asleep and Shiloh took them into one of the tents as soon as it was set up.

Exhaustion tugged my bones towards the ground and I struggled not to give in. Akhíta kept shooting distrustful glances my way and while I didn't *think* she'd leave me behind while I slept, I wasn't sure enough to chance it. I had to see Royal awake first. I thought about going to Akhíta and telling her my plan, but she vanished into her tent before I could.

Most of the others went to sleep as well, after watches were decided. No fire was lit, as it would have led anyone within miles towards our exact location with its glow. Eventually it was Pedro and I alone in the chilly night, and he didn't pay me any mind, his eyes sweeping the land to the east, back where we'd come from. It was still pitch black and, though the stars provided a fair amount of illumination, there was enough tall scrub that it would be easy for a group of lawmen to sneak up without warning. The thought made me a bit sick. I kept playing the afternoon over and over in my mind, wondering what I could have done differently, aside from not coming out here at all. I tried to pull out my rosary for comfort, only to find it caked with blood as well. There was no comfort to be found in it now, so I tucked it back in my pocket.

Shiloh came out awhile later and spotted me sitting off near the horses, woven blanket wrapped around my shoulders. I couldn't see his expression, but I could tell he was watching me. After several minutes of contemplation that made me want to pull the blanket up over my head, Shiloh came over and sat down next to me without a word.

"I'm sorry," I whispered.

"Hmm."

"How's Royal?"

"Alright. I got some food in them awhile ago. That'll help."

I nodded, returning us to silence. I honestly wasn't sure why Shiloh had even come over.

"What you said earlier, about it being Royal's decision if I should leave or not—"

"Mhmm?"

"—It's my decision too. I'll leave in the morning. I just want to see that Royal's alright first."

Shiloh sighed, going silent again for a time until eventually he twisted around to point south behind us. "About twenty or so miles that way is Empire Station, the fort that marks the start of the Allmen Pass." He twisted to point north. "Forty or so that way'll put you back in Whiskey Hole." Again, this time to the southeast. "Eighty or so that way, you'll be at Lost Lake, but that's hardly a town at all, just a church and a few scattered homesteads. A hundred or so miles beyond Lost Lake would put you in Pearl."

"So?"

"So pick which one you can survive walking too, because Akhíta will not give you a horse, no matter what Royal has to say on the matter."

"Oh." I curled in on myself under my blanket. "She really blames me that much?"

"You scare her," Shiloh said like it was the simplest thing in the world.

I turned a confused expression towards him. There was no way I could scare Akhíta. I didn't need to have known her long to know she was smart and brash and sharp and a skilled thief. Sure, I could probably beat her at reciting poetry, or embroidery, but that hardly mattered, let alone inspired fear, and I told Shiloh as much.

"What do you see when you look at Akhíta?" Shiloh asked.

"I just said, didn't I?"

"What else?" Shiloh pressed.

"Is this another 'life isn't books' conversation?" Clearly I was missing some point he was getting at.

"Sort of. More a 'your perception of the world is very narrow' conversation. You scare her because you're white. Because her father was a former slave who died in the war and her mother is Lakota. You scare her because your whiteness blinds you to the dangers those around you face day in and day out. When the law comes for her, as they have many times, it is so they can kill her. If the law comes for you, they'll send you home with a stern warning because your father is a rich, respected white man."

Oh. "I didn't realize—"

"Exactly," Shiloh said, voice a little harsher, accent a little deeper. "You don't realize, and that's why you're dangerous. You don't understand the danger you've put this entire group in. You don't understand how the world works outside your books, outside your beautiful house in your beautiful town. Every single one of us is here because, for one reason or another, the world doesn't want us. You, though. The world wants you. A pretty, vivacious, young white woman. Sure, you're a bit too smart, a bit too fond of other women, but those things can be hidden. Tucked neatly away in a chest of drawers to make your future husband happy. None of us have that sort of option. There is no room for us in towns and cities and universities. The only room we've got in this world is the room we carve out for ourselves, and sometimes that is messy, bloody work, which only digs us in deeper."

I pulled my knees up to my chest, resting my chin on them and wrapping my arms around my legs. The fabric of my skirts cracked where the blood had dried, bits of it flaking off, underlining Shiloh's point.

"I didn't realize," I whispered, holding back tears. We fell silent for a long stretch before I spoke again. "What are the chances Akhíta would even let me try to apologize before I left?" I asked.

"None. You made her a promise, and you broke it. That's a line you don't cross with Akhíta."

Guilt curled through me, pressing the tears out of my eyes and air out of my lungs. A dozen excuses and justifications died on my lips. Everyone kept telling me I didn't know what I was doing and they were right. It was time for me to shut up and listen.

"Okay," I said, voice shaking. "That's fair. Like I said, I'll leave as soon as I see that Royal is alright."

Shiloh nodded and stood up, brushing dirt off his pants. "Get some sleep, Clarabella. You've got a long walk tomorrow."

In the end I did manage to nod off, head resting on my saddle. Someone kicking my boot woke me, revealing a looming silhouette backlit by the rising sun. It took me several seconds of staring blearily upward before I realized the silhouette was Royal.

"The ground? Really?" Royal said.

I scrambled upright and swept my eyes over them. Their skin was still somewhat pale, and there were bags under their eyes, but otherwise they looked alright. They'd changed into a clean shirt and simple reddish brown skirt, leaving their hair loose and wild. They hadn't even bothered with shoes.

"How are you?" I asked.

Royal shrugged. "I've had worse."

I opened and closed my mouth a few times. "That's…that's not a comforting answer, you know that, right?"

Royal shrugged more dramatically. "You asked."

"Of course I asked! You got shot because of me! And then lied about it and spent the whole afternoon just quietly bleeding out!" It was amazing how quickly I could flip over to being annoyed when it came to Royal. Sort of comforting in its normality, though.

Royal grinned sheepishly, fiddling with their ring, something I was beginning to realize was a nervous habit. "Sorry about that. If it makes you feel better, I legitimately didn't realize it was that bad."

"Didn't real—HOW?"

"Adrenaline?"

I put my hands on my hips, eyes narrowed in suspicion. "Why does that sound like a question?"

"Uhh…."

"Was it more magic?" I asked. "Because I still can't quite wrap my head around all of that."

"Well—"

Royal was interrupted by Akhíta striding up behind them and shoving my pack into my arms. "You've seen Royal is alright now. Time for you to go. There's five days of food and water in the pack, if you're careful."

"Akhíta—" Royal started.

She turned and shook her head at them. "No. I am not traveling with this čhakála anymore."

"She's my sister, Akhíta," Royal said.

"She nearly got you killed."

"I nearly get me killed at least once a week," Royal returned.

"Hiyá." With that Akhíta turned and walked off.

Royal sighed and held out a hand towards me, waggling their fingers until I handed over the pack. They unceremoniously dropped it in the dirt. Akhíta turned back around and glared at Royal, who just held up their hands slightly, fingers spread wide.

"Look, I get it. She can't stay here. That's fine. Take everyone up to your mother's until things blow over here, and I'll stay with my sister and finish helping her on my own like I originally planned—"

This was met with a loud chorus of nos from the rest of the group who had clearly been eavesdropping. Royal groaned, scrunching up their face and making little frustrated grabbing motions in the air.

Shiloh stood from where he'd been eating around the campfire and sidled up next to Akhíta. "Look, as much as I am always amenable to paying a visit to Mama Standing Bear, we are not doing that."

Akhíta nodded in agreement. "So it is time for Clarabella to leave."

"We're not doing that either," Shiloh said.

Akhíta turned to stare incredulously at Shiloh while Royal looked mildly surprised to be getting some backup. I was pretty sure I looked even more surprised. After our conversation last night, Shiloh was the last person I expected to be coming to my defense in any form.

"Royal isn't willing to just send their sister off with nothing but a pack, and I think we can all agree, given her lack of experience out here and thus high likelihood of death, that is completely understandable, can't we?" Shiloh directed this at Akhíta who didn't nod, but she didn't show any sign of disagreement either. "And the rest of us aren't willing to let Royal go off with Clarabella alone, given that she's likely to get them into more trouble and Royal is likely to let it happen because they're a little blinded by being a protective older sibling."

"Hey! I am not blinded by anything," Royal said.

"Yes you are," Shiloh said. "We *all* are. Who here hasn't done something reckless to protect someone else in this group? Royal and Akhíta especially."

No one said anything.

"Exactly," Shiloh said. "We're all human, and we all have people we get a little stupid for. Mistakes were made yesterday. Emotions are high. Let's stop going in circles about it and figure out a real next step, agreed?"

Everyone looked to Akhíta who, after several tense moments, gave a begrudging nod before leveling a finger at me. "You are on very thin ice."

I nodded, none too sure what was supposed to happen now. No one else seemed to really know either and it took a bit for conversation to resume. I looked to Royal who shrugged and gestured towards breakfast. My stomach growled, desperate for something after not eating since breakfast the day before. Cautiously I followed Royal over, graciously accepting a bowl of what appeared to be oatmeal from Theo, who smiled jovially like he hadn't had a gun on me the night before.

"The gang comes first, you know?" Theo said, tone light and conversational.

"Err...yeah," I said, shuffling away.

I went and sat next to Royal and Shiloh.

"Shiloh?" I said cautiously once I was settled. "Last night...you made it sound like you agreed with me leaving?"

He smiled. "No. I told you where you could go if you did, and I said Akhíta wouldn't let you take a horse. I never said I couldn't talk Akhíta out of making you leave in the first place."

"Then why not just say that?" I asked, frustration leaking into my tone.

"You needed to feel guilty for awhile. No point in wiping away a mistake before you've learned from it," Shiloh said.

Royal gave a long-suffering sigh. "Always a game with you."

"A learning experience!" Shiloh admonished, taking Royal's bowl and getting up to heap another serving's worth on top of what was already there. Royal chuckled and accepted the bowl, along with a kiss.

"What about the fact that Akhíta doesn't trust me?" I asked.

"Nothing for it," Shiloh replied. "But that doesn't mean she won't let you stick around for now, just that she is going to be very particular about it."

Royal gave a grimace and a shrug. "Sorry. It's just how she is."

I nodded. "Fair enough."

I finally looked down at the oatmeal, which had been making my mouth water ever since I sat down. I didn't even like oatmeal. But it smelled so inviting. Warm and appley.

Royal winced as they shifted their weight and I opened my mouth to ask if they were alright. They said they were fine before I could get the words out.

I eyed their abdomen, wondering how true that was. "Are you sure? I mean. Yes, the external wound healed, but the bullet was still in there, wasn't it? Could the...magic...have really gotten rid of that? Fixed all the damage it did inside?"

"She does make a fair point, for once," Shiloh replied. "Those bandages heal wounds, but a bullet itself isn't exactly a wound."

Royal drummed their fingers against their stomach, staring contemplatively down at their food. "Well, I do feel fine. Just wrung out, which I'm guessing from the state of Clarabella's skirts is from blood loss."

Grimacing, I glanced down at the stains. I should have changed the night before, but I hadn't had the energy.

"That doesn't really count as a wound either, come to think of it,"

Shiloh said. "The result of one, yes, but not a wound itself."

"Exactly," Royal said, pointing at Shiloh with their spoon. "Anyways, I think I'm good. I promise to inform someone if things change, or if I cough up a bullet."

Royal and Shiloh continued to chatter back and forth about what counted as a wound and what didn't, heatedly debating the limits of magical healing. At one point Royal even dug a journal bound in soft leather out of a pocket in their skirt and started taking notes. The journal looked well loved and Royal was already most of the way through it. I wondered if it was all notes on magic, if there was really enough in the world to fill a whole journal. It was one thing to accept a few bits of magic hidden here and there, vestiges of an old world, but to contemplate that maybe that old world wasn't so old made my head spin.

Of the things I had always discounted as fiction—potions and curses and fairies and so much more—which of them might be real? And how had I never realized?

I pulled at every thread of memory my mind offered up, trying to follow one to something that felt like magic. Nothing came. I'd spent my whole life in sunny Altora, a town as normal as it got. Tree-lined brick avenues, church on Sundays, and quaint houses full of everything ordinary. Sure, some strange drunks wandered through from time to time, the occasional snake oil salesman, but that was true of anywhere.

Except, I realized, that wasn't exactly the old world, was it? That was, in fact, all very new. Altora had only been founded thirty years ago. A speck of time, no matter how quickly it had grown. It felt like this was getting me closer to the answer, but the final pieces eluded me, hanging vaguely out of reach.

Something Royal said earlier popped into my mind. That the railroad was the worst thing to ever happen to this country.

I broke back into the conversation between Royal and Shiloh. "The other day, you said the railroad is the worst thing to ever happen to this country. What did you mean by that?"

Royal leveled their pencil at me, looking impressed. "Now you're asking the right questions. The railroads are destroying magic. All of them are, in every country that has them."

"But why?" I asked. Coming to the realization that the two things were connected did not mean I understood it.

"Our theory is the iron rails," Royal replied, eyes bright.

"Oh no, you've gotten them started," Shiloh said with a tone that made it clear he was only teasing.

Royal plowed on like Shiloh hadn't spoken, voice fast and hands dancing in the air. I couldn't tell if they were signing for Little Mountain who was several feet away, or just gesturing in general. Maybe both. "See the magic in the world, it runs in these sort of...rivers, all over the world. Or perhaps veins would be a better analogy. Yes, veins. Veins under the surface. But iron interrupts this magic. Blocks it. This was never really a problem, and in fact served as a protection for much of history, but until now humanity has never created anything in the realm of rail travel. Now there's huge lines of iron cutting through the veins, blocking them like a tourniquet. And, just like if you block blood from a portion of the body, if you block magic from parts of the world it begins to wither and die."

"Okay," I said slowly. "I can follow that, I guess. But...none of this is dead?" I gestured out at the land around us. Sure, it wasn't the prettiest stretch of country, but it was full of living things.

"But is any of it magic?" Royal returned, one eyebrow arched high.

They had me there.

"What are the Pits, then?" I asked.

"A wound," Royal said. "Sort of. If we're using the vein analogy, anyway. They're a way to get inside the body where more blood—more magic—is. The deeper you go, the more blood, the more magic, there is."

Little Mountain clapped once to get Royal's attention and started signing. Royal watched her and translated. "My people say the Pits were formed when Coyote angered the sun with a silly prank. The sun vanished from the skies, sending the world into cold and darkness. Coyote regretted what he'd done and began to dig and dig, trying to find where the sun had gone when it slipped below the horizon for the last time. He didn't know he was digging into the next world until it was too late and the next world began leaking out. He turned around and ran home in fear, only to find the sun had returned on its own. But he never filled his holes back in and so they remain, letting bits of the next world into this one."

Royal nodded, turning their attention back to me. "The Ute seem to know the most about the Pits, since most of the central range is their land, but even they won't go very deep into them, not even for religious ceremonies. There's other stories of their origins as well. The Navajo say the Pits were carved by a fire that burned for a hundred years. The Lakota say a great herd of buffalo dug them to survive a terrible winter. I think the Lakota name for them is 'Kin Ošme Makoskan,' which means 'The Deep Wilderness,' but I'm sure Akhíta will tell me I've pronounced that wrong."

"My head is spinning," I admitted. "I never saw any reason to think the Pits were more than just an aspect of geology we didn't yet understand."

"Technically they are," Shiloh said. "It's just that current science isn't the way to understand them. Royal is determined to change that, though. Hence that little journal, and the dozen or so that came before it."

Royal held the journal up and gave it a shake. "And I'll do it, too. The answers are out there somewhere."

Little Mountain shook her head, looking amused. "It is going to bite you," Shiloh translated.

Royal waved her off. "Bah. That will just give me more data."

I chewed my lip. "Is there some sort of magic that could help me find Emilia?"

"Probably," Royal said. "We used to have a compass that could point you to your true love, but we sold it ages ago."

"What about, like, spells or something?" I said, frustrated. How could magic suddenly be real, yet unable to help me? "Books always have a spe—but this isn't a book." I puffed out a frustrated breath.

"She's learning!" Shiloh said brightly. "Magic isn't like it is in your books either. Far as we know, spells are hogwash. Or maybe they just are now because magic has been weakened so much. Hard to say."

I groaned and flopped back in the dirt. Royal patted my knee sympathetically. "There's other ways to find lost things."

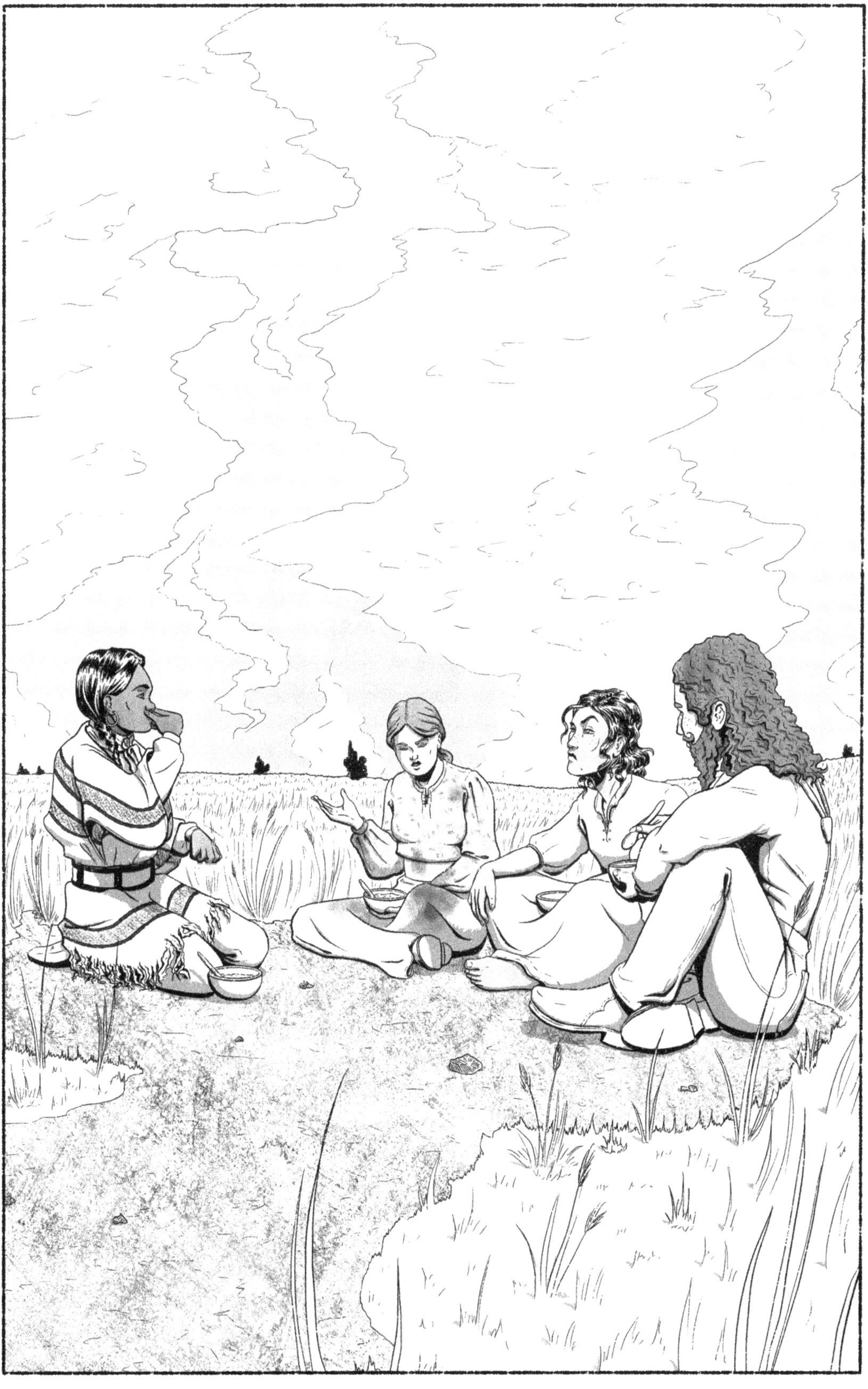

"Like what? A search party couldn't find Emilia over at least the last few days. And I love her, but I wouldn't exactly say she's skilled at evasion. She doesn't even know how to ride a horse or start a fire."

"That greatly narrows the search, then," Little Mountain signed, translated for by Shiloh once again. "She wouldn't run off into the plains, so we'll have to look in the towns."

"Or on the trains," Royal mused, leaning back on their hands. "That would make the most sense, I think, if they weren't able to find her in town. South, probably, away from home and her father."

"She could be anywhere then," I said. Despair leached into my mind. I was never going to see her again.

"We could always ask—" Little Mountain signed. Royal cut off translating with a shake of their head.

"Ask who?" I said, looking between them.

"Another...gang...of sorts, we know," Royal said, reluctance weighing down every word. "Know of, I should say. But their information wouldn't be worth it, trust me."

Little Mountain glared and made a flurry of signs that no one translated. Royal signed right back without speaking. After a few silent exchanges Little Mountain threw up her hands and got up, leaving the three of us alone. Everyone else seemed to have wandered off as well, all spreading out to do different things.

"What was that about?" I asked, now extremely suspicious.

"Nothing," Royal said.

"Royal."

"They can't help and even if they could, you wouldn't want them to," Royal said.

"Well what are we doing, then?" I asked.

Royal didn't answer, seeming unsure.

"I'd say we have two likely options now," Shiloh said. "Either she took the train south, or perhaps she decided to go west and make the crossing on her own. West would certainly be the last thing her father would expect, given she ran away to avoid exactly that."

"So we check the Station first," Royal picked up, "and if no one has seen her there we continue south."

Shiloh nodded.

"Wonderful. Good plan," Royal said, getting up. "I'm going to take a nap." They seemed a little too eager to move the conversation away from whatever Little Mountain had been advocating for. Clearly they weren't going to be honest about that, nor was Shiloh it seemed. Maybe one of the others would. I just had to find a way to ask.

Chapter 8
The Fort

Fox seemed like my best bet, even though he'd been avoiding me, so I changed into fresh clothes and wandered around until I found him fishing in a small creek away from camp. Attempting to fish, anyway. His line had gotten tangled, resulting in a lot of mumbled cuss words. I came and sat next to him on the bank, silently holding out my hand. Fox eyed my hand, and my face, for several moments before handing the mass over.

I turned it over in my hands several times before I started gently prying at it to loosen the knots. Fox watched with interest, leaning in close to study what I was doing.

"I take it your hair wasn't curly when you wore it long?" I asked.

Fox shook his head. "Nope. Straight as a stick. But yours isn't that curly either? And neither is Royal's?"

I continued tugging here and there, undoing the mass one loop at a time. "Our little sister, Josephine, has a head full of curls. Combing them out when she washes her hair is a nightmare."

"Ah. Makes sense."

The conversation felt so stilted, but I didn't know how to fix it, let alone ask about this mysterious other gang. It wasn't exactly like Fox and I had been good friends before Royal had been shot, and we certainly weren't friends now. Awkward silence continued to hang until, finally, I pulled the right strand and the whole knot fell apart in my hands.

"Thanks," Fox said, reeling the line up before casting it out again.

"So…you're sticking around?"

I glanced over my shoulder towards camp. "I guess? I'm at least not walking off into the sage right this moment."

"Hmm."

"Do you want me to leave?"

Fox shrugged. "Last night sucked, but it isn't the first time one of us has been shot. Not even the first time this month that Royal specifically has been shot."

I groaned. "Do they *really* get in that much trouble?"

Fox snickered. "Yeah. Poker games, pick-pocketing, general robbery. Royal's always up to something. We all qualify as outlaws, probably, but Royal is the one who really lives up to it."

We were interrupted by Akhíta appearing out of the brush behind us. My spine snapped straight and I watched her approach, wondering what was about to happen, but she didn't even acknowledge my presence.

"Fox, pack up. We're heading for the fort."

With that she turned around and left.

Fox glanced at me. "Well. She didn't shoot you and say the coyotes got you when Royal wasn't looking. That's something?"

It didn't really feel like anything.

"What's at the fort?" Fox asked, gathering his fishing equipment.

"News of Emilia, maybe."

Fox paused, tilting his head to look at me. "You really love her?"

I nodded.

Fox fiddled with his fishing pole, looking down at his feet. "Until I met Royal and Shiloh…I never thought someone like me could have something like that." Fox finally looked up and gave me a slight smile. "I get why you want to find her so much."

Now was my chance. "Earlier…Little Mountain said something about another gang that might be able to help. But Royal seemed really wary of them and kept insisting they couldn't help. Do you have any idea what that was about?"

Fox thought about it for a minute, then shook his head. "No, sorry. Guess it's something from before I joined up."

I sighed. "Oh well. Maybe I can manage to wheedle it out of Royal if the fort doesn't give us a lead."

Arriving back in camp, we found that it had been entirely packed in our absence. Royal was already mounted up, redressed in the same black duster, pants, and silver rimmed hat as when I'd found them in Whiskey Hole.

When we reached the fort after a few hours' ride Royal pulled me aside and undid my hair, leaving it loose around my shoulders.

"What are you doing?" I asked, feeling uncomfortable. I hated my hair loose, especially when I was riding.

"Changing your appearance a little," Royal said, turning to their saddlebags. They stuffed one arm down inside, far deeper than it should have been able to go, and pulled out a lovely, embroidered, pale pink riding jacket. Holding it up in front of me, Royal looked thoughtful. "Eh, a bit big, but it'll work."

I took it and slipped it on, wishing it wasn't a little big. It really was lovely. "How did you do that with the saddlebag?"

"Been like that ever since I found it. Holds a shocking amount, without ever getting heavy, but sometimes things come out a bit singed. Not really sure why."

I resisted the urge to ask more questions. Magic was easier to take in little doses.

"Hó, uŋyáŋpi kte," Akhíta said. Shiloh was standing at her shoulder.

Royal turned and quirked an eyebrow at both of them. "What do you mean '*let's* go'? You two don't need to come."

"Recent bullet wounds result in supervision of all endeavors for at least the following week," Shiloh proclaimed.

Royal looked to Akhíta.

"What he said. But you're not the one I'm supervising." She leveled a look that could have frozen a river at me. I swallowed heavily, barely resisting the urge to hide behind Royal. I also got the distinct sense she was speaking Lakota because she didn't want me to be fully privy to the conversation.

Royal shook their head, rolling their eyes dramatically and gesturing towards the fort a short distance away. "Well, let's go then."

It was a huge wooden structure made up of two compounds, one on either side of an equally large wooden arch that spanned them. The one to the south had a sign over the entrance that said "departures" while the one closest to us had a sign that said "arrivals." Wagons, horse riders, and people on foot were all lined up at the arch, being inspected and questioned before they were allowed to pass through. The din was even louder than it had been in Empire. Guides shouted their rates, preachers shouted offers for last rites just in case, soldiers shouted instructions, kids cried.

Akhíta no longer seemed worried about standing out, but I did notice she'd twisted her hair up into a large bun, tucking all the bullet casings on the tips out of sight. Shiloh, who was apparently the most familiar with the fort, led us to the compound to the south and in through the gates. Inside was somewhat calmer in the level of noise, but not so much in the level of activity. Shops and offices ringed a wide courtyard, people dashing to and fro between them getting last minute supplies and documentation. Shiloh started weaving us towards a storefront with a sign on it that said "Registration."

"And you really think the railroad won't be an improvement over this?" I asked after I was run into for the third time. Cutting off the magic or not, providing a better way to cross the continent without going nearly all the way up to Canada or down to Texas had to be done.

"The only thing wrong with this place is bureaucracy," Royal said. "They started charging to take the crossing about ten years back, and it has made a right mess of it all."

"Charging for *what*?" I asked.

"They say they want records of everyone making the crossing, to make sure no one gets lost and all deaths are recorded," Royal explained. "So to create those records, they put a permit system in place. Cross without one and you get fined, but to get one you still have to pay."

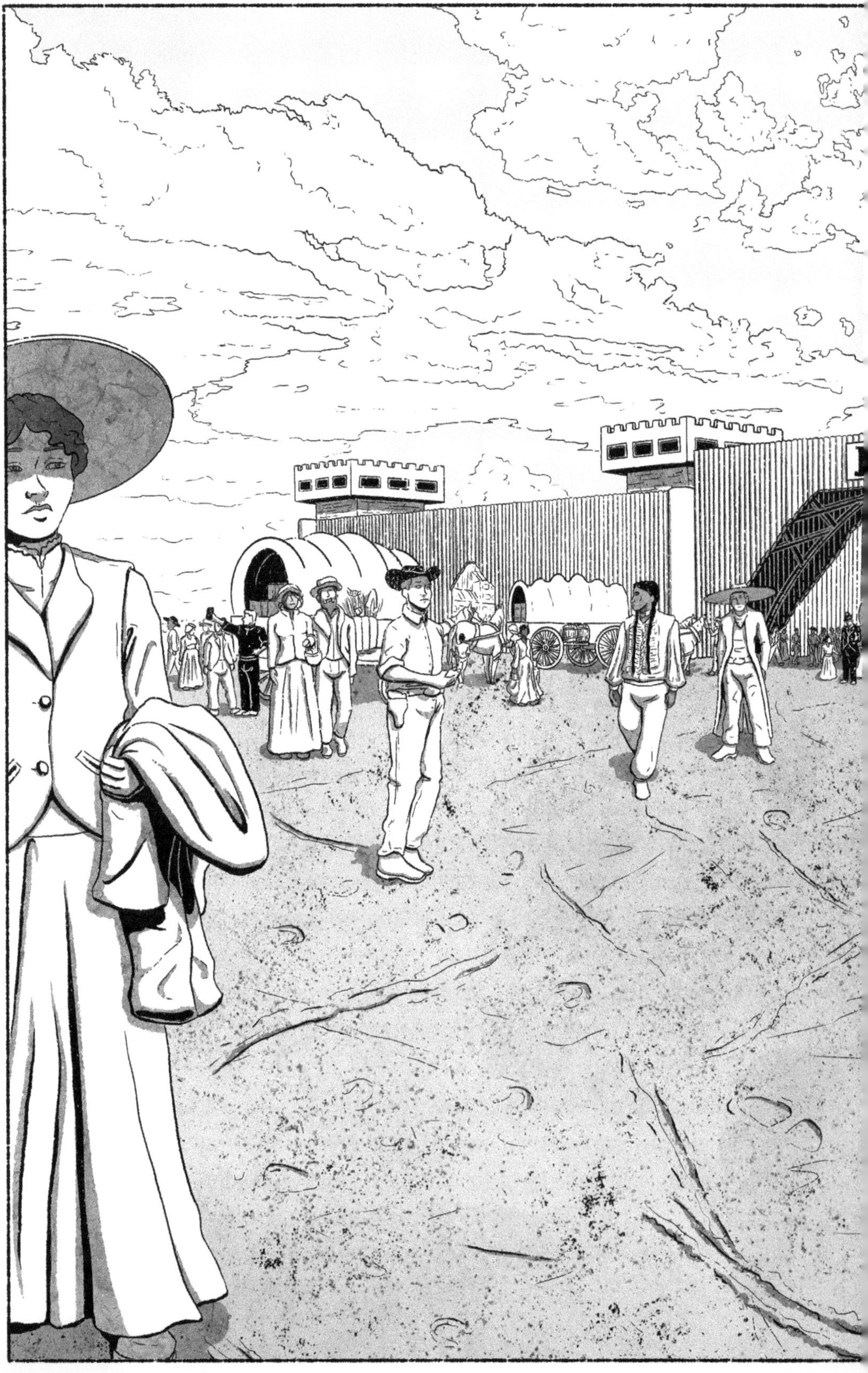

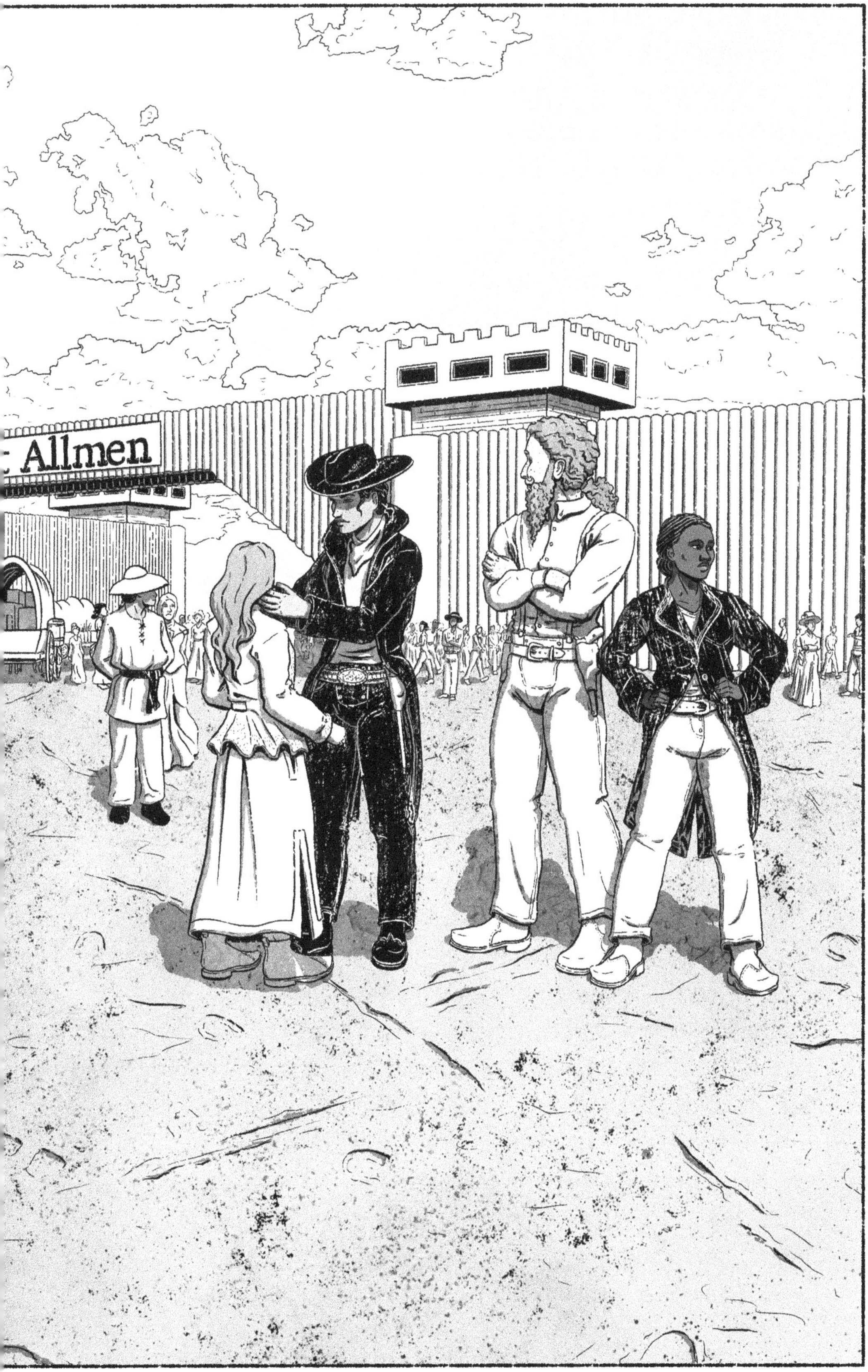
Allmen

"One of these days I'm gonna burn it down," Akhíta muttered. "You people are so fond of counting and cataloging everything. Everything must have a name, a system, a number, a piece of paper. It's ridiculous."

"Everyone behave," Shiloh said, stepping through the open door of the information office.

Inside were three very hassled looking men, all trying to help a crowd of people who were, by and large, all shouting at them.

"Obnoxiously busy as always," Shiloh observed.

Royal nodded to Akhíta, jutting their chin out to the right side of the room. Akhíta nodded and went that way, while Royal continued to the other side, leaving Shiloh and I by the door.

"Now what?" I asked.

Shiloh shrugged. "I stopped asking those two 'now what' ages ago. They'll figure it out and shout if they need us."

Within moments I'd lost sight of both of them in the crowd. Not even Royal's height was enough to keep them visible. Shiloh's height, and bulk, however, were enough to buy the two of us some room as we got jostled over into a corner at the front, pressing us up to the glass storefront.

"I never got the chance to say thanks," I said. "For convincing Akhíta to let me stay."

"Everyone makes mistakes," Shiloh said.

I nodded and took a deep breath. "Shiloh?"

He glanced down at me without saying anything.

"Tell Royal I'm sorry, for leaving without saying goodbye."

I'd made up my mind on the ride over. It was clear that my leaving would be best, but that Royal wasn't likely to let it happen. They had a good thing going with these people, even if it was dangerous some of the time, and I was messing that up. I'd slip out now, find somewhere to hole up, come back to the information office once Royal was gone, and continue on my own.

"Royal won't like that," Shiloh said after a moment.

"I know." I slipped out of the pink jacket and handed it to Shiloh. "But it's what's best."

Shiloh sighed and took the jacket. "I'll try and buy you some time.

Royal will follow, though."

"Thank you," I said, fighting a few tears.

Turning to leave, I got a look out the front windows, freezing at what I saw. There, in the courtyard, were two of the men from the judge's hotel room. They were holding up a piece of paper to everyone and even from this distance I could see my picture sketched onto it, along with Royal's. Before any thought of what to do could cross my mind one of the men turned and looked directly at me. He squinted for a moment before his face shifted to a glare and his hand came to rest on his pistol.

"Shiloh!" I squeaked.

He turned, took in the man shoving his way through the crowd, and immediately grabbed me around the waist, pushing me deeper into the crowd in the building. Angry shouts came from all around us but Shiloh didn't stop, pushing me ahead of him through a side door. This didn't get us outside, however, only into the next building, which seemed to be under renovation and had no one in it. Shiloh grabbed a desk and dragged it in front of the door we'd come through.

"Royal and Akhíta," I said, voice shaking. Both were still in the information office.

"They'll take care of themselves," Shiloh said. "Here." He reached into his left boot and produced a small revolver, holding it out to me.

I held up my hands and shook my head. "I don't know how to shoot."

"Pull the hammer back, point it at someone you don't like, and pull the trigger," Shiloh said.

I took it gingerly, nearly shooting the floor when something slammed into the door Shiloh had barred.

"Breathe," Shiloh instructed in a whisper. "Stick to my back. We're going through the shops to the gate. Get on the first horse you see and bolt west. There's a series of rock towers, the Gates of Purgatory, that mark the start of the pass. They're a maze, and you can't miss them if you ride west from here. We can lose them there and hide. I'm right with you."

I swallowed and nodded. Somehow this was so much worse than yesterday. I hadn't had time to think yesterday and the whole affair hadn't lasted more than a minute. But this. Plans and horses and mazes and a terrifyingly heavy gun in my hands, bullets in its chambers. This was too much. And yet, what else was there to do?

Shiloh turned and made for the next wall, the next door, kicking his way through when he found it locked. The next building looked to be a moderately busy fur shop, the one after that a dress store, then a general store. Our crashing, stomping entrances earned a lot of angry shouts and affronted yelps, but no one tried to stop us. Nor, did it seem, was anyone trying to follow us. I hated that even more, not knowing where the men were.

When we reached the last shop right next to the gates—a cluttered but uninhabited, seemingly closed place selling all sorts of funeral things, caskets included—Shiloh stopped and looked out the windows. Sucking in a breath of air through his teeth, he let out a quiet curse. Both men were standing at the gate, checking everyone who left.

"That's the only way out?" I asked, peering around him.

"Forts aren't exactly made to be easy to get into, and thus are not easy to get out of either," Shiloh muttered.

The sound of a gun cocking turned us both around, finding the shopkeeper with a shotgun aimed at us over the counter.

"Get along," he said firmly. "Before I put you in one of these fine pine boxes."

No idea what else to do, and very much not wanting to be forced outside, I did the only thing I could think of and dropped my gun, held my hands up, and gave in to the stress that had been making me want to cry ever since I'd first seen the men.

Gulping in air, I stepped away from Shiloh, who looked confused and didn't lower his own pistol.

"Help me, please!" I said to the shopkeeper. "Please! I don't want to be here anymore!"

The shopkeeper gave me a once over, then jerked his head in indication for me to come forward and get behind him. I dashed over, turning to see that Shiloh looked murderous. With the shopkeeper's attention still on Shiloh, I grabbed a large brass paperweight and crashed it down on the shopkeeper's head. He dropped like a rock, chin bouncing off the counter and gun clattering to the floor on the other side.

Shiloh's mouth fell open and I just stood there, staring down at the moaning man, my hand still hovering in the air with the paperweight. I felt guilty, but there hadn't been time for anything else. Nothing that wouldn't result in my immediate arrest, anyway.

I looked back up at Shiloh. "Like Royal said, they never suspect the woman."

Shiloh broke into a huge grin and laughed. Within moments he'd come over and bound up the shopkeeper, gagging him as well. The man, now fully conscious once more, glared at both of us.

"Any thoughts on the gate?" Shiloh asked, handing the little revolver back to me.

I looked around the shop, trying to come up with something. There wasn't really anything useful in here. Just caskets, bibles, some black dresses, and other funeral related things. But it didn't matter what I came up with, because in that moment an explosion shattered the previously controlled chaos of the courtyard.

"This is our chance," Shiloh said, grabbing my hand and dragging me out the door into the chaos.

There was a crush of bodies at the gate, everyone screaming and shouting and crying. We shoved our way in, Shiloh clearing a path. I caught sight of one of the men after me, but he couldn't get to me through the crowd.

The other side of the gate was just as chaotic and filled with a lot more soldiers. They were pulling people out, trying to get them out of the way so they could get inside. None of them paid Shiloh and I any notice. We were just another pair of scared people to them.

"Those," Shiloh said, pointing at a pair of saddled chestnut quarter horses tied to a post several yards away.

Feeling guilty I yanked on the reins of one to free them from their knot around the post, then swung myself up into the too large saddle. We were on the east side of the fort but, remembering what Shiloh said earlier, I turned south and went around the structure until I was able to head west. For the moment, I kept my horse at a trot, not wanting to draw attention. Shiloh did the same. It was all for nothing as, within moments, four men were on our tails on horses of their own. Two of them were the original men, the other two were soldiers.

Shiloh and I both took off at a gallop, my hair whipping around my face. I couldn't tell if I was really hearing gunshots over the thunder of hooves, and I didn't bother to turn back and check. If I got hit I'd know.

Like everything else about the Pits, the Gates of Purgatory couldn't be seen until we practically fell into them. A steep path of loose red dirt plunged us down into a shadowy world of towering sandstone pillars. It couldn't have been the main path in, as it wasn't wide enough for a wagon.

Shiloh took the lead, weaving between the pillars. My horse struggled to keep up, stumbling twice over the loose rock and sand. This wasn't a trail horse and if we kept going like this the horse was going to break a leg. I chanced a glance over my shoulder and couldn't see anyone, though it wouldn't have been hard for them to be just out of sight.

Yelling for Shiloh I pulled up the reins, dismounted, and smacked the horse's butt, sending it running off.

"What the hell?" Shiloh said, circling back. His horse was frothing at the bit, sides heaving.

"These horses can't take this terrain." I yanked the laces of my skirt and let it fall to the ground, leaving me in my petticoats. Scooping the skirt up I used it to brush my footprints out of the sand. "Let them follow the hoof prints."

"You're much more impressive today than you were yesterday," Shiloh said, dismounting and smacking his horse to send it off as well.

I didn't feel very impressive. Just scared.

Shouts could be heard echoing around us, syllables shattering against the rock, sending fragments bouncing in every direction and completely obscuring their origin. Shiloh led the way down several thinner paths, far too thin for horses, and I followed, brushing away our tracks as we went. I wanted to ask about Royal and Akhíta, if Shiloh thought they were okay, but didn't dare speak for fear of how far my voice would carry.

Shiloh stopped and I bumped into him, turning to see that our path had ended. In front of us was a broad, washed out expanse. Several other paths could be seen branching off from it, but there was no cover between us and them. Voices could still be heard, seemingly somewhere close.

"Should we turn back?" I whispered. It would mean going quite a way. There hadn't been another way to turn for a good distance.

Shiloh looked between the expanse in front of us and the thin path behind, debating. The question was answered for us by a loud shout of "There!" and a bullet slamming into the rock above Shiloh's head, sending sand raining down on us. Before we could properly react others rung out from above, slamming into the opposite wall. Shiloh grabbed me and dragged me to the ground, putting his body over mine. I could barely see what was going on; our pursuers had emerged from one of the crevices across the wash, and they were firing up at someone on top of a pillar. With some twisting I managed to catch a glimpse of a person up there, silhouetted by the sun, sun that glinted off the silver rim of a cowboy hat. Royal. Thank god.

Several other people appeared next to Royal, but I couldn't really tell who was who. Shot after shot rang out and suddenly Royal started to back up before running full tilt towards the edge. Before I even had a chance to scream they'd jumped into the air, curling their body forward and to the side, putting their shoulder between them and the ground. Just before they slammed into the dirt and inevitably death, a bubble of light shimmered around their body, a barely visible opalescent sheen, and shattered against the ground, shards dissolving in bright sparks. Royal took the impact as if it was nothing, as if they'd taken a fall of only a few feet rather than fifty. One smooth motion and they were rolling to their feet, both pistols drawn and already firing before they were even fully up.

Shiloh cursed in what I assumed was Irish and scrambled to his feet, raising his own gun and trying to cover Royal. The whole world slowed to a crawl when the last pursuer standing, one of the soldiers—bleeding from a wound to his shoulder—raised his pistol and took aim at Royal's head. There was enough time for Royal to flinch, but not enough for them to dodge. I screamed. Shiloh yelled. The gun went off.

And the bullet slammed to a stop inches from Royal's face, opalescence rippling out from it before it dropped into the sand. Everyone froze, but Royal regained their composure first and shot the soldier through the heart.

Everything went still. Royal, shoulders heaving with heavy breaths that echoed as loud as the gunshots, eyed the now still bodies of our pursuers. None of them moved. Royal put away one pistol, kept the other drawn, and slowly advanced until they reached the bodies. One by one, Royal toed at them. Only once they'd reached the last body did they seem to relax.

"They're all down," Royal shouted.

Several whoops sounded from above us. Shiloh, however, looked far more shaken than pleased. Whatever had just happened, it didn't seem like something that should have.

"Shiloh and your sister?" Akhíta called.

I was surprised at how relieved I felt to know she was okay. Also a little confused that she seemed to care if I was.

Royal turned and looked around, clearly not sure where we were.

"Here!" Shiloh called, stepping out into view. "We're good!"

A few more whoops went out as Royal ran over. They scooped me up in a bone-crushing hug, kissing my forehead, before releasing me to hug Shiloh just as tightly. Stepping back, they kept one hand on each of us as they looked us over.

"Not hurt at all?" Royal asked, voice shaky.

"Fine," I said.

"What the hell was that?" Shiloh asked.

"Are. You. Hurt?" Royal returned.

"No. What. Was. That?"

Royal opened their mouth a little and shook their head, hands held out palm up.

"It was that thing you used to jump, wasn't it?" I asked.

Royal and Shiloh both turned to me, looking confused.

"It couldn't have been," Royal said. "That's just an old charm to protect from falls. It doesn't protect against bullets."

Shiloh gave me an assessing look. "What makes you think it was that, Clarabella?"

"Well...they sort of looked the same. The bubble that protected Royal from the fall, and the shimmer that radiated out from where the bullet stopped." I thought they'd looked the same, anyway. Maybe I'd been mistaken.

Royal shook their head. "I don't know. We'll figure it out later. I'm just glad you're both alright."

Shiloh didn't seem quite as ready to move on, hovering protectively close to Royal. He did drop it, though, bringing the conversation back to everything else. "Clarabella could give you a run for your money when it comes to getting out of a sticky corner, Royal."

"Okay, interesting, will ask more about that in a moment, but first: Clarabella, where the hell is your skirt?" Royal asked.

I looked around and didn't see it, turning back to Royal with a shrug. "I was using it to brush away our footprints," I explained. "I dropped it when the shooting started. I'll find it in a minute."

Royal let out a deep breath and nodded, pulling me back into a hug. This time they didn't let go and I let my head rest on their chest, feeling their pulse beneath my cheek. It was going a mile a minute, but slowing down.

Shiloh stepped away, giving Royal's forehead a kiss first before going over to examine the corpses. I was trying not to think about them. About their families. They'd just been doing their jobs, after all. The soldiers, anyway.

"You scared me," Royal muttered. "I knew you were with Shiloh, and that he'd look after you, but...fuck. Akhíta and I set off that stick of dynamite to buy you a way out, but we weren't sure if it worked."

I pulled away a bit. "No one got hurt in the explosion, right?"

Royal shook their head. "We found an empty office."

I glanced over at the four dead men. Shiloh was pulling them all into a line. Royal glanced over as well.

"It happens," Royal said. "It isn't good, soldiers especially, but it happens. We'll bury them here to keep the animals away and get a letter to the fort about where to find their bodies."

I nodded, still feeling guilty. All this just to find Emilia. Would I even be able to look her in the eye now?

Chapter 9
Post Fight

The rest of the gang made their way down to us, arriving with all the horses and gear. Everyone was clearly on edge, despite the victory. A lot of glances were sent over shoulders, and conversations were kept to low tones. Akhíta marched straight up to Shiloh, demanding to know what happened. I answered for him.

"I was trying to leave," I explained. Royal, who was still hovering at my side, made a shocked noise and I forced myself not to look at them. "I figured that was best, and that the only way I could do it was when Royal was elsewhere. But when I turned to go, I saw two of the men from the hotel—" I gestured to their bodies—"they had a sketch of me and were asking people about it. One of them spotted me through the window, so Shiloh grabbed me and we ran through the shops—"

Shiloh picked up, laying out the rest of the story and giving me far too much credit throughout, like he was a proud parent bragging about his child's arithmetic skills. Akhíta listened in silence, and I was still forcing myself not to look at Royal. Meanwhile, several of the others had pulled shovels out of their packs and were preparing to dig the graves.

"Excuse me," I said, stepping away from Akhíta, Shiloh, and Royal. Their conversation paused as they all watched me.

Making my way over to Pedro, I held out my hand for his shovel. He glanced over at Akhíta, seeming to silently ask permission. I couldn't see how she responded, but he handed the shovel over. As I moved to start digging, I saw Royal disappear down a crevice, Shiloh on their heels. Hesitating a moment, I eventually decided to let Shiloh handle it.

The digging was exhausting, sweat rolling over every inch of my skin and hair hanging lank around my face. We could only get the four graves so deep in the sandy soil, having to call it after a few feet. Before the bodies could be moved, I went over and kneeled next to them. The first man, one from the hotel, was maybe in his thirties and black, a bullet hole in his cheek. Gently, I patted his pockets, searching for something that might identify him. I found it; a little pocket bible with a name scrawled on the first page. Jeremiah Harrisburg. I set the bible on his chest, placed one hand on it and moved to the next body.

"What are you doing?" Akhíta asked, coming to stand next to me.

I glanced up at her. "Enough people in this country have been buried without their names, don't you think?"

She didn't answer for a moment. "My father was buried without his." She opened her jacket to reveal a scrap of rough blue fabric sewed into the lining over her heart. "One of his fellow soldiers saved this and sent it to my mother so she'd have something at least, but his body was never recovered. At best he's in some mass grave somewhere. More likely his body was strung up and desecrated by the southern soldiers."

"I'm sorry," I told her.

She continued to watch me as I checked over the three other bodies. The soldiers were easy; both had little silver plates with their names, ranks, and family names engraved on the surface. Such things had been popular to carry during the war and it seemed the practice had not fallen out of favor. The second man from the hotel, though, had nothing except a necklace with a Star of David pendant.

"I don't know what last rites are for a Jewish person," I admitted to Akhíta.

She looked over her shoulder and whistled. "Theo!"

Theo trotted over, looking to Akhíta. She nodded at the body of the last man. I tilted the pendant up so Theo could see.

"What do we do for him?" Akhíta asked.

Theo peered over his spectacles. "Well, as I am the only Jewish person here, and not a Rabbi, there is not much we *can* do. But I will say a few words."

One by one, we wrapped the bodies in blankets, then lowered them into the graves. When we reached the Jewish man, Theo whispered "Baruch dayan ha'emet," along with several quieter phrases I did not catch. Royal and Shiloh still hadn't reappeared by the time we finished piling the dirt back on, marking the graves with stones, and it was getting dark. I stared off towards the crevice they'd vanished down, knowing full well my chances of finding them without getting lost were minimal.

At some point someone had retrieved my skirt, draping it over my saddle. I went and slipped it on, taking my time tying the laces.

"Well," I said, looking out over the group. "If someone will tell me the way out of here, I'll be going."

No one said anything. Most looked to Akhíta. Akhíta glanced over at Royal and Shiloh, then surveyed the rest of the group.

"No judgment on your answers. Who is in favor of Clarabella staying?"

Fox raised his hand first, then Hazel. Dahlia raised her hand just because her mother did. One by one everyone else's hand went up. My heart twisted.

"Why?" I asked.

"Shiloh made it pretty clear you saved him today," Daiyu said. "Once in the shop, and once with sending the horses off."

I looked to Akhíta, who had not raised her hand.

"I don't like you," she admitted. "And I still don't trust you. But you've earned yourself some...tolerance, today."

I nodded, still unsure if it was a good idea to stay. "Thank you."

We mounted up, heading down the path Royal and Shiloh had gone. Little Mountain walked ahead of us on foot, tracking Royal and Shiloh and making sure the path was safe—and wide enough—for the horses. After about fifteen minutes we found the two of them in another, smaller, wash, sitting side by side next to an old, extinguished campfire ring. Royal didn't look up when we arrived, but Shiloh did. He got up and whispered something to Akhíta, who whispered back. Shiloh looked pleased, then came over to me.

"I hear you're staying for now?" He said it loudly, clearly intending for his voice to carry.

I glanced at Royal and, though I couldn't see their face, I could see that their posture was rather stiff.

"For now," I said.

Shiloh smiled. "Good. In that case, come with me."

I followed, feeling confused. He led me to the side of the wash that was still bathed in sunlight, near a crevice that branched off to the east, and handed me the same little pistol from earlier.

"You have got to learn to actually use this thing," Shiloh said. "Even if you don't like it, you at least need to understand it."

I puffed out a breath and nodded. Handing it back for a moment, I dug around in my skirt pocket until I found a stray bit of ribbon to tie my hair with so it wouldn't be in my face. Once done, Shiloh held the gun up for me to see, demonstrating how to load it, how to rotate the cylinder, how the sights worked.

"Won't the shots give away where we are?" I asked after the explanation.

"Nah, they'll echo too much." Shiloh pointed down the long, straight crevice to where it made a sharp left turn. "Now, see that whiteish stripe about five feet up from the ground? Aim for that, straight ahead," Shiloh told me.

Warily, I raised the gun in both hands, staring down the length of the barrel. It was so heavy, especially after digging for so long. The tiny square sight peg at the end danced back and forth, never quite settling on the right spot. Shiloh stepped behind me, using his feet to nudge mine around and resting one hand under my wrists to steady me.

Taking a deep breath, I squeezed the trigger. My ears rang with the noise and every bone all the way up my arms shook, but I managed to keep the gun from flying back towards my face which felt like a major accomplishment. I did not, however, manage to hit anywhere near the white line. I wasn't even sure where I'd hit until Shiloh pointed out a pockmark several feet higher.

"Try again," Shiloh said. "Shoot between breaths and don't let your hands move until at least a second after you've fully pulled the trigger."

I nodded and took aim again. This time I was much closer, but still not within the stripe. Without prompting, I took a third shot. This one, finally, sort of, hit where I intended. It was still high—I'd been aiming for the center of the stripe—but it was at least within the white.

"Try and hit that same spot again," Shiloh prompted.

The attempt was made, and was not successful. I was high once again.

"You're overcompensating for how tired your arms are, and it's making you shoot high," Royal said, appearing at my other side. They didn't actually look at me, just at the pockmarks from the bullets.

When I'd decided to leave without saying goodbye, I knew it was going to hurt Royal. They'd never liked to be alone, which was why they usually were. Better to cut people off before they cut you off. The problem was, Royal never would have let me go, even if it was the right thing.

Carefully, I handed the gun to Shiloh, who nodded to us before walking off to give us space, then I turned to face Royal. "I know you're hurt, but I'm not sorry. I need to finish this myself, so no one else gets put in harm's way. Four people died today, you nearly died yesterday and again today, and we have no idea if more people died yesterday as well."

Royal continued looking at the pockmarks. "What about Emilia, then? You can't find her on your own, especially now. That's why you came to me in the first place."

I stared down at my feet, swallowing heavily. "I love her. I'd give a lot to find her, but I've realized there are things I wouldn't give. You're one of them."

"So you'll let her go?" Royal asked.

I shook my head. "I'll wait. Send out some ads in the papers, hope she sees them. Keep an eye on the judge, maybe he'll find her after all. Write some letters to people in California, see if they know anything. It would have been better to find her quickly, but we didn't, so. This is what's left."

Royal sighed and reached around to pull something out from under their coat where it had been tucked into their waistband; a medium sized leather-bound book with the word "Register" stamped on the cover in gold. "Here. There's no Emilia Pierce listed, but do any of the other names in that from the last week ring a bell?"

I took the book and tilted it towards the last of the light, scanning down the most recent few pages. Each crossing was recorded along with the names and ages of everyone going, the numbers of horses and wagons, the reason for crossing. None of the names rang any bells. That didn't mean one of them wasn't her, though.

"Thanks for trying," I said, returning the book to them.

"Are you leaving or not?" Royal asked.

I glanced over at everyone else. They'd gotten camp set up and were starting a fire now that it was dark enough for the smoke not to be noticed. They were keeping the flames low, though, to help hide the light.

"I'm not sure what point there is to staying," I admitted. "Everything else I can do on my own."

Royal made an unhappy little noise. "You don't *have to*, though. Just because it isn't some flashy gunfight doesn't mean I, we, can't help you with this."

"Royal, I need to go home."

"No, you *don't*," Royal said, finally turning to face me. There were frustrated tears in the corners of their eyes.

"Royal, Mother and Father are waiting for me, and our siblings—"

"Please, Clarabella. Mother and Father aren't good people. If you go home…a few more years and I won't recognize you at all. Please."

"Our siblings—"

"We'll get them too," Royal begged. I'd never seen Royal look this vulnerable. This afraid.

"I…" I tried to come up with an answer. Something I could say that would make this better. Something that would make Royal understand I had to go home.

They shook their head, taking a step away. "Forget it. Go home then."

With that they stalked off, dropping into the dirt next to Shiloh.

Shiloh took one look at them, then looked over to me with concern. I swiped a few tears away from my own eyes. This shouldn't be so hard. I had to go. I couldn't live this life, and Royal made it clear years ago that they couldn't live mine.

But I couldn't leave things like this either.

Daiyu seemed to be in charge of dinner for the night, so I went over to her. "I was wondering what ingredients you have?" I asked.

"Quite a few. Royal isn't the only one with special saddlebags. What do you need?"

"Flour, salt, baking soda, baking powder, bacon grease, and buttermilk?"

"Everything but the buttermilk," Daiyu said.

"How about lemon juice or white vinegar and regular milk?"

"I can do milk and a lemon."

"Perfect. Can I use a bit of all of that, and a large bowl?"

She bowed slightly and started assembling the ingredients for me. Watching with interest, I realized that one of her saddlebags had frost all around the edge, and this was the one she took the milk from. I took a dented tin cup as well, some utensils, and a cast-iron skillet. I'd never done this over a fire before, but there was a first time for everything. Taking my bounty I went and folded myself into the dirt next to Royal.

"Pay attention, this is Mother's biscuit recipe," I said.

Royal looked confused but didn't say anything, watching as I poured out a healthy measure of milk, then squeezed half a lemon into it before setting the cup aside to curdle. I was doubling the recipe so there would be enough for everyone, and the bowl was barely big enough as I mixed together all the dry ingredients. Carefully, I started cutting in the bacon grease, mixing it in bit by bit until it was the right consistency. Finally, I finished up by mixing in the curdled milk.

Dusting my hands with flour, I gently gathered the dough and folded it over itself several times so the biscuits would have layers. Then, with the help of a knife to keep the dough from stretching, I pulled it apart into little palm-sized balls, dropping each one onto the skillet. Once they were laid out, I smeared more bacon grease on the tops. The whole process was silent, Royal watching over my shoulder.

"There. No idea how long they'll take over an open fire like this, but that's about it," I said, getting up and arranging the skillet over the coals Daiyu had dragged away from the main fire for cooking.

"Why'd you show me?" Royal asked when I came and sat back down next to them.

"Because I didn't want to leave with us fighting, and you said you wanted to know the recipe, so." I shrugged.

Royal sighed, leaning over to thunk their forehead against my shoulder. "Thanks. But I still don't think you should leave."

I didn't say anything. My mind was made up.

The biscuits came out perfect. Golden and crispy, the layers peeling apart to allow for Daiyu's meaty gravy to be stuffed inside. Royal didn't try to hide how much they were enjoying them, eating three without even a drop of gravy.

With dinner finished, everyone spread out, lazing in the soft sand. It must have been a nice change from the normal, hard dirt.

"Story night?" Nadir asked, looking to Royal. The statement was met with a chorus of agreement.

"Any requests?" Royal asked, getting up and going to their saddlebags.

"Poe," Oliver said, again met with agreement.

Royal rooted around their bags until they pulled out a frayed dime novel. The cover had no adornment nor illustration, just the words "Selected Works of Edgar Allan Poe" in heavy black letters. Royal settled with their back against a small log and flipped through the pages until they reached a bookmark. They studied the page for a moment, stealing a quick glance at me before clearing their throat and beginning to read in a soft voice.

"'The chateau into which my valet had ventured to make forcible entrance, rather than permit me, in my desperately wounded condition, to pass a night in the open air—'"

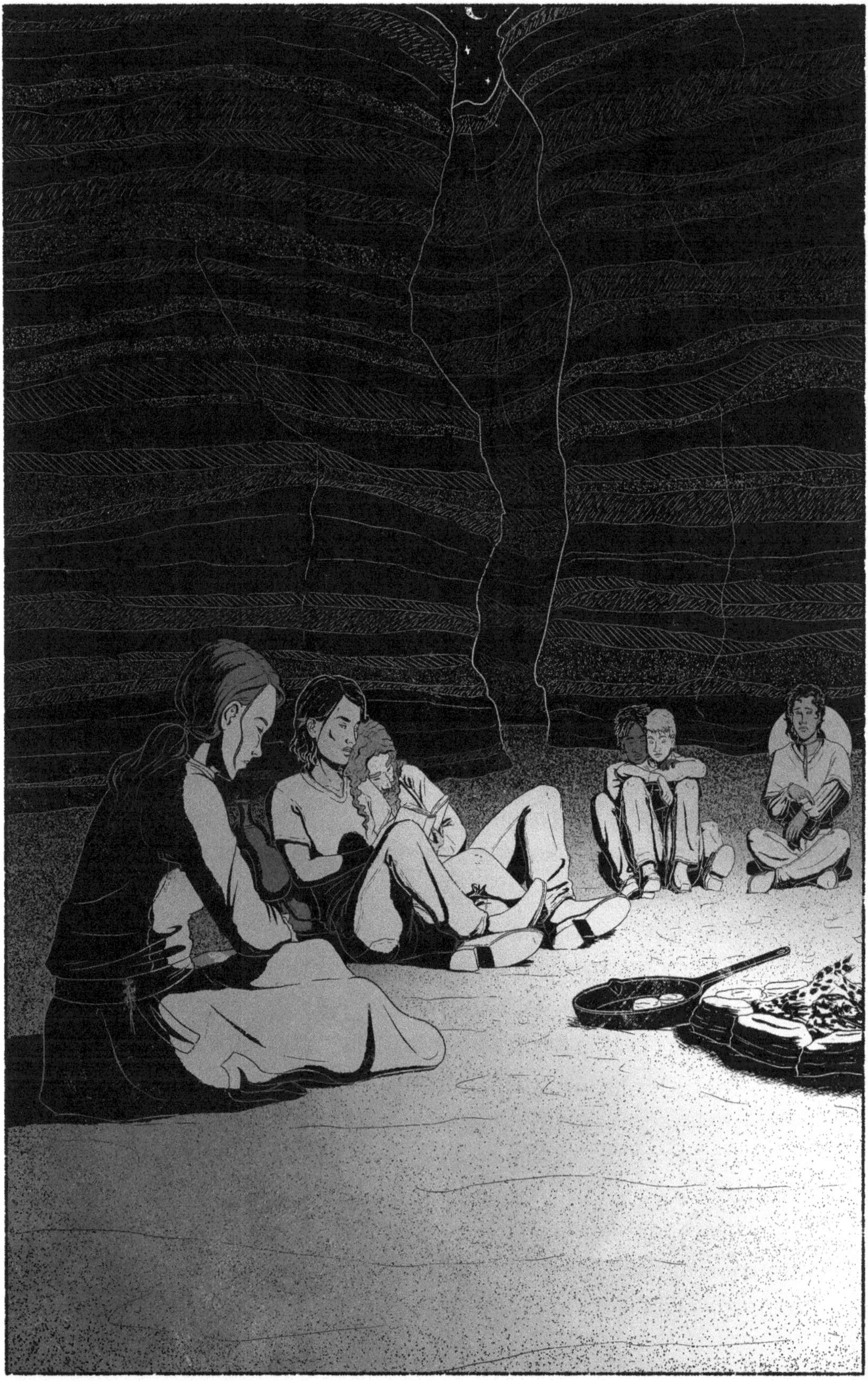

I'd forgotten how good Royal was at telling stories. They knew exactly what to do with their voice to send shivers down everyone's spines at exactly the right moments. The whole gang sat enraptured, though Hazel put Dahlia to bed before the reading began.

The story was short, though, and didn't take long to get through. Akhíta shot down the idea of reading a second one, saying the day had been long enough and everyone needed to rest.

"I'll take first watch," Royal offered.

Everyone grumbled playfully and thanked Royal for the story, peeling off for their tents. Soon it was Royal and I alone by the dying fire. With no voices to overpower them, the sounds of the night crept in. The crackle of the fire, the whistle of the wind through the pillars, the distant yip of a coyote.

"Did you figure out why the bullet didn't hit you?" I asked after awhile, just for something to say.

Royal shook their head and pulled out what, at first glance, seemed to be an unremarkable stone from their pocket. It was hardly bigger than a quarter, and not much thicker, pale gray in color. When the firelight hit it right, though, I saw a red gouge that nearly cut the stone in half. Royal tossed it to me and I managed to catch it. Barely.

"It's nothing special. Took us weeks to figure out what it did, and that was only on accident. My horse spooked at a snake and threw me, and that bubble appeared, taking the impact for me," Royal said. "Kept testing it and, far as we can tell, it just protects from falls."

I turned the stone over in my hands, running my thumb along the groove. "Maybe protecting you from getting shot is another property of its magic that you didn't know about?"

"Then why didn't it stop the bullet in the hotel?" Royal reasoned. "I had it then too. I love Ranger, but she's a damn chestnut mare and acts like it at every opportunity. I always keep that stone on me now."

I chewed my lip. "Maybe...because that wouldn't have been immediately fatal?"

Royal gave a little sideways nod and shrug. "I suppose that's a possibility, but something about it still just...doesn't feel right. Every magic object we've ever found, it does one thing, and one thing only."

I handed the stone back, and they tucked it away. "Protecting from fatal wounds is one thing."

Royal hummed. "Mmmmm. Yes, but that feels a lot like saying all of medicine is one thing, because it all helps heal people. It's...too big. Magic isn't like that. Not anymore."

I shrugged, out of ideas, and we fell back into silence.

"You sure I can't talk you into staying?" Royal asked eventually, voice stiff. "We'll keep looking for Emilia."

I shook my head. "This isn't the kind of life I want, Royal. I can see now why it is the life that works for you, but it doesn't work for me."

Royal sighed and nodded, eyes focused on the fire. "We need to see one another again, though. Somehow. I refuse to let Mother and Father be the only influences in your life."

"I would like that," I said, ignoring the comment about Mother and Father. Clearly we were never going to see eye to eye on that. "We'll figure something out."

Royal let out another longer, slower sigh. "Okay. Before you go... there's one more thing I think we need to try. It will, at the very least, tell you for sure if Emilia stayed in the area or made the crossing."

I frowned. "Why didn't you say anything about this before?"

"I *did*," Royal said. "It's the other gang Little Mountain brought up. Well, they're not a gang, exactly. People call them The Preachers, but I don't know if they have a name for themselves. They're a group of women. Scorned women, chased out onto the plains by abusive husbands, mostly, or so the stories say."

"That doesn't sound so bad," I said. "Well, why they're out there certainly does, but they themselves don't."

Royal looked at me out of the corner of their eyes. "They aren't human anymore, Clarabella. I'm not even sure all of them are alive, or if they're just...shells filled up with magic."

I felt my eyes widen. "Oh."

Royal nodded, focusing back on the fire. "They're not...dangerous, exactly. Unless you look like a man. It's said they collect the sins of men and wield them like weapons. No one knows how long they've existed out there, but Little Mountain's people say the first ones appeared only after the first settlers invaded the area."

"Do you really think they could help?" I asked.

"They know things," Royal answered. "But there's a price to pay for the information."

"What kind of price?"

"Depends what you want to know."

I stared into the fire as well, focusing on the twisting flames. "Do they tell you the price before or after they answer your question?"

"I have no idea," Royal said. "I've seen them, but I've never had anything to ask. It's up to you. If you want to try, I'll take you to them. They aren't far."

"Let me think on it for the night?" I requested.

Royal nodded. "Go get some sleep. And wake Shiloh up to come take watch, please."

I leaned over and gave Royal a kiss on the cheek before getting up to head for our tent.

"Clarabella?" Royal called. I glanced back. "Thanks for the biscuits."

Chapter 10
The Preachers

Ghostly women and oval portraits of Emilia danced through my dreams all night. Or maybe Emilia was one of the ghostly women. By the time I woke up, I couldn't quite remember.

Royal was lounging next to me; they'd never been much of a morning person, always preferring to laze in bed when possible. Shiloh was on their other side, snoring softly.

"What time is it?" I muttered, not moving to get up either.

"Morning."

"Helpful."

"Early morning? I don't know. Sun's up."

Flailing around, I freed one of my legs from the blankets and kicked Royal in the ankle.

"Brat," Royal said, kicking me back. The admonishment lost a lot of its heat when Royal gave a wide yawn at the end.

I burrowed deeper into the blankets, debating the merits of trying to go back to sleep. My whole body ached down to my bones. How could Royal live like this all the time?

"Have you thought about The Preachers?" Royal asked.

I let out a long, slow breath. "I dreamed about them. I don't know if that counts as thinking." Royal didn't respond, letting me work through the problem. "It's so hard to decide, without knowing more about them. About what the cost would be. But if they can give me even an inkling of where Emilia is...I think I want to try?"

"You need to be sure," Royal said.

We laid in silence for awhile as memories floated through my mind. Emilia helping me do my hair. Her managing to tell off a rude professor without getting in trouble. Kisses stolen in empty hallways, the risk of being discovered making the kisses sweeter. Giggling as we set up strings and coins over the door of the room we shared to serve as alarms so we could sleep in the same bed without getting caught. The nights felt so lonely without her.

"I'm sure."

―

This time, splitting up was the only option. Anyone who appeared to be a man couldn't come with us, at least not all the way. Royal changed into a loose, light pink prairie dress patterned with the outlines of flowers, and put on a long, curly blond wig tied loosely with a gray satin ribbon. Akhíta was coming along as well. Everyone else would make camp partway there, letting the three of us continue on alone. I was surprised how little protest Akhíta gave to the plan. Maybe it was because she knew I'd finally be leaving after.

We got going around noon as, apparently, The Preachers were impossible to find in daylight. I'd attempted to clean myself up somewhat before we mounted up, twisting my hair into a bun and changing into the only other skirt and shirt I had. Hopefully The Preachers wouldn't care too much about everything else. Like how bad I smelled.

I was surprised by how short the ride out of the Gates was, but once we emerged I saw why we'd spent the night within them. Off in the distance—far enough away that everything looked miniaturized—was a wagon train heading down a gentle slope. It stretched back farther than I could see. Voices floated out from it when the wind was right, though nothing was distinguishable about them.

"How deep does the pass go?" I asked, remembering what Shiloh had said about Astro being born just deep enough to be strange.

"Not very," Royal said. "Maybe a thousand feet below the plains, at its deepest. Things don't start to get noticeably strange until around 2,000, depending on which Pit you're in. Some get weirder quicker, presumably because they're deeper and thus have more magic leaking out."

"Things can still happen on the pass, though," Shiloh added. "Strange animals wander across, people hear screaming and babies crying off the trail, that sort of thing. That's why the wagon trains are so big. More people means more protection."

Akhíta turned us away from the train, heading south.

"Why don't people talk about what they see?" I asked.

"They do, but people like you don't believe them," Akhíta answered.

I supposed that was fair. I couldn't imagine trying to convey, let alone convince, anyone of the things I'd experienced over the last few days. Any of my friends back in Altora or at school would have laughed and reacted exactly the way I had, believing that such things were silly superstitions and the domain of the uneducated.

To our left, the Gates continued for several miles until they gave way to a sloping hill that we followed the contour of. To the right, the land fell away, going deeper and deeper. Thick pine trees began to appear several hundred feet below us once we were beyond the Gates. The first few rows were small, runty things, but when you looked deeper you could see them getting larger. It was hard to tell their real height, without knowing where the land sat underneath. Their green branches rippled in the breeze, swaying like water and just as thick.

The dirt crunched behind me and I turned to see Royal pulling their horse up next to mine. Their profile was sharp in the afternoon light, tanned skin painted gold and blue eyes blazing. Any trace of the aftereffects of being shot seemed to have vanished.

"This is the first time you've even seen a Pit, isn't it? Let alone been in one?" Royal asked.

I looked out over the land stretching down and away an unfathomable distance. "I've seen pictures."

Royal shook their head with a huff. "Sketches don't do the Pits justice. Photographs don't either."

I hummed, tucking a loose lock of hair back up with the rest. "I suppose it's hard to comprehend that, beyond what we can see, the land keeps going down leagues beyond where anyone has reached. From here it just looks like a forest in a canyon."

It was Royal's turn to hum. "That's what the first settlers thought. Thought they could hike down and hike back out the other side to access the grand lands to the west. Thought they were lucky. Thought the Pits would be easier to cross than mountains, that they wouldn't face cold or snow or lack of food and water. They were never heard from again because of those mistaken assumptions."

I'd heard those stories. As a child they'd been scary bits of make-believe. When I'd gotten older they'd become fables meant to keep myself and my friends from getting too curious and wandering off only to be swallowed up by the ground.

"Is it true a few people did come out, but they'd gone mad?" I asked.

Royal nodded. "One man, he went down there to try and mine, not to cross. He wandered out after a year. His eyes were gone, and he spent the rest of his life babbling in a language no one recognized."

I shuddered. "That's horrid."

"He didn't respect the place," Royal replied. "Not that I'm saying he deserved it, but trying to mine down here is about the stupidest thing you could ever do. He tried to take things that didn't belong to him, so the Pits took things from him as punishment. Plenty of people go into the Pits, despite the danger, but the smart people know not to go too deep, or to take what doesn't belong to them."

"How deep have you been?" I asked.

"Few thousand feet," Royal replied. "Just enough to search for trinkets." In response to my confused look, Royal continued. "That key, the bandages that saved me, my saddlebags, the stone. They're all things we've found in the Pits. People leave ordinary objects there, sometimes intentionally, sometimes not. Once the objects have sat within a Pit for long enough, they become slowly imbued with magic. Because those things aren't actually from the Pits, we can take them back without having to pay a price. Never really know what we're going to get, though.

There's no rhyme or reason to it. Things left down here for decades are as ordinary as when they were dropped. Other things turn magic within a day. One set of saddlebags might hold half a house, another might bite your arm off when you reach inside."

"Well that sounds like a rather terrifying gamble."

"Testing the stuff is half the fun," Royal said with a grin.

I pinched the bridge of my nose, rubbing at the skin there. All of this was giving me a headache. Whenever this was over, I was going to have to write it all down. Not to share, just to get it all out of my head and into some sort of order. Or maybe I *would* publish it. Some version of it. Finally get Royal and Shiloh into a book like they wanted.

Royal, Akhíta, and I left the others after a quick dinner at the new camp. The ride to The Preachers wasn't far, only about half-an-hour. When we arrived at the large meadow Royal said was the right place, there was no one to be seen. Just a large pile of rocks around the base of a jagged, ten-foot tall, whitewashed wooden cross that listed to the side. Dozens of scraps of fabric in all different colors, many of them faded and falling to threads, were knotted around the beams, fluttering in the breeze. The rocks below were streaked with some sort of dark stain. In the falling light I couldn't tell what had caused it.

All three of us dismounted, leaving the horses back a ways. Royal brought their saddlebags slung over their shoulder, and we made our way to the cross. Royal produced a short knife, but Akhíta held out a hand to stop them.

"It's her question," Akhíta said, nodding towards me.

"It's also mine," Royal returned. "I want to know where Emilia is for Clarabella's sake."

Royal and Akhíta stared at one another silently for several seconds, then Akhíta dropped her hand, scuffing a foot angrily through the dirt. Royal shook back their sleeve and, before I could protest, sliced a neat line across the top of their forearm. Holding it out over the rocks, several drops of blood dripped down to splash against the stone, answering the question of what had streaked their surface. Looking closer now, I realized there had to be hundreds of stains. Layer upon layer covered every trace of the rocks' original colors.

Royal nudged me and I looked up. No longer was there an empty expanse of meadow backed by forest. A dozen women were standing there, all silent. They each had lengths of fluttering, gauzy black fabric over their heads, tied loosely around their necks to create a rippling bubble of fabric that obscured their features. The ends cascaded down, hanging in tatters to their ankles. They wore no other clothing underneath, and the thin fabric hid nothing of their forms. All had loose hair, or dreadlocks in the case of one woman.

Their eyes were white. Not their irises, not their pupils, because they had neither. Only white. Nothing but sclera. And yet, I somehow knew they could see me. I could feel their gaze raking over my skin, flaying it from my bones as they judged me.

At the center of the group, a woman stood out. She did not have gauze over her head. She did not, in fact, have anything resembling clothes at all. But she was covered. The only description I could think to put to it was that the woman seemed to be covered by clouds of ink, rippling and billowing as if it had been dripped in water even though she was not in water. It swirled over her skin, slid down her waist, thinned and thickened as it moved. Only rarely did it allow an unobscured glance of skin, of face. Unlike the others her eyes were solid gold and she had no hair at all.

"Wanderers," the ink covered woman said in a voice like honey. It clung to my skin, warm and inviting. I wanted to curl up in the sound until I drifted off to sleep.

"I have a question," Royal said, raising the pitch of their voice a bit.

The woman was silent, staring straight at Royal who stood stiff at my side. Akhíta, on Royal's other side, was taking long, slow breaths that seemed very deliberate. Gliding forward one measured step at a time, the ink-woman came closer and closer, her attention entirely focused on Royal. Royal swallowed heavily and did not move. Akhíta's hand twitched. I had the distinct impression she wanted to draw her gun but didn't dare do it.

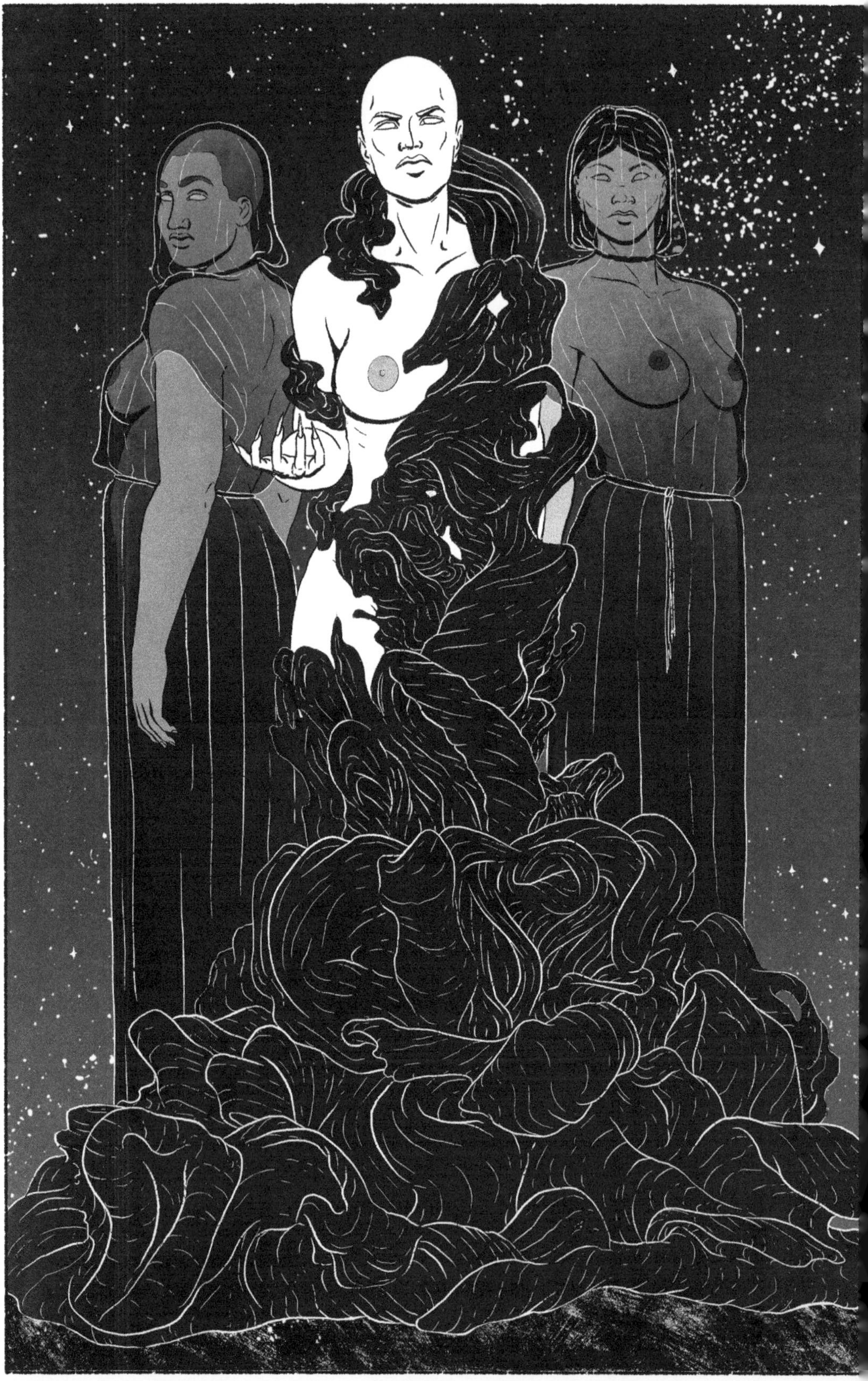

A breath away, the woman stopped and held up one hand, revealing sharp nails as gold as her eyes and hovering it in the air above Royal's cheek. With her first finger, she made a light tapping motion. An opalescent sheen radiated out from the spot, just as it had when the bullet had nearly hit Royal in the exact same spot the day before.

"Interesting," the ink-woman murmured. She did not step back. "Is your question about this?"

Royal hesitated. "No."

She smiled. It was the coldest smile I had ever seen. A predator's smile. Thin and curling and crooked. "That is probably wise. Ask your true question then."

To Royal's credit, they kept their face and tone even. It didn't matter, though. I could see their pulse fluttering faster than a hummingbird in their neck. "Only if you promise not to answer until you've told me your price, and I have decided if it is worth it."

The woman nodded once.

"We're looking for a girl," Royal said. "She ran away from her father several days ago to escape an arranged marriage, and he may have asked her to do something else, we aren't sure. We'd like to know where she is, if you have that information. Her name is Emilia Pierce."

She stared at Royal for another immeasurable length of time, then pointed to the ground at their feet. "The mask in your bag. The stag."

Royal swallowed and kneeled down, fishing around. Their hands were tense but steady, struggling to pull something large out of the opening of one of the bags. They had to turn the thing around several times until suddenly a large antler appeared, followed by a stylized deer face and the second antler.

"We don't know what it does," Royal said, handing it over. "None of us wanted to risk putting it on without knowing."

She took it. "That was wise. It changes faces. It will be very valuable for the women who choose not to remain with us."

"I'm glad you have use for it," Royal said.

She nodded, handing the mask off to another of the women, that woman's hands sliding through tatters in the fabric she wore so that she could take the thing.

I couldn't help but feel a little glad as well. If that would help women escape cruel husbands, but also save them from whatever fate had befallen these women, it had to be a good thing.

Silence fell as the ink-woman assessed us. Something deep in my gut told me not to break the silence, that if I did the outcome would not be in my favor.

"Emilia Pierce?" The woman said finally.

Royal nodded.

"We have seen her, three days past. One of us found her being escorted by men she did not trust and helped her slip away."

Not even the soporific tone of her voice stopped those words from slicing through my heart. I'd thought, at best, they might know if she'd made the crossing or not. No part of me had imagined they might have actually seen her. And if they had seen her three days ago, where was she now?

Royal reached out and squeezed my hand, eyes still focused on the ink-woman. "And then?"

Silence fell once more, along with the last of the daylight, plunging the world into tints of blue. My heart was a jackrabbit in my chest, desperate to escape before the fangs of whatever the woman was about to say sunk in.

A smile more dangerous than she'd had before curled up her lips. A smile that said, without words, that she knew more than us. "We offered to ferry her across," she said. "But Miss Pierce requested a different outcome. She has left to undertake the trials. She will join us if she survives."

I gasped, spinning to look at Royal for reassurance. In the seconds my eyes were off them, The Preachers vanished once more.

"What does that mean? What does that mean?!" I asked, knowing my voice was shrill and unable to stop it.

"Breathe," Royal said, holding me by the elbows.

"*What does that mean?*" I repeated, shaking in Royal's hands.

Royal opened and closed their mouth a few times, so I turned to Akhíta instead. She didn't like me, so what qualms would she have about saying something upsetting? Or so I assumed. Even she looked hesitant.

"Tell me!" I shouted.

"There's a ritual—"

"Akhíta," Royal said, warning in their tone.

"Coming here was your idea, Royal. You knew there might be consequences. Clarabella deserves to know," Akhíta replied before turning her attention back to me. "There's a ritual, to become one of The Preachers. Some women choose to do it, rather than just accepting The Preachers' help. No one knows what the ritual is, aside from the fact that it involves descending into this Pit. When they reemerge—if they reemerge—they are a Preacher. Or so the stories go."

A sob escaped my lips and I stumbled forward, letting Royal envelop me in their arms.

She was gone.

Emilia was gone.

Chapter 11
Rescue Plan

Somehow, we got back to camp. I wasn't really paying attention. Part of me realized Royal and Akhíta were having a heated, whispered conversation the whole way. It didn't matter. None of it mattered. Without acknowledging anyone else, I dismounted and stumbled into Royal's tent. Once there, though, I had no idea what to do next.

Fear started to shake its way up my spine and I grabbed onto the wool blanket under me, trying to let the rough fibers ground me. Breathing started to feel like snatching at the air only to not find enough of it there. Biting my lips, I tried to stifle the sobs.

Why?

Why? Why? Why?

WHY?

What had made her do this? They'd given her the option to cross the Pits safely in a way her father never would've been able to follow, so why had she given up? Why had she picked them?

I wanted to pull out her letter, read it again knowing what I knew now. Was there a hint in there somewhere that I'd missed? Something that said my love for her wasn't enough to keep fighting? My hands were shaking too much, though, and I was terrified I'd rip it.

Akhíta had said the ritual wasn't always something people survived and all I could think about was how little Emilia knew about the world outside of a town. She was so smart in so many ways, but surviving the wilderness wasn't one of them. It wasn't one of them for me either.

In that moment I realized that what I wanted more than anything else was to be Royal. Full of purpose and understanding backed up by the right sort of skills. I knew, without a doubt, that if it had been me lost in the Pit, Royal would come to get me without a second thought. Except that was the problem. That had been the problem ever since I'd found Royal. They would go too far to protect me.

When I'd told Royal that I was okay with finding Emilia taking a long time, I'd meant it. That, however, had been predicated on her being alive. On her being human. Without those things….

I'd already lost her, I realized, and I wasn't willing to risk Royal's life attempting to find her.

One by one, I pried my fingers off the blanket and began to pack my things. The tent was at the edge of camp, and it was dark enough now that if I was careful I could slip away without anyone knowing if I went out the back.

As I reached for the flap of the tent, bag slung over my shoulder, shouts echoed from out front. For a split second I thought we were under attack again, until I realized it was Akhíta and Royal shouting at one another.

"You didn't feel it, Akhíta!" Royal snapped.

"I don't care!" Akhíta snapped back.

Hesitantly, I let my pack slide to the ground. This didn't sound like a disagreement among friends. It sounded like a real fight, which was the last thing I could picture Royal and Akhíta having.

Making up my mind, I left the pack and went out the front of the tent instead. Royal and Akhíta were standing next to the fire a few feet apart, fists clenched and still shouting back and forth. Everyone else was clustered off to the side looking extremely alarmed. Spotting me, Shiloh dashed over, eyes wide.

"What *happened*?" Shiloh asked. "Neither of them will tell us."

"I…uh…" I glanced over at Royal and Akhíta. Honestly, the events of the evening had gone somewhat fuzzy. It was hard to tell if that was from whatever magic the women possessed, or because of the earth-shattering revelation they'd given me. I managed to stumble out an explanation anyway, reiterating everything that had occurred. Shiloh looked more and more alarmed as I laid it all out.

"It was where Royal almost got shot in the face? You're sure?" Shiloh asked.

I nodded. "And it looked the same, too. An opalescent sheen that radiated out from the spot."

I'd managed to gather at this point that Royal and Akhíta were now fighting about this occurrence, and what it might mean. Royal was adamant they had to know. Akhíta was adamant that something very dangerous was going on and the best way to handle it was to get as far away from here as possible.

"Okay, that's enough!" Shiloh shouted, striding over to insert himself between the two of them. "We're leaving."

"No!" Royal said.

Shiloh spun to face Royal. "Yes. I'm not saying we won't try and figure this out, but we sure as hell aren't doing it here. We are getting the hell out of this Pit and going somewhere very, very far away." There was real fear in his voice.

"What he said," Akhíta agreed.

Royal pressed the heels of their hands to their temples, taking a shaky breath. "O—Okay. Fine. Let's go."

For a moment all the tension seemed to lift. Shiloh reached out to pull Royal into a hug. Akhíta's shoulders dropped and she ran a hand through her dreadlocks. The rest of the group started to shift out of their tight cluster. Even I felt better, knowing the choice of not journeying into the Pit wasn't resting on my ability to resist asking Royal to go.

But before Shiloh's arms could close around Royal, a shudder ran through them and they swayed, falling to their knees with a gasp. Shiloh didn't even have time to catch them, he was so caught off guard by what happened. Everyone shouted, dashing to Royal and circling around. They were bent over on their hands and knees now, coughing great, heaving coughs, and clutching at their stomach. Shiloh and Akhíta were both struggling to pull them upright, roll them over, something so they could figure out what was going on.

I shoved myself through everyone else and dropped down in front of Royal, taking their face in my hands and tilting it up to the light. Their lips were stained with blood, globs of it mixing with spit and running down their chin.

No one seemed to have any idea what to do, all scrambling around trying to come up with something. There was a general consensus that this had something to do with Royal getting shot, but there was no visible wound left to treat and, it seemed, no healing magic left either. Shiloh's arms wrapped protectively around Royal, working to keep them somewhat upright and out of the dirt. Akhíta, having given up on getting Royal into a better position for being examined, laid down in the dirt and was trying to look up at Royal's stomach, attempting to pry their hand away.

Royal kept struggling to say something, but they couldn't get the words out around the coughs. A pool of blood was forming in the dirt beneath their mouth, their skin going ashy pale once more.

I looked around, just as desperate as everyone else for an answer. Most of the others were at the pile of saddle bags, digging through them in what was clearly a desperate hope to find some bit of helpful magic that had been forgotten about. Little Mountain was at the edge of the group, digging as frantically as the others.

Seeing her gave me an idea, at least for understanding what Royal was trying to say, and maybe realizing what they were trying to say would help somehow.

I tilted Royal's face up to mine. "Royal, sign it. Whatever you're trying to say, sign it."

Royal nodded, finally prying away the hand they'd been pressing into their stomach and making two quick motions with it.

"'I'll stay,'" Shiloh translated. "Wha—"

Before Shiloh could get the word out a wave of…something went out over the camp. Some sort of feeling. I didn't have words for it, except that it felt a lot like what standing next to the Preachers had felt like. Warm and sedate in a way that seemed like it might be a trap.

Royal instantly stopped coughing and took several deep, gasping breaths. Shiloh was finally able to haul them upright, pulling Royal onto his lap and bringing one hand up to cup Royal's face. There was no trace of blood anywhere on them, no sign that their skin had ever gone gray. The only sign at all that something had been wrong were Royal's wide eyes and crooked wig.

No one spoke, the only sound in the camp Royal's heavy breaths. Shiloh was shaking, arms tight around Royal, and Akhíta looked terrified, breathing nearly as hard as Royal.

"You...you can't leave the Pit," I realized.

Royal gave a shaky nod. "I can't leave the Pit."

If everyone had been alarmed before, it was nothing compared to how everyone was now. Akhíta reacted first, telling Pedro to take Hazel, Dahlia, and most of the others out of the Pit now. They all objected but Akhíta told them it wasn't an option, that she could only worry about so many people at once, so some of them needed to go. Reluctantly, those who had been told to go did so, working quickly to pack up and get going. With them gone, there was less than half of the group left.

Shiloh had not moved the entire time, nor let Royal get up. Royal didn't object, resting their head against Shiloh's chest. I stayed kneeling next to both of them, unsure what else to do and not wanting to leave Royal's side. Neither of them said anything until those who were leaving were gone.

"Clarabella?" Royal said once the hoofbeats faded. "Can you grab my journal? It's under my blankets somewhere."

I nodded and went to retrieve it. The leather was soft in my hands. As soft as the edges of Emilia's letter. Coming back I handed it to Royal, intending to also throw another log on the fire to give Royal more light to read by, but all they did was clutch the journal to their chest, wrapping both arms around it.

Everyone that remained—Akhíta, Little Mountain, Daiyu, Theo, and myself—came to sit around Royal and Shiloh.

"How did you know you had to stay?" Akhíta asked, tone forcibly even. She'd sat so that she was backlit by the fire, and I couldn't make out her expression. Theo took up translating everything for Little Mountain.

Royal shrugged, the fabric of their dress rasping against Shiloh's shirt. "It happened the second I said I'd leave. So I figured if I said I wouldn't leave, maybe it would stop. And it did."

"What's happening?" I asked, looking at each of them. They all gave a shake of their heads and a shrug.

"The Pits don't keep people," Little Mountain signed. "Not like this. They steal from them. They make them go mad. They kill them. But they don't keep them."

"Could it have been something the Preachers did? Not the Pits?" Shiloh asked.

Akhíta shook her head. "No. We paid their price. They may be dangerous, insane even, but they have rules and they stick to them."

"I agree," I said. "I may not know anything about the Preachers, but the way the leader spoke to Royal...she said whatever is going on with them was '*interesting.*' It just...it didn't sound like something she had *done*. More like something else was already happening and she was just...observing it."

Royal nodded. "That's the sense I got too."

"Any other useful senses you'd like to offer up?" Shiloh asked, speaking for the first time. His voice was rough, still shaking somewhat. Royal snuggled closer, tucking their head under Shiloh's chin, but didn't answer. Shiloh gave them a squeeze.

Akhíta turned to me, gaze assessing. A good part of me suspected I was about to get blamed, only for Akhíta to go the exact opposite direction, catching me off guard by asking me what I thought.

"I hardly know anything about magic," I said.

"That's why I'm asking," Akhíta returned. "You're more objective to it than any of us. Just. Throw out ideas. You might have noticed things we didn't."

I cast my eyes around, running through the events in my mind, trying to pick out bits and pieces that jumped out. "Royal was...coughing up blood, just like when they got shot. But the external wound didn't come back, only the internal one."

Royal straightened up, still staying within the circle of Shiloh's arms. "Like we were talking about over breakfast the morning after. Just because the external injury was healed doesn't mean the internal one was. The deep one…."

"Uh…sure?" I said. I really hadn't been going anywhere with the point when I'd brought it up.

Royal's eyes bounced around, thoughts flying behind them. After several seconds, and some resistance from Shiloh, Royal got up and started pacing, muttering to themself.

"Love, I'm going to need you to share your thoughts," Shiloh said.

Royal flapped a hand in Shiloh's direction, continuing to pace. "In a second, they don't make sense yet."

Shiloh sighed and we all sat back to wait, watching Royal pace and mutter. Finally, Royal stopped, facing towards the Pit, hands on their hips and back to the rest of us. A soft breeze rose up out of the Pit, wrapping the pink dress around their legs and fluttering their still crooked wig.

"That was a consequence, right?" Royal said, clearly not talking to any of us. All of us glanced around, equal parts confused and wary whenever any of our eyes met.

"Royal…" Shiloh said, earning another hand flap in his direction.

"A consequence for using your magic without paying a price?" Royal said.

They were talking to the Pit, I realized. Shiloh and Akhíta seemed to both have the same realization at the same time, scrambling to their feet. I joined them. New to this or not, it seemed like common sense that trying to have a direct conversation with a large, unknowable source of magic couldn't be wise.

"Don't," Royal directed at us, holding out a hand to keep us back but not turning to look at us. "We're already in this. The only way out is through."

Shiloh clenched his fists, but stopped as requested. Akhíta stopped for a moment, then continued forward. She didn't try to reach for Royal, but she did stand next to them, giving a curt nod.

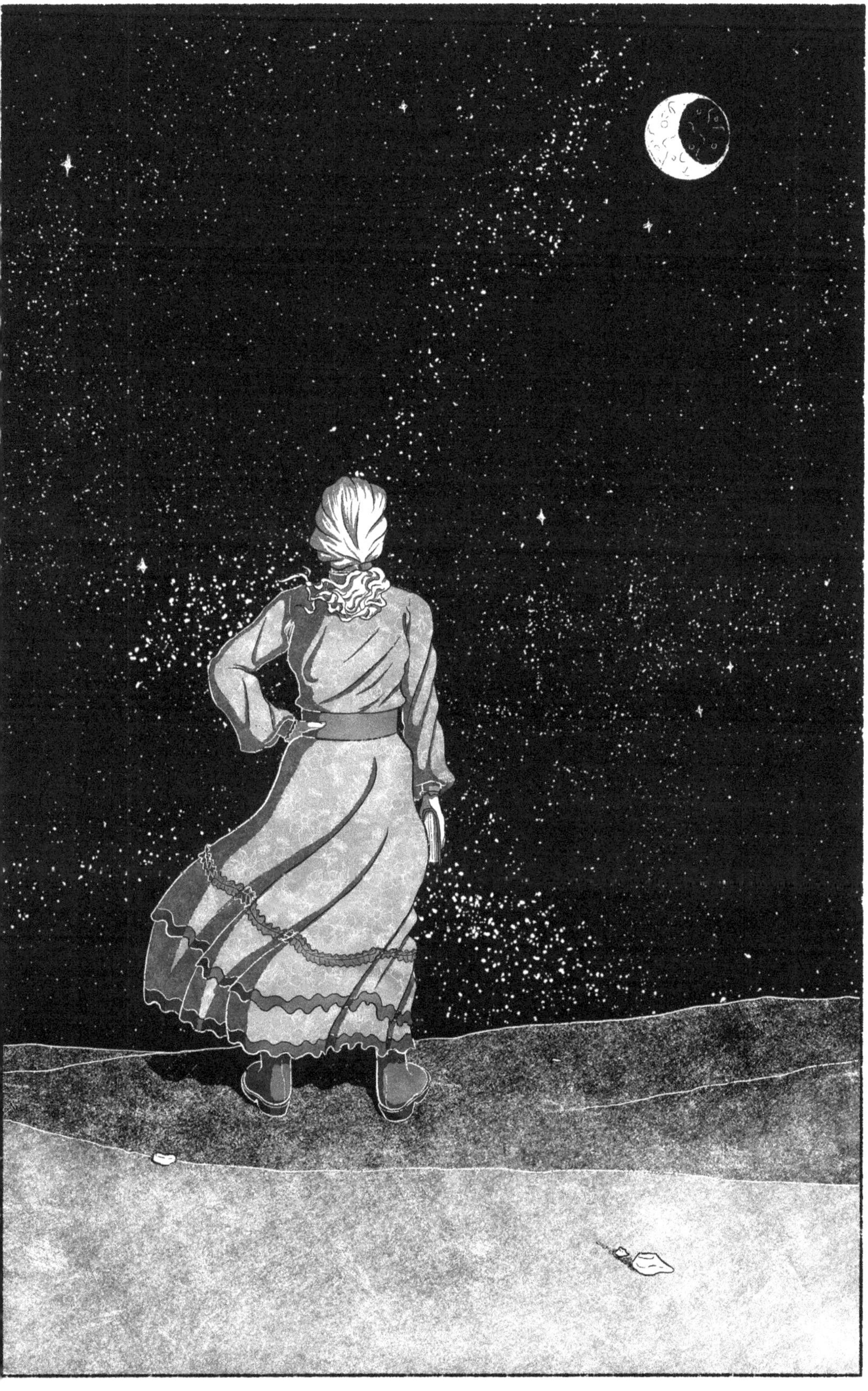

Royal nodded back and continued. "Is the price that I have to stay?" Royal let out a little yelp, clutching at their stomach again. "Okay, okay, wrong guess!" Royal gasped out, swaying a little.

Shiloh made a pained noise but stayed where he was. I hovered next to him, unsure what else to do. Everyone else continued to watch warily from the ground.

Steady once more, Royal took a few deep breaths. "Okay. So. I have to stay, for now, I guess. But not forever. Because I didn't pay a price for the magic I've used."

"I thought you only used magic that didn't require a price?" I asked. "Using things that were made magic by the Pits but didn't come from them."

"I thought so too," Royal said. "I must have been wrong…somehow."

"We've all used just as much magic as you, Royal. You've never done anything different than the rest of us," Daiyu said. "Some of us have even used more, I'd wager."

"Yes, but…" Royal trailed off. Their journal was still dangling in one hand and they brought it up, thumb running over the cover. "I'm the only one who has tried to understand it."

"Is that significant?" Theo asked.

Royal shrugged, finally turning to face everyone. "It's the only thing I can think of that's different."

"Well what are we supposed to do about it?" Shiloh asked. "If you can't leave, but don't have to stay…what the fuck does that mean?"

"It means the Pits want something else from them, some other price. And they'll protect them until they get it, or kill them if they don't," I reasoned. "That's why the bullet stopped before it hit Royal's face, and why their old wound came back when they tried to leave."

Royal nodded. "As soon as I came into the Pit, this, whatever it is, started. I'd guess that, if our fight in the Gates had happened up on the plains, that bullet wouldn't have stopped and I'd be dead now. The stone had nothing to do with it, it was some other magic. Magic we don't know about, and that I haven't paid a price for."

"How the hell do we figure out the price then?" Shiloh asked.

"And the answer is not allowed to involve you asking the damn Pit more questions. I'm not watching you put yourself in pain, or worse, all night."

"Trust me, I am completely open to other suggestions," Royal replied.

"The Preachers?" Little Mountain signed.

"No," Akhíta said, voice firm. "Whatever game this is, I don't want them on the board."

No one else seemed to have any other ideas.

Royal sighed. "Sleep on it?"

No one seemed keen on this, all of us remaining standing where we were. Still, no other ideas were offered and eventually we realized that sleep was indeed the only option at the moment. Akhíta instructed that watches were to be taken in pairs; Theo and Little Mountain, myself and Daiyu, then herself and Shiloh. Royal protested not being given a watch only to be immediately shut down by everyone else.

Shiloh was first in the tent, rearranging it so that he'd be at the back and I'd be at the front, rather than the other way around as it had been set up before. Royal huffed, realizing they were being contained.

"I'm not going to run off," Royal said.

"Not of your own volition," Shiloh replied. "But at this point, who's to say your volition is what would be making that decision?"

Royal grimaced and nodded. "Unsettling. But fair enough."

"All of this is unsettling," Shiloh muttered.

Royal shucked off their wig and dress, flopping onto their bedding with a dramatic sigh in just their underthings. I laid down next to them, not bothering to even take off my shoes.

Royal raked an assessing gaze over me. "Not planning to sleep."

"I'll sleep," I said. "But if I have to run after you in the middle of the night because you're in some sort of magical trance, I would prefer to do it with my clothes and shoes on."

Royal groaned. "Can you two stop being so...so...*morbid* about this? There is absolutely no reason to think I'm going to go into some trance."

I rolled onto my side, propping myself up on one elbow. "Look. An hour ago...my whole world shattered, aside from several tiny pieces. You are one of those pieces so, until we figure this out, I am going to continue to worry and be morbid. And Shiloh clearly loves you to death, so I figure he also gets a pass on being worried and morbid."

"That I do," Shiloh said. He laid down next to Royal, throwing a protective arm over them and tugging them closer.

Royal's face softened, attention still on me. "I'm sorry. About Emilia. I meant to come talk to you about it, after you'd had a little time to yourself, but then Akhíta and I started fighting, and, well."

I laid back down, sniffing. "It is what it is. I want to go get her, to save her from whatever she's gotten herself into, but it's probably too late now."

"I'd take you to find her if I could," Royal said. Before I could respond that I knew that, and it was why I hadn't asked, Royal yelped, curling up into a sitting position and wrapping their arms around their stomach. Shiloh moved just as quickly, alarm clear on his face even in the dim light provided by the fire shining through the crack in the front of the tent.

"It's over, it's over," Royal said, though their voice was shaky. "It was just a flash."

"What the hell *was* it?" Shiloh asked, arms tight around Royal once more. "You didn't ask a question."

"They didn't ask a question the first time either," I realized, resting a hand on Royal's shoulder. "When they said they'd leave. They just said it, and the magic didn't agree, so it punished them."

"But all they said this time was that we aren't going after Emilia!" Shiloh returned.

"Then...does that mean we should go after her?" Royal asked, earning an annoyed nose from Shiloh, likely for daring to ask the question and risk more pain. Nothing happened, though.

All three of us looked at one another in confusion. Why in the world would the Pit want Royal to go after Emilia?

Chapter 12
Gearing Up

This was an unnerving enough revelation to get everyone back out around the fire, Royal shrugging back into their dress first. It was not, however, a revelation that really provided anymore answers than we'd had before.

"Why the hell would the Pits want *you* to go after Emilia?" Akhíta asked for the third time since we'd come back out. "Not Clarabella, her girlfriend. You. Who has never even met the girl before."

"Does it matter?" Royal asked, sounding tired. "I clearly don't have the option not to go."

Shiloh sighed. He'd been hovering at Royal's shoulder the entire time. "Not that I wouldn't follow you to hell and back, but I was hoping that would never have to be literal." Royal opened their mouth, a look of protest on their face, but Shiloh interrupted. "You going alone isn't an option. Don't even suggest it."

Royal had enough sense to know this wasn't an argument they could win, so they didn't bother to try. It was quickly decided that Akhíta and I would be going as well. Emilia was my girlfriend and Akhíta clearly wasn't going to stay behind. Everyone else would go meet up with the rest of the group, making camp at an agreed upon spot so we could find them later. If we lived. No one said that last part aloud, though.

Theo brewed up a large pot of Arbuckle's coffee that smelled dangerous, handing out large cups. Not one for coffee, I slugged it back anyway, realizing I'd need it. We didn't have time to waste on sleep. Royal, meanwhile, pulled Daiyu aside, then disappeared into her tent with her. When the two of them came back out, Royal had a bundle of clothes and pair of boots in their arms, all of which they handed to me. I tilted the bundle around, trying to discern in the dark what all was in the pile without dropping anything.

"There's a lot of things you can do in a skirt, but this journey isn't one of them," Royal said.

"*Pants*?" I said, incredulous. "I have never worn pants in my life!"

Royal shook slightly with a suppressed laugh. "They don't bite."

"But they're...they're..."

"Skirts with a couple extra seams," Royal said. "It's not like you're wearing them to church. Hurry up and change."

I stood there for a moment, trying to come up with another argument. Failing, I gave in and went into the tent to change. It took me a moment to get everything figured out in the dark, having to go by feel. They at least seemed to fit, no matter how awkward they felt. There was a shirt as well, something made of a tougher fabric than my blouse and with short sleeves. Last came the cowboy boots. Except, I realized, they weren't last. There was something else that had fallen out of the pile as well. I couldn't tell what it was in the dark, except that it felt like a bunch of leather cords and some sharp bits of metal.

Exiting the tent, I held them up. "What are these?"

"Climbing spikes," Royal said, shimmying around me to go into the tent. "Shiloh will help you."

Shiloh waved me over, indicating for me to sit. I did, handing over the contraption. Shiloh took it, untangling the cords to reveal that it was actually two contraptions. He set about attaching them to my boots, tightening all the buckles until everything was snug. Three rows of thick metal spikes now ran across the bottom of the front half of each of the boots.

I could sort of feel the spikes underneath me when Shiloh held out a hand to pull me to my feet, but mostly they sunk into the dirt. Between the need for pants and now climbing spikes, I was starting to seriously doubt my ability to get through whatever this was going to entail.

Before I could say so, a coil of bound up rope sailed through the air and nearly hit Shiloh in the head. He managed to catch it just in time.

"Teach her knots!" Royal shouted from the tent, their arm that had thrown the rope before disappearing back inside.

"I know knots," I said, feeling a bit relieved. "Some knots."

"Better than no knots," Shiloh said.

He uncoiled a length of rope, taking me step by step through how to tie it into a harness, which sent me right back to doubting everything. I very much did not want to do anything that involved a harness. There was no going back now, though, so I did my best to memorize all of it. Shiloh undid the one he tied and handed the rope over, walking me through doing it myself.

"You're a good teacher," I said. He really was. Patient, clear, willing to correct without scorn.

He smiled and I was surprised to see that he looked sad. "Thank you. I used to run a schoolhouse, actually. Just a little thing. No one else where I lived at the time was willing to do it, so I took it up when I turned seventeen. Until I left, anyway. Taught the kids how to read and know their numbers. Simple stuff."

Before I could decide if I wanted to ask for more detail, or if I even should, Akhíta announced it was time to go. Hastily, I reached up and finger combed my hair before working it into a simple braid. Royal reemerged, back in their silver rimmed hat, dark jeans, and spiked boots. Their duster was nowhere in sight, though, and they'd put on a faded green button up shirt, the sleeves rolled to their elbows.

Daiyu and Little Mountain had been making up packs for all of us and they handed them over now, explaining that each carried five days of food but only a single canteen of water as Akhíta instructed that the packs needed to be light. As the other three each strapped on a couple of guns, Theo shoved more coffee at each of us. We took it gratefully before setting off.

No one said goodbye.

After the flurry of activity that led to leaving, our walk felt positively sedate. We hiked in silence and I kept stealing glances at Royal, catching Shiloh and Akhíta doing the same. Royal, for their part, ignored this.

For awhile we were just trekking through scrub, then through scraggly, scattered Juniper trees. They were the sort of stunted, twisted little trees that, were we on a mountain range, you would expect to see near the tops, scattered at the edge of the alpine level where it became impossible for them to grow. There was no path under our feet until, suddenly, there was. It was thin, winding away into the darkness of the forest that grew thicker and thicker. I would've given anything for a full moon. As it was, all we had was a single oil lantern, and not that much oil. Akhíta moved to light it before the trees could close in over our heads, only for Royal to shake their head.

"Save it. Right now, this is just a path, and one we have taken before. We can handle just a path," Royal said.

Akhíta nodded.

None of us moved.

Royal puffed out a long breath. "Last chance for anyone to turn back."

This was directed at me and, for a moment, I almost considered it. The thought of turning around flitted through my mind, gone as quick as it had come. I could never do that. Somehow, even if I didn't understand it, I'd gotten Royal into this. So I was going in.

When I didn't say anything Royal nodded once, squared their shoulders, and headed into the black.

We all formed a line, hands on the pack of the person in front of us. Part of me wondered if there was some sort of magical light source we could be using. That seemed like something that would exist. A lantern that never went out nor needed more oil. A rock that glowed when you held it. Something.

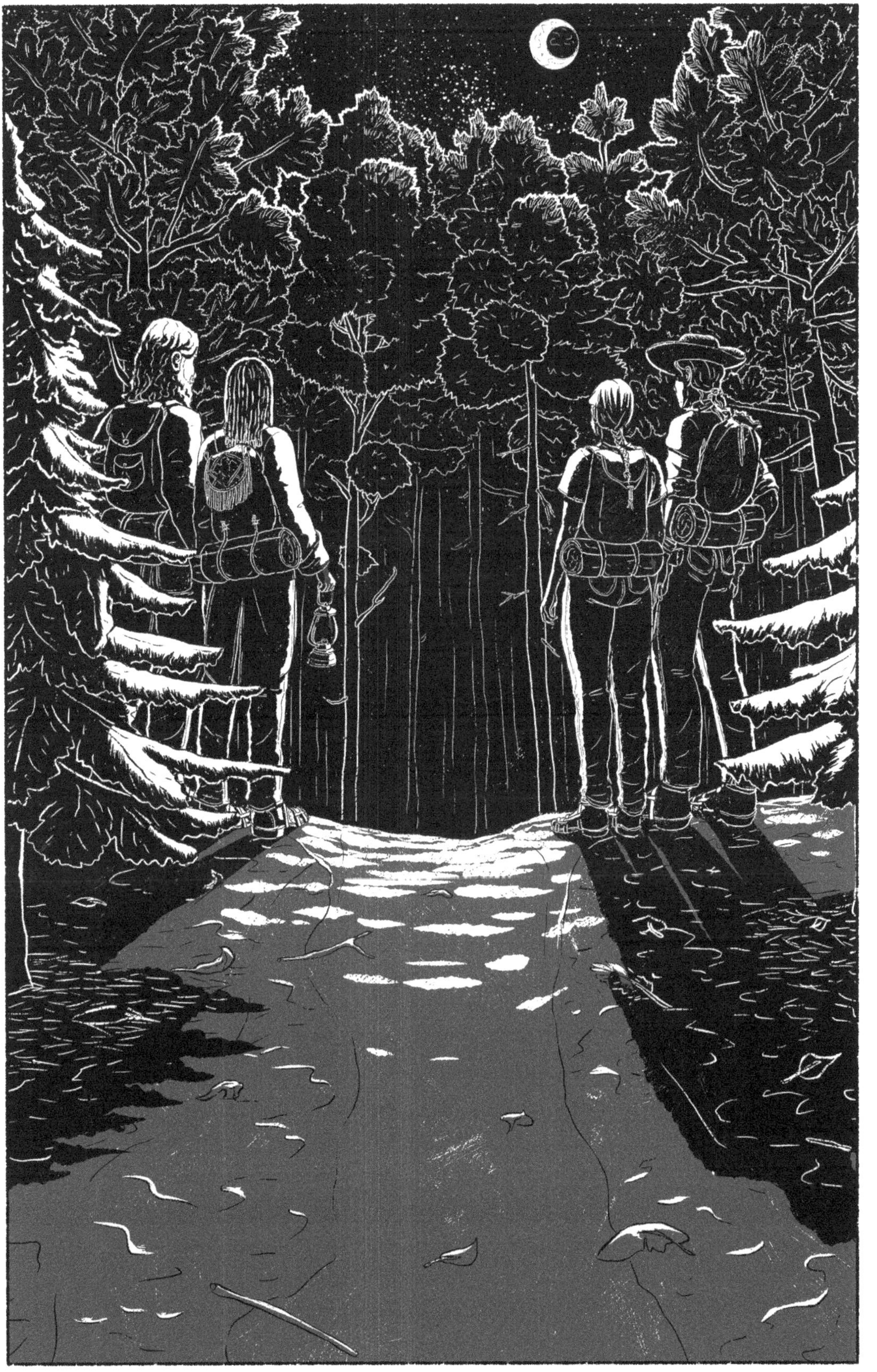

The smarter part of me, however, the part that was starting to understand all of this, realized that it might not be smart to use magic right now. The rules had changed, or at least Royal had been wrong about them. There might be a price now, and we didn't know what it was.

"Where did this path come from?" I asked softly. I wasn't sure if it was the darkness or the situation that made me unwilling to speak at full volume.

"Hard to say," Royal responded from in front of me, their voice just as soft. "It has been here as long as we've been coming down."

"How many times have you been in this Pit?" I asked, trying to be comforted by the fact they knew it at least somewhat.

"Maybe a dozen times," Shiloh answered this time. "It has always had the best loot, changed things in the most interesting ways. We suspect it may be one of the deepest Pits."

Nope. No comfort to be found in this conversation. Back to silence it was.

Royal had other ideas, though. "Tell me about Emilia."

"What?" I asked.

"I'm trying to figure this out," Royal said. "But I don't know anything about her."

I had no idea what to say. Nothing I could think of about Emilia made this make any sense.

"Does she believe in magic?" Akhíta asked from the end of the line.

I thought about it. "I don't think so? She always teased some of the other girls at school who did."

"There's something I haven't understood ever since we spoke to her father," Royal said. "He said he'd paid those men to escort her. But where? Why not take her himself? He clearly tried to take her on the crossing himself."

I hadn't even remembered that, but the conversation came back to me now. "They tried to make the crossing, but she fought him so he took her back to the hotel. Then he said he gave her a choice, do him a favor or go to the Duke—"

"And if he wasn't escorting her to the Duke anymore, then she must have chosen the favor," Royal picked up.

"What favor could his teenage daughter do him that would be more valuable than marrying her off to a Duke?" Akhíta wondered.

"What were his exact words?" I asked Royal. "Something about it being a 'more direct manner of helping recoup his lost investment in the railroad', I think?"

Royal hummed in agreement. "Still, Akhíta's right. He also said the marriage was specifically because this Duke had connections to the railroad, so what could she do *aside* from being married off that would help her father? Presumably, he lost a lot in the recent railroad market crash, which kicked all this off, so…what?"

None of us came up with an answer.

"What was her relationship with her father like?" Shiloh asked.

"She adores him," I admitted. "Her mother died when she was very young. Emilia doesn't even remember her, and she is an only child. Her father has always doted on her. I think…I think that's why she must have gone with him when he came to get her from college. No matter how much she didn't want to be married off, she loves her father enough that it would have taken a lot for her to object."

"She did, though. Something happened when they attempted the crossing that made them turn back," Shiloh pointed out. "And again when he sent her off with those men."

"Maybe that was when It became real for her," Akhíta suggested. "The crossing, I mean. She may have finally realized the kind of man her father is."

It seemed as much a possibility as anything else.

"He hardly seemed like the caring sort when we spoke to him," Royal said eventually. "And he was a snake's ass when I knew him as well. Whatever happened, however she ended up where she is now, I think we can assume he doesn't care if she makes it out alive as long as he gets whatever it is that he wants."

"Exactly," Akhíta said. "She loved him, but he owned her. He had no reason at all to be kind, because he'd twisted up her concept of love so much he knew it didn't matter."

"Yet, she still ran," Royal mused. "Whatever her father asked, she considered it terrible enough to finally break that bond. So what changed?"

"Whatever it was, she ran away from her father and chose the Preachers instead," Shiloh reasoned.

"And now the Pits have decided *I* have to go after her," Royal muttered. "Which *doesn't make sense.*"

"We're missing something important," I said. "Until we figure that missing piece out, we'll just be beating our heads against the wall."

Royal sighed. "Yeah."

The path continued to slope down under our feet, slowly getting illuminated by the rising sun. Not much of it managed to reach us directly, aside from a few small beams, but it was enough for us to finally see where we were going. Now that I had the opportunity, I looked around.

There was a small forest to the west of Altora, but it was nothing like this. It was very cleaned up and even had several cobblestone walking paths winding through it. This forest, though. This forest was wild and thick. Chest high grasses rose up on each side of the path, interspersed with thorny bushes and thick fir trees. Birds twittered in the branches, though I couldn't see any of them, and bugs buzzed amongst the plants. It was all so green. So alive.

Yet, none of it seemed magical. I still wasn't sure what magic would look like, aside from Royal's various trinkets, but all of this looked normal. Sounded normal. Smelled normal.

Bit by bit my ears started to pick up another noise, one I couldn't quite put a name to. The wind, maybe? No one commented on it so I didn't either.

"Almost there," Royal announced sometime later. The sun was fully up now, turning the air hot and humid.

"Where?" I asked. As far as I knew there was no actual destination on this journey, just the vague endpoint of finding Emilia.

"The river," Royal said. "It'll save us a day, maybe two, before it becomes too dangerous to ride."

"We don't have a boat," I pointed out.

"There's always a boat," Shiloh said cryptically.

Royal paused for a moment, turning to look at all of us. "Once we're in the river, that's when this really starts, so we need to be clear about something. If any of us gets split up from the others, from me, you go back. No questions asked. Searching for one another in here isn't a possibility, and it would only slow things down to try."

"We're searching for Emilia," I said.

"Not willingly," Royal said, wincing slightly. They waved off everyone's worry before we could say anything. "Semi-willingly," Royal amended. "Anyways. You get separated, you leave. Head up and out. Agreed?"

"No," Shiloh said simply.

"Also no," Akhíta said.

"Third no," I finished.

Royal looked pissed but ended up just shaking their head, turning around and walking at a faster clip now.

"They don't really believe we'd leave, do they?" I whispered to Shiloh.

He contemplated Royal's retreating back, frowning as he did. "No, and that scares them more."

Chapter 13
Canoe

The river wasn't visible, only audible, thick brush obscuring its banks. Royal seemed to know what they were doing, though, continuing to follow the path until a passage through the bushes was revealed. I would have missed it if it weren't for Royal. It wasn't big, hardly wider than my shoulders and short enough that Royal had to duck, which meant Shiloh probably didn't fit at all. Indeed, I heard the branches scratching against him behind me.

Underneath me the ground began to turn slippery, the dirt more and more saturated. I couldn't help but notice that no footprints other than ours marred its surface.

My spikes didn't make much of a difference, not having anything solid to dig into, so I held my arms out as much as I could for balance, trying to treat it like skating on the pond at Christmas. It all felt so awkward. The weight of the pack on my back, the rough fabric around my legs, the sweat on my skin.

It was so hot in this little tunnel. Hot and humid. Sticky. I'd never been this sticky. The light now was entirely green, filtering in through the verdant leaves. Still, though, nothing seemed out of the ordinary. It was just an overgrown forest. Somehow this was worse. Magic was not only easier to take in small doses, it was also easier to take when I could see it. Knowing it was out there, lurking somewhere below us and slowly dragging Royal in, that was worse. And who knew what it might be doing to Emilia, who had already been here for days with no foreknowledge to guard her against what was coming.

We reached the river quite suddenly, and without ever leaving the tunnel. It arched over the entire river now, branches trailing down into the slow, shallow water. The river wasn't very wide either, maybe fifteen feet. Two wooden poles stood several feet apart but only a couple feet tall, right at the edge of the water. To each was tied a two-man canoe, both looking surprisingly modern. I wondered how they'd gotten here, and why they were here at all. Shiloh had said there'd be boats, though.

Royal waded in and pulled one boat up onto shore, Akhíta the other. Without having to consult one another, they started lashing the boats together side by side. Neither seemed to mind how wet they were getting in the process.

"Uh…question?" I said, eyeing the water. It just looked like water. It wasn't even muddy, providing a clear view to the rocky river bottom and the long, fluttering strands of algae clinging to those rocks.

"What?" Royal asked, looking around to try and spot whatever they assumed I'd seen.

"You said people who take things from the Pits suffer consequences, right? And Akhíta told Daiyu not to pack us too much water…but…can we drink this, or would that count as taking something from the Pit?" I said.

Everyone else stilled, all of us now looking at the water. The plain, boring, water.

"I wish you had kept the question to yourself," Shiloh remarked.

Akhíta shook her head slowly, turning to look upriver. "No…the spring for this river isn't in the Pit itself. It's quite far away, in fact. The water came here the same as we did."

"I find that believable enough," Royal replied. "And thus, I'm going to stop thinking about it now."

I chewed my lip, unconvinced. "What if we're wrong? Or, what if we're right *now* but become wrong later once we're deeper? At some point, the water has to become part of the Pit, doesn't it?"

"What is there to do about it if you're right?" Shiloh asked.

I contemplated a moment, still watching the water. "Pay for it?"

"How?" Akhíta asked.

I shrugged, holding out my hands. "I don't know. All of you understand this better than me, I'm just making things up as we go."

"Blood?" Royal suggested. "Giving a bit of our life for the thing we need to stay alive?"

I was reminded of the wound metaphor Royal kept using. It made blood seem even more like the right answer, so I nodded. Royal reached around and slid their hunting knife out of its sheath on the back of their gun belt. There was already a bandage wrapped around where they'd cut themself to summon the Preachers, so they shimmied back the edge and sliced a new line, tilting their arm so the blood would drop into the water. As it hit, the water shimmered with opalescence in a way boring, normal water would not have, and the blood vanished. It didn't mix into the water, it just vanished.

"Seems that was the correct answer," Royal said.

"That was the correct answer for you, but I don't think you make for the best benchmark at this point," Akhíta said, holding her hand out for the knife.

"Yeah, that's fair." They handed the knife over.

Akhíta took it, wiped it on her pants to get Royal's blood off, then rolled up her jacket sleeve and slit a clean line across her arm in the same spot Royal had. When her blood hit the water there was no strange shimmer, but it did vanish in the same way. The same thing happened for Shiloh, who wiped his blood off on his own pants, then handed the knife off to me. I took it, feeling the heft. It weighed as much as the little pistol Shiloh had given me. I'd given that back, though, still uncomfortable with it.

"Keep it shallow," Royal said. "I'll do it for you, if you need me to."

I shook my head, holding up my left arm and setting the blade against my skin in the same spot as the others. "It wouldn't be my payment that way." Taking a steadying breath, I dragged it across in a quick, light slice. Blood beaded up, catching in the fine hairs across the back of my arm. I was surprised at how little it stung.

Stepping forward, I tilted my arm over the water, letting several drops of blood fall. Part of me was surprised to see the same thing happen as had happened for Shiloh and Akhíta. Somehow I'd been expecting that, because Royal and I were related, because we shared the same blood, the magic might be doing something to me as well. That didn't seem to be the case, though.

Three new cloth bandages were pulled out of a bag and wrapped around our arms to staunch the wounds. No point sacrificing more than necessary.

Royal and Shiloh took one canoe while Akhíta and I took the other, with me in the front. Between our bodies and our packs, there wasn't room to spare in the little boats. Nor, I realized, were there any oars. It didn't seem to matter, though. As soon as we were all in the canoes the boats moved of their own accord, sliding off the bank and drifting to the center of the river.

Shiloh yawned wide and loud, shimmying so he was sitting in the bottom of the canoe, leaning back to rest against his pack and propping his legs up on the sides. Royal caught his yawn and leaned back to rest against Shiloh's chest. Shiloh immediately wrapped his arms around Royal and within moments both were asleep, breaths slow and even.

Akhíta looked at them, then at me. "I don't like you enough to do that."

"Should we be sleeping at all?" I asked.

"We have to at some point," she replied. "In shifts."

I nodded and turned to face forward. This, however, meant I could feel Akhíta's eyes on my back, but not see her, which made my skin crawl. At this point, I had no idea how much she did or didn't blame me. Just because she seemed to be tolerating me at the moment didn't mean things would stay that way.

"Your mother," I said, desperate for some sort of conversation. If she was talking to me I at least had some idea of her mood. "What's she like?"

"What?" Akhíta asked, confusion clear in her voice.

"Your mother. Everyone kept talking about going to stay with her until things cooled down. It made me curious."

"She's a nurse," Akhíta said eventually. "Or she was during the war, anyway. They'd take anyone they could get once things started to drag out. It didn't matter that she was Two Kettles Lakota. But once it was over no one would hire her anymore. She lives in a cabin quite a ways north, nearly to Canada. Mostly treats travelers now. Helps deliver babies on the surrounding homesteads. It's why she hasn't been dragged to a reservation. As long as she has value, they let her stick around."

I was beginning to pick up on the forcibly even tone Akhíta used when talking about difficult things, and she was using it now. I tried to steer the conversation back to more neutral territory.

"How often do you see her?"

"Whenever I'm bringing her people who need help finding a new home."

I puffed out a breath. So much for neutral territory.

"What?" Akhíta asked.

"Nothing. I don't want to make you keep talking about hard things. I'll shut up."

It was Akhíta's turn to sigh. "I doubt we'll have many conversations down here that aren't about hard things. It goes both ways, though. What's *your* mother like? I've only ever heard Royal's accounts."

I opened my mouth to answer, then didn't. What *was* she like? A week ago I never would have had reason to question that, yet after everything Royal had expressed on the matter, I did have questions now.

"Can I ask you something else before I answer that?" I said instead.

Akhíta hummed her consent.

"Your mother...you love her?"

"Very much."

I turned around to face her now. "Why? What...what's that like for you? What...makes her a mother worthy of being loved in your eyes?" I needed to know. Needed something to compare my own answer to.

"I've never really thought about it like that before," Akhíta admitted. "She just...is. She tucked me in every night, told me stories, taught me to hunt and cook. She knows exactly how I like my meat prepared, and that I prefer elk over deer. She made sure I learned to read, soothed my nightmares. She sought out other black women so she could learn how to do my hair, since it is so different from her own. It's…all those little things, I suppose."

I chewed the inside of my lower lip, rolling it between my teeth as I played out memories of childhood in my mind. The only one who'd ever soothed my nightmares was Royal. The only one who ever did my hair, other than myself, was Royal. The one who helped me learn to read, aside from my teachers, was Royal. Mother taught me to cook, but it was only ever when she needed help doing so for a church bakesale or a town potluck. Royal bandaged my scraped knees, snuck me extra dessert, threw rocks at my bullies. It was always Royal.

Until they left.

"I don't know what my mother is like," I admitted, swallowing heavily. How hadn't I noticed?

Akhíta watched me assesingly. "I'm sorry."

I faced forward once more, glad that Akhíta let the conversation drop. Her gaze on my back no longer felt quite so piercing either.

With a little work, I managed to arrange myself in a comfortable enough position to doze off without fear of falling off into the water. I woke to the boats jostling slightly as Royal and Akhíta swapped places. She laid down the opposite direction from a still sleeping—and snoring—Shiloh, tossing her legs up over his shoulders. Royal, meanwhile, sat behind me where Akhíta had been.

We were out of the tunnel of bushes now, surrounded instead by steep walls of rock. I was surprised to find that the sun was falling, painting the sky pink above us.

"Keep an eye on them. Royal isn't allowed to take watch alone," Akhíta said, eyes already closed.

Royal rolled their eyes. "Oh, *now* you trust my sister?"

"With some things," Akhíta said cryptically.

I looked too Royal for clarification, only getting a shrug in reply.

Rooting through a pack, Royal produced some jerky and handed over a large slice. I nibbled on the edge, not really that hungry despite not eating all day. Nerves, I supposed.

I shifted to sit sideways and watched Royal out of the corner of my eye as we drifted, trying to gauge if they were alright. They were certainly being quieter than they usually were, their eyes sweeping up and down the surrounding cliffs. I looked as well, trying to see what they did. To me it just looked like rocks.

"How deep are we?" I asked softly, not wanting to disturb Akhíta and Shiloh.

Royal didn't look at me, still focused the cliffs. "Hard to say, exactly. Not very, though. We won't start going deep until we leave the river in the morning."

"Why are you so tense, then?"

"I don't know the rules anymore," Royal muttered.

I couldn't help but feel sorry for them. They had been working so hard to understand all of this, and now it had all been turned upside down. For someone like Royal, I knew that had to be painfully frustrating.

Glancing up at the sky, I asked how long we'd been on the river. It really didn't feel as though I had slept long enough for it to be sunset.

"No idea," Royal said. "I was dead asleep to be honest." They glanced over at Akhíta. "I kind of hope it gets fully dark soon, though. She never sleeps well unless it's dark."

The second their words ceased, darkness enveloped us. There was no dusk, no lingering warmth. It was day and then it wasn't anymore. I couldn't even see a rough silhouette of Royal a few feet away. The darkness was solid. Heavy. Royal swore softly and I heard them rummaging around in a pack while I was still trying to process what was happening.

"Give me the light back," Royal muttered. I was confused for a moment until a few clicks sounded, bringing sparks with them as Royal fought with their lighter. The brief flashes of light danced across my eyes, lingering there and layering upon one another with each iteration until Royal managed to get the oil lamp going. When I tried to speak they put a finger to their lips and handed the lamp over before drawing a pistol and holding it ready at their side.

I swung the lamp around in a slow arc, wishing it threw the light farther. As it was, it didn't even make it to the cliffs, just provided a limited bubble around us over the river. My ears strained, trying to pick up something, anything, other than the soft swish of the boat through the water. When there was finally something to hear, a little splash, I nearly dropped the lantern in fright.

Royal reached out and gently tapped my leg, mouthing the word "breathe" when I looked over. Nodding, I rolled my shoulders, trying to release some of the tension.

There weren't stars, though I didn't remember it being incredibly cloudy, but I thought my eyes were starting to adjust enough that I could pick out the top of the cliffs where they sat roughly thirty feet above us. Or perhaps my mind was just inserting what I assumed to be there. After awhile, though, it was hard to be concerned anymore. While the sudden onset of this darkness was still unsettling, nothing else had happened. Royal seemed to have relaxed somewhat as well, resting their pistol across their lap now.

I waved to get Royal's attention and mimed putting out the lantern, quirking an eyebrow in question, trying to communicate that we didn't seem to need it and should save the oil. Royal swept their eyes all around us, then gave a nod. I lifted up the glass and blew it out, plunging us back into darkness so complete it felt heavy, like being underwater. It pressed against every inch of my skin, making it tingle.

I heard Royal shuffling once more, sensing they were getting close to me until, suddenly, their back was resting against mine. I was grateful for the contact, leaning into them as well. Shiloh and Akhíta slept on. I was starting to wonder about Shiloh but for all I knew he'd been awake while I slept earlier.

When the orange dots appeared, it had been dark for so long it felt like my eyes didn't quite remember how to see. First there were two, hovering about ten feet above the water ahead of us and off to the side, where I thought the cliffs had been. Then there were four. Then six. As they moved they left smears of orange light behind. Eventually it occurred to me I might need to be worried about the dots, so I elbowed Royal.

Whatever the dots were, they weren't providing any real illumination, leaving me to guess at what Royal was doing. I felt them turn behind me and, after a moment, heard the click of their pistol. They did not speak and neither did I.

The closer we got, the more dots appeared. There were dozens of them on both sides now, and we were only feet away from the first ones. We crossed in front of the first and a sharp yip echoed out, soon joined by a cacophony of others.

Akhíta and Shiloh both shot up, tangled together from their odd position. Royal dropped their pistol and lunged over, clapping a hand over both their mouths. All around us the cackling yips and barks continued. It was clear now they were coyotes, dozens and dozens of them. They raced up and down the cliffs, light trailing from their eyes, and I still couldn't actually *see* them.

One by one the coyotes peeled off, rising up to the top of the cliffs and vanishing from view over the top, until there was only one left. It was silent and watching us from just above the waterline as we drifted closer. I heard someone shifting, relatively sure it was Royal. Some deep-seated sibling instinct told me they were about to do something stupid. Reaching out, I attempted to grab a fistful of their shirt only to find empty air where I expected them to be.

"Hello?" Royal called.

Akhíta, Shiloh, and I all made noises of protest.

The last coyote, now just ahead, grinned. I shouldn't have been able to see it grin, except that its mouth was full of shimmering specks of white and blue light flickering behind its fangs. Its mouth opened wider and wider, far beyond what a normal coyote could do. There was blackness among the light now, lighter than the blackness that surrounded us somehow, and I realized the lights were stars. They ballooned out with the new, lighter darkness, growing larger and larger until they consumed the river in front of us.

There was no way to stop, no way to turn, nowhere else to go. The boats sailed into the stars.

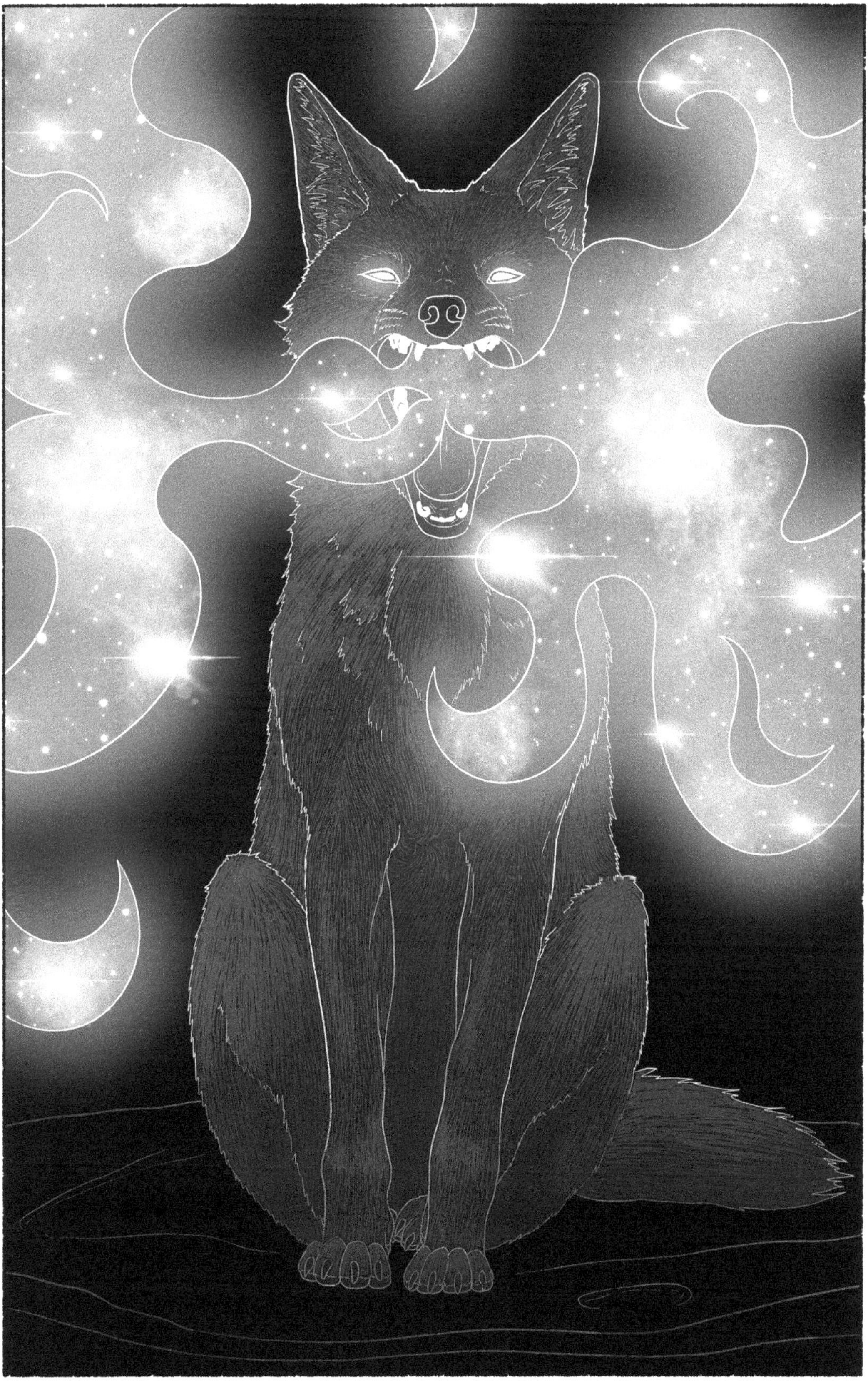

I don't know what I'd expected to happen, but it wasn't for us to still be in the river, except now in a meadow lit by the earliest hints of dawn. Royal was crouched at the rear of our boat, looking behind us to where the end of the canyon stood, now lit just like everything else. Even from behind, I could tell Royal was grinning.

"How many times do I have to tell you not to talk to the damn coyotes, Royal?" Akhíta said witheringly.

Hearing someone else speak made me flinch. The sound of it felt foreign after the long silence of the canyon. Somehow, Royal's voice hadn't had the same effect. Maybe it was because we'd still been in the canyon then. In the dark.

"Are you telling me you knew those coyotes would be there?" I asked, feeling miffed. Some warning would have been nice.

"No," Shiloh said. "We've seen coyotes down here before, but never like that."

"Never seen darkness like that either," Royal mused. They were still watching the canyon as it shrunk into the distance.

"So why the hell did you talk to it?" Akhíta asked. "I've spent two years trying to keep you from getting eaten by things in the dark and you keep trying to make friends with them. It is exhausting."

"I was curious," Royal said, distractedly.

"About?" Shiloh asked.

Royal didn't answer at first until eventually they said, "Intention."

Despite being pressed they didn't provide any clarification. Akhíta, Shiloh, and I all shared another glance Royal didn't seem to notice, clearly also sharing the same concern. What was really going on with Royal?

Chapter 14
Cliffs

When the sun reached the same position as it had been in when we boarded the boats, both turned for the bank, bumping up onto the shore. The moment the last of our things were out both boats vanished. I stared at where they'd been, mulling over the fact that it should be at least confusing, but I was beyond caring at this point.

Royal, standing next to me, chuckled. "And to think, a few days ago you didn't even believe in magic. Now you're on a *quest*."

"This is not a quest," Shiloh said.

Royal threw their arms out and started walking backwards down the gentle slope of the meadow. "This is most certainly a quest! There's even a damsel."

"They're going to trip," Akhíta observed flatly.

Royal tripped, sprawling backward head over heels.

"At least they didn't have the lantern," Shiloh said.

"And they're not talking to the wildlife anymore," I added.

"Give it time. They'll find a bear or something to make friends with soon enough," Akhíta replied. She hefted on her pack and set off towards Royal who was still sprawled out in the grass, trying to act like they'd intended to fall and were just resting.

"Hello," Royal said conversationally.

"Úŋnišike," She kicked their boots until they got up, groaning dramatically the whole time. The two of them set off down the path together.

"If the coyotes eat light, what do the bears do?" I asked Shiloh.

He shook his head. "I'm hoping we don't find out."

We were back on some sort of path and, according to Shiloh, had saved a couple days of walking by taking the river. The consensus was that Emilia probably hadn't taken the river, given how hidden it was and, as far as anyone knew, the boats only appeared in one place. If true, this meant Emilia could only be a day, day-and-a-half at most, ahead of us. Maybe less, given she wouldn't be moving with any speed. Royal was sure she was on the same path, though, given that it was the only one in this area and it would make sense for her to have stuck to it.

This was far too much guessing and supposing for my tastes. I wanted something, anything, solid, both for Emilia's sake and Royal's. Some indication that we were at least on the same path. I was so far out of my depth here, though, that there was nothing I could do save trusting the others knew enough to be right. That trust was hard to hold on to, though, given that everything all of them knew about magic had been turned upside down.

Once, when I was about ten years old, a balloonist had come to town in a great red and orange balloon, touching down in the town square and offering rides for a quarter apiece. I had desperately wanted to go but my mother forbid it, feeling balloons were far too dangerous. That was the closest I had ever come to being higher than a few floors off the ground.

Until now.

The meadow ended abruptly, the ground vanishing. Royal, Akhíta, and Shiloh approached like this was completely normal. I followed right up until I saw what the drop off actually was. A cliff. A cliff that made the ones along the river look like skipping stones.

If the swooping in my stomach was any indication, my mother had been right to forbid the balloon ride. Safe or not, my ten-year-old self would have ended up a blubbering mess on the bottom of the basket. My seventeen-year-old self wasn't doing much better.

I couldn't even estimate how tall the cliff was. It was craggy and jagged the whole way down, ending in a steep pile of scree that flowed out into the beginnings of a forest. Taking a few steps away I swallowed heavily, tilting my head up to look at the clear blue sky so I couldn't see the cliff at all.

"It isn't going to go away just because you aren't looking at it," Royal called from where they were kneeling over a pack a ways away.

"Says who?" I called back. "We just watched a coyote release daylight from its mouth."

"Well, if it was going to go away just because you wanted it to, it would've done it already," Royal replied.

I groaned, my head still tilted back. "So how long is it going to take to go around?"

Akhíta laughed and I finally looked away from the sky. She was pulling an absolutely massive coil of rope out of a crevice between several boulders. Making what felt like very deliberate eye contact, she tossed it over the edge, one end still trailing back into the crevice.

"Welcome to our general store," Akhíta said. "We're not going around."

"What?" I said, not wanting to believe her.

Royal held out a hand in my direction. "Come 'ere."

I shook my head, eyes going wide. When I'd pictured climbing in the Pits I had imagined a bluff or two, maybe cliffs like the river ones. Not something several dozen times taller than the tallest building in Altora.

Royal came over and got me, slipping my pack off my shoulders and draping an arm over them. "I've got you." They walked me closer to the edge of the cliff, pushing lightly to keep me going. "Nope, no closing your eyes."

That was a lot to ask for. I managed to pry my eyes open anyway, a wave of dizziness washing over me as I looked down the cliff for a second time. Flailing out I wrapped an arm around Royal's waist.

Royal gave my shoulders a squeeze. "Breathe. You'll be completely secure, and we'll be down before you know it."

"Why'd Akhíta call it your general store?" I asked, hoping the answer would make the cliff seem less intimidating somehow. My voice came out higher than I'd intended.

"Look closer," Royal said. "At the actual rocks, in places where they're flat."

Moving my eyes felt like tugging at a stuck door. They just didn't want to do it. At first all I could see was the dark gray rock, shot through with veins of white. After a moment, I thought I saw what Royal might mean. There was a doll there, weatherbeaten with a cracked porcelain face. In another spot lay a jar filled with something blue. There were dozens of objects scattered all over as far down as I could see.

"Oh," I said, realization washing over me. "This is where you get the magic things you sell."

"A lot of them, yes," Royal replied. "In the other Pits we tend to find things that were accidentally left behind. This is the only place we've ever found that is deliberate."

"How did they all get here?" I asked, searching out more. A book, warped by rain. A pearl necklace, the pearls loose on the rock, string having dissolved away. A muddy yellow dress, caught and torn.

"Do you remember what the Preachers said? About Emilia leaving to do the 'trials'?" Royal asked, a note of hesitation in their voice.

I did now, but was a little alarmed I hadn't even considered Emilia up to this point. What would she have done when she reached these cliffs? Before I could spiral into my thoughts, Royal kept speaking.

"These cliffs, they mark the start of the Preacher Path. I don't know what the trials actually are, but I know the women who undertake them, their path through starts here. The bottom of these cliffs is the deepest any of our gang have ever gone. The objects, far as we can tell, are either things the women have left behind, or things that have been left here as offerings to the Preachers," Royal finished.

"Emilia—"

"Made it down," Shiloh interrupted, appearing on my other side. He'd been walking the length of the cliff while Akhíta continued to ready the ropes.

I spun to face him, forgetting about the cliff entirely. "What? Did you see her down there?"

"No," Shiloh said. "Which is sort of the point...."

I looked at him in confusion.

He shifted, looking uncomfortable. "There's fresh footprints, small ones, a little ways south. And she wasn't...at the bottom. So she survived the climb."

The dizziness now was for a whole new reason. He was saying she hadn't fallen to her death. Which was, of course, good, but I hadn't even considered the possibility until now. I just wanted a sign that she was okay, something other than the absence of her body at the bottom of this cliff.

Not knowing what else to do I made the sign of the cross and sent out a quick prayer. I realized it was the first one I'd said in days. Since I'd first seen Royal use magic. This was starting to be too many feelings to deal with at once, and I was almost glad when Akhíta called out that it was time to go. Except for the fact that it would, in fact, involve going.

Royal gave me a squeeze and steered me over to Akhíta. She had four ropes laid out, each trailing back into the crevice she'd pulled them from. I looked and saw that they were all wrapped around a thick pillar of rock within the crevice. The ropes were fanned out, each a few feet apart, except for one that was still coiled up. Thick, folded pieces of canvass protected the ropes where they went over the edge. Several more shorter, thinner lengths of rope sat at Akhíta's feet. She'd already taken one and tied it into a harness around her waist. Before I could say I hadn't paid enough attention when Shiloh taught me how to tie a harness, Royal grabbed one of the remaining lengths and started doing it for me.

"Just take it slow," Royal instructed as they tied. "Keep your eyes on the rock in front of you. Going down is the easiest part. Like walking backwards. There's a few places to stop and rest on the way down, you don't have to do it all in one go."

Going down was the easy part. Which meant that, by default, at some point, if this went well, we would have to go back up, and that would be the hard part. Great.

"You tripped walking backwards not even an hour ago," I pointed out.

"And I was fine," Royal said.

They continued to give me instructions, attaching my harness to a thick metal ring that was already threaded through with a larger rope. Lastly, they handed me a pair of small, fingerless leather gloves. I slid them on, trying to keep my hands from shaking, and Royal laced them tightly around my wrists.

"You can still go back," Royal whispered so that only I could hear. "I'd feel better if you did, honestly."

I shook my head. "Not a chance."

They sighed. "Yeah, I figured."

After Akhíta shucked off her jacket and packed it away, she and Shiloh lowered our packs down first using the large rope that hadn't been tossed over yet. Then she and Royal went over, telling me to take the rope between theirs and hers while Shiloh took the one on Royal's other side. Shiloh guided me backwards, being gentlemanly enough not to comment on my method of getting over the edge. Royal and Akhíta had simply leaned back in what looked like a barely controlled fall until they slid out of view. There was no chance in hell I was doing that so, instead, I laid on my stomach and scooted backwards until my legs were dangling into open air. Fingers of my non rope holding hand tangled in the grass, I tried to figure out what to do next.

Royal figured it out for me, thankfully, grabbing my boot and pushing it forward until my toes made contact with the rock. I felt the spikes dig in and brought my other foot forward until it connected as well. Taking a deep breath, I pried my fingers up one by one, and fed out the rope with my other hand the way Royal had showed me. Soon enough I was, essentially, sitting, my legs straight out in front of me and butt supported by the harness.

Royal grinned from next to me. "Good job."

I didn't dare look down to figure out where Akhíta was.

Within seconds Shiloh joined us.

"One step at a time," Royal said. "I'm right next to you."

"Less than a week with you and I'm making the worst decisions of my life," I muttered.

Royal chuckled, taking it for the stress induced jab that it was.

We hadn't even done anything yet and my arms already ached with tension. I knew I should relax them, not use up all my energy, but I found it entirely impossible to do so. Hopefully the first break wouldn't be too far down.

I took my first step. Then another. And another.

"Do you want to talk?" Royal asked. "It might help."

"Nope." I wanted to get down.

I needed something to occupy my mind, though, so I started a running list of the objects I saw as we passed them, wondering what magic they might contain. A single earring; maybe it let you hear whispered conversations. A hairbrush; maybe it helped your hair grow longer. A pack of cards; maybe they always won. A wooden jewelry box; maybe it protected your jewelry from theft, hiding it from people with bad intentions.

I kept doing it, going through object after object. It wasn't really making the climb any easier, but it at least kept me from panicking.

"First break," Royal said, pulling me out of my head.

Their definition of a break was a ledge that was barely a couple of feet wide. I did not quite agree that this counted as a break. A break would have been a nice cave I could crawl into and forget about the cliff entirely for several moments.

"You're doing great," Royal said. They reached over and put a hand on my back rubbing it up and down soothingly. Exactly like they did when I used to have nightmares.

I rested my forehead against the rock, enjoying the coolness of it and trying not to think about how much cliff was left. I honestly had no idea.

This time there was no option for me to scoot over the edge on my stomach. I had to do it the way everyone else did. Why this seemed so much worse than actually making my way down, I didn't know, but it did. Royal stayed right next to me, going the exact same speed. We tipped over together until our legs were straight out in front of us, feet flat on the rocks.

"Not so bad, is it?" Royal said.

"I can't believe you do this willingly," I gasped out.

"You'll be okay, I promise," Royal assured.

Sure.

An old miner's hammer; maybe it got warm when you got near gold. A ball of yarn, half fallen apart and tangled around the rocks; maybe it knitted itself when you put it on the needles. A necklace with a simple, circular charm; maybe it...maybe it....

I stopped, staring at the necklace. The charm. It was tiny and gold, sparkling in the sun, and the charm had a small heart cut out of the center as its only ornamentation.

I knew that necklace. I'd felt it run dangle against my skin dozens of times, a cold accent to warm kisses.

It was too far away for me to reach unless I folded my knees and brought myself closer to the cliff. Technically, I only needed one hand on the rope to keep myself secure, but the idea of taking my other one off even to grab the necklace still felt terrifying.

"Clarabella?" Royal called. They were a few feet below me now.

Making up my mind, I folded my knees inch by inch. When I was close enough, I unlatched my hand and reached forward.

"Whatever it is, leave it!" Royal said, worry in their voice. Akhíta and Shiloh said something as well, but they were farther down and I was too focused to understand them. Royal let out a curse and I heard them scrabbling on the rock below me.

My fingers brushed the chain, and the world fell out from under me. Someone screamed. Maybe it was me.

I didn't fully comprehend that I was falling before I suddenly wasn't anymore.

"Put your arms around me, put your arms around me!"

Akhíta.

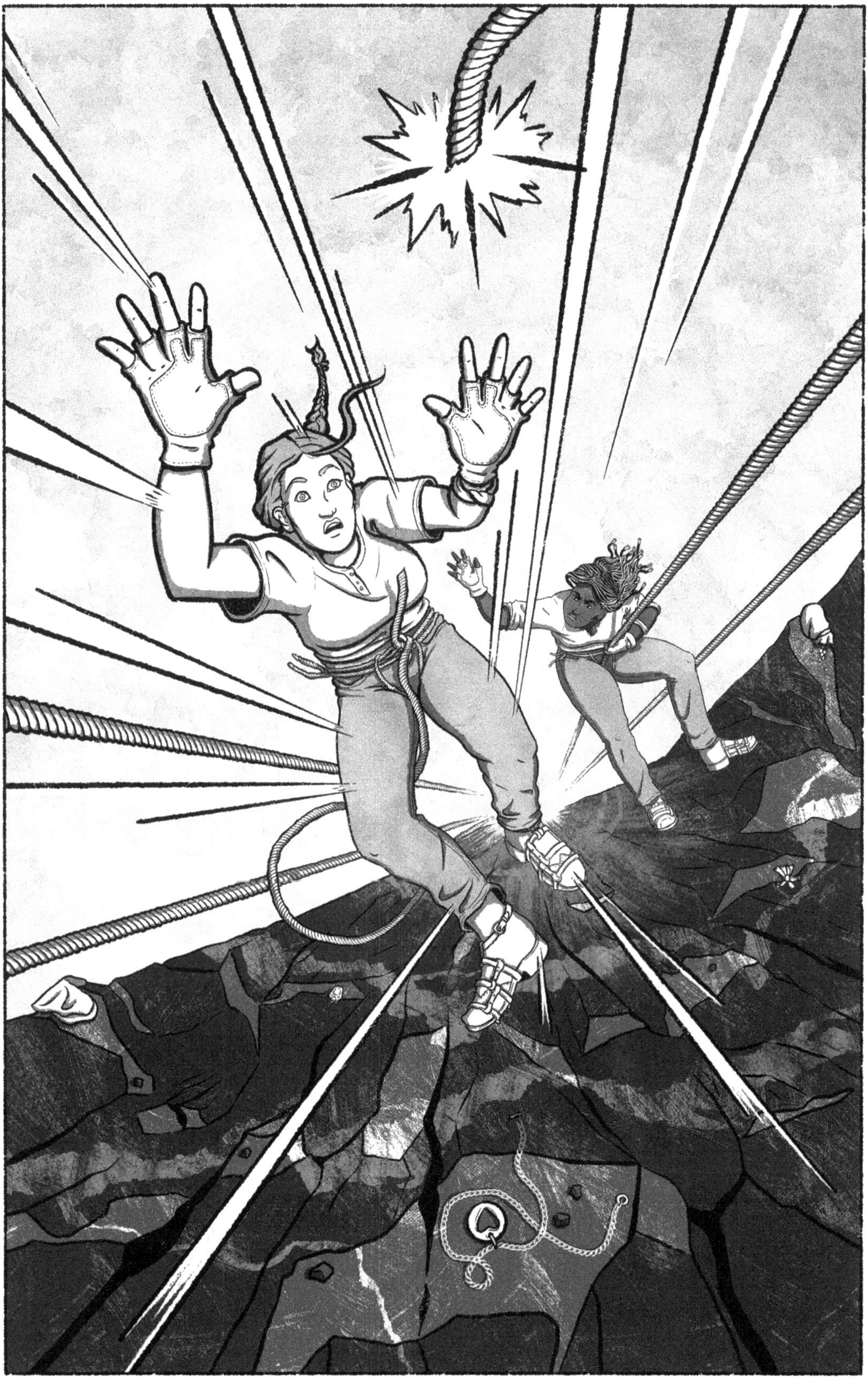

She'd caught me, one arm under one of mine and wrapped across my back and around my side, hand fisted in my shirt. Her other arm was twisted up in her rope to keep us in place as we dangled sideways.

I stopped thinking and tried to do what she said, terrified that any wrong move might make her drop me. My limbs refused to move the way I wanted, making it even harder. Finally I managed to swing one arm up and across her chest, bringing my other one up over her back, and clamped my hands together on the other side of her neck.

"Hook your right leg over mine. Royal, shut up!" Akhíta instructed. Royal had been shouting my name over and over, I realized.

I did as she instructed and, with a lot of awkward wiggling and sliding, we managed to get into an arrangement where I was sitting on her lap, her legs stretched back out to place her feet against the cliff. My arms remained locked around her and I clamped my legs around her waist, ankles hooked together. Chancing a glance up I saw Royal maybe twenty feet above us, being held in place by Shiloh. Royal was paler than they'd been even after getting shot and, despite the distance, I could tell they were shaking. I realized with alarm that there was no sign of my rope anywhere between where I now was with Akhíta and where Royal was.

"Are you secure?" Shiloh called.

"Yeah," Akhíta replied through gritted teeth. I wasn't sure I agreed.

Shiloh released Royal after an admonishment to go slow; we didn't need someone else falling. Both they and Shiloh were at our level in moments.

"What happened?" Royal asked immediately. They were too far away to touch us, but Royal reached out towards me anyway.

"We'll figure it out on the ground. Akhíta, can you get down with her like that, or do you need me to take her?" Shiloh said.

"I highly doubt we could pry her off of me," Akhíta answered. She was correct. I couldn't have let go of her if I wanted to. "I'll manage, let's just get down."

No idea what else to do, I tucked my head into Akhíta's shoulder and waited for it to be over.

When we reached the scree I still couldn't disentangle myself from Akhíta, even when I started sobbing. Royal was there in seconds, prying me off until I was clinging to them instead. They were holding me so tight it hurt. I didn't care.

"What happened? What happened?" Royal asked.

I didn't know.

"It's been cut," Shiloh said somewhere behind Royal.

Royal turned, pulling me with them. "*What?*"

"Her rope," Shiloh said. "Hang on."

There was the sound of shifting rocks, something being dragged over them. I peeked out to see Shiloh rapidly running what was left of my rope through his hands, stretching it out one arm's width at a time. When he reached the end he looked up, muttering numbers to himself.

"It...it wasn't cut at the top. It had to have been cut...just above where she fell from," Shiloh said, confusion clear in his voice.

Royal looked down at me, immense concern and fear on their face. "What happened? You were reaching for something. What was it?"

"Em—Emilia's ne-necklace," I managed, struggling to find my voice.

"And you fell when you tried to grab it?" Royal said.

"When—when I touched—it."

"The Pit must not have wanted you to take it," Shiloh said.

"No...no...I don't think—" My thoughts were a mess. I thought I understood what had happened now, but I couldn't get it out.

"Let's get off the rocks," Akhíta said, speaking for the first time.

I turned to see her standing behind me rubbing at her shoulder of the arm she'd used to grab me.

"You caught me," I said.

"Of course I caught you."

"You don't like me."

She huffed. "There is quite a distance between not liking someone and letting them fall to a gruesome death."

"Are you hurt?" I asked.

She rolled her shoulder, then shook her head. "I'll sleep it off."

Royal, one arm still around my shoulders, reached out their other arm until Akhíta came over and accepted a hug.

"Thank you, thank you," Royal muttered over and over, face buried in Akhíta's hair.

Chapter 15
Rest

Royal and Shiloh each took two of the packs, refusing to let Akhíta or I have one. Royal also refused to let go of my hand as we shuffled sideways down the loose rock. I didn't object. The slippery, shifting rocks hardly felt better than hanging off the side of the cliff.

Bit by bit my shaking subsided, and my breathing evened out. By the time we reached the edge of the scree and stepped into the forest I felt somewhat normal again. Still shaken, but functional now.

Around us stood thick, towering pines. It would've taken three grown men to wrap their arms around the trunks. The ground was clearer here as well, all but the hardiest of plants shaded out. Warmer air than expected filled my lungs, filled with the taste of being among so many living things.

"We camp here," Shiloh declared, dropping his two bags.

Akhíta shook her head. "We've got hours of daylight left. We shouldn't waste it."

Shiloh shook his head right back. "You're hurt. Clarabella and Royal are both a mess. We need to rest and regroup."

Royal dropped both their packs in agreement. Akhíta gave in and moved to the packs, seemingly to help make camp. Shiloh waved her off. Royal and I were waved off as well, shoed over in the direction of a fallen log it was clear we were meant to go sit on while he set up camp alone. Royal sat pressed up close to my side, one arm tight around my shoulders, chin resting on top of my head.

"I know what happened," I said.

Royal made a questioning noise.

"What you said, back on the river, about intention? You think we're influencing the magic here somehow, don't you?" I asked.

"I think *I* am," Royal muttered. "Because of what's happening to me, whatever it is."

"Well...it might not just be you. Before we came down the cliffs, I was thinking about how I'd give anything for a sign that we were on the right path. That Emilia had really come this way, gotten this far. Then her necklace shows up, except...Shiloh said her footprints were to the south of where we came down, so how did the necklace get there? Even if she dropped it intentionally, the chances of it being directly on the path I took down...."

"But that doesn't explain your fall," Royal said.

"I didn't pay for it. I just wanted it."

"How the hell is your death worth a stupid necklace?" Royal said, anger in their tone. "That's not a fair price. And, if you're right, you didn't even have a *chance* to pay."

I shrugged. "Maybe I'm wrong. All I know for sure is I wanted a sign, and when I touched the necklace I fell."

Royal hummed and didn't press it any further.

Shiloh, seeming intent on mothering all of us, handed out some fruit leather and jerky once camp was set, along with the small canteens of water we'd brought. As the food was consumed he made Akhíta sit on the log like it was a horse, taking a seat behind her in the same way. Gently, he peeled back her shirt and prodded at her shoulder. She winced.

"Well, it isn't dislocated," Shiloh declared. "No idea how. I still can't believe you managed to catch her, to be honest."

"Neither can I," Akhíta admitted.

"I owe you my life for that," Royal said.

"I think you owe me nine lives at this point," she replied.

Royal's lips twitched in a poorly suppressed smile. "Will you accept a cat instead, if we really are up to nine?"

The rest of us groaned. Some of the tension lifted, though.

Shiloh insisted Akhíta wear her arm in a sling, at least for awhile. She wasn't pleased, given that she was right handed, but Shiloh threatened to tell her mother that Akhíta wasn't treating an injury properly. This got Akhíta into the sling so fast it was almost funny.

Royal made me tell the others my theory about why I fell, then added on. "Back at the river, I had the passing thought that I wished it was darker, because I know you never sleep well when there's still light out, Akhíta, and I wanted you to be able to rest. As soon as I said it, all the light vanished. It didn't *get* dark, it just *was* dark. It reminded me of before we came down, when we were trying to figure it out, how I'd say things and the magic would react. Except, then I tried to ask for the light back and nothing happened, so I thought I must be wrong."

"So?" Shiloh asked.

"Well, now Clarabella is saying the same thing happened with Emilia's necklace, even though she didn't say it out loud. She thought about wanting a sign, and then, later, she got one. And she paid a price for it," Royal said.

"I follow you," Akhíta replied. "But if you're right, what was the price for the darkness?"

"It was *too much* darkness," I suggested, remembering how it had felt on my skin, how little the lantern penetrated it. "The price was the danger of it. But when Royal asked for light, they didn't pay another price. Wait…no…."

"No?" Royal said.

I screwed up my face, trying to remember exactly what happened. "You asked for the light back, but…you did it while you were digging for your lighter, didn't you?"

Royal frowned for a minute, then swore. "So it *did* give me *a* light, just not the light I wanted."

"What we want…but wrong," Shiloh mused.

I nodded.

"Wonderful," Akhíta said.

"And we're barely into the Pit," Royal pointed out. "We need to be very, very careful about our thoughts, our words, going forward."

This was like being told not to think of an elephant. As soon as you were told not to, all you *could* think of was the elephant. From everyone else's expressions, I guessed they felt much the same.

"What about the coyotes?" Akhíta asked. "The last one especially. It gave you back the light without a price."

"I think it has been long established that coyotes have their own rules," Royal said. Akhíta didn't disagree.

With nothing else to do, we all agreed to get some rest. Shiloh tried to argue that he could take the first watch alone. Royal disagreed, insisting on staying up with him. Shiloh seemingly gave in, tucking Royal up under his arm where the two of them had settled with their backs against the log. Shiloh winked at me over Royal's head and started gently running their knuckles up and down Royal's arm.

"Don't do that," Royal yawned.

"Do what?" Shiloh asked innocently.

"*That*." Royal yawned again.

"I have no idea what you mean."

"Asshole," Royal grumbled.

I smiled and rolled over onto my stomach on the bedroll Shiloh had laid out, pillowing my head on my arms. Right as my consciousness slipped away, I wondered if dreams counted as intention.

"Hey, hey, Royal, you're alright, you're alright," a soft, urgent voice assured.

I couldn't quite get my bearings, waking up in the darkness. For a second I thought we were still on the river, that the cliff had been a bad dream. But it wasn't the same darkness. Flickering orange light danced around me on the tree trunks, and a firefly drifted past in a lazy, bobbing path. Sharp pine needles littering the forest floor poked up into my arm where it had fallen off the bedroll.

"You're alright," the voice said again. Shiloh.

Twisting around I looked until I found him, arms wrapped tightly around Royal, rocking them gently and stroking their hair. Neither seemed to notice me looking. I stayed still, trying to figure out what was going on.

"It was just a dream," Shiloh murmured. "Just a dream. Shh."

"Akhíta didn't catch her," Royal gasped, tears in their voice.

"She did, Clarabella's fine," Shiloh assured, continuing to rock Royal.

I wasn't sure if I should get up or stay put. On the one hand, my fall was what had caused Royal's bad dream. On the other, this sort of seemed like the kind of thing a partner would be better at fixing than a little sister. I decided to stay put, watching them through half closed eyes over the crook of my elbow.

Shiloh continued to rock and sooth Royal until, several minutes later, Royal pulled away with a shaky breath. They ran their hands through their hair, pressing their hands to their eyes and sniffing a few times. Shiloh reached out and rubbed their back.

"I can't lose her, Shiloh," Royal whispered.

"I know," Shiloh said, just as quiet.

Royal's voice still shook somewhat. "I've been trying to think of a way to get her away from home ever since I left, to convince her to come with me, and then she just shows up in Whiskey Hole? Fuck. It felt like a miracle."

"I know."

"And she wants to find her girlfriend, sure. I never thought we'd find her, but I figured, hey, it'll buy me time to convince Clarabella to stay."

"I know."

"And now, now I *have* to find her, and the magic is changing, and somehow it nearly killed Clarabella. And I don't *get it*. I don't get any of it."

"I know."

"I *hate* not understanding." Royal was talking faster now, still quiet. "I've spent the last three years trying to understand the magic of this place, and now it's turning on me? Putting my sister in danger? *I don't get it.*"

"Maybe that *is* it," Shiloh offered. "You've tried to understand it. I've never seen anyone study it like you have. Use it, exploit it, trade it, worship it, sure. But study it?"

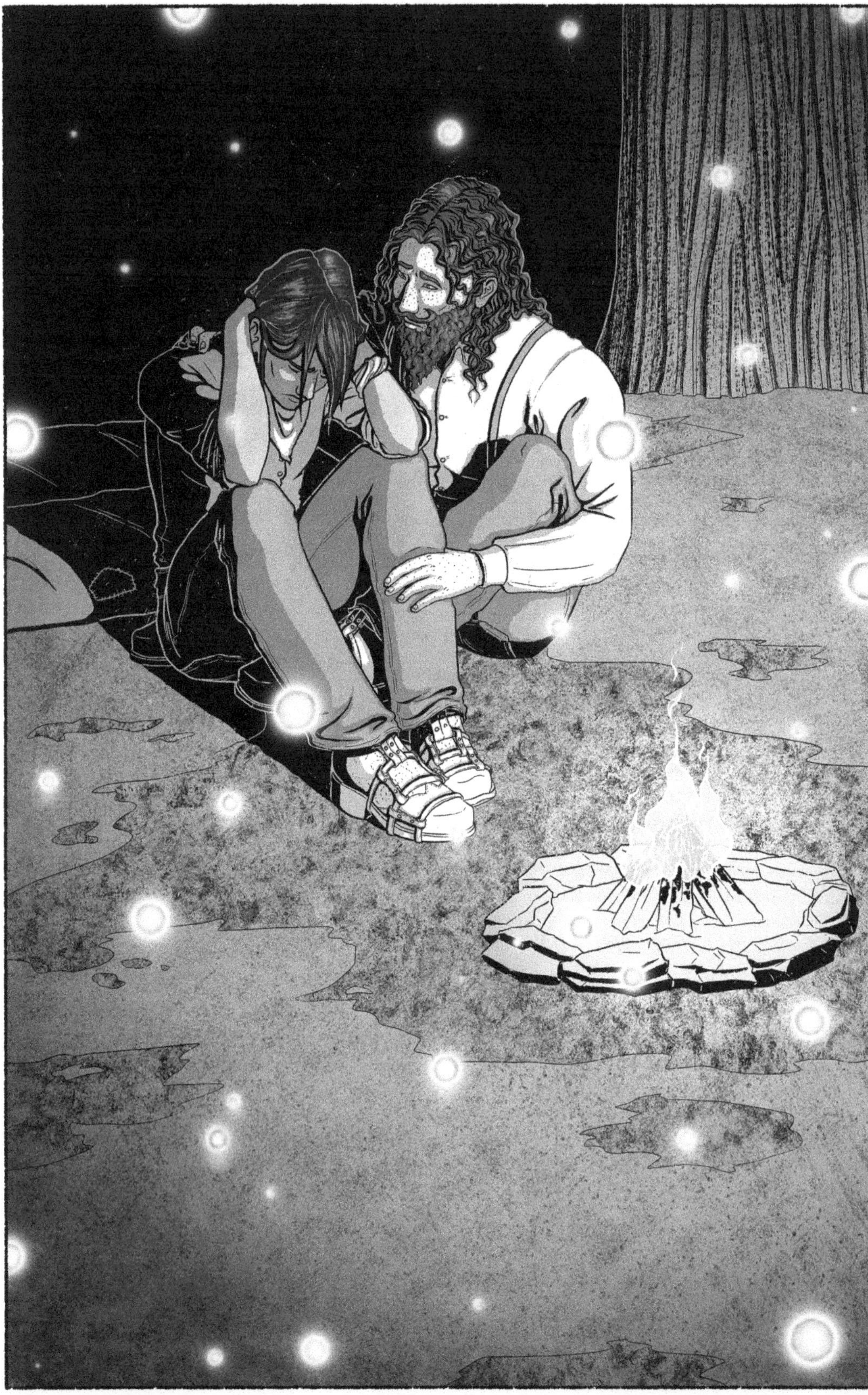

"So what?" Royal said, frustration in their voice and set of their shoulders. More and more fireflies were coming out, casting dancing spots of light across their face.

"Maybe this is your price for trying to understand."

Royal didn't have an answer for this, staring into the fire with their eyebrows drawn in consideration.

I regretted my decision to eavesdrop. There was only so much guilt one person could take in a day, and this put me over my limit. I tried to imagine it, Royal slipping in through my window one night, trying to convince me to leave with them. I didn't think I would have gone, and knowing how much my refusal would have hurt Royal hurt me.

How had we ended up like this? Was it really because of our parents? Even if I had started to see what Royal meant about them, I couldn't wrap my mind around how it led to where we were now.

At some point I drifted off, only to be awoken when it was still dark by Akhíta. It was our turn on watch. Shiloh and Royal sunk into the bedrolls. I almost said something to Royal about what I'd overheard, but decided it would be better to let them rest. Hopefully it would be without nightmares this time.

Akhíta and I did not speak, and I didn't mind. I did wish I had a book, though, even if keeping watch and reading weren't things that should be done at the same time. The problem was that keeping watch was rather boring.

The fireflies were everywhere now. Out of nostalgia, I reached out and grabbed one, cupping it between my hands and bringing them up to my face so I could peek through my fingers. I'd caught plenty of fireflies before—it was one of Royal's favorite things to do on warm summer nights when we were little—so I knew what they were supposed to look like. A thin brown body, the back end a glowing bulb, two long antennae, and six skittering legs.

Whatever was in my hands did not have most of these things. All it had was the light.

I shook my hands gently, trying to reposition it. This made no difference, however. It remained nothing more than a slowly pulsing yellow orb. Keeping my hands together I got up and went to Akhíta, kneeling down next to her.

She looked curiously between my fingers, letting out an interested, "Hinú."

Reaching out, she caught one of her own. We both looked between her fingers to find a floating orb exactly like mine. Distracted by her orb, I didn't notice the growing heat in my hands until suddenly pain lanced up my left one.

I yelped, letting the orb go. Tilting my hand towards the fire, I found a shiny red welt in the center of my palm, about the size of a quarter. Akhíta, seeing my hand, instantly released her orb as well.

"Wassup?" Royal said blearily, rising up on one elbow to look over at us.

"The bugs are not bugs, and they burn," Akhíta said, examining my hand.

She grabbed her canteen and poured some water over the burn. I hissed and resisted the urge to pull away. Royal came over, examining my hand as well.

"Nobody *asked* them to burn, right?" Royal said.

I shook my head. "I was thinking about catching them when we were kids, that's it."

"They may just be part of this place," Shiloh offered, sitting up and rubbing his eyes. "Like the coyotes."

Royal sighed and went over to the packs. "Did we bring any sort of salve? We could use the plants here, but then we're back to having to pay a price."

"Getting burned isn't a price?" I muttered. My hand was throbbing now, every beat of my pulse grinding through it.

Royal sat back on their heels. "It...could be?" They looked over at me. "Do you want to chance it?"

The throbbing in my hand made up my mind for me, and I nodded. It wasn't like I could fall down a cliff this time if we were wrong.

Royal led me over to a large, leafy bush at the base of one of the trees. It was taller than both of us, the stalks as thick as my wrist near the ground and tapering out as they got higher.

Royal tapped a branch of it, about waist high. "Break this one off and dribble the sap that comes out over the burn."

I reached out and did it, hesitating a moment once it was off. Nothing happened, though. The ground didn't open up and swallow me, no trees fell on my head. I let one drop of sap fall onto the burn. It felt cool, chasing away the edge from the pain. When nothing else happened, I let more fall over the wound until I could hardly feel it at all. It was still there, however, so Royal brought me back to the fire and wrapped a bandage around it. My second of this trip. And now I was down a hand as well.

"Any idea what time it is?" Shiloh asked.

Akhíta pulled a pocket watch out of her coat pocket, frowning at it, then shaking it a little.

"Already stopped working?" Royal asked.

Akhíta sighed and put it away. "Yeah. I'd hoped it would work a bit longer, but I suppose we shouldn't be surprised. We'll have to go by the sun."

"What?" Royal asked.

"The sun? The big white thing in the sky during the day?" Akhíta said.

"No, not you," Royal replied. "You." They toed Shiloh's boot, trying to get his attention.

Shiloh didn't answer, staring off towards the cliff with a frown.

"Shilohhhhh," Royal said.

Shiloh leaned forward and pulled a burning branch out of the fire, holding it aloft like a torch. Light jumped and danced around the clearing, bringing the forest into motion. The rest of us were on edge now, tensely looking where Shiloh was.

"Shiloh, share," Akhíta ordered, voice low.

He shook his head like he was unsure, then got up and walked swiftly to the edge of the clearing we'd entered through, stopping at the tree-line. With the torch in hand, there should have been enough light to see the scree we'd come down, perhaps even some of the cliffs. We hadn't gone far into the forest at all, no more than a dozen feet so we could make camp without having to move a bunch of loose rocks out of the way. Except now, on the other side of Shiloh's light, there was nothing but more trees.

I knew we'd come in that way, felt the aching presence of that stupid cliff ever since I fell from it. More concretely, the log we'd sat on earlier was still there, the roots still pointing towards where the cliff had been, and now no longer was.

I swallowed heavily. "What was that you said about going back if we got split up?"

Chapter 16
Wolves

Morning came slow, none of us willing or able to go back to sleep. Camp was packed up in silence and, after quickly filling our canteens in a creek, we set off at a healthy pace, trying to make up time.

There was no more path now. This, at least, was expected according to Royal, unlike the cliffs disappearing. The point of the Preacher Path was that it was a challenge, not any sort of direct route. As for the cliffs, none of us knew what to do with that except to hope they came back when we were on the way out, or that we could find another path. Given the way the magic was behaving, I refused to let myself consider any other options. We were going to keep going down. We were going to find Emilia. We were going to fix whatever was going on with Royal. We were going to get back out. We were all going to be fine.

We were all going to be fine.

Royal took the lead, moving with a level of purpose that seemed slightly suspicious. Or maybe I was being paranoid. Our only real direction was "downhill" at this point, after all. It was hard to even navigate by the sun, with all the trees twisting the light around and obscuring its origins before it made it to the ground.

"Oh sweet lord!" I yelped, arms pinwheeling as I staggered back. My feet went out from under me anyway and I found myself on my ass, thankful for the spongy clover covering the forest floor. In front of me, exactly where my face had just been, hovered a shimmering blue dragonfly the size of my arm. Its blurred wings were completely, eerily, silent. It bobbed up and down a few times, then turned and lazily fluttered off, back into the trees.

Royal was watching me with a mischievous little smile. "You good?"

"That thing was as big as a child," I said, pressing a hand over my heart.

"It was just a bug," Royal returned.

I scrambled to my feet. "That was *not* 'just a bug'!"

They chuckled and continued walking.

Huffing, I followed.

Akhíta and Shiloh were a short distance behind us, but never out of eyesight, and I slowed down to walk with them instead, finding them in the middle of a whispered conversation. The conversation dropped immediately once I was with them.

"What?" I asked.

Akhíta and Shiloh glanced at one another.

"Opinions on Royal's choice of direction?" Shiloh asked, voice quiet.

I frowned. "What?"

"They're moving very...purposefully," Akhíta said.

I watched Royal's back, contemplating. Maybe it hadn't been paranoia earlier.

"Why haven't you said anything?" I asked.

The two of them glanced at one another again.

"We figure," Shiloh said, "that if Royal is being led, it's by whatever magic brought us here in the first place. We're going to end up where it wants one way or another, so it is probably better to just...not resist."

I'd begun to reach a point where there were too many things to be alarmed by, and thus I was not really alarmed at all, which held true when Royal suddenly disappeared after this statement. After a quick second my brain caught up and I realized they'd just kneeled down, examining something under a bush covered in fat red berries. The three of us came over, trying to see what they were looking at.

It was a handkerchief. White, though a bit stained, with an

embroidered design of lilacs. I could still feel the needle against my fingers as I pushed it through the cloth over and over again to create the design not even a month earlier for Emilia's birthday.

I kneeled down next to Royal and picked it up with shaking fingers. No words were needed for everyone else to realize what the object was. Who it had belonged to.

Royal stood up and pulled me into a hug as I held the scrap of cloth to my chest, trying not to cry.

"Did you ask for that?" Royal asked gently.

I shook my head. They nodded, gave me a squeeze, then stepped back. Pressing the fabric to my nose, I was sad to find it didn't smell like her. Just dirt with a hint of sweetness, probably from the berries, some of which had dripped juice onto the cloth. Still, though. It was a piece of her. I didn't want to put it back, even if there was a price.

It was just a thing, though. It wasn't her, and I wasn't willing to risk it preventing me from finding her. Reaching out, I tucked it back under the bush. Before anyone could say anything, I took the lead and continued walking, not looking back.

The bugs weren't the only things getting bigger. Everything else was too. Trees would've taken four men to wrap their arms around the trunks now, the branches layered so thickly above us only hazy, indirect light made it to the ground now, making any shadows fuzzy and indistinct. At one point a hare whose head reached my waist bounded between the trees in front of us, making everyone jump and earning me a little vindication for being startled by the dragonfly.

We ate lunch while walking, debating how long this might take. The Pits couldn't really be bottomless, could they? Akhíta didn't think so. She was convinced there was a lowest point somewhere. Magic or no magic, it wasn't like they went through the entire planet. Shiloh, however, was of the mind that just because they didn't go through the planet didn't mean they weren't bottomless. This launched a debate between he and Royal about alternate dimensions, something that got quickly shut down by Akhíta lest the two of them give the magic any bad ideas.

A low rumble stopped us all in our tracks, frowning as we looked around for the source. Just as we were about to discount it and keep going, another one sounded accompanied by what, mostly, appeared to be a wolf stepping out from behind a tree. Everyone went for their guns, whipping them out, except for me, as I didn't have one. The wolf didn't move, though, staring at us from its spot twenty yards off, so no one fired.

"The fucking thing's got eight legs," Shiloh hissed.

With the initial shock of the moment gone, I realized he was right. Except it didn't just have eight legs, it had four on its underside and four on its back, curling up into the air like they were resting. It was also about the size of a draft horse, maybe bigger.

"We are never telling my mother about anything that happens down here," Akhíta muttered. "She'll never let us out of the house again."

"Any suggestions?" Royal asked.

Akhíta, pistol still raised in her left hand, carefully slipped out of her sling and drew a second gun. "Nope."

"The trees," I whispered. "Look at the trees."

Stretching out to the left and right, there was a distinct line of trees, each with a heavy black mark at their base. They weren't in any language I knew and all looked like they'd been burned there. The line was about halfway between us and the wolf.

Shiloh, seeing what I was getting at, undid the bandage over the cut on his arm, balled it up, and lobbed it across the line. The effect was instantaneous; the wolf lurched forward, teeth bared and jaws snapping. It tore into the blood tinged fabric, shredding it until nothing was left but threads dangling from its teeth. Teeth still bared, it retreated slightly, never taking its eyes off of us.

"Well," Royal said, holstering their guns, "at least now we've got time to think this through, since it won't cross the barrier."

"*They* won't cross the barrier," Akhíta said. She gestured with one of her guns, pointing to several spots among the trees. It took me a moment, but one by one I began to pick out more of the strange wolves, all just as big. There were six I could see and, I assumed, plenty I couldn't see. Several were shaggy gray, two white, and one—the first one—solid black. When the wind shifted it brought their musky odor to us, and it wasn't one I would've ever associated with any sort of dog. It smelled, if anything, like copper. Hot copper. The scent of a penny after it had been placed on the tracks by a child and pressed flat by a passing train.

Shiloh and Akhíta holstered their guns as well, all of us watching the wolves watching us. Royal paced back and forth, right on the line, staring into the trees. The wolves tracked their progress but did not move.

"Do we have anything to give them?" I asked. "A price?"

Royal shook their head. "I don't think so. Not enough to buy passage for all of us."

"I doubt any payment would suffice," Akhíta reasoned. "I'd guess they're like the coyotes. Not just magic, but something with a will of its own."

"Too dangerous to bargain with, then," Shiloh said.

Royal, who had continued to pace, stopped, pointing at something beyond the line. "What's that?"

We all crowded together, trying to see what they saw. Once I did see it, I was surprised it took me as long as it did to notice. The scrap of shiny, bright blue satin was like a beacon against all the green. There was no way to tell from this distance what the fabric had been, but the tattered ends gave a good indication as to the fact it suffered the same fate as Shiloh's bandage. After the first scrap, it was easy to see that there were others littered around, most of them muslin in an even lighter shade of blue, though there were other bits of satin as well. Some sort of ribbon.

An uneasy feeling settled in my gut. The bits could have been from anything. Yet, what else could they be from but Emilia?

"There's no blood on them," Shiloh said before I could fall into panic.

He was right. The uneasy feeling retreated slightly.

"No blood we can see," Akhíta returned.

The feeling came back full force.

Royal crouched and squinted, eyes going from piece to piece. "I think...I think it was a dress. Look at that bit with the buttons, and there's a bit of lace around what I think is a cuff over there."

"Does it matter?" Akhíta asked.

"It's *just* a dress," Royal said. "All the fabric looks like it came from one thing. No undergarments, no shoes."

"Still don't see why it matters," Akhíta said.

"I don't either," Royal admitted. "Clarabella, start throwing out ideas. Whatever comes into your head."

"Why do you have to keep making me do that? I don't know either."

Royal snapped their fingers and twirled their hand in a circle in my general direction.

I threw out my hands. "I don't know! It's probably Emilia's, because why wouldn't it be at this point? But, like Shiloh said, there's no blood we can see, and like *you* said, it looks like it's only a dress. So, I don't know. She took her dress off and gave it to the wolves the way Shiloh tossed his bandage in? But I don't know why that matt—"

I was cut off by Shiloh snapping his fingers. "Back up, back up. The way I tossed my bandage in. I have an idea. Part of an idea. We need something bigger than a bandage."

"Well we didn't exactly bring extra clothes, and I'm not stripping," I returned.

"You took off your skirt in the Gates," Royal pointed out.

"When I had petticoats on!"

Shiloh, ignoring us, reached into his bag and pulled out the only spare blanket we'd brought. Ripping off a length, he tossed it in. The same thing happened as with the bandage, except this time three wolves went for it, tugging it to shreds between them for nearly a minute.

"So...what now? We strip our way through the forest, leaving them bits of clothing to chew on instead of us until we end up naked on the other side?" Royal said. "That seems like quite the gamble, given we have no idea how far their territory goes and, I don't know about the rest of you, but I am not wearing that many layers."

Shiloh shrugged. "I wouldn't mind seeing you naked."

Royal gave him a fond but withering stare and twirled a hand at me again.

"I've got nothing," I said.

Shiloh, lips pursed to the side, kneeled down and rooted deeper into his pack. Pulling out a smaller satchel, he undid the leather tie and laid it out flat, revealing an eclectic collection of objects. A stub of a candle. Several coins. A few vials full of liquids and powders. A little cat statuette. A broken bit of mirror.

The use of magic seemed unwise, but what else was there to do at this point? Humming in contemplation, Shiloh selected the largest vial. It was several inches long and filled nearly to the top with a shimmering blue powder.

"I don't know if that will be enough," Royal said. "If we blow it into the air it'll only buy us a few minutes. If we get them to eat it, well, how do we get all of them to eat it?"

"What is it?" I asked.

"Powdered sapphires," Shiloh answered. "Used to be a necklace that would wipe the wearer's memory of anything that happened the last few days. We never managed to sell it and then, one day, it just sort of... dissolved. It still effects memory, but not as much."

I thought this through. "Who ate it to figure this out?"

Royal snickered. "A very fine banker named Julio. Poor man woke up forgetting our lovely night together and without the county's debt records in his safe."

"Poor man indeed. No one deserves to forget a night with you." Shiloh winked.

I groaned, pinching the bridge of my nose. "Can we just do this, please?"

In the end, it was decided we'd give up our bedrolls. They were cumbersome, heavy, and it was warm enough down here that we all felt we'd be fine without them. Each of us cut off a piece of cloth to cover our faces with so we wouldn't be effected by the powder, and Shiloh dusted about two-thirds of the vial over everything that was left. It glittered even in the indirect light, throwing out sparkles against everything around us, and had a faint scent of burned ginger.

Keeping the rest of the vial in his hand, thumb over the opening, Shiloh lined us all up right on the boundary. Each of us had a ball of bedding in hand, ready to throw on his signal.

"Go quick, but don't run. Startling them with rapid movement might undo the powder's effects. Don't look back, and stick together. Ready?" Shiloh said. We all nodded. "Three. Two. One."

I threw my ball as hard and far as I could off to the left, which admittedly wasn't that far. There was no time to regret it, though, and we all took off as soon as the wolves were on the fabric. I felt the barrier slide over my skin, like stepping through a thin sheet of water. Shivering, I held my breath and glanced at the wolves. Eight of them stood around our scattered bedding, heads dipping between the ground and looking at us, like they couldn't decide what was more important. According to Royal, we had about an hour before the effect wore off. On a human.

"They see us," Shiloh muttered. "They know we're here, but they can't remember for long enough to act on it."

It was impossible not to keep glancing back at them as we progressed through the forest. Giant and eight-legged or not, they were enough like regular wolves for my instincts to be screaming at me about not keeping my back to them. Several stumbled after us, staying within sight. They never managed to get close before a dazed look came over their faces and they stopped.

The ground under us was getting steeper, our spikes keeping it manageable. I wanted to grab a stick to use for balance, but there wasn't time, nor did I have a payment.

A low, louder than ever, growl froze us all in our tracks. There was no sign of its source. Shiloh slowly slid his thumb off the vial, holding it up as we waited, putting our backs together to cover all sides.

When the creature leaped out from behind a tree, it was only feet away. I thought I heard Shiloh curse, knew I felt his arm move next to me, and then suddenly the wolf was stopped a couple feet away. Blue powder sparkled over its brown muzzle and it shook its head like it was trying to get rid of a fly.

Without speaking we all skittered away and kept going, faster now. That had been our one and only Hail Mary. The powder was gone. And this wolf had only inhaled it.

Despite our best attempts, we did start to separate a little. Not much. Only a handful of feet between everyone as we made our way down the ever steepening hill. We couldn't even walk straight down it now, having to stand sideways and go at an angle to keep our footing. Briars scratched and grabbed at my clothes, the sound making my skin crawl. What else might hear it?

I kept stealing glances at the trees, hoping for more marks that might indicate the edge of the wolves' territory. There were none to be found. We were nearly at the bottom of the slope now, though, which was a relief. I could see the ground flattening out a short distance from us. We'd be able to move quicker once we were there.

When the wolves came, it was silent. We weren't being warned away anymore. We were being hunted. Over a dozen poured out of the trees above us, loping easily across the terrain that we could barely stand up on.

"Go! Go!" Royal screamed.

They didn't need to tell us, everyone taking off. I had half a mind to throw myself down the rest of the hill. It seemed like a better option than getting eaten. Several shots rang out, I didn't know who from, and a wolf went rolling past, crashing through the brush. It landed at the bottom where it attempted to stand, only to find one leg unable to take its weight. Without hesitation it laid back down, rolled over, and stood on its second set of legs, twisting its head around until it was upright. Snarling, it charged back up towards us, splitting Shiloh and I off from Royal and Akhíta.

"Don't lose sight of them!" Shiloh shouted.

The bottom of the hill was so close. I knew I still couldn't outrun them, yet the flat ground seemed safer. More shots rang out and I was so focused on watching Royal and Akhíta, and making it to the bottom of the hill, I almost missed the sound of Shiloh letting out a pained yell behind me. I spun, nearly losing my balance and toppling over.

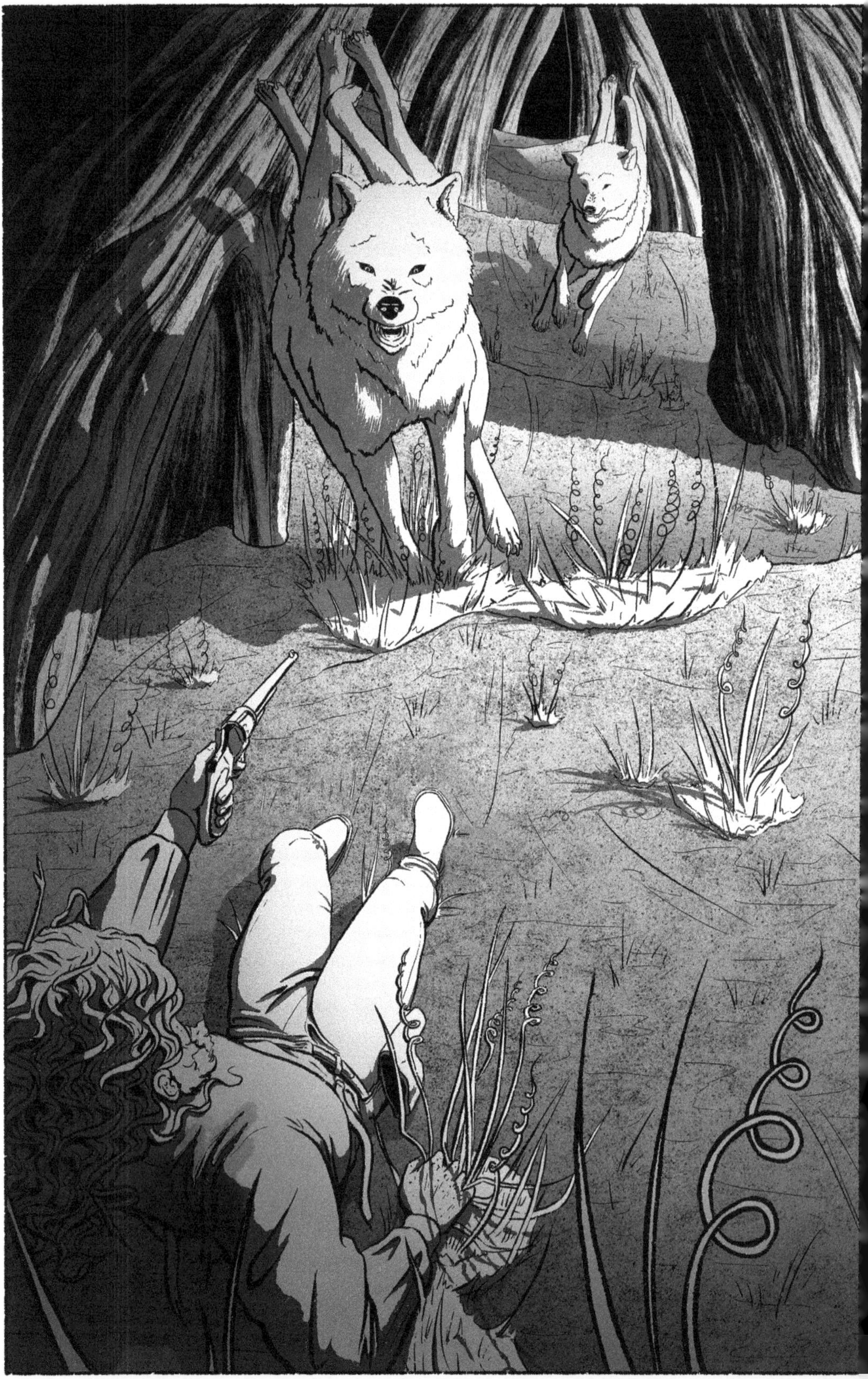

Searching, I found him sprawled out on his back, head pointed down the hill, one hand clutching a bleeding shoulder and the other firing up at a wolf leering over him. Freezing, I stared, no idea what else to do as time slowed down around us. The wolf seemed mostly unbothered by Shiloh's bullets, snapping and snarling but not retreating as they dug into the fur of its shoulder, which it had turned towards Shiloh. I almost felt like it was aware of exactly how many he had, and of the fact that Shiloh didn't seem able to aim well from his position and with a wounded arm.

A spark of light sliced into my eyes and, for a moment, I thought it was somehow more of the powder. But no. It was a gun. Shiloh's little backup gun. The one he'd used to teach me how to shoot. It must have fallen out of his boot. Scrambling back up the hill, I snatched it out of the dirt, pulled back the hammer, and prayed that it was still loaded.

This time, my arms weren't tired. And I wasn't bleeding out upside down on a hill.

One steadying breath and I pulled the trigger, the sights set between the wolf's eyes as it lunged for Shiloh. Its movement made me miss the head, but the bullet still hit home, slamming into the center of its chest. Instead of landing on Shiloh, it sailed over him, falling limply into the dirt and skidding down the hill until it got caught in the bushes.

Shiloh rolled onto his side, looking at me with wide eyes, his chest heaving with heavy breaths. Using the plants as handholds I pulled myself up to him.

"Get up, get up," I ordered, grabbing his uninjured arm and pulling. Several more wolves were circling, hackles up and teeth bared.

It took a couple tries for him to get turned around and get his legs under him, and even then he struggled to stand. Before I could figure out what to do, Royal and Akhíta appeared, each throwing one of Shiloh's arms over their shoulders. Shiloh's gun still tight in my hand, we tripped and stumbled our way down the last of the hill, nearly falling on our faces when we reached the flat ground.

"Why are you stopping?" I shouted when Royal and Akhíta stilled, gasping for breath.

"We're out," Akhíta panted, gesturing off to the side.

There was, once more, a line of trees stretching out to each side, each with a large black mark at its base. Looking back, I saw the wolves pacing on the other side, unwilling or unable to cross. Even the one I'd shot had managed to struggle back to its feet.

I hadn't even felt the barrier pass.

Chapter 17
Patch Up

Shiloh was quickly lowered to the ground, grunting in pain. His pack was gone—torn off or dropped, I didn't know—and blood soaked the back of his shirt, one side of his suspenders hanging loose from where it had been ripped in half. Akhíta tore off her coat and shoved it against the wounds while Royal pressed up against the front of Shiloh's shoulder to keep the pressure on the wound. Shiloh tucked his head into Royal's shoulder, taking heavy breaths through his nose.

"Tell me what to do," I said, kneeling next to Akhíta.

"Get his shirt off. Tear it."

I did as instructed, gently working it out from under Akhíta's coat without her having to let off much of the pressure. With the shirt pulled down and hanging from where it was tucked into Shiloh's pants, we waited a few more minutes, giving the blood time to clot. Feet away, the wolves paced.

Royal spoke softly into Shiloh's ear, giving reassurance. Chancing it, Akhíta pulled off the coat to check on the wound. Three long slashes curved from his collarbone, over the top of his shoulder, and down to the bottom of his shoulder blade. They were clean cuts, not what I would have expected from the relatively dull claws of an animal, let alone one so big. Blackened clots clung to the edges, redder drops continuing to bubble up out of the deepest parts of the wounds which went over the curve of his shoulder. Even there they, thankfully, didn't seem that deep.

"Can you move your hand?" Akhíta asked.

Shiloh rolled his fingers into a fist a few times. "Yeah."

"Here, hold this," Akhíta said, pushing the coat back up against his wound and indicating for me to take it. I did, leaning my full weight against Shiloh's shoulder.

Shiloh grunted. "At this rate, Clarabella, I'm going to owe you my life as many times as Royal owes theirs to Akhíta."

Royal snorted, turning their head to kiss Shiloh's hair. "No you're not, because neither of you are allowed to get hurt or nearly die ever again. It is officially forbidden." They shifted their eyes to me, voice softening. "Thank you, though."

"Honestly, I can't believe I made the shot." It still felt like my bones were shaking from it. Or maybe they were shaking from everything else. It was hard to really calm down with the wolves still so close and not losing interest, even if they couldn't get to us.

Akhíta returned, a needle and bobbin of silk in hand. "Clarabella, I need you to try and keep pressure on the areas I'm not working."

I nodded.

"Wait," Royal said, releasing their half of the pressure and fumbling off the little silver and turquoise ring they wore. It must have been tight, as they winced when it slid off.

"Put that back on," Shiloh ordered, swaying as he straightened up to glare at Royal.

"You need it more at the moment," Royal said. "This is going to be a lot of stitches, and we don't have anything else."

"Put. That. Back. On."

"No." Royal grabbed Shiloh's hand and jammed the ring on. It should not have fit, given how much thicker Shiloh's fingers were, but it slid on easily, forming to the right size.

I'd never seen Shiloh and Royal look like they might be legitimately pissed off at one another, but they did now. Royal looked away first, placing their hands against Shiloh's chest to return their half of the pressure we were keeping on the wounds.

I glanced at Akhíta, eyebrows drawn in confusion. She gave a slight shake of her head, looking somewhat angry as well. Shifting the coat to expose part of the wound, she poured some water over the top of the first cut, then began quickly stitching it up. She didn't bother to make it pretty, just functional.

Shiloh, for his part, didn't react to the procedure nearly as much as I would have expected. I'd never had stitches myself, but I had accidentally stabbed myself with needles while embroidering enough times to know it wasn't pleasant. When I thought about what it must feel like to have a needle and thread sliding all the way through your skin like that, I shuddered involuntarily.

"Look away if you need to," Akhíta said. "We can't afford you passing out."

"I'm fine," I replied. Dealing with the wound itself wasn't what was bothering me anyway.

After the first cut was finished, Akhíta sat back, shaking out her hand and rolling her injured shoulder.

"Trade me," I said, holding out a hand for the needle and silk.

"Have you done stitches before?" She asked. "On a person?"

"No," I admitted. "But I help my father embroider saddles, and I just watched you do it for twenty minutes, so. Yell at me if I start getting it wrong."

"'T's fine," Shiloh said. "Just get it done."

Royal remained silent, mouth drawn tight.

Akhíta handed the supplies over, trading places with me. I threaded a new length of silk, pinched the top of the second cut together slightly, took a deep breath, and set to work. It was not at all like embroidering saddles. There were no awls pre-punching holes to give the needles easy passage. Instead the skin clung to the little metal spike, bowing in and out as the needle went through one side and out the other. Thankfully the needle was curved, which helped immensely. I doubted digging around with the needle, trying to get it to come back out in the right place on the other side, would be appreciated.

By the time I reached the bottom of the cut my fingers were tinged red, the stain weakening as it stretched towards my palms. I handed everything back to Akhíta to finish up the last one. The second the last stitch was tied Shiloh yanked off the ring and shoved it back onto Royal's finger.

Royal groaned and fell backwards, fists and eyes clenched shut, taking short, measured breaths.

"Wha—" I started, trying to figure out if Royal had been hurt and I somehow hadn't realized.

"Talk to your sister, because that was stupid and I don't have the energy for it right now," Shiloh said, standing up only to immediately almost fall over. Akhíta caught him, slinging his good arm over her shoulders.

"What is happening?" I asked, looking between the three of them.

"Will you talk to her?" Akhíta asked, addressing Royal. "Because if not I'll send her off with Shiloh and then you and I *will* talk."

"It wasn't stupid," Royal muttered. They were breathing somewhat better now, their body beginning to relax.

Akhíta sighed and hefted Shiloh off into the trees a ways, setting him down against a log before shoving the last of the water at him, demanding he drink it all.

"Well?" I said, still kneeled where I'd been before, hands on my hips as I stared down at Royal.

They sighed, opening their eyes and staring up at the canopy. It was now so thick I couldn't make out even a sliver of sky anywhere. Lifting their hand off the ground, they tapped the ring, back on their left pinky, with their thumb.

"We found this a little over a year ago. It masks pain," they said.

That explained Shiloh's lack of reaction to the stitches. It didn't explain what was happening to Royal right now.

Royal dropped their hand to lie across their stomach, closing their eyes and continuing without prompting. "Do you remember how I always used to have days where I just stayed in bed reading?"

"Sure. You were always buried in books."

They shook their head. "That's not what I mean. I mean those days I never came down for breakfast, never got dressed, didn't even go to school."

I thought about it. "Yeah, I guess I remember a few days like that."

"There were more than a few," Royal said. "I didn't stay in bed because I wanted to read, I stayed because I couldn't make myself get up."

I frowned. "What?"

Royal sighed. "Ever since I can remember, I hurt. Some days are better than others, but the older I get the more bad days I have. Had. Sometimes I didn't even have the strength to hold up books so I just laid there."

"Why didn't you say anything?" I said, aghast. "Tell Mother and Father?"

"I *did* tell them," Royal said. "All the time. They said it was in my head, that everyone ached after a hard day, that I needed to just stop being lazy. Eventually I started to figure they must be right, since no one else seemed to struggle like I did, so I tried to ignore it."

"Royal...." I felt tears building in the corners of my eyes.

Taking a deep, shaky breath they continued. "By the time I was a teenager I was pretty good at ignoring it, at pushing past it. Problem was, it usually caught up to me every few months or so and I'd go down for days. The first time it happened after I met Shiloh and Akhíta, they hauled me up to her mother's. Mama Standing Bear spent an hour bombarding me with questions—she's even more terrifyingly protective than Akhíta, trust me—and by the end of it she'd mixed up some sort of tincture. I was too exhausted and uncomfortable to care at that point, so I took it without question.

"I passed out and, when I woke up, I felt kind of drunk. It took me a minute, but I realized it was because I wasn't in pain anymore. I hadn't even realized what that felt like. How much pain I'd actually been in."

I pressed my hand over my mouth, forgetting about the blood. Tears were flowing down my face now as I struggled to wrap my head around all of this.

"Mama Standing Bear taught Akhíta how to make the tincture and, after a few days of resting and taking it, I felt better than I ever have in my life. I kept taking it after that, but overtime it was clear it wasn't having as much of an effect. We'd found other magical items that helped with medical things, and we kept hoping we'd find one that would help with this. Then we finally did."

"Royal, I...I don't even know what to say. I'm so, so sorry I didn't know. And Mother and Father...I can't even...that they'd say that to you, without ever trying to help...I...."

Royal shrugged, shoulders scrapping against the dirt.

"The ring really helps?" I asked, scooting closer.

They nodded. "Yes. Except it doesn't...treat the pain, the way the tincture did. It just masks it. Dulls it to a manageable level. With the ring on there is very little difference between the pain of, say, getting shot in the gut and just stubbing your toe."

My eyes widened. "Oh. That's what you meant when you said you didn't realize how bad the gunshot was."

They nodded again, eyes still closed. "I still take the tincture sometimes, when I think I might end up in a situation where it would be dangerous not to feel pain. It works a lot better when it's only taken occasionally. Can't always anticipate what may cause pain, though. Plus, the effects only last a day at most, and some of the ingredients are hard to come by."

"So...why is Shiloh mad at you, then?" I asked. Reaching out, I gently lifted Royal's hand and turned it back and forth so I could examine the ring. It was well made, the turquoise shot through with a vein of black and the silver untarnished.

"Because he loves me," Royal said. "He doesn't like me taking the ring off without the tincture. We've fought about it several times. And...."

I set Royal's hand down and glanced over at Akhíta and Shiloh. She was going at her bloodied coat with a knife, shredding it into strips. Shiloh was very pointedly not looking at us. Akhíta took the strip with a patch of her father's uniform, the patch miraculously unstained, and tucked it into a back pocket of her pants.

"And what?" I asked.

Royal swallowed heavily. "And when I take it off, putting it back on... the effect isn't instantaneous. Not for me, anyway. It takes a few days to build up."

I blinked several times, thinking through all the implications of this. "Okay. I might…have to agree with Shiloh. We can't exactly afford for you to be suffering right now, Royal."

"It's done," Royal said. "He can be mad at me if he wants, so can you and Akhíta, but I don't regret it. I won't sit back and watch the people I love be in pain."

"So we're supposed to watch you be in pain instead?" I asked, voice harsher than I intended.

This, finally, got Royal to open their eyes and they looked up at me, eyebrows drawn.

"Don't look at me like that," I said, glaring down. "You're too smart to think that you caring about any of us is a one way thing."

"I didn't mean—"

"I don't care," I said. "You know, you've got a hell of a martyr complex sometimes. For the record, I don't appreciate it, and it seems like Shiloh and Akhíta don't either. What's the point of protecting the people you love if by doing so it hurts them even more?"

With that I stood up and strode over to Akhíta and Shiloh, plopping down next to them. Akhíta looked between me and where Royal was still splayed out on the ground. She didn't say anything.

Royal made their way over awhile later, sitting quietly next to Shiloh, who had fallen asleep after Akhíta bandaged his shoulder. Royal gently stroked Shiloh's hair, looking forlorn.

The wolves had given up over the course of the last two hours, trotting off into the forest one by one until none were left. Sometimes, though, my skin still prickled like one might be watching from somewhere I couldn't see.

Akhíta didn't break the silence, busying herself with cleaning and reloading all the guns. I didn't break it either. I didn't even know how. Instead, I gathered up the remains of Shiloh's shirt from where Akhíta had placed it off to the side and took it to a shallow brook within sight. Kneeling down, I dunked it in, running the fabric between my knuckles to get the blood out. The stain wasn't going anywhere, but at least the crusted, dried blood itself would be gone.

Holding it up, I examined the damage. It wasn't as bad as I'd expected. Overall, aside from the three cuts and the tears I'd made to get it off him, the garment was relatively intact. I could probably fix it, at least enough to function. It wasn't like we had another shirt for him, and he needed something.

Going back to camp, I laid it across my lap, not caring that it was wet, and started gently picking at the tears with the tips of my fingernails, freeing a few threads. Taking the stitches needle from where Akhíta had laid it on her pack, I went to work.

By the time Shiloh woke up, I was nearly done. He groaned and stretched gingerly, staring blearily up at Royal who had still been stroking his hair. Royal hesitantly pulled their hand away. They and Shiloh stared at one another for a long moment.

"How are you?" Shiloh said finally.

"Regretful," Royal replied.

Shiloh looked surprised, sitting up carefully with Royal's help and turning to face Royal. "Really?"

Royal nodded. "Y'all are right, it wasn't a smart decision. Not down here. I didn't think it through. I'm sorry."

Shiloh visibly deflated, reaching out with their good arm to pull Royal into a hug. "Thank you."

Royal snuggled closer, looping their arms around Shiloh's waist. Shiloh kissed the top of their head and rubbed their back a few times.

"Seriously, though," Shiloh said. "How are you?"

Royal hummed. "Tired. I think laying down for awhile afterwards helped, though."

"Well, better than nothing," Shiloh sighed.

Shiloh didn't have much appetite, and with his pack gone we were starting to run low on food, but Akhíta wouldn't hear any excuses, forcing him to eat the last of the jerky and drink another skein of water from the brook. After making the bandages, she'd emptied Royal's pack, redistributing the supplies into her and I's. Taking Royal's pack, along with the intact portion of Shiloh's suspenders, to make Shiloh a sling. Nothing else we had was big enough.

Shiloh shook his head. "I'm fine without it."

"I'll tell my mother," Akhíta said, repeating the same threat he'd given her when she wouldn't put her own arm in a sling the day before.

It seemed Mama Standing Bear was as much of a threat for Shiloh as she was for Akhíta, because he put the sling on immediately. Compared to what Royal had said about our own mother's reaction to their pain, I wondered what it must really feel like to have a mother who cared so much not only about you but everyone associated with you.

"Okay," Shiloh said. "I understand that I passed out for an unknown, to me, amount of time, and I am also suffering from blood loss, but... shouldn't it be starting to get dark?"

"No!" Royal said quickly and loudly. "No, we do not want it to be dark!"

Shiloh winced, realizing his mistake as we all tensed up, waiting to see what might happen. Nothing did, though.

"Shiloh's right," Akhíta said after a minute. "I think. I kind of lost track of time too, but it does feel like it should be evening."

Debate over the matter stopped at the sound of something swishing through the leaves out of sight. The sound did not come from the side of the barrier the wolves laid claim to, though that was little comfort. Who knew what else might be out here now that we were deep enough to be encountering giant, eight-legged wolves. Royal helped Shiloh up and together we all backed against a tree, waiting with bated breath as the sound grew closer.

When I finally saw it, I thought it was a little group of spindly trees somehow walking through their taller relatives. Until I looked up. The thin brown stalks were not trees. They were legs. Deer legs. The creatures towered above us, totally unaware of our presence. They had to be at least twenty feet tall at the shoulder. A buck led the group, his antlers glowing a soft red color. Behind him trailed three does, only a bit smaller.

Prancing among the group were three fawns, their spots beginning to fade with age. Even they were larger than I could wrap my mind around, though somehow also smaller than I expected, their shoulders level with my eyes.

When a howl sounded from the other side of the barrier in a long, low note that made my ears ache, the herd froze, looking off towards the sound. The buck let out a sharp huff, steam billowing from his nose in huge clouds. He scored the ground with one hoof, digging a trench nearly a foot deep with one swipe. Another howl sounded and the whole herd sprung into motion, turning and bounding deeper into the pit with a cacophonous crashing.

"We all saw that, right?" Shiloh asked once the noise faded.

"The giant deer?" Royal asked. "Yeah. We all saw them. Can you imagine how much we could sell that rack for?"

We all groaned. "Royal!"

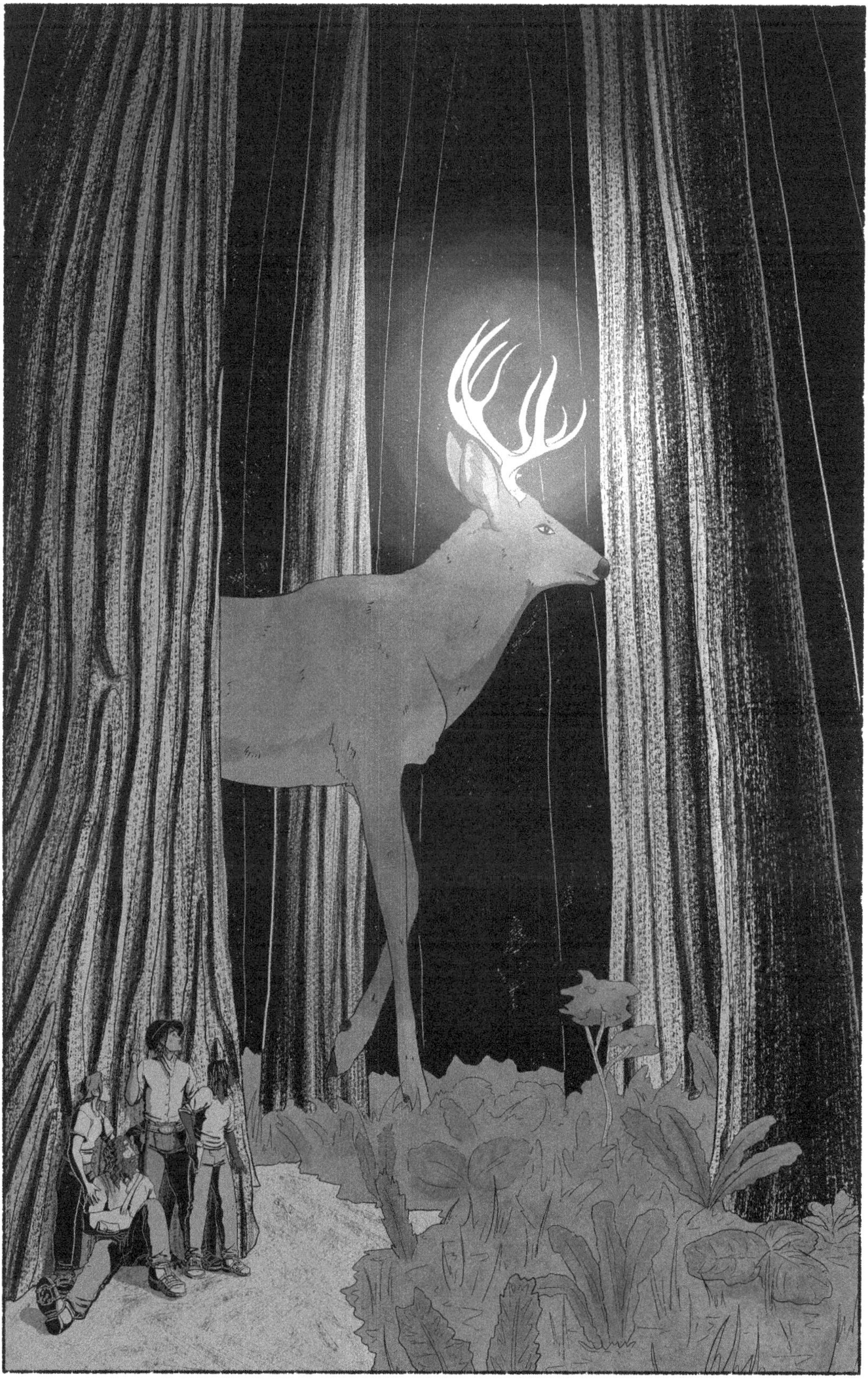

Chapter 18
The Cave

None of us were willing to camp so close to the wolves. Even knowing they couldn't get us, none of us thought we'd be able to rest with them so near. Akhíta and I took the remaining packs, surprisingly with no protest from Royal and Shiloh. Both of them seemed entirely wrung out.

Akhíta made Royal take the lead again, insisting she needed to be in the rear to make sure neither Royal nor Shiloh keeled over. We didn't intend to go far, knowing how much the two of them and—frankly—how much all four of us needed to rest. My fingers still ached from all the sewing, especially the stitches in Shiloh's back. His shirt was holding up, though, despite a few gaps.

Royal wanted me to take Shiloh's backup gun, but without a belt for a holster I had nowhere easily accessible to put it. I suggested we get to wherever we were going to camp, then we'd figure something out. Something that didn't come with a price. Royal agreed, insisting I stick to Shiloh's injured side so I could draw the gun if needed. It sat loose in one of the holsters for his bigger guns, that gun lost on the hillside.

After several minutes of walking, Akhíta tapped my elbow. I looked back and she slowed her pace, indicating for me to do the same. Once Royal and Shiloh got a little way ahead, Akhíta spoke, her voice low.

"How is your hand?"

I examined the burn. It hadn't blistered, surprisingly, but it still stung when I opened and closed my palm.

"Not too bad," I told her.

"Mmm."

"What?"

"My shoulder's killing me," she admitted. I realized she'd never put it back in a sling. "I definitely tore something, and putting pressure on Shiloh's wounds didn't help."

I winced.

"Save it, you didn't choose to fall," Akhíta said. "Also, did you know you look exactly the same as Royal when you feel guilty?"

I huffed.

"Anyway. My point is…all of us are hurt. You've got the least of it, but you still are. Hand injuries are worse, in a lot of ways, even if they're minor. They can prevent you from doing a lot."

"No one ever said this was going to be easy," I observed.

"No, and I didn't expect it to be. Yet…I don't know. I just think we need to be aware of it."

"And you're telling me?" I asked.

She glanced over. "You've saved the life of one of my best friends twice now. That's earned you some leeway. Some."

I suppressed a smile. "Thanks?"

"Just keep your head about you."

"Fucking rocks. Why are there fucking rocks?" Royal said from ahead of us, drawing our attention.

There were indeed, very suddenly, a lot of large rocks. A whole wall of them tumbled about like they'd been tossed there by a child. Some were as small as a horse cart, others as big as a house. Mossy paths wove between them for a short distance until they piled up, blocking any easy passage as far as we could see in either direction.

All four of us bunched up, staring at this new obstacle. On any other day, climbing them probably would've been strenuous but manageable. Akhíta was right, though. We were all injured, or in Royal's case, extremely worn down.

"We camp here," Akhíta declared. "We'll figure it out in the morning."

No one objected, Shiloh sinking to the ground so quick I thought he'd passed out. Royal, seeming to have the same concern, jumped over and caught him before he made it all the way down.

"More water," Akhíta ordered, pulling out a skein. Before handing it over she pulled out a thin glass vial of white powder, dumping some into the water and shaking it up.

"What is that?" I asked.

"Salt," she said.

"Just...salt?"

She laughed. "Yeah, just salt. It helps, as long as there isn't too much."

"Tastes terrible, though," Shiloh muttered.

"Too bad," Akhíta replied.

Shiloh sighed, taking a swig and wincing at the taste. He took a few more, then scooted down to lay his head in Royal's lap, instantly falling asleep. Royal laid down as well, one hand splayed over Shiloh's chest, and fell asleep just as quick.

"You should rest too, if your shoulder is bothering you," I suggested to Akhíta. I got the exact response I expected, which was an eyeroll. "Would it work to threaten to tell your mother?" I tried.

"You don't know where she lives."

I gave up.

It did, eventually, get dark. It did not, however, stay dark.

"Being constantly unsettled is getting exhausting," Akhíta remarked, looking up towards the sky. There was no way to even guess how far away it was now, the trees soaring up far beyond heights we could comprehend, their branches tangled together in a solid mesh. I could no longer tell how many men it would take to wrap their arms around the trunks. At least a dozen. Yet light was still coming from somewhere above, and it had returned what felt like less than an hour after darkness fell.

I didn't even have the energy to agree with her. I wasn't tired, exactly. Nothing in me felt like I needed to sleep, it was more that I felt weary. Thinned out. This was somewhat unsettling in its own right.

Given the events of the day, the stress and exertion of them, I should've been struggling nearly as hard as Royal and Shiloh to stay awake. I hadn't even eaten since this morning. Yesterday morning? Awhile.

I thought about The Preachers. About the stories of people going into the Pits and coming back changed, if they were lucky enough to come back at all. Aside from The Preachers, had anyone ever gone this deep and made it back out, in *any* form?

"I think we need to get going," I said.

"Why?" Akhíta asked.

"Because isn't the whole point of this path that it changes people? I just... how much longer we've got down here?"

We stared at one another, faces both tense with worry. I could tell she knew I was right.

"Here." She took off her belt and laid it across a flat rock near us, drawing a knife from her boot. With a careful, deliberate motion, she sliced the belt in half down its length. Handing one half over, she nodded towards Shiloh's holster that held the little gun.

He didn't move as I undid his own belt and slipped the holster off, rebuckling his belt afterwards. There was no buckle for my belt, but I was thin compared to Akhíta's stout build, providing enough excess length to tie the strip in a knot sturdy enough to hold the gun in place at my hip.

Before I could wake Shiloh and Royal, Akhíta grabbed my shoulder and turned my back towards her. I had no idea what she was doing until I felt her fingers running through my hair, undoing the braid I'd put it in before we came down. After everything, the braid had become a suggestion at best, strands pulled out every which way, many dangling in my face. Akhíta quickly and efficiently gathered all the strands and braided them up tightly, rebinding the end before patting my shoulder.

"Thanks."

She nodded.

Royal and Shiloh were both slow to wake, and Akhíta made both of them drink some of the lightly salted water this time. Neither of us told either of them how little time had passed. Easier, and probably better, to let them think they'd gotten a decent amount of rest.

Still, with so little time passing, no one had come up with a solution for the rocks blocking our way.

"Maybe there's a path through?" Shiloh suggested. He and Royal were sitting on a low rock while Akhíta and I paced the wall a short distance in either direction.

"We could walk for ages before we find it," I said.

"What if we *are* meant to go over the top?" Royal asked.

"Well then the Pit shouldn't have beat us all up," Akhíta said.

I paused, thinking this over. "You're right. It did beat us up. And we've also seen it change the landscape, making the cliffs vanish overnight. So why would it give us an obstacle we can't pass?"

"Because it's a di—"

Shiloh clapped a hand over Royal's mouth before they could finish. "No. Do not go insulting the place now."

"Maybe just gag 'em, Shiloh. We all know how quickly Royal's mouth can get ahead of them," Akhíta suggested.

Royal, mouth now free of Shiloh's hand, stuck their tongue out.

"Anyways," I said. "There has to be a way through, one we aren't seeing."

I turned to the wall, studying it more intently, no idea what I was looking for. It was just rocks. Mostly brown, with a few lighter stripes. None of them stood out.

"Maybe I can climb up a little ways, and see if I can see something from up top?" I offered.

"Carefully," Royal insisted. "And not far. Remember you have to get down."

"My favorite part," I muttered, heading for a rock that seemed to have a manageable slope. Water had carved a series of divots almost like steps into the side. Or magic had. Going on my hands and knees, I scrambled up until I was sitting on the top, about fifteen up. I stood carefully, trying to see over the top of the formation, but I couldn't make anything out. The rocks went on as far as I could see in every direction, fading away into dim haze.

"Anything?" Royal called.

I shook my head. "Just more of the same."

"Come back, please!" Royal said. "I don't like you being up there alone when we can't get to you."

I nodded, turning around to go down. As I looked over the edge, unbothered by so little height as compared to the cliffs I'd fallen down, I noticed something strange around the base of one of the rocks. The rock looked the same as all the others, as did the dirt and moss around it, but unlike many of the others the moss faded out a few feet away.

"Akhíta, that rock about ten feet to your right, are those scrape marks at the base?"

She went over and kneeled, brushing her fingers through the dirt. "Yeah, I think they are."

Carefully, I slid down the rock on my butt, using the spikes on my boots to control my speed. By the time I made it down, Royal and Shiloh had come over to inspect the rock and drag marks as well. The stone wasn't that large, only around seven feet tall and three feet wide. Hardly bigger than a door.

"Oh!" I said, realizing. "We need to move that. Somehow. I think the way through is on the other side."

Shiloh ran his eyes up and down the rock. "Even on my best day I couldn't move that. Maybe all four of us if we were all on our best day, but even then I don't know."

"Well it moved somehow," I reasoned. The scrape marks were easy to make out now that I knew what to look for. The rock had clearly slid several feet to the left at some point.

Waving all of them out of the way, I stepped up to the wall and started running my hands over it. Sliding my fingers around the curved sides and pressing them against the larger rocks it sat against, I moved my hand carefully up and down each side as high as I could reach, searching for some sort of gap. On the bottom of the right side, I found one, hardly bigger than my hand.

"Whatever you do, do not stick—oh good, you stuck your hand in there," Royal said.

I patted around, feeling only dirt, until my fingertips brushed up against something smooth and cool. Resisting the urge to yank my hand out, I reached in farther and probed the object, trying to figure out what it was. It moved and I realized it was actually two objects.

"Shoes!" I said. "There's a pair of shoes in here."

Hooking my fingers into the tops, I pulled them out. It was a pair of white Sunday riding boots, expensive ones that went up over the ankle and laced with strips of creamy silk. The heels were torn up, the leather scuffed and stained, and one of them had split open at the toes.

"Those are Emilia's?" Royal guessed.

I swallowed heavily and nodded, running a thumb over the now tattered laces. Little thorns were stuck in several places, evidence of the plants that had snatched at the silk, unraveling it as Emilia walked.

"I think we've been missing the obvious," I said.

"What do you mean?" Shiloh asked.

I laid it out piece by piece. "The necklace. It was her grandmother's, one of her most treasured possessions. It bought her safe passage down the cliffs. The handkerchief was a gift from me, given up to buy her the berries on that bush because she needed something to eat. The dress her best protection against the elements, given up to get her through the territory of the wolves. Her shoes, another bit of protection down here, given up to buy a way through the rocks."

How had she learned the rules of this place so quickly? And what would happen when she no longer had things to give?

"Then we need to buy passage through as well," Shiloh said. "What else do we have to give?"

"What else *can* we give?" Royal returned. "None of us are giving up our shoes like she did. We're actually planning on getting out of here, she wasn't."

Royal gasped and doubled over, clutching at their stomach. Akhíta and I dashed over, Akhíta catching them before they could topple forward off the low rock they'd gone to sit on.

"I told you not to take off the damn ring," Shiloh said, voice thick with worry as he came to sit next to Royal.

"I don't think that had anything to do with the ring," Royal panted.

I brushed the back of my hand along their forehead, finding it hot. "Does it still hurt?" I asked.

Royal shook their head, straightening up. "No. It was just the one… pulse."

Resting one hand on their shoulder, I turned to stare at the closed passageway. "The prices have gotten bigger and bigger the deeper we've gone. We need something that is worth a lot."

Akhíta's hand drifted towards her back pocket.

"No, not that," I said firmly.

She looked confused, as did the other two.

"I saw you put the piece of your father's uniform in your pocket earlier," I admitted.

Royal turned to her. "Don't even think about it. Getting a damn rock to move is not worth that."

I nodded in agreement. There had to be something, though. What else did we have? The guns. Our clothes. The canteens. None of that seemed like nearly enough. It had to be something sentimental. Something with meaning. Something like….

I slid my hand into my own pocket, feeling the bumps inside. In the mad dash to leave after the magic started hurting Royal, I'd nearly left my rosary behind in the tent, only remembering it at the last second. I ran my fingers over the beads now, counting them with my thumb. Bits of Royal's dried blood flaked away under my fingers. I'd never had a chance to wash it off. Once I'd gone over every bead, I pulled the whole thing out, tangled around my fingers.

Royal's eyes widened. "Clarabella, be careful. We don't know if the magic will see that as just an object, it might see it as your faith entirely."

I shook my head slowly. "It's not *my* faith, though, is it? It's Mother and Father's. And they…they aren't who I thought they were." I looked down at the light pink quartz beads. "I'll figure out my own faith later. But this…I'm okay with giving this up."

Royal swallowed heavily, hesitating before giving a single nod.

Akhíta and Shiloh each nodded as well. Everyone stood, crowding around the rock; who knew how long it might stay open?

I crouched, hand hovering near the hole I'd pulled Emilia's shoes out of. "Ready?"

Everyone said they were, so I shoved my hand in, dropped the beads, and sprung to my feet. The rock was already half open by the time I was fully up, revealing a dark, thin passage behind it. I dove in, the others dashing in behind me. Whether the doorway closed because we were all in, or because it indeed hadn't been meant to stay open long, we all barely made it in time.

Crowded into the tiny space, no bigger than a closet, we all waited in the dark, catching our breath. Shiloh's elbow dug into my arm, my face was in Akhíta›s hair, and Royal›s gangly limbs were somehow woven between all of us. I could feel an opening to my right, but I wasn't willing to go down it yet. Not without getting a better idea of where it might lead.

"It occurs to me," Royal said, voice muffled like their face was pressed against something, "that we perhaps should have figured out a light *before* we came in."

"The lantern is in my bag," I said. "There's still a little oil left."

"Wonderful. And do we know where my lighter ended up?" Royal asked, being met with silence. "We're doing so good."

Akhíta sighed, shuffling around to face me and indicating for me to turn around so she could get into my pack. With a fair amount of wiggling to get it free, she handed the lantern to me over my shoulder, then kept digging. When she couldn't find the lighter I handed everything over to her instead and dug through her pack. There wasn't a whole lot left. I pushed my fingers into every little nook and cranny until they brushed up against a cool piece of metal, rough with an engraving. Snatching it out, I passed it to Akhíta. She flicked it open and the small space filled with warm orange light.

Royal, pressed up against Shiloh's side, waggled their fingers until Akhíta handed over the lighter, and they tucked it into their back pocket.

"That," Shiloh declared, looking over my head, "is a very small passage."

I twisted around to look, finding that he was right. The opening was only perhaps a foot wide and seven feet tall. The floor of it sloped steeply downwards, covered in loose dirt and pebbles. I might've been able to go down straight forwards, if I curled my shoulders in, but everyone else would have to shimmy sideways.

"Well, I doubt we're going to be let out the way we came in," Royal said.

"How much oil do we have left exactly?" I asked.

Akhíta shook the lantern, the fuel inside sloshing. "Maybe an hour, if we're lucky."

"So…half-an-hour?" Royal grumbled.

"Better get going then," Shiloh said.

I had to go first; there was no room for us to shuffle around so anyone else could. Taking the lantern, I curled my shoulders in and started down, stopping a few feet in to wait for the others. Akhíta was forced to carry her pack in her hand and go sideways, unable to make it down the passage any other way.

Royal's estimation of the timing on the oil turned out to be optimistic. Within fifteen minutes the lantern started to flicker before going out with a puff of smoke, the last embers of the wick fading out until we were left in complete darkness.

"Well. I guess it isn't like we can get lost," Royal observed.

They weren't wrong, so we linked our hands together just in case and kept shuffling on.

When the light started to return, it was strangely blue and rather dim. It was also, for the moment, sourceless. Hoping it was the way out, we all shuffled a little faster.

"The floor," Akhíta said.

I looked down, finding a small, whiteish crystal no bigger than my pinky sticking up out of the dirt. The faintest shimmering light emanated out from its center, not even strong enough to light up the surrounding dirt. After a glance back at the others, I kept going.

More and more crystals started to poke up out of the dirt, getting bigger and brighter as we went until there was almost no path left at all, just sharp gems. They were all that same whiteish color, shimmering light at their cores. It wasn't quite the same opalescent sheen I'd seen coming from other instances of magic, but it was similar.

Emilia had gone through this without shoes, I realized.

As quickly as the passage had started, it ended, dumping us out on a ledge the size of a stage at a fancy theater.

"Holy shit," Royal breathed, falling to their knees and taking off their hat to run a hand through their hair.

"Má lé má," Akhíta echoed, her tone as awed as Royal's.

I knew I looked equally awestruck, as did Shiloh.

The ledge was halfway up the wall of a cavern bigger than all of Altora. Across all of it splayed a tangle of crystals, some as big around as the trees. They jutted in all directions, crossing and merging with one another over and over, going into and coming out of the walls, floor, and ceiling. Each one glowed from within, bathing everything in that soft, shimmering light. It was, easily, one of the most amazing things I had ever seen.

"Can we tell your mom about this part?" Shiloh asked.

Akhíta gave a slow nod. "Yeah, we can tell her about this part."

"We've got to find a way through it first," Royal pointed out.

Tearing my eyes away from the crystals, I looked around the ledge. It was maybe forty feet above what I assumed was the ground, though it was somewhat hard to tell. Several crystals did lean up towards the ledge, but none were close enough to get to. A large fracture ran through the ledge as well, about two feet from the edge, but it seemed old, the edges smoothed out and the crevice it created packed with dirt. Between the crack and the edge were two large divots that almost looked like footprints, save for the fact they were twice the size of normal feet. They were as worn at the edges as the crack.

I'd reached the point where I was willing to try just about anything, risky or otherwise, so without giving myself too much time to think, I crossed the crack and stood in the divots to see if anything happened. Nothing did, except for Royal telling me off and hauling me away from the area.

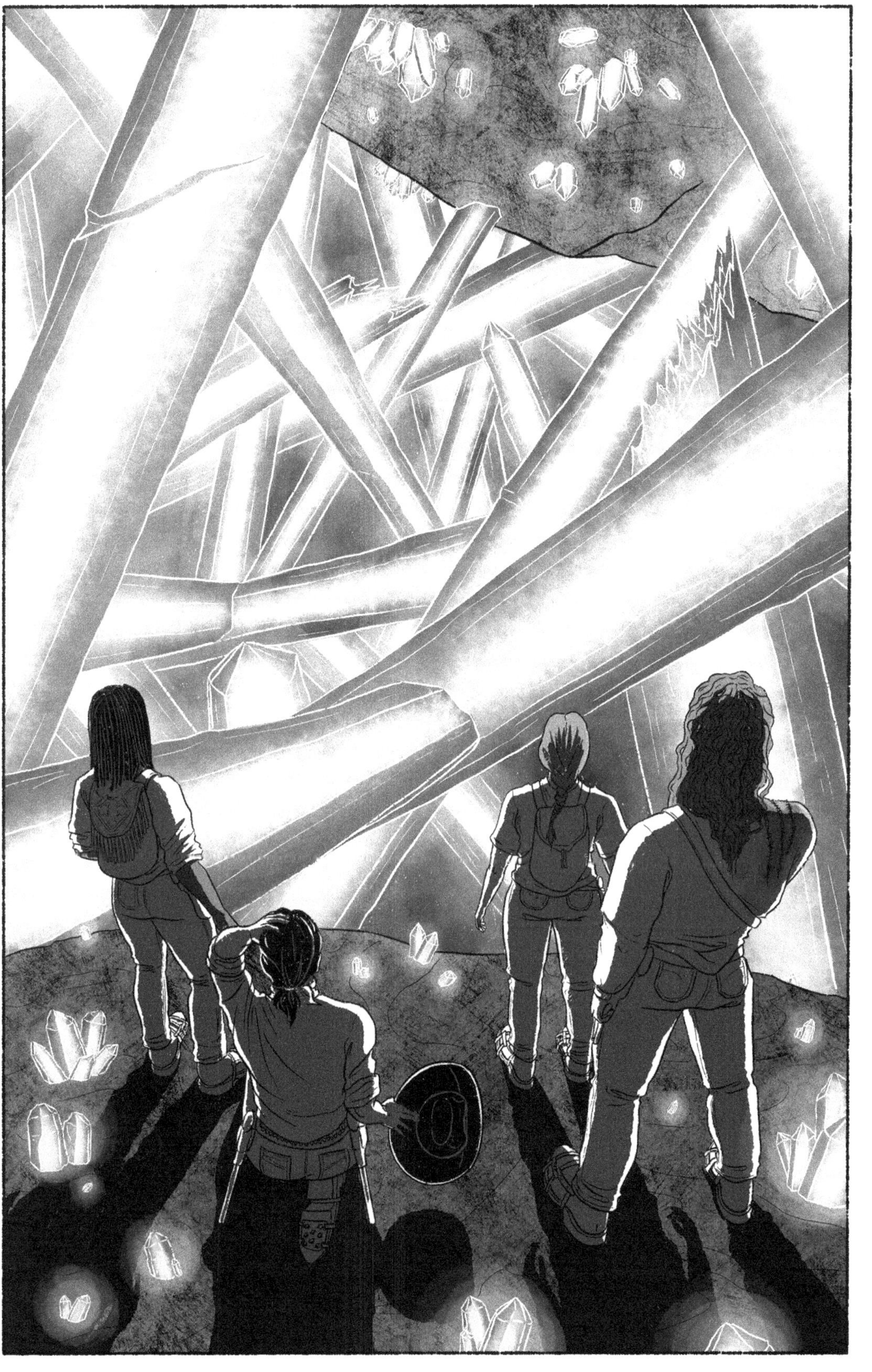

With some more searching, we found a path off the side of the ledge. It was steep, with several dropoffs that took some effort to navigate down, especially for Shiloh, but it did get us to the ground. The lower we got, the hotter and more humid it got as well. By the time we were at the bottom it felt about like swimming.

Heat and humidity or not, being among the crystals was even more humbling than being above them. While everyone caught their breath and drank some water, I reached out and brushed my fingers over one. It was as smooth as glass, as warm to the touch as skin. Smoky white fractures ran through it, catching and refracting its light in strange patterns.

"We need to move," Akhíta said. "This heat is dangerous, especially with so little water."

This was difficult. There was, sort of, a path to follow. It involved a lot of ducking under crystals, shimmying around them, and sometimes clambering over top of them. I didn't know what we would do if we came across one that was too big to get over. Their shape and smoothness meant there was no way to really get a grip, even with our spikes.

"Akhíta?" Shiloh called.

I looked around, finding that she had stopped and was now staring intently at one of the crystals off to the side. Sweat was running down her face in rivulets, and she did not appear to have heard Shiloh.

"Hey," Shiloh said, going back and shaking her shoulder.

She jumped and shook her head. "Má!" She shook her head again, clenching her eyes shut as she did. "Sorry. I just...sorry."

"You alright?" Royal asked, frowning.

She opened her eyes and gave a nod that was too slow to be convincing.

"Go in front of me," Shiloh insisted.

She glanced at the crystal once more before doing as asked without protest.

There was no time for more concern, so we kept going.

A large crystal crossed the path and, with a boost from Royal, I was able to swing my leg up over the top to straddle it, pulling them up after me.

"Shiloh, you next!" Royal called. "Akhíta can help you stay stable while Clarabella and I pull you up, then we'll pull her up."

Shiloh didn't respond. He, just like Akhíta, was staring into one of the crystals in a daze. Royal and I both scrambled down, finding Akhíta already pulling Shiloh away.

"What happened?" Royal asked, putting a hand on Shiloh's hip and staring up into his face. Shiloh looked more out of it than Akhíta had, his eyes unfocused and blinking. Rivulets of sweat ran over his skin and soaked his shirt, his normally wild red hair hanging lank around his face from the humidity.

"His mom," Akhíta said, voice tense.

Royal turned to her in confusion. "What?"

"His mom…in the crystal," Akhíta said. "I only caught a glimpse of her, but she looked just like the portrait he has. Earlier…I thought I saw my father in one, but I assumed it was the heat. I think it was him, anyway. I don't have any pictures, just some sketches my mother did."

"She told me to go home," Shiloh said, voice slurred. "That I'd done enough and it was time to go back."

"Shiloh," Royal said, voice gentle. "Your mom is dead. She died in a house fire when you were six."

"My father told me the same thing," Akhíta said, voice shaky. "That it was time to go back."

"Okay, we need to *go*," I insisted.

Royal nodded, throwing an arm around Shiloh's waist and steering him down the path. In his dazed state we almost couldn't get Shiloh over the large crystal, but with some effort we did all make it to the other side.

"Fuck," Royal muttered.

Akhíta had stopped now, her eyes clenched shut.

Royal swore again and told me to take Shiloh while they went and slung an arm around Akhíta. She came easily, keeping her eyes closed.

"It was my mom that time," she said. "She was crying."

"Just go, just keep going," Royal told her.

I tugged Shiloh along, trying to go as fast as possible without making him topple over.

I wasn't surprised when I looked back and found Royal frozen, their eyes locked on a crystal this time. Akhíta, too, looked dazed, staring into another crystal.

"Don't move," I ordered Shiloh, unsure if he was even aware of my presence.

I yanked on Royal's arm, trying to get their attention to no avail. Akhíta was no more responsive.

"Darling, you know your father and I love you dearly. Just come home. All is forgiven." The voice was like silk and yet all wrong. But I still knew it.

Swallowing heavily I turned to find a shimmering image of my mother staring at me out of the same crystal Royal was focused on. She looked resplendent in her Sunday best, her smile soft and warm. Her arms were held out, like she was inviting us in for a hug.

This vision wasn't meant for me, though. It was meant for Royal. All it did for me was send a shudder down my spine at the wrongness of it. I tried to spin Royal around, but it was like they'd become one with the ground. Not knowing what else to do, I reached over and pulled their knife from its sheath at their back. Quickly, I slipped Royal's ring off and poked the tip of the knife into the back of their hand. They gasped and I jammed the ring back on.

"Go to Shiloh," I ordered as they reeled away from the crystal, swaying and gasping for breath. "Now."

They listened, stumbling off and collapsing against Shiloh's side. I poked Akhíta's hand next, getting the same reaction. Pushing her forward, I started to herd the three of them ahead of me, keeping the knife in hand.

"Clarabella?" I froze, fighting the urge to turn back. Something in me, something I was pretty sure wasn't me at all, forced me to turn anyway.

Emilia was standing there, dressed in a blue muslin dress tied with a satin ribbon, white Sunday riding boots on her feet, my handkerchief in hand, and a little gold necklace around her neck. Her beautiful blond hair was in perfect ringlets, set over her shoulders like she was about to pose for a portrait. She smiled wide, her eyes crinkling at the corners.

"I missed you," she said.

This vision was meant for me, and I couldn't resist it. Everything else faded away until it looked like the real Emilia was standing there in front of me, not a reflection in a crystal.

"I'm coming to get you," I said. Or thought. I couldn't tell.

She laughed, reaching out to brush a hand against my face. I gasped when her fingers touched me, shocked at how real they felt. All I wanted to do was melt into that touch.

"Darling, you don't need to come get me. I've already gone home," she said. "Turn around, and we'll be together again."

It wasn't true. I knew it wasn't. Yet the tug towards home was so strong. Surely she'd be there? Back in our room, splayed across her bed with the latest edition of Harper's Bazaar propped on her knees.

No.

"Please, darling. I miss you," Emilia said, bringing her other hand up to cup my face.

"I miss you too," I said. Even as she drew in all of my attention I tried to take a mental inventory of my body, tried to fight for some bit of control. Right foot, nothing. Left foot, nothing. Left hand, nothing. Right hand...knife.

I still had the knife.

"So come home? Please?"

I managed to curl one finger tighter. "You don't want to go home."

She tilted her head.

I curled another finger tighter. "Your father is there." Another finger. "You ran away from him. He'll—he'll just send you off to marry the Duke or—find another—find another way to make you do whatever—whatever else it is he wants."

"Oh. Well, I suppose we'll just have to run away then, won't we?" She smiled, but this time the expression in her eyes didn't quite match the one on her mouth.

I tightened my last finger and my thumb.

"We will run away together," I said. "Me, and the real you."

I twisted my wrist, jabbing the knife into my thigh.

It wasn't deep, but it did draw blood and proved to be enough.

The vision in front of me shattered like broken glass, shards of Emilia's face fading back into the depths of the crystal.

Gasping, I turned to find the others standing where I'd left them, all still looking dazed and seemingly unaware of anything that was going on.

"Go!" I said, shoving at all of them into motion.

The path didn't get any easier and I kept seeing flickers of Emilia out of the corner of my eyes. Soon, there was no ground left at all, just crystal after crystal. Sometimes the others were somewhat lucid, but never all at once and never for long. Between the humidity and our sweat, the surface of the crystals was dangerously slick. We all fell over and over, Shiloh leaving behind dots of blood from where a few of his stitches had burst.

At one point my foot slipped between two crystals and I heard something pop, pain lancing up my leg. Whimpering, I freed my foot and kept going. I wasn't standing at this point anyway, just sliding from one slick surface to the next.

"There," Royal gasped, the first thing they'd said in I didn't know how long.

I looked up and saw they were pointing at a small yellow dot off in the distance. It took a minute for my eyes to adjust, allowing me to realize that it was an opening in the cavern wall, a sliver of forest floor visible on the other side.

I nodded, unable to form words.

The last stretch proved to be the hardest. Visions danced around all of us, their voices echoing off the walls. A tall, regal looking woman with Shiloh's fiery red hair. A woman with Akhíta's eyes and two braids hanging over her shoulders. My mother. Emilia. A black man in a Northern Civil War uniform.

More than once I had to grab one of the others and poke them with the knife before shoving them in the direction of the exit. Only once did I have to do it for myself.

When we finally reached the little opening, only a few feet tall and wide, we crawled through and collapsed one by one onto the soft, cool moss.

Chapter 19
The Final Push

I laid there, fingers digging into the moss as I sucked in air, relieved to find it cool and dry. The others, scattered out around me, were doing much the same.

"What the fuck was that?" Royal gasped.

"Shiloh's bleeding," I answered. "Check his shoulder."

Struggling to my knees, I crawled over to Akhíta who was on her back, one hand tangled in her hair and shaking.

"Are you hurt or just…?" I asked, gesturing vaguely as I had no words for what else she might be.

She shook her head and sat up. "Not hurt. Except for where you stabbed me. Repeatedly." She held up her hand, which had several little rivulets of blood running down the back."

"It was necessary," I said.

She dropped her hand and nodded. "I know. Thanks. How's Shiloh?"

"Alright, I think," Royal said. They were kneeling behind Shiloh who was sat up but curled forward, head resting on his knees. "Only a few stitches popped."

"We should put new ones in," Akhíta said, looking around for the packs. Only they weren't there. She looked at me and I shrugged. I had no idea where they'd gone.

"I'll be alright," Shiloh said, straightening up and running a hand through his hair to pull it away from his face. It was still dripping wet.

Each of us looked like we'd been dumped in a lake and nearly drowned.

"Both of you c'm'ere," Royal said, holding an arm out to Akhíta and I.

We crawled over and, after throwing their other arm around Shiloh, Royal yanked Akhíta and I into the hug. All four of us collapsed together, unable to do anything else.

"We need water," Akhíta said eventually.

"I'll try and find some," I said.

"And put it in what?" Shiloh asked.

I didn't have an answer to that, so I pulled away to look around, hoping to find something. For the first time, I really saw where we were. It was the forest. A forest. The trees were as big around as houses now, stretching up so far they faded away into darkness. Everything was covered in moss and lichen in dozens of colors. White flowers with thousands of petals hung from thick vines, ferns writhed in a wind that was not there, unseen creatures called back and forth, and all of it was suffused with a soft golden light.

And the ground was perfectly flat.

"We're at the bottom," Akhíta whispered.

As we watched, a little blue creature skittered out on a rock several feet away, stopping to stare at us with a single large eye. It was about the size of a frog, and sort of built the same way, except for the flickering opalescent fire that enveloped its form. It let out a meep and skittered on out of sight, leaving a trail of smoldering black spots in its wake. The moss was too damp to ignite, though, only letting out thin wisps of smoke.

"I take it back," Akhíta said. "We are not telling my mother about *any* of this."

"I appreciate the belief that we still might make it out of here," Royal muttered. No one chastised them for the statement.

The bubbling of a creek drew my attention and, still not sure what I'd put the water in, I moved to stand. The second I tried to put weight on my right foot I collapsed with a yelp, lightning screaming up my leg and pushing its way out in the form of tears. I'd completely forgotten about the pop I heard earlier.

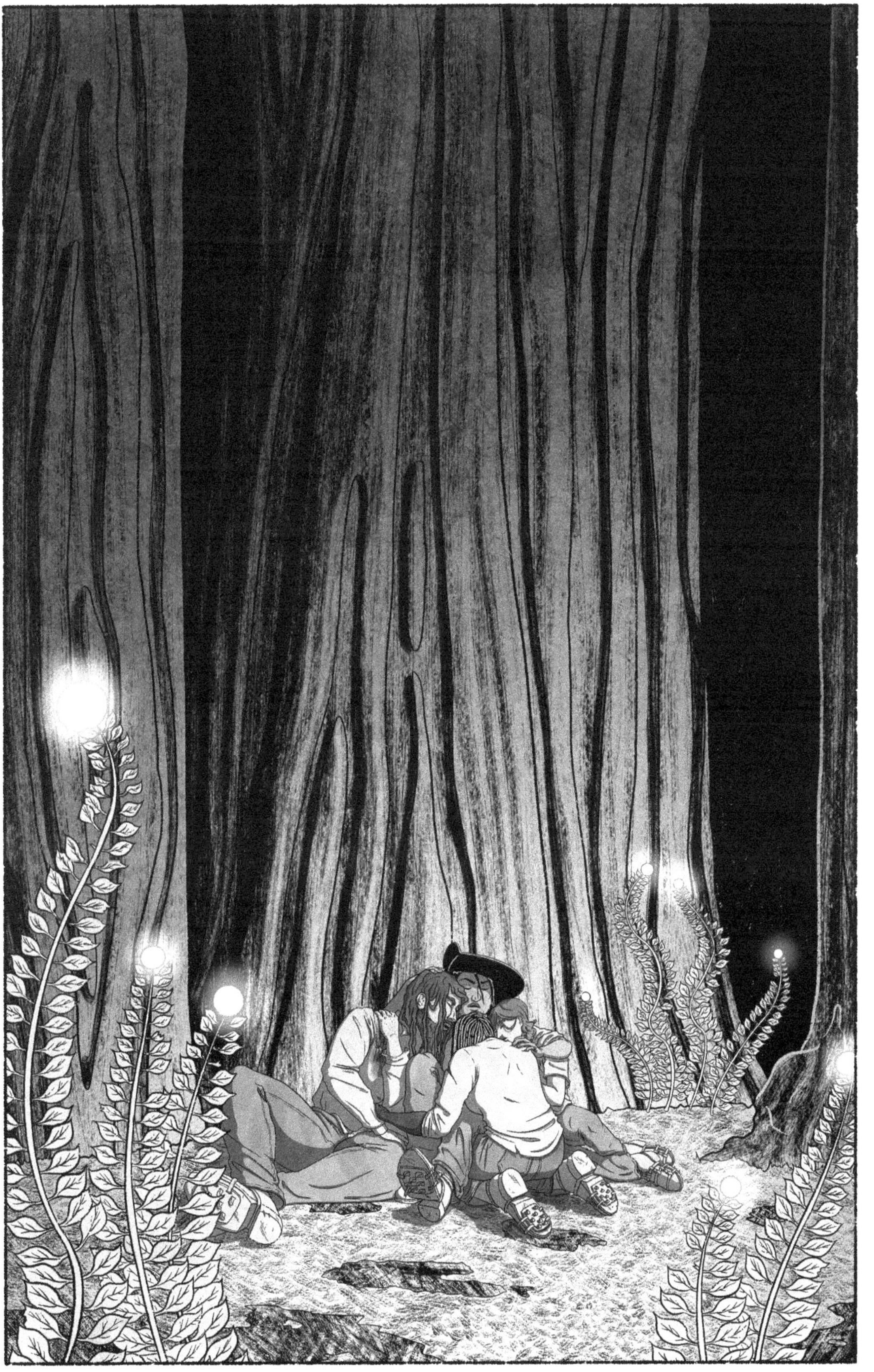

No one managed to catch me before I hit the ground, but Royal was at my side as soon as I was down. I clasped my hands around my calf in a desperate attempt to stem the pain.

"Where?" Akhíta asked, leaning over my foot.

"On the—on the right side of my ankle," I told her. "My foot slipped between two of the crystals during that last stretch, and I heard something pop."

Akhíta frowned, supporting my foot with a hand on the heel of my boot. "I don't think there's anything we can do except leave your boot on to help keep the swelling down."

"I can't walk," I realized.

"Don't get mad at me, any of you, but what about my ring?" Royal asked.

Akhíta shook her head. "It wouldn't help. The actual injury would still be there. If she walks on it it'll make it worse, potentially much worse."

Royal growled in frustration, standing up quickly, stumbling as they did. "Fuck this. Fuck all of this. I'm done."

"Royal!" Shiloh said, looking alarmed.

Regaining their balance, Royal made it over to where I'd dropped their knife and snatched it up, nearly falling over in the process.

"Stop them, stop them," I said, pushing Akhíta in Royal's direction.

She wasn't doing any better on her feet than Royal was, however, and ended up falling to her knees. Shiloh didn't seem able to get up either.

Royal strode out of reach of everyone, a grim and determined look on their face, continuing to shout into the forest. "I'm done with your damn games, I'm done with your damn prices, I'm done with you hurting my family. You forced *me* here, not them, so leave them the fuck alone." They snatched up a thick stick from the ground. "This is mine now, so my sister can walk." Tossing it towards me, they reached out for a plant with leaves the size of wagon wheels next. With a quick slash of the knife they cut through one stalk. "And I'm using this to get us water." A couple deft slices cut off the leaf itself, leaving only the hollow stalk, open at one end. Royal went and dunked it in the water, coming back and holding it out to Akhíta.

She didn't take it. Royal didn't move.

"What you just did...was phenomenally stupid," Akhíta said. "Tákuwe héčhanuŋ he?"

"Like I said, I don't care. I'm done with this."

Akhíta still didn't take the stalk.

Royal let out a sharp breath through their nose, then drank the water themselves. They went and refilled it, holding it out for Shiloh this time. Shiloh took it, but didn't drink, staring up at Royal instead.

"I know you're scared," Shiloh said, voice gentle. "We all are. Don't do anything like that again."

Royal cast their eyes to the ground and nodded.

Shiloh drank and handed back the stalk.

Royal brought me a drink next and I downed it, ignoring the strange taste that came with. There was an edge of sulfur, but there was something else too, something that was more feeling than taste. Sharp.

Akhíta finally gave in and drank some as well.

Royal helped me up, letting me balance on one foot as they measured the stick against my side. It took a sharp right turn about five feet up its length, so Royal broke off a couple feet from the bottom, putting the angled part of the branch right at the height of my armpit. After they broke off the extra length from the top half as well, I hobbled about to test it. It wasn't comfortable, digging into my armpit and not providing a good area to hold on to, but it worked.

The water helped all of us a lot, and Akhíta made everyone drink a second stalk's worth. There was nothing to do now but get up and go. Except now, without a slope, there was no indication at all as to which direction was which.

"How big do you think the bottom of the Pit is?" I asked. Emilia couldn't be that far now, could she?

Royal shrugged. "I'm not sure somewhere like this even has an actual size."

Still. "Emilia?" I called, as loud as I could.

"EmILiA!!!!" Something echoed. It was my voice, except distorted, distorting more and more with every echo until it faded away.

"Nope!" Royal said. "Nope. Nope. Not doing that again."

"Agreed," Shiloh said.

Akhíta sighed. "Let's just walk. At this point we either find her, and a way out, or we don't."

With no other ideas forthcoming, we did as she suggested. It was extremely slow going. The water had certainly helped, just not quite enough.

"Is the ring really helping you *that* much?" Akhíta asked Royal. She'd paused to lean against a tree and catch her breath.

Indeed, Royal seemed to be doing better than the rest of us. Walking quicker, swaying less.

They shook their head. "The ring isn't helping at all. I feel like I've been repeatedly trampled by an angry horse. But, unlike all of you, I'm used to that. I've had a lot of practice pushing through it."

Akhíta grimaced.

Royal shrugged. "It is what it is."

"Try not to hurt yourself," Shiloh said. "Please."

"Doing my best," Royal told him.

Hobbling along on the crutch was exhausting. It took both my hands to keep it steady and moving the way I wanted and sometimes it sunk deep into the mossy ground, nearly making me fall. Royal tried to help at one point, offering to let me lean on them instead, but they were too tall and it just didn't work. Akhíta was only an inch or two taller than me, but she could barely stand herself.

"Any guesses how long we've been gone?" Shiloh asked.

"Three days?" I said, entirely unsure. Between sleeping at random times and the eventual loss of the sun, I'd completely lost track.

"Sounds right enough," Shiloh replied.

When an owl as big as Akhíta swooped silently from above and landed in front of us, we all just stared, unable to muster up any other response. It was gray and white, tufts of feathers sticking up like ears on either side of its head. It turned its head in a jerking motion, revealing another entire face on the other side. The beak clacked once, then the head kept going, making a full circle to reveal the first face again.

"If this thing starts asking us to solve riddles, I'm done," Royal declared.

It clacked its beak once more, then took off as silently as it had come.

Shiloh gave Royal a withering look.

"What?" Royal said. "I didn't ask for anything or address anything directly. I just. Voiced my annoyance."

Shiloh shook his head and started walking again.

I caught several more glimpses of the owl in the branches above us. It was always perched right on the edge of the darkness that consumed the upper levels, staring down at us with wide yellow eyes.

"Clarabella."

I looked down from the trees and found Royal bending over a neatly folded pile of cloth on a waist high rock. Hobbling closer, I ran my fingers over the stained fabric. It was a set of underclothes. A chemise and petticoats. Dirt and blood stained the bottom edge of the petticoats.

"Footprints," Shiloh said.

He was pointing at a spot of mud among the moss. Right in the center was one small, bare, footprint no bigger than my own. The impression of the heel of the other foot was visible as well, where the ground went back to moss, and a couple muddy footprints trailed out over the moss too.

Dropping the petticoats, I followed the footprints. They didn't last long before the mud ran out, leaving us standing in a stretch of forest that looked exactly like everywhere else.

"Why did she take them off?" Akhíta asked, catching up to me. "Was she paying for something?"

I had no idea. But... "Her corset wasn't there."

"What?" Shiloh asked, panting a little as he stopped next to us.

"She always wore a corset," I said. "We've found every other piece of clothing she might have had on, but not her corset."

"Maybe she took it off before she came down," Royal suggested. "Or it is down here, we just didn't find it."

"Maybe..." I trailed off.

A soft splash sounded somewhere off to our right and all of us went silent, turning towards the sound. I couldn't place exactly where it came from, but if I strained, I thought I heard the soft swishing of something moving through water. Tentatively, I took a few steps towards where I thought the sounds were coming from. When they didn't get any quieter, I kept going, picking my way forward one measured step at a time.

What I saw first, I did not recognize. Corsets were stiff garments, not something that was capable of being crumpled into a ball and tossed aside. Yet, there it was, lying on the ground in front of me, the laces trailing out behind it.

What I saw second was Emilia. Her back was to me, entirely naked, hair nearly ice white in this light and cascading down to her waist, ends spreading out on the water of the perfectly circular pond she was half immersed in. The pond stood alone, no source of water flowing into it that I could see. In each hand Emilia held a cluster of what I realized were the whalebones from her corset, all of them carved with strange black markings.

Chapter 20
The Pond

Royal's arms were locked around my waist before I could think to do anything. I shouted Emilia's name over and over again without getting the slightest reaction from her. Slow ripples emanated out from her body with every breath she took, reaching the edge of the pond without bouncing back.

"Clarabella, stop, stop, we need to think this through!" Royal said, giving me a shake.

I sucked in a deep, hitching breath and nodded.

"I'm going to let you go," Royal said, "but if you make one move towards that pond, I will tackle you. Is that understood?"

I nodded again.

"Okay." Royal released me and took a very small step back.

Akhíta was circling the pond, which was about fifty feet across, staring intently at Emilia.

"What part of her do you see?" Akhíta called.

"Her back?" Shiloh responded. He'd stayed with Royal and I.

"Me too," Akhíta said. "Walk around the edge and watch her. She never moves, she never turns, but you can't see anything except for her back."

I did, hobbling as fast as I could, eyes locked on Emilia's back. Akhíta was right. She didn't move, she didn't turn, yet, somehow, in a way that made my head ache, all I could ever see was the same angle of her back.

"What's on the bones?" Shiloh asked once we reached Akhíta.

She shook her head. "I can't make it out from here."

"Okay," Shiloh said. "Okay. We've found her, but that's not entirely why we're here. Royal, how are you feeling?"

All three of us turned to Royal, but I kept Emilia in the corner of my eye.

Royal wiggled a little, clearly trying to feel out their whole body. "Fine? Not great, obviously, but there's no new pain all of a sudden or anything like that."

"I wish that were a comforting answer," Akhíta muttered. "I don't like it, though. It doesn't feel right, not after the magic forced you down here."

"Can't say I disagree," Royal replied.

We all turned to stare at Emilia. She was as still as ever, hands full of bones still hovering just above the water.

"To bad we don't have some damn rope," Shiloh said. "We could try and lasso her."

Royal crouched down at the edge of the pond, staring at it intently. The edge, like the rest of the pond, was perfect. Smooth and curved, no water lapping over it. The mossy ground just ended, revealing an inch of dirt that went straight down to the water which itself was inky black, revealing nothing of what was underneath.

"Going in there is not an option," Akhíta declared.

Royal hummed, standing up. "Shiloh's plan might be the only option, then. We don't have rope, but there's vines everywhere."

"And how do we pay for them?" I asked.

"Like I said, I'm done paying for things," Royal declared. "I'm a damn outlaw, after all."

Taking out their knife once more, they placed the blade between their fingers, swung their arm back, and whipped the knife in a perfect arc up into the trees. It sailed, spinning end over end until it sliced through a thin vine about thirty feet up, then dropped and stuck, point down, in the moss. The vine fell with a thump, coiling into a heap.

Shiloh and Akhíta shared an exhausted look, but neither one argued.

There was no point anymore.

Royal picked up one end of the vine and began running it through their hands, stripping off the leaves and flowers. If my estimation of both its length and the size of the pond were right, it would barely be enough to reach Emilia.

"May as well get another one," I told them.

They nodded, retrieving the knife for another throw. Meanwhile, Akhíta was circling the pond again. Shiloh had found a rock to sit on, clearly out of energy to stand. I was trying not to think of what it might take to get us all out of here, if we even could.

Having stripped the second vine, Royal knotted the ends together and tossed one end to me. "Tug. Put your full weight into it."

I did, only able to use my unburned hand as I leaned back, my fist wrapped around the woody surface. Royal did the same. It held. Royal looped one end back on itself, tying a smaller loop around the body of the vine to make a lasso.

"That's a lot heavier than lasso rope," Shiloh observed.

"I'm aware," Royal said.

"Also, you are shit at lassoing," Shiloh added.

"Yes, thank you for the commentary, dear. May I remind you this was *your* idea?"

"No," Shiloh said, looking slightly amused. "I said it was too bad we didn't have rope to try it with. Real rope. Not a bendy stick masquerading as rope."

Royal shook their head and hooked their finger around the knot that created the loop, striding over to the edge of the pond, stopping a few feet away. Akhíta had made it back around to us and stood back to watch. Royal gave one low swing at their side, using the momentum to bring the loop up over their head for a few more swirls before they let it fly. It sailed only as far as the edge of the pond before it suddenly stopped and crumpled to the ground.

"What just happened?" I asked.

Royal shrugged and strode forward, sticking their arm out ahead of them. Nothing stopped their progress. Their arm went out over the water without anything happening. Akhíta came up and held out her arm as well, nothing stopping her either. Stepping back, Royal tried the lasso once more, only to get the same result.

Frustrated, I leaned down and scooped up a rock, chucking it towards the pond to see what might happen. It, like the lasso, reached the edge of the pond and dropped straight to the ground.

Royal chucked the lasso to the side and sat down at the edge with a frustrated growl, staring intently at the water and muttering to themself. It sounded like they were going over everything that had happened so far. The canyon, Akhíta catching me on the cliff, Shiloh getting injured by the wolves, me getting injured by the firefly and, more importantly, by the crystals.

"I'm the only one not hurt," Royal said eventually.

"Like hell you aren't," Shiloh said.

Royal shook their head. "No, I'm not. I'm suffering, yeah, but only in the way I always am. I never actually got hurt down *here*."

None of this could argue with this.

Royal looked back over the water and startled, pulling everyone's attention back to Emilia. She hadn't moved, but the strange black marks on the corset bones were crawling up both her hands, vanishing from the bones as they did.

"Emilia!" I screamed. She still didn't respond.

One of the bones, completely free of marks now, slipped from her hand and slid silently into the water. All of us gasped involuntarily, the air sucked from our lungs for a fraction of a second before we could pull more back in.

"Wh—" Akhíta started, only to be interrupted by a long, low wail. The sound made my ears ache even when I clamped my hands over them.

Another markless bone dropped and another breath was stolen from us. This time it was much harder to find another one. The wails ceased like they'd been turned off and a shudder went through every plant around us, leaves raining down. None fell into the pond and the water remained still, its only movement the ripples from Emilia's breathing.

"We can't let her drop another one of those," Royal said, ripping off their gun belt and letting it clatter to the ground. They tossed off their hat as well and pushed up their already rolled sleeves, leaning down to grab the vine and pulling it over their head, cinching it tight around their waist.

"I'll go!" Akhíta said. "We still don't know what this place wants from you."

Royal shook their head. "Akhíta, you *know* how bad I feel right now. You've seen how little strength I have when I'm like this. Your shoulder may be hurt, but with Clarabella's help, and whatever help Shiloh can give, you can pull me back in. None of us could pull Shiloh in, with her bad hand Clarabella can't pull you in even with Shiloh's help, and Clarabella can't even walk either. It has to be me."

"Royal, please, don't," Shiloh begged, good hand shooting out to clasp around Royal's wrist. He looked terrified. "Please."

"I have to," Royal said, clasping their other hand over Shiloh's and squeezing gently. "I don't know what's happening, but whatever those bones are, whatever's on them, I think it's killing this place. And I'm not going to let that happen."

I lurched forward, letting my crutch drop and wrapping my arms tight around Royal. "No, Shiloh's right, don't do it, please."

I knew this would mean losing Emilia. My heart ached knowing I was giving her up, but I still had a chance to save Royal. Besides, part of me suspected Emilia was already gone in every way that mattered.

Royal pried me off, shaking their head. "I'm going."

Shiloh sobbed and tried to get up from the rock, only to sway and fall back onto it. Royal leaned over and pulled him into a fierce kiss, prying his hands away after and stepping out of reach.

"Love you, Shiloh," Royal said. "You too, Akhíta. And Clarabella?"

I sniffed, tears rolling down my face.

"Thanks for coming to find me."

I let out a sob of my own, reaching out for Royal. They stepped away from my hands, towards the edge of the pond, only to duck and roll across the ground, dodging the blow Akhíta aimed at their head. Royal swung a leg out, knocking Akhíta's legs out from under her and sending her sprawling out backwards onto the ground.

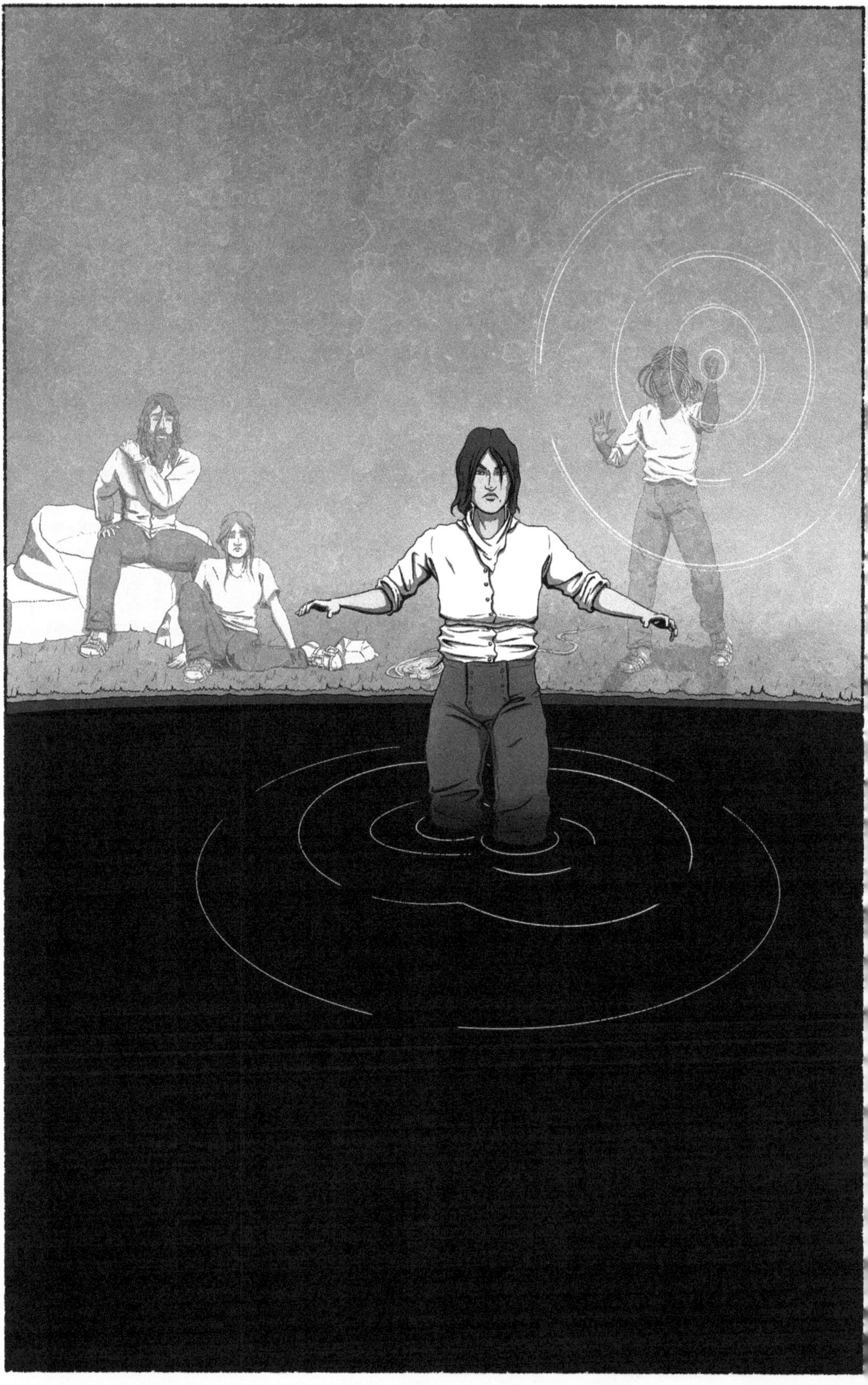

"Love you enough that you're predictable, Akhíta," Royal said, scrambling back to their feet and grabbing most of the vine as they did.

Before anyone else could do anything, Royal stepped over the edge and into the water.

I don't know what I expected to happen, maybe for them to vanish, maybe for the pond to violently throw them back out, but nothing did. They were just standing there, ankle deep in water. Royal looked back at us, hands held out slightly, and shrugged. Akhíta lunged forward, hands stretched out to grab Royal, only to slam into whatever barrier had stopped the lasso and the rock before. She cursed in a very colorful combination of French and English, slamming her fists against the barrier we could not see.

"Sorry," Royal told her, looking at Shiloh and I as well. They turned around to face Emilia once more, taking a tentative step forward, the water rising to the top of their boots.

Shiloh kept calling out Royal's name as they advanced forward. Akhíta kept smacking at the barrier. I just…sat down. Watched.

The vine, at least, seemed to be holding, trailing out over the water behind Royal, a few feet still outside the pond. Akhíta, seeing this, bent down and yanked it hard. It went taught against the barrier while the other side remained loose. No matter how much she tugged, the barrier would not release the vine.

The black marks had now consumed Emilia's fingers, beginning to coil up her wrists. Another bone, nearly blank, was hanging at the tips of her fingers. Royal lunged, grabbing it before it could hit the water. Emilia did not react, but neither did the magic or the forest around us. Things remained as they were.

Slowly, Royal took the bone and, after a moment of contemplation, stuck it in their mouth, holding it between their teeth. Hands now free, they took a deep breath and mirrored Emilia's pose from behind her. Reaching out an inch at a time, they slid their hands under Emilia's, then clasped onto her, forcing her hands closed so no more bones could drop.

It was hard to see exactly what was happening with their backs to us, but it didn't seem like Emilia reacted to this either. Royal pressed a little closer, bringing Emilia's hands up in front of her until Royal was able to take both of her hands in one of theirs. No longer wrapped around her, Royal managed to turn her around and, for the first time, I saw her face.

It was expressionless, her eyes filmed over with white.

I was right.

She was gone.

We never should have come here.

Making sure to keep her hands out of the water, and the bones gripped tightly, Royal started to lead Emilia back to us. Akhíta nearly fell when the improvised rope went slack. I scrambled up to help her pull it in, putting all my weight on my uninjured leg and not caring as the rough vine tore at my burn. Shiloh managed to get up as well, twisting the end of the rope around his left fist. It didn't matter, though, as we could only pull the rope as far as Royal had walked. We couldn't actually pull them in.

Little by little Royal and Emilia emerged out of the water. When the two of them were a few feet away Royal took the bone from between their teeth and chucked it off into the forest, then took the rest of Emilia's and did the same. Whatever magic those bones had, the effect seemed to only matter in the water, and they all fell harmlessly to the ground.

Royal pushed Emilia forward and, instinctively, I reached out for her. No resistance met my hand and I almost fell forward into the pond in shock, managing to catch myself on my bad foot. Yelping, I pushed past the pain and grabbed Emilia's shoulder, pulling her towards me. The sooner she was out the sooner Royal was out.

Emilia placed one foot on the moss, inky black beads of water dripping off her skin. Lifting her other foot free from the water, she placed it on the moss as well. A crack like the loudest thunder I'd ever heard ripped through the air, the ground, a single, huge ripple emanating from the center of the pond. Shiloh lunged for Royal, only to slam against the barrier once more. I tried too, only to be met with the same result.

Royal, eyes wide, opened their mouth to say something, but they didn't get the chance. Their feet flew out from under them, seemingly pulled backwards by something, and they vanished under the water.

Chapter 21
Hum

Everyone screamed except Emilia, who remained unmoving. The vine was limp in Akhíta's hands, no longer caught in the barrier, and she yanked it towards her, only to reveal a frayed end. Shiloh threw off his sling and slammed against the barrier with his other shoulder. I pressed my hand up against the barrier, hobbling around the edge of the pond in search of some break, not caring how much it made my ankle scream. Royal's name echoed back and forth between all of us.

The pond itself was as smooth as glass now, and just as dark as it had always been.

Making the full circuit, I grabbed Emilia by the upper arms, shaking her. "Emilia? Emilia, what is happening? What did you do? EMILIA!"

She stared right through me, eyes still filmed over, body rolling limply through the movement of my shaking.

Shiloh fell to his knees, gasping for breath. Akhíta was on the ground now as well, shoving her fingers into the moss and tearing it away, like she was trying to dig her way under the barrier.

Another boom sounded, even louder than the first, and a single, large, ripple rolled out from the center of the pond once more. When it reached the edge a sound like shattering glass followed the last vibrations of the boom. Shards of magic shimmered in the air, opalescent as always. Cracks radiated out across the barrier from dozens of points, revealing it at last. Shiloh struggled back up, moving to slam his shoulder into it once more. Before he could the ground pitched up under all of us.

I screamed, arms pinwheeling as I was thrown violently backwards. Emilia crumpled into a heap next to me and didn't move. Twisting around I saw that Akhíta and Shiloh had been thrown as well, both struggling to get back to their feet. Shiloh's shoulder was bleeding freely now, his shirt hanging off where my repairs had given way.

The ground continued to pitch and roll, as wild as waves, preventing any of us from getting up. Even crawling didn't work. Every movement we made towards the pond got rebuffed with a sharp roll that sent us flying backwards. I caught glimpses of the pond through the chaos, and it was still once more. It was becoming harder and harder to see, though, the cracks in the barrier continuing to glow and spread.

Birds, or things that might have been birds, screamed and swooped all around. Other creatures, ones I didn't have any word for, stampeded among the trees which swayed and crashed into one another, sending debris raining down.

The light from the barrier grew brighter and brighter, whiting everything out. I had no idea where any of the others were anymore. Where I was. Closing my eyes made no difference against the blinding light. It seared into me until another boom sounded and suddenly everything was dark, a cool, soft breeze blowing over my skin, the ground still and flat underneath me. It was rough now, though, all trace of the spongy moss gone.

"Akhíta?!" Someone called, shock clear in their voice.

I knew that voice.

Daiyu.

It was Daiyu.

Her voice was joined by several others, all shouting, and I pried my eyes open, amazed when I found that I could still see. Not far away a cheerful little fire flickered in the middle of a ring of tents, a large pot hanging over it, bowls tipped over and abandoned around the ring. Stars sparkled in a blue-black sky above us, the night not all consuming yet.

"What's going on?"

"Shiloh's hurt!"

"Who's the girl? Is this Emilia?"

"Where's Royal?"

Royal.

"Royal!" I sobbed, struggling to my feet and spinning around in search of them. There was Akhíta, fighting off Little Mountain's help and spinning around to look as well. Four people were crouched around Shiloh, telling him to stay still. Daiyu had gone to Emilia who was sitting up, rubbing at her eyes and looking around in confusion.

Royal wasn't there.

Fox was at my side, trying to reach out for me but unable to grab hold as I continued to move.

"Clarabella! Clarabella, what's going on?" Fox demanded, finally snagging one of my elbows and forcing me to still. "Where's Royal? Why are you back already?"

I looked at him in confusion. "Al—already?"

"Yeah. You guys only left this morning. The sun has barely set. You haven't been gone much more than half a day," Fox said.

"No." I shook my head. "No. That's…no. It's been days." I looked over to Akhíta who shook her head as well, looking just as confused.

It had been days. It had to have been. There was no way all of that could have only happened in a handful of hours.

"Clarabella?"

I looked down and saw Emilia staring up at me, her eyes clear and blue. Someone had brought her a blanket and wrapped it around her shoulders to cover her. There was still something about her that seemed dazed, though.

"Where's Royal?" Fox demanded again.

"The pond took them," I said, knowing it would make no sense to Fox or any of the others who hadn't been in the Pit with us. "The pond took them."

Akhíta tore away from Little Mountain and started ranging out, stumbling as she went and screaming Royal's name. My chest heaved, senses going numb, everything around me starting to feel more like a play on a stage. Little Mountain, and now Pedro as well, were following

Akhíta, trying to get her to calm down. She acted like they weren't even there. Shiloh was groaning in pain as Theo poured some sort of liquid over the wounds on his shoulder. Emilia's eyes kept snapping back and forth, silently taking in everyone's faces. And the stars kept spinning by above us.

I lost track of what was happening, finding myself sitting by the fire with no idea how I got there. Fox was kneeling in front of me, pressing a cup to my lips, dribbling a bitter liquid down my throat. I didn't have it in me to resist.

One detail at a time, I regained awareness of what was going on around me. Emilia was at my side, holding her own cup and still wrapped in the blanket. Someone had put a blanket on me as well. Shiloh was laid with his back to the fire, Hazel re-stitching his wounds. Akhíta was sitting across the fire from me, Pedro's arms wrapped tight around her on one side and Little Mountain's on the other side. Nadir and Oliver were crouched in front of her, trying to talk to her but not getting any response. She just stared over the fire, straight at me.

"Clarabella?" Fox said, voice gentle. "You with me?"

I gave a weak nod and broke eye contact with Akhíta to look at Fox, finding his face full of worry.

"Can you tell me what happened?" Fox asked. "Shiloh's unconscious and Akhíta won't respond to anyone."

I glanced at Emilia who, much like Akhíta, was just staring straight ahead.

"She won't say anything either," Fox said. "We need to know what's going on, Clarabella. Where's Royal?"

"The pond took them."

"You said that," Fox said, voice still gentle and slow. "What does that mean?"

I didn't have any idea how to explain, so I just said it again.

Fox brought the cup back up to my lips and forced me to take another, larger drink. I could tell now that it was some sort of tonic, not some sort of alcohol, but it still burned a bit. It was a lot like bad tea. Maybe it was bad tea. Whatever it was, it brought a little more clarity to my mind.

I took a shaky breath, trying to put my words in some sort of order. "There was a pond. Emilia was in it, and she had these…these bones…from her corset. They were doing something to the magic." I glanced at Emilia, expecting another nonresponse. Except, this time, she swallowed and her shoulders shifted under the blanket. She didn't look at me, but I was sure she heard me.

"What happened then?" Fox asked.

I kept my eyes on Emilia as I spoke. "Royal…Royal got Emilia out. No one else could do it. We were all hurt. And then something…something pulled Royal under, and everything went crazy. The whole world started shaking and rolling. We couldn't—couldn't get to Royal."

"Okay. Then?" Fox said.

"There was light, and thunder, and it kept getting brighter and brighter and then we were just…here." I doubted this made things any clearer for Fox, but it was all I had.

"So the last time you saw Royal, they'd been pulled into this pond?" Fox asked.

I nodded. "At the very bottom of the Pit. They vanished under the water."

Emilia was still not looking at me. I pulled a hand out from under my blanket and reached out, resting it over her knee. She shuddered.

"Emilia, please," I tried. "Please. Tell me what happened. Did the Preachers give you those bones?"

She didn't answer.

"Emilia, please," I repeated, tears building in my eyes. "Please, I need to know what happened to Royal."

I was answered, not by her, but by a building hum off in the distance. The whole camp stilled, all looking off towards the noise. It built and built until it was recognizable as words. Singing. Dozens of female voices harmonizing in a language I couldn't recognize.

Out of the gloom of the night emerged a Preacher. The fabric over her body rippled in the breeze as she continued to sing. One by one more

Preachers joined her, ringing the camp at the edge of the firelight, their song coming from every direction now. Akhíta was on her feet, head spinning to look at all the Preachers. There were far more of them than when we'd met them by the cross. All the men in the group shrunk down, eyes on the ground. Hazel clutched Dahlia to her chest, arms wrapped tight around her as Dahlia cried.

Two of the Preachers parted, making room for the ink-woman to step between them and into our circle. Both Preachers stepped back into place once she was in, closing the gap. Next to me, Emilia's breathing sped up, becoming as rapid as a rabbit's. Her spine had gone ramrod straight, the blanket tumbling off her shoulders. I realized that the blackness that enveloped her arms when she was in the pond was no longer there, leaving her skin as pale white as ever.

No one moved and the singing continued as the ink-woman stared Emilia down. Based on how tight my own body felt, I wasn't sure anyone *could* move. Slowly the singing faded away until there was only a low, melodic hum coming from the Preachers.

The ink-woman strode forward, walking through the fire like it wasn't there, sparks mingling with the ink sliding over her skin. She kneeled down in front of Emilia. I was sure now that Fox couldn't move; he looked utterly terrified with her only inches away.

She reached out one hand, caressing Emilia's cheek with her sharp, golden nails. "Did you think we didn't know when we took you in?"

A small, scared noise bubbled out of Emilia's throat.

The ink-woman shook her head and smiled. "Ignorant child."

She dropped her hand, leaving several drops of inky water running down Emilia's cheek.

"Where. Is. Royal?" Akhíta ground out, struggling to force her way through the words.

The ink-woman turned and contemplated her. "Royal made their choice."

"That's not what I asked!" Akhíta said. She was leaning towards the ink-woman, fighting against whatever was holding her in place. "Tell me! I'll pay your damn price!"

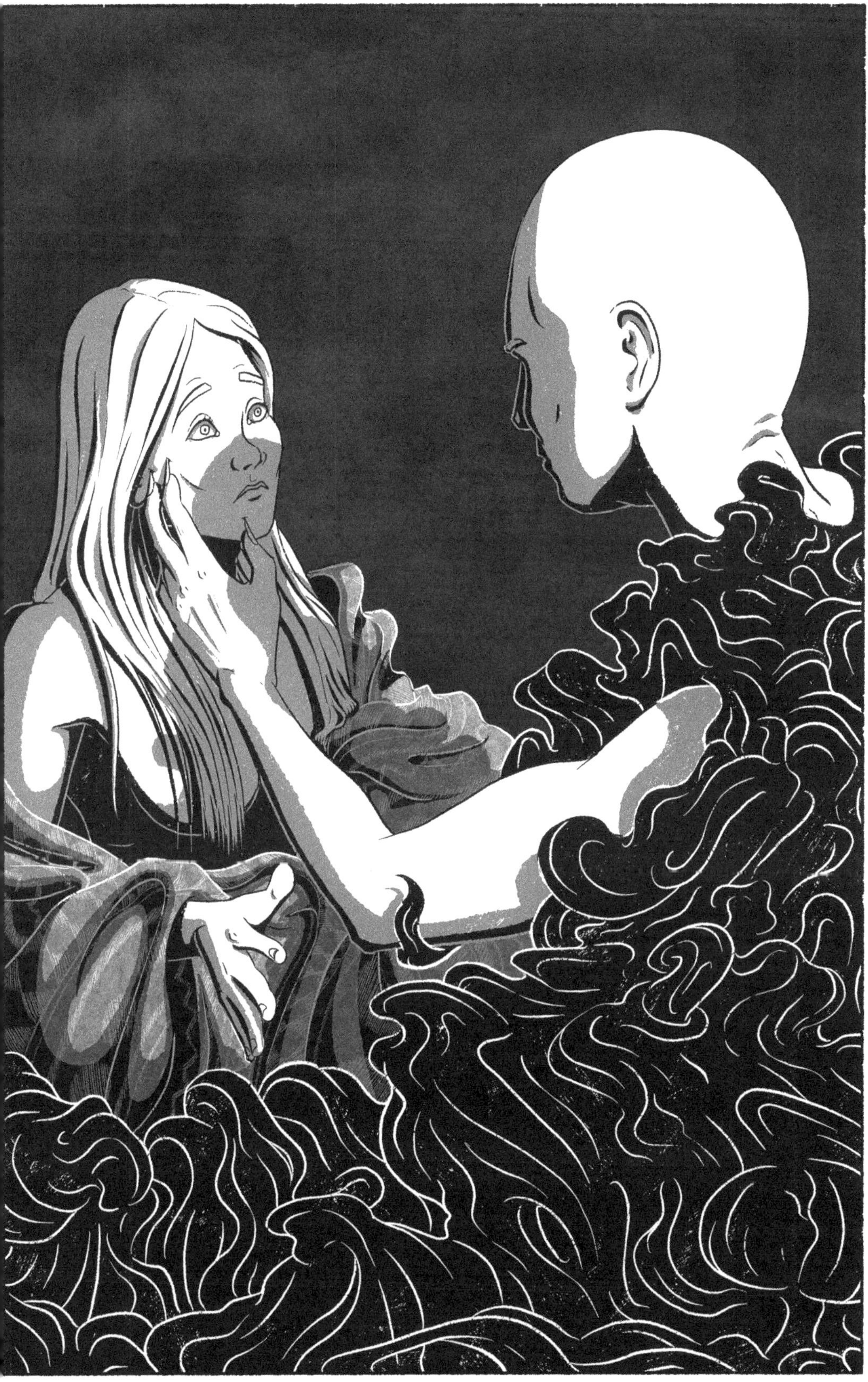

The ink-woman tilted her head, silently watching Akhíta struggle. Akhíta managed one step, then another. The fire was between her and the ink-woman, yet it didn't seem like Akhíta cared. She looked just as ready to walk through it as the ink-woman had.

"You have already paid a heavy price by choosing to go with them," the ink-woman said.

"Then tell me!" Akhíta screamed. She wasn't struggling to talk nearly at all now, but she could still hardly move, only managing a couple more steps. "Tell me what happened to my friend!"

"They died."

Chapter 22
Escape

Akhíta fell to her knees, screaming as she went. The ink-woman watched. Then, in the blink of an eye, she and the other Preachers were gone, the night ringing with silence in their absence. Released from whatever had been holding me, I fell forward with a gasp, throwing out a hand to catch myself before my face slammed into the dirt.

Shouts built up over one another, everyone trying to make sense of what happened. Only Emilia was still, staring where the ink-woman had been. There was still a drop of dark water clinging to the line of her chin. A bang silenced everyone once more. Looking over the fire, I saw the solid black hole of a gun barrel leveled at my face, Akhíta's thumb pulling the hammer back for a second shot. I didn't think she'd hit me with the first shot, at least not in any immediately fatal way. Maybe she'd sent the first shot wide on purpose, getting my attention so I knew exactly what was coming.

I didn't move out of the way.

Pedro leaped at her, shoving her hand to the ground as Little Mountain grabbed for the gun. Theo raced over, trying to help restrain her as well, while Akhíta howled and screamed at them to let her go.

"Ignú! She did this!" Akhíta shouted, eyes locked on me. Little Mountain managed to twist the gun out of her hand and threw it well out of the way, removing Akhíta's second gun as well. "She never should have come looking for Royal!"

My body shook, and I had no idea what to do. She was right. This was my fault. Royal was happy. They had friends. A life. A boyfriend who adored them. All of that was gone now, sucked into a pond at the bottom of a Pit because they'd tried to save the girl I loved. The girl who sat next to me now, maybe with answers but unwilling to give them.

Whatever grief was consuming Akhíta, it wasn't losing any steam. Any exhaustion and pain she had been in before didn't seem to have any effect either as she continued to fight against her other friends.

"Get up," Fox said, reaching down and hauling me up. He reached for Emilia and hauled her up too, both our blankets falling to the ground. Fox didn't stop to get them, dragging us both to a tent and pushing us inside. My ankle continued to throb and pulse. I had no choice except to ignore it.

The tent looked like Hazel and Dahlia's, though it was hard to make much out with only the faint firelight coming in around the flaps. Fox rooted around, pulling out a dress. He shoved it at Emilia and told her to put it on. She did, which somehow felt surprising. Fox shoved some shoes at her next and she put those on as well while Fox shoved a bunch of other things into a pack. This, he gave to me.

"Go north." He pointed that way. "You'll be back at the fort in a day. There's enough water in there for that. Lay low until dark, then steal more once you get there. Then get the hell out of here. Out of this territory. Out of this country even."

"Fox—"

He shook his head. "Don't. I'm doing this for Royal. Akhíta will kill you if she gets away from the others. Just go."

"I'm sorry," I said, tears finally rolling down my face. "I'm sorry."

"Go."

I did, pushing Emilia out the back of the tent ahead of me.

"Clarabella?"

I turned back, only able to make out the edges of Fox's face.

"The rest of us will kill you too, if we ever see you again."

Emilia and I stumbled out into the darkness together. She didn't question it when I threw an arm over her shoulder, wrapping one of her arms around my waist and helping me take the weight off my bad foot.

It took a long time for Akhíta's shouts to fade into the distance, and neither of us said anything as we walked. I wondered what Akhíta would do, was doing, in response to Fox helping us leave. There was no doubt in my mind she could chase us down if she wanted. We hadn't made it far.

"Stop, stop," I gasped, the pain in my ankle finally becoming unbearable.

Without a word, Emilia lowered me to the ground and kneeled next to me as I sobbed, clutching at my calf. It was all too much. I just wanted to curl up in the dirt and stay there. Let the sun come up and pull the life out of my body until all that was left was food for the crows.

Emilia did nothing, just watched. I wanted to shake her again, shake her until she gave me answers. Why was she just sitting there? I couldn't get any words out, though. Instead I gave in and let myself fall sideways, the dirt grinding into my cheek, turning to mud as my tears soaked into it. Emilia laid down next to me, staring up at the sky, with her hands folded over her stomach.

"You came for me," she said softly.

I struggled up onto an elbow, looking down at her. Before all of this I would have responded with, "of course, of course I came for you." Now, though, there was so much more to it than that. I'd been fully prepared to walk away until the magic brought Royal's gunshot wound back, and again once we reached the pond and I thought Emilia was already gone.

All I managed to say was a strangled, "What?"

"You came for me," she repeated. "You shouldn't have."

I shook my head, not comprehending anything anymore.

"I went down there willingly, you know."

She sounded like she was commenting on the weather, still looking up at the stars, bright blond hair fanned out around her in the dirt.

"Daddy asked me too."

My heart jittered in my chest and I repeated the only word I seemed capable of: "What?"

"Daddy asked. When I refused to marry the Duke, he locked me up. Told me that it was my duty to the family to marry well." The words rolled off her tongue like water. Simple and clear. "I sobbed and sobbed, begging him not to make me do it. Finally, he offered me another way to better the family. Daddy wants the railroad built. He's paid so much to see it done, you know. Lots of rich men have."

Ice slid through my veins. "Emilia...what did you do?"

She went on like I hadn't spoken. "Did you know magic was real? Remember how much we used to tease those who believed?" She laughed, the sound high and tinkling. "So ignorant. Daddy knew, though. All the rich men do."

"Emilia." I was crying again, a picture I didn't want to look at building in my mind.

"Daddy bought me a new corset and promised that if I went down into the Pit with it, I would be free to do whatever I wanted with the rest of my life. I asked him why the corset mattered. He said the bones inside were special. That they'd help him build his railroad." Emilia started to hum quietly, the tune almost the same as the Preachers, but not quite.

The story felt so wrong. It didn't even sound like her words, the sentences too choppy and simple. Too childish. This wasn't the girl who could verbally spar with our professors for hours without pause.

"I told Daddy I didn't want to do that either, that I had no idea how to go into a Pit, that I was scared. But Daddy promised it would be fine. He paid some men to take me. I didn't like them though. The lady dressed in dark clouds showed up outside of camp one night, and offered to take me away from those men, to take me across the Pit and give me a new name. I told her I didn't want to disappoint my Daddy. She told me she could help me do what he wanted, but that it was dangerous."

The ink-woman.

Emilia carried on. "She told me about a special path down into the Pit, and how I could get down there safely. She said I had to pay with things I cared about, things that were important to me. I had to give up that handkerchief you gave me when I got hungry. I'm sorry."

Every word continued to be addressed towards the stars. I wasn't even sure she knew I was next to her anymore.

"I think Daddy lied, though." This was said in the same even tone as everything else. "It was so strange down there. So scary. Why did you come for me?"

"I—I love you," I stuttered, knowing it wasn't true anymore. At least not for this thing that was in front of me now, because I was no longer sure it even was Emilia.

"How strange."

She sat up and finally turned to face me, hair wild around her face, twigs and dirt sticking out of it. Her eyes bored into mine and all I wanted was to run away. To hide. This was not my girlfriend. It wasn't even a shell of her. When she reached for me, I tried to scramble backwards out of reach, only for her to catch me by my injured ankle.

I screamed in pain or fear, I didn't know which. She twisted my foot around, examining it as I sobbed and tried to pull myself free.

"Stay still," she said. I did, out of fear or force, I didn't know which.

I gasped for breath, watching as she slowly closed her eyes, letting out a long, slow breath of her own. A warm, orange glow began to emanate from her hand where it cupped the back of my ankle. The heat soaked through the leather, through my sock, and into my skin. It got brighter and brighter, hotter and hotter to the point it almost burned. Then suddenly it was gone.

Emilia dropped my foot into the dirt. It didn't hurt. The rest of my body still ached, but my ankle felt fine. It was almost disconcerting how fine it felt compared to everything else.

"Wh—what?"

She opened her eyes, staring at me just as intently as before. "Daddy is going to kill us both now."

Then she was gone, as quickly as the Preachers. I spun around, not daring to call out for her, finding only empty land around me, the breeze warm and the smell of sage heavy. Somewhere, a coyote yipped.

Sobbing, I curled back up in the dirt.

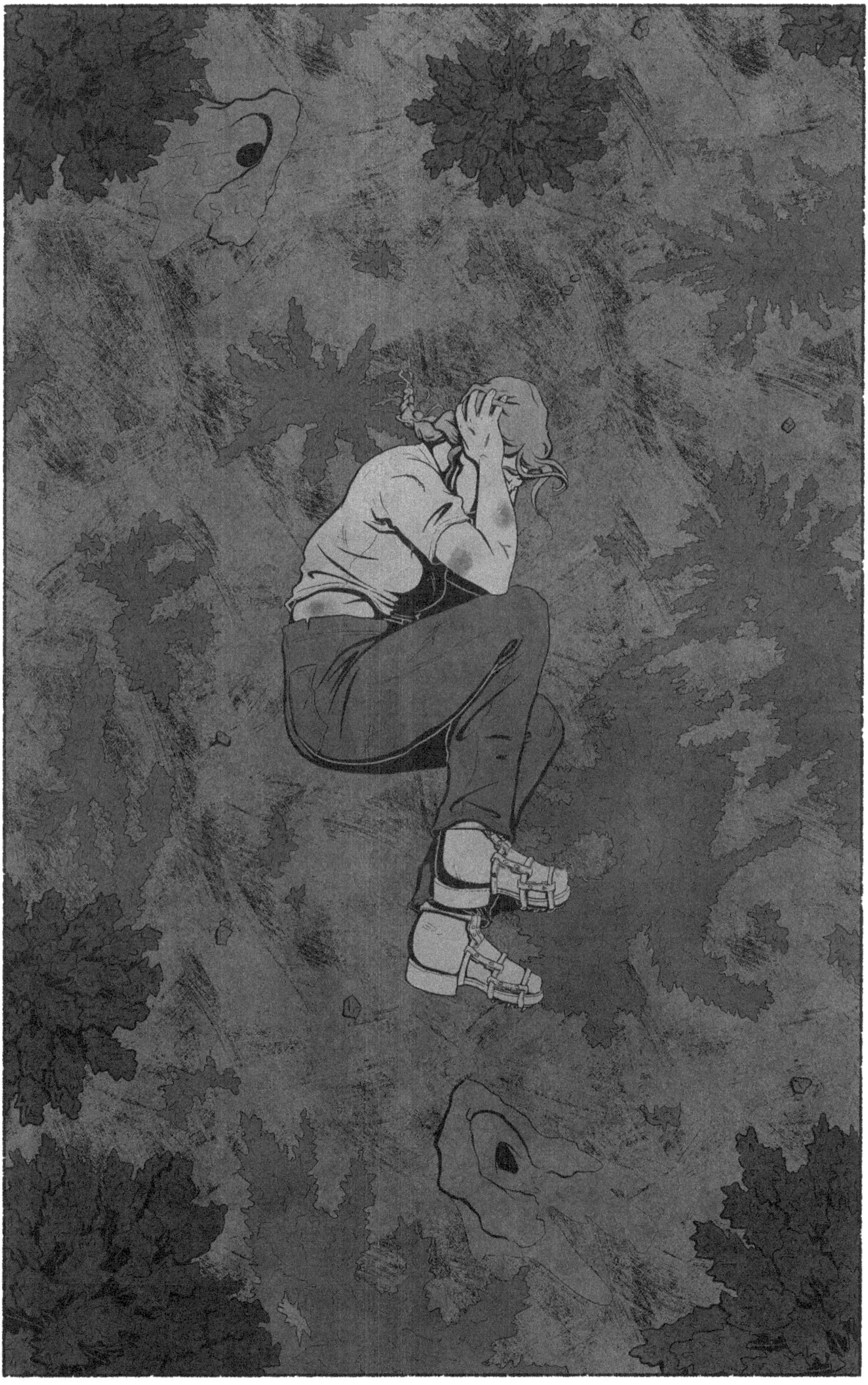

Epilogue

The ground had stilled. Broken branches, leaves, and cracked rocks were littered everywhere save for the still surface of the pond. Several animals lay dead, crushed by huge fallen branches or speared by slivers of fractured rock. To one side, an abandoned gun belt lay, half full of bullets, one gun slid halfway out of its holster, the other with its cylinder knocked open, all the bullets fallen out. Some distance away lay a felt hat, one side of the wide brim folded up and a ring of silver around the edge.

A rabbit the size of a large dog with tangled, root-like horns sprouting from its head hopped over and sniffed at the hat. It nudged it a few times, then lost interest and bounded on. Several more creatures did the same, examining these strange objects that had never been seen in their domain before. One was small and blue, something like a frog with fire flickering along its back. It singed a small hole through the flat side of the brim before bounding on.

As they came and went, none seemed to pay any mind to the pond in their midst. None drank from its dark waters. None looked at it. None noticed the red glow slowly building under its surface.

The light pulsed like a slow heartbeat, no sound accompanying it, and the water remained still.

Something skittered across the ground and over the hat, moving so fast its form was undiscernible.

The pond continued to pulse, a deep sound beginning to accompany each pulse, growing louder with each one.

A bird with three heads landed next to the belt, pecking at one of the guns, metallic tings ringing out as it did.

The pulsing ceased abruptly, the pond dark once more.

Everything stilled, all the animals turning to stare at the pond they hadn't acknowledged before. They waited.

When the surface of the pond exploded every animal began to scream and call, yet none ran away as the black water rained down on them. It immediately flowed back into the pond, but not before a hand shot up and latched onto the moss at the edge. The limb was charred black, cracks like veins giving a glimpse of fire flickering beneath the skin. On the littlest finger sat a slim silver ring, a bright bit of turquoise nestled in the center.

Backers

Thank you to everyone from Patreon and Kickstarter who has supported this project over the last two years. It would not have come to life without you.

Patreon:
Tanya Stere | S.R. Harper
KJRaeside | Lydia Rogue
Katie M. | Stefanie H.
John R. | Courtney T.
Ashley | Arashi Senshi
Margaret B. | Adam
JDR. Cricket | Hannah T.

Kickstarter:
An Old Submariner
Annalee Greusel
Autumn
Carrie Anderson
David Gerald King
Veronica Wolanin
Elle Dimopoulos
Holly Aeryn
Raine Barker
Kat Moon
Kelly A Larson
Kody H.Shishido
Meghan Snyder
Olivia Smith
seelieAce
VOID says hi
Suzanne M.

Acknowledgements

This is one of those bucket list projects that I've been dancing around for years. The characters and plot are all new, but I've wanted to write a Western for quite a while. I grew up in Colorado, the child of a barrel racer from Montana and a cowboy from an old Colorado ranching family. Western aesthetics and stories have been in my life from day one, in both good ways and—unfortunately—bad ones. It is a genre that can easily tip over into a lot of horrible tropes and themes, but it is also such a rich period of history with so many stories that deserve to be told. Obviously, this is a Weird Western rather than just a Western, so there are plenty of fantastical liberties taken, but I did my best to weave those liberties into real events from the time without glossing over the sharper edges. At the same time, I was not at all interested in focusing on those sharper edges. Sometimes you just need a story that goes, "Yep, that's going on over there, but WE are gonna go get chased by some magic wolves in a hole in the ground." So that's what I wrote and, Reader, I hope you loved it as much as I do!

Thank you so much to everyone who helped to bring this book to life, from my supporters on Patreon who were there for the whole writing process to the backers on Kickstarter that helped create the beautiful special edition and funded the first round of printing. Swifty, thanks for always letting me toss ideas at you and being appreciative of the random half-finished illustrations I dropped into the chat at all hours. Thank you to Maggie Stiefvater for hosting such an awesome writing workshop that really helped bring this book to life. The plot of this book is so much stronger thanks to your advice, though the characters might disagree as it went much less favorably for them after said advice. Thank you to Jamie as well, who I met during said writing workshop, for hooking me up with the printer who brought the special edition to life; it is even more beautiful than I could have imagined. Lastly, shout out to True Grit Texture Supply for the Rusty Nib brush set for Procreate. These illustrations exist because you created the inking brush set I've been dreaming of for years. I love it so much.

Other Works by Katy L. Wood

Novels:
Glory is Poison Book 1: Poison in the Blood

Artbooks:
Into the Background: A Seek & Find Artbook

Visit Katy L. Wood on her website to learn more about her other projects and join her newsletter to be the first to hear about new projects.

www.Katy-L-Wood.com

About Katy L. Wood

Katy L. Wood is a queer author and illustrator who lives in varying areas of Colorado with her two cats, Rumble and Rebel. The majority of her childhood was being handed a bear-whistle, pushed out the door into the forest, and told to be back for dinner. Occasionally she would have cousins with her, occasionally she'd be alone. There were many adventures to creepy abandoned trailers with bones in the front yard (which she learned as an adult were not actually abandoned, making them ten times creepier), up creeks while making rudimentary maps, and into old mineshafts. Honestly, it is probably a miracle she survived to adulthood. She is now taking bets on if she'll make it to middle-age, given that her habits have not changed the slightest.

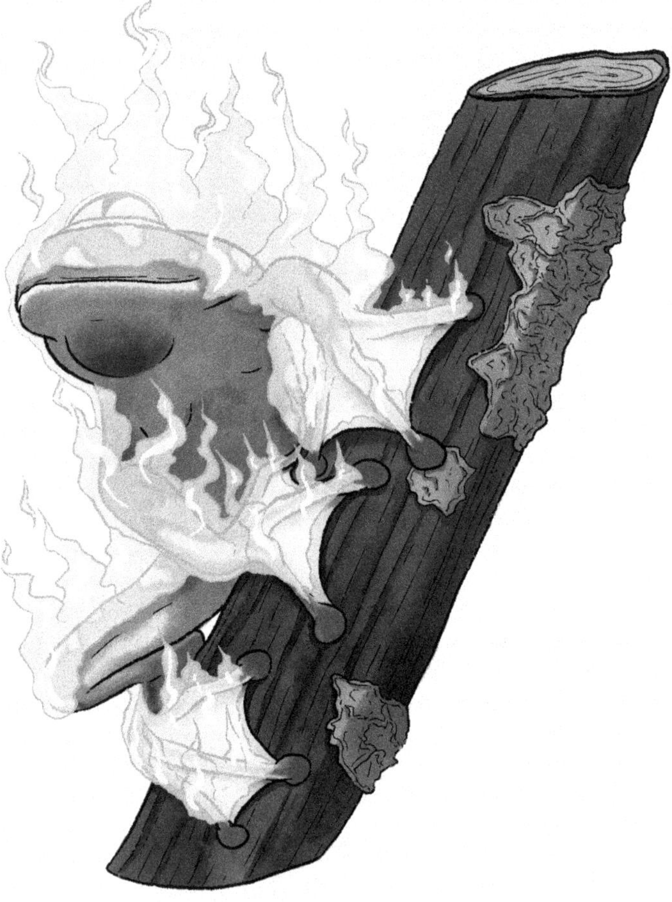

Milton Keynes UK
Ingram Content Group UK Ltd.
UKHW042318031123
431778UK00027B/109/J